W9-CNX-057

■

BY THE SAME AUTHOR

FICTION

Axis

Promise The Earth

NONFICTION

Anatomy of a Scandal

True Brit

Crossroads of Civilisation

■

Comrades

Comrades

CLIVE IRVING

VILLARD BOOKS  NEW YORK 1986

 Published in the United States by Villard Books, a division of Random House, Inc., New York, and simultaneously in Canada by Random House of Canada Limited, Toronto.

Library of Congress Cataloging-in-Publication Data
Irving, Clive.
Comrades.
1. Spain—History—Civil War, 1936–1939—Fiction.
I. Title.
PR6059.R914C6 1986 823′.914 85–40735
ISBN 0–394–53937–0

Grateful acknowledgment is made to the following for permission to reprint previously published material:

Warner Bros., Inc.: Excerpt from lyrics to "Let's Do It, Let's Fall in Love," by Cole Porter. © 1928 (renewed) Warner Bros., Inc. All rights reserved. Used by permission.

Warner Bros., Inc.: Excerpt from lyrics to "You're the Top," by Cole Porter. © 1934 (renewed) Warner Bros., Inc. All rights reserved. Used by permission.

New Directions Publishing Corp. and Penguin Books, Ltd.: Excerpt from "The Faithless Wife," from *Lorca: Selected Poems* by Federico Garcia Lorca. Rights in the United States and Canada administered by New Directions Publishing Corp. Translated by Steven Spender and J. L. Gili. © 1955 by New Directions Publishing Corp. Rights in the world excluding the United States and Canada administered by Penguin Books Ltd. Translation by J. L. Gili. (Penguin Poets, 1960), pg. 46. Copyright © 1960 by J. L. Gili. Reproduced by permission of the publishers.

Manufactured in the United States of America
9 8 7 6 5 4 3 2
First Edition
Book design: Jessica Shatan

■

"... however much you deny the truth, the truth goes on existing, as it were, behind your back ..."

—George Orwell, *Homage to Catalonia*, 1938

■

Comrades

1

MADRID, NOVEMBER 1936

Three men against three tanks with only a bridge between them and Madrid. She brought the Leica into focus on the men and she left the tanks out of focus, finding an image that seemed as hopeless as the struggle. One tank pulled ahead of the others. Its turret gun canted down, not at the men but at the mines. They had to pick off the mines before they could move. There were other men on the bridge, dead. And one broken but still alive. Above him a single bulb shone yellow through the mist, a light morning mist like grain on a film. Blood ran down a gutter, but she thought in black and white: black and white pictures took the blood out of war. The three men ignored the tanks and went to their comrade under the lamp.

The tank detonated a mine with one shot and moved around the crater. The three men had the wounded man swinging between them and they started to run. The other two tanks began to follow the first.

She was at an empty gun embrasure at the barricade on the east side of the bridge. Outside the barricade some men were trying to aim an ancient field cannon at the tanks, and locking a shell in its breech. *"No pasarán! No pasarán!"* It was the women screaming from the barricade—women militia. She had five pictures now, and wound on for a sixth.

The three men with the wounded man were going to make it. The old cannon fired over their heads. The shell fell uselessly into the river. Men and women came out from the barricade to help bring in the wounded man.

The lead tank picked off another mine. It did not detonate. A dud. The tank began to roll over the mine and range its gun at the barricade—the gun seemed to level with the Leica's viewfinder. There was the smell of blood and cordite. They were trying to load the old cannon again.

Then two explosions, a small one, under the tank—the mine was not dud—and, as the tank slewed, a larger one from within the tank, a burst of brilliant light and then pouring black smoke. Shards of steel flew. Some hit the sandbags around her, cinder hot. Burning oil hemorrhaged from the tank's belly across the bridge. The old cannon fired again, and again the shell fell in the river. But the other two tanks had stopped. Something vaguely human appeared from the burning tank's turret and fell back into it. The other tanks began reversing back over the bridge, and the women cheered. But the broken man was dead, on a saturated litter, by the barricade.

■

"The censor won't clear stuff like this." Max Praeger held up a print, still wet. "They're putting out that Franco hasn't crossed a bridge."

She had wrapped the bare bathroom bulb in red acetate. Praeger's face looked healthier in that light.

"They *didn't* cross the bridge."

He went to another print. "You take risks. Too many."

"The Leica was made for this war. Fast as a bullet."

He saw the body under the tank. "Tell me—" He looked up. "—tell me, how do you do it?"

"What do you mean, Max?"

She moved one print to keep it from sticking to another.

"You know what I mean."

"We both do the same job. We both get bylines."

"When you look through that camera, don't you feel anything?"

"Hell with it, Max. You know I feel something. What am I supposed to do? I'm not doing the killing."

"So young."

"Listen." She began pegging prints to a line to dry over the bath. "Listen. Two months ago I was the society reporter on a lousy paper in Boston. Mug shots—COAL BARON'S HEIR STEPS OUT WITH GOOD-TIME GIRL. That kind of thing. A real career. Then a guy says, 'Anybody here speak Spanish?' Abracadabra. Here I am. War. So I'm young."

"America," he said, extruding it into a sigh. One of his comprehensive opinions.

"Listen, Max, you mysterious middle European scribe. Don't get superior. What side are you on, anyway?"

"Side? I don't have a side. I have a newspaper."

"Yes. I know."

"Max." She decided to concede to his years, to his wisdom. "Max—do you *really* think the censor will block this stuff?" He liked being appealed to. "After all, nobody expected that bridge to be held, and it was."

"They don't encourage optimism, these pictures," he said. ". . . No, Barea wouldn't clear them. He couldn't."

"Damn. My best stuff. There might be another way."

"How?"

"The embassy. I know a guy at the American embassy. He could put them in a pouch. Other people do it."

"What happens when it gets published? They would throw you out."

"By that time," she said, gathering the prints, "it won't matter. Either Madrid will have fallen—or these will look like a victory."

"Mary," he said, as she opened the door, "what would you do if the fascists took Madrid? Assuming that you survived. Would you stay?"

He looked jaundiced in better light. "That's not what you mean, is it, Max? You mean, would it make any difference to me, do I *care,* if the fascists take over?"

He waited.

"Either way, Max, it's a story."

But he knew she was lying.

■

She had to wait at the gates of the American embassy while a Marine made a call; then she was waved inside by a white glove. The place felt glacial, impervious to the war. He came clipping down a marble hall to meet her, Tom Esposito. As smooth as ever, but possibly fatter than she remembered, definitely balder.

"Mary."

No—he hadn't been able to forget that, the last time, she had not joined his list of conquests. At least she was three years older now and so out of his usual range.

"Mary Byrnes. All grown up."

"Hello, Tom."

He took her by an arm and steered her down a corridor.

"You haven't moved the pictures," she said.

"They're not ours to move. We rent the place."

"Six Goyas. *Six.*"

"They haven't moved the pictures in the Prado."

"No, they haven't." She stopped at one of the pictures. "Did you ever *really* look at this?" She gave him the same attention. "No. I guess you didn't."

He took the elbow again and squeezed it lightly. "Let's cut the smart stuff, shall we?"

"Philistine."

"Come into my office, for God's sake."

The office had huge windows looking out on the gardens. The desk had gold gargoyles and was as big as a pool table.

"Not bad for a mere commercial attaché," she said.

He guided her to a chair but, instead of going to the desk, he paced the parquet, heels snapping. "Okay, Mary. You said on the phone that it was urgent."

She pulled the envelope from her bag. "These are my best pictures.

The censor would kill them. Can you get them to Paris in the pouch?"

He surveyed her, leaving the offered envelope in the air. "I'm not supposed to do that."

She put the envelope on the desk. "I need a drink," she said.

"Sure," he said, and moved to a cabinet. "Sherry okay? We're out of bourbon."

She nodded.

"You know," he said, taking up a decanter and pouring two glasses, "I have to admire the way you—the way you've *matured*."

"What's that supposed to mean?"

He gave her the glass. "You're really serious about this reporting racket, aren't you?"

"Of course."

"Okay." Finally he sat behind the vast desk. "Then I'll give you some advice. Don't get involved."

"Involved?"

"I read the stuff that gets filed from Madrid and I wonder if those guys are in the same city I'm in. You haven't been here that long, but those who have been here from the beginning, they're presenting this like it was clear-cut, black and white, good and evil—a people's democracy versus the filthy fascist Franco. Jesus, they're so damned innocent."

"You prefer Franco to the government?"

"*What* government?"

"The *elected* government."

"Don't be sophomoric. This government has ceased to function. Can you imagine? Anarchists. Marxists. Trotskyists. Socialists. A government?" He paused and tasted the sherry with epicurean care, then said, "With family connections like yours, I would think you would get the picture."

"What I get the picture of," she said, with deliberate firmness, "is that Franco has badly miscalculated. When he led the military insurrection—and that *is* what it was, an insurrection—it was all supposed to be over in weeks. The civil war has been going on for three months. *Three months*."

He didn't concede. "And you think Madrid is going to hold out—against tanks, against planes?"

"I don't know."

"But what would you prefer?"

She sighed. "You're the second person to ask me that in two hours."

"What was the answer last time?"

"Either way, it's a story."

He looked at the envelope lying on the desk, and then amiably at her. "I'll break the rules for you, Mary Byrnes, if you'll do something for me."

■

The censor's office was on the fourth floor of the tallest building in Madrid, the Telefónica. Praeger thought that Arturo Barea, the censor, had decided that the best way to kill off journalists in one stroke was to gather them there, in the best artillery target offered to Franco—and that the soulful Barea didn't mind the idea of being blown up with them. Yet, however many shells were falling, the Telefónica somehow remained unscathed. It even came to feel safe.

Barea's office had, that morning, the smell of a place recently vacated by a crowd—the taint of tobacco, alcohol, and the other contagions that went with journalism in war or peace. Barea seemed to be there alone, slumped at his desk.

"Why are all those cars lined up outside?" asked Praeger.

"You were not told? You should have been told," said Barea.

"Told what?"

"Evacuation. To Valencia. If you want to get out, it is the last chance."

Praeger, surprising himself, thought of Mary Byrnes, who hadn't been told either. "Who's going?" he said.

"Almost everybody. Except him." Barea nodded to a body that Praeger had so far overlooked. A reclining figure on a cot, fully clothed, in the shadows.

"Does he know?" said Praeger.

A shell fell somewhere close enough to shake the windows.

"Two bottles, at least. He'll sleep for a day."

"Did you know," said Praeger, "that Portuguese radio is reporting that Franco rode up the Gran Vía this morning—on a white horse?"

"Ah," said Barea, with stirring passion. "Some of the shits cannot wait." He searched through a pile of typescripts and telegrams. "Look—this telegram arrived addressed to His Excellency Generalissimo Francisco Franco, Madrid. Congratulations to the conqueror. Signed by the president of a piss-pot Spanish American republic. I'm returning it, with a service note, 'Unknown at the above address.' "

"Are you staying?"

The joke had already drained from Barea's face, and suddenly he was almost appealing to Praeger, getting up from the desk, pulling out a pack of small cigars.

"Here," he said, giving one to Praeger and lighting it for him as he spoke. "I tell you something. The others don't know it yet. But the government is going with them, to Valencia."

"What?" Praeger's breath almost extinguished the lighter.

"Yes," said Barea. "The government is leaving Madrid." He waited until his own cigar was alight, and drew on it with placid pleasure. "I have no orders. But I'm staying. I look out the windows, I do not see the people running."

With less composure, Praeger sucked at the cigar. There was heavier gunfire from the west, and smoke drifting up past the fourth-floor windows from the direction of the river. "If the government is going," he said, "who is in charge of Madrid?"

Flynn, on the cot, began snoring.

■

Esposito led the way into a sitting room, small but exquisitely furnished. A woman rose from a sofa. She was as tall as Mary, though more slender, almost too slender; taffeta hung from her without sound anchorage.

"Mary, this is Señora del Olmo; Christina, may I present Miss Byrnes, Mary Byrnes."

The woman's face, when it became clear, was heavily powdered and looked bloodless. She took Mary's hand lightly and said, "It is good of you to come."

Mary already felt that in some subtle way she had been misrepresented: the woman looked at her with too much hope.

"Let's sit down, shall we?" said Esposito. "Señora del Olmo is the wife of a distinguished businessman, Manuel del Olmo. Señor del Olmo managed the Spanish subsidiary of an engineering corporation in Baltimore. Two months ago he was arrested, with many others. He is being held—*they* are being held—in the Model Prison, without charges. Señora del Olmo has not seen her husband since. At first, there were letters. Now they have stopped."

The woman had the curious aridity of someone obliged to deal in things which had probably never troubled her before.

"I thought," said Esposito, "as a reporter, you could make inquiries. They worry about American opinion. I can give you other names, all with American connections."

"Is Señora del Olmo living here, in the embassy, with her family?"

Esposito seemed uncomfortable. "Yes—there are refugees in all the embassies."

"Political refugees?"

The woman finally spoke from ruby lips. "My husband has no politics."

Esposito nodded. "I can vouch for that."

Mary thought that the woman's bearing was, in itself, a political statement. "I don't know what I can do," she said, "but I'll certainly try."

Outside, Esposito was less formal—he took her arm again. "Thanks. You're in the Gran Vía Hotel, aren't you?"

"Yes."

"Isn't that a bit dangerous?"

"Where isn't?"

"You could come here. There is room. We're down to a skeleton staff. The ambassador decamped to France."

"Thanks, but no thanks."

"Why not?"

"Too cozy."

□

■

Praeger watched the cars leave, taking more than half of the press corps with them. Mary, even if she had known, wouldn't have gone—he was sure. And he was glad. She carried a kind of danger that enlivened him, that he hadn't known for years: the great mop of red hair, the open white face with its band of freckles, and the loose, loping walk he found so hard to keep up with. She was the clever innocent, seeing things too simple for him to notice, ingenuous in an adamantly moral way. Like her perfect teeth, she had brought innocence across the Atlantic to a place where it was exotic. Futile to lust after her; he felt neuter under that vigorous gaze, though there was a sting of regret in conceding it.

He crossed the Calle de Hortaleza, twenty yards from the Telefónica. There was a poster on a wall, of a priest with a seed pouch at his belly, sprinkling not seeds but crucifixes that, when they settled in rows in the earth, became the crosses on graves. Simple, powerful visual propaganda, a kind of political literacy in a country of mass illiteracy—that was clever. The wall that bore the poster was all that remained of an apartment house. A shell had opened up the building's guts, and two cold, damp nights with rising wind had already peeled paper from the walls; dyes from the paper bled into the rubble and the plaster smelled like sour milk. There was a family photograph on a sideboard, four people; Praeger paused to stare up at it. Secure faces behind fractured glass.

■

Walking back from the embassy, Mary stopped amid the trees of a square. The sun had come out, for the first time since the battle began. People were back in the cafés. Some seemed never to have left; the old men playing dominoes kept their jackets on and their eyes on the tables.

There was some problem with the traffic. It was jammed in the exit to the square. Horns blared, men got out of cars daubed with the various party allegiances. There was a banner draped across an apartment building, DEFENSA MADRID. The banner rose in a great wind, the building began shaking, seemed to move in slow motion, then its facade collapsed, one floor buckling on top of another—so slowly, it seemed, that she fixed on a detail, that the banner was split neatly between the words as it sank. The traffic noise had drowned the explosion, but now there was a lick of flame from within the building, and everybody was running. She ran out of the trees, across the street, and into a doorway. There was a huge explosion, much closer, and the blast bounced back off a wall and blew her over. She slid facedown over marble, glass showering around her.

Someone fell on top of her, pinning her down. In her eyeline across the marble in the street she saw her camera case, lying in the gutter. And feet, many feet, running. It was a man on top of her. Acrid smoke drifted in, but there were no more explosions. The man rolled from her and, almost shouting, said, "Nobody looked up. *Nobody looked up!*" He was young, dressed like a peasant in corduroys and canvas shirt. But it was not the voice of a peasant. He looked at her. "Are you hurt?"

"No," she said, puzzled by his anger.

"You did not look up."

"Look up?"

"At the sky. Bombers. *They were bombers.* Not artillery."

"You were shielding me," she said, picking herself up.

"Bombers," he said, "this is how it will be. We have no defenses against bombers."

He wore a red and black neckerchief—an anarchist. Then she realized, as though recalling a dream. "I think I've seen you before," she said. "On the Segovia Bridge." She remembered him in black and white, on the print. "*My God!*" she said, aware of how hysterical it sounded in Spanish. "You were on the bridge. You brought that wounded man off the bridge."

He looked her over with more attention, and less concern.

"You are American, I think."

"Yes." She looked across to the gutter. The camera case remained there. Beyond it, in the street, two horses, still tied by halters but with only a splintered beam left from their cart, were trying to stand up. A leg of one had been sheared away. The uninjured horse had a crazed energy as it dragged the other a few feet. She had to get the camera case; blood from the horse was lapping it.

"That is yours?" he said, seeing the case.

"Yes."

He went to the street and picked up the case, holding it out for her; it was still dripping blood.

She went to take it, but his face fell out of focus, the square and the noise faded, and she collapsed at his feet.

■

Arturo Barea had watched the Junkers bombers from the fourteenth floor of the Telefónica. There was nothing to oppose them in the afternoon sky. They were very clear, three of them making a loop over the city. Now smoke drifted in the southern wind.

He went down. On the fourth floor the switchboard girls had arrived for the five o'clock shift. Their lipstick was bright and their hair neat. Luis was with them—Luis the orderly in his commissionaire's uniform, looking like a Ruritanian general and fighting to keep his nerve.

"You saw the bombers," said Barea. "It's not safe here. Shells, bombers. Any of you are free to go if you want to."

The girls shook their heads.

"I'm a government employee," said Luis. "I have my rights, I cannot leave my post."

Barea suppressed a smile. "Very well." He saw a curtain flapping in the breeze from an open window. "Very well. But we must make this place safer. We cannot stop shells coming through the window, but blast is dangerous. I want mattresses at the windows by the journalists' desks and—" He went to close the open window. "—and tape on the other windows, to keep the glass from fracturing in blasts; you've seen it being done in other buildings."

The girls, thought Barea, would have made a good poster—BUSINESS AS USUAL.

□

■

Someone was sweeping up glass. It was the first sound Mary heard as she came around. Then people talking. She heard water. Hosing down. A woman bent over her.

"You see," said the woman. "She is all right."

There was another woman there—both were in black waitresses' uniforms. The one bending over her was dabbing her brow with a towel that smelled of coffee.

"What happened?" she said, in English, then repeated it in Spanish, elbowing herself up.

"You fainted. That is all. The shock. You are all right."

She remembered. She remembered the man with the anarchist colors at his neck, the way his dark brows knitted over olive eyes. They had put her on a banquette in the café. She felt that she had melted and was slowly resolidifying. Several men were sweeping glass, but the café's patrons were back at their tables. The street was being hosed down. She remembered the camera case. And saw it—by her feet. No blood.

"Where is he—the man?" she said.

The woman with the towel grunted and looked curiously censorious. "*That* man."

"Where is he?"

"Don't you worry about him. So many like him these days. So full of themselves."

The other woman brought a glass of water.

Mary sat up and sipped it. Nobody took any notice of her—and, though a fire burned in the square, the traffic was moving again.

She walked back to the Gran Vía Hotel. She had never seen so few people in the lobby. Praeger, at least, was in the bar, like a dependable fixture. He raised his glass of cognac to acknowledge her.

"Max. Where is everybody?"

"Gone," he said, and in the gloom she saw, for the first time, how collapsed he seemed.

"Gone?"

"To Valencia. You didn't get the word?"

□

"I need a drink. Several." She swung onto a stool beside him, and the old bartender, without her asking, poured her a cognac. "I've had a bad time, Max. I was caught in the bombing, had no damned idea it *was* bombing. It all happened so fast."

"Ah," he said, "you do look shaken. I've never seen a cognac disappear so fast."

"So," she said, "why didn't *you* go?"

He peered into his cognac as though looking at a crystal ball. "Over the years, whenever the retreat has sounded, Praeger has remained on station." His eyes moved from the glass to her. "I am, as you see, not inclined to evacuation. They were German bombers, by the way. Junkers. I think that's significant. Until now they've been very reluctant to show themselves. Franco must be less sure of himself, to be so blatant with his German bombers."

"You are quite drunk, aren't you?"

He smiled. "Of course. Would you care for another? You do look very pale."

"Oh God," she said, quietly. "I don't know how I feel about this. I mean, being left here. With people like you."

"I'm quite harmless," he said.

"Okay," she said. "Okay."

■

A ringing bell jarred her awake. At first she did not remember that she was in Praeger's suite—Praeger's arrival in Madrid, even before the civil war had begun in July, had got him the best rooms in the hotel. She had slept on a sofa, a sofa with almost all its springs exposed that smelled of Praeger's tobacco. The bell was real enough, somewhere near on the Gran Vía. There was weak light through the gap in the heavy curtains. She was puzzled by another sound, almost in beat with the bell. It was like marching, but oddly impressed. She pulled herself up, feeling giddy, and went to the window.

The Gran Vía was veined with ice. Drizzle had frozen as it hit the streets. There was no traffic, but the Vía was lined with people, some with children lifted to their shoulders. Others were at windows.

The sound was of boots cracking into the ice: a column of men, as wide as the Vía, marched west, to the river and the front line. But they were like no army she had seen before—ill-sorted in old uniforms that looked vaguely French.

A cry went up. *"Viva los rusos!"*

The leading file of men was lightly armed, but behind them others carried heavier equipment, ammunition, and dismantled machine guns.

"Viva los rusos! Salud! Salud!"

"No," said Praeger, who had materialized at her side. "No. They are not Russians."

"Who then?" she said.

"Old French machine guns. Old British rifles, some German. A ragbag. Flotsam in boots."

Praeger looked, in the gray light, as bad as she felt.

"God, they look raw," he said, as though pleased by seeing a condition worse than his own.

The crowd continued its acclaim, but the column was not distracted. The faces in the sharp wind had the look of directed zeal, of a religious procession, underscored by the bell. That was, she thought, all they did have in common: a kind of faith.

"I'd heard about them," said Praeger, "being trained somewhere in the north. They've all come across the Pyrenees, in the night. Volunteers, from everywhere. They can't be ready for the front."

"The people think they're the Russians."

"Yes." Praeger looked at her. "The Russians won't look like that, when they come. They call these people the International Brigade. Communist cannon fodder."

"You're very cynical, Max. Look down there. Look at the—the *hope*."

But Praeger had turned away, and pulled his dressing gown more tightly around him, and fumbled with a desk light. Suddenly she felt gauche, using a word like *hope* with Praeger; Praeger didn't even bother to show his contempt for it.

■

The wrecked tank remained on the bridge, on Tarmac seared where the oil had burned. Now, with a skin of ice, the tank had a lacquered glint—as though coated for permanent display, a trophy and a warning. No more tanks had tried to cross the bridge. The fighting had moved a mile or so farther north. The militiawomen huddled at a brazier in their black, one-piece *monos,* the zippered overalls that somehow emphasized sex instead of suppressing it. Only a few men remained with them. And in the morning chill the women's faces and voices had the assumption of independence in them, the independence that war had delivered to them when nothing else could have.

Nicolás Cordón, huddled at the barricade with scalding coffee for warmth, remembered the American woman with the red hair, and how she had looked when she passed out.

"Nicolás." It was Aneta Ferrer, in not a *mono* but a man's greatcoat.

"Aneta."

"Nicolás, you look without spirit."

"Tired. Just tired. You make it sound like a lapse of faith."

Her smile was mocking. "I am not a priest."

"No. But you would gather me, if you could."

She squatted beside him, leaning against the damp sandbags, and took the coffee from him to take a sip. "Oh, Nicolás. If only your mind would follow your heart."

He put an arm around her. "What does it matter?"

She passed the coffee back. It seemed to have intensified her. She stayed within his embrace but offered no weakness. "Nicolás, I'm serious. As an anarchist, you're always suspect. The war doesn't allow your kind of dream. The people who will prevail are those who understand power—how to *take* power."

He tightened the embrace. "Aneta. In bed we are lovers. Out of bed—out of bed, I am an anarchist, you are a Marxist. And Spain is big enough for both of us."

She shook her head. "No." She was angry. "No, no, *no.* You don't understand."

A loudspeaker above the barricade began to crackle with static. *"Comrades!"* The woman's voice assembled itself and their attention in the one word. "Comrades, people of Madrid." All the women's faces were upturned now. "Men and women of Madrid, this is La Pasionaria. The glorious victory of Madrid can be ours. The line is holding. Comrades and workers, you are valiant. I speak to you for comrade General Miaja. The loyal army is with the people. Victory will be ours. *They shall not pass.*" The voice was abruptly swallowed in music, and the music in the cheers of the women.

Ferrer said, "*Dolores!* Dolores understands."

Her face was freshly dedicated and as zealous as a nun's in the sharp morning air.

The elevator girl at the Telefónica held herself aloof in a prissy, varnished way. Mary could see that the girl must have picked up Praeger's cognac-tinted breath. The elevator, impaired by one of the frequent drops in voltage, moved slowly.

"Max," said Mary, "have you ever wondered about this building? A novice could hit it from two miles. Wouldn't it be the first thing you would knock out, if you were Franco?"

In confinement Praeger felt nauseated. "It *has* been hit," he said.

"Oh, sure. A stray shell. You know what I'm getting at, Max. You know the place is run by an American outfit, International Telephone and Telegraph."

"So?"

"Don't play dumb, Max. Every telephone line in Madrid goes out of here. Every international call in Spain. Franco doesn't want to touch it. It must be too damned useful."

They crawled from the third to the fourth floor.

"Mary, you have a very devious method of thought."

"Not at all. Not at all. I'm not half devious enough for this place."

The girl opened the doors, and Praeger scuttled out ungallantly ahead of Mary.

Windows had been blocked with mattresses, and Barea sat with a fitful desk light reading a newspaper. He glowered at Praeger but smiled at Mary.

"Miss Byrnes," he said, getting up.

"Arturo." She nodded to the mattresses. "It feels like you are under siege."

"I do not mind the guns or the bombers." He picked up the paper and showed it to her. It was in English. "It is *this* that I mind." He looked from her to Praeger.

The paper's headline was REDS RAPE NUNS.

"That's not my paper," said Praeger.

"No, but why do they print these lies? The man who wrote this piece has never left Franco's side." He began to calm down, and looking at Mary again said, "You always write the truth, Miss Byrnes. But I do not see the American papers, so I do not know if it is printed. And I am puzzled. Why does America, the world's greatest democracy, not support the elected government of Spain?"

"America is neutral, Arturo."

He assessed her, shook his head slowly, and said, "*Nobody* is neutral."

"I can't answer for it, Arturo."

"No."

"Arturo, I need your help." She handed him a piece of paper. "Do these names mean anything to you?"

He held the paper nearer the light and scanned it, then shook his head.

"They are all prisoners, being held in the Model."

Now he was more alert. "*Fascists,*" he said, "only fascists are in the Model." He looked at the piece of paper more carefully, noting its quality. "Where did you get this?"

"From my embassy. They've asked me to check on these people. According to the embassy, these men are only held on suspicion; they have had no trial."

Rarely for him, Barea was openly, even dismissively, sarcastic. "The American embassy? Businessmen, for sure. They were put into the Model for their own good. Otherwise they would have been pulled through the streets. I don't understand. What has your embassy asked you to do about them?"

"They haven't been able to make any contact with these men. They want an assurance that they are okay; they cannot get any answer out of the Foreign Ministry, since the ministry went to Valencia."

"Do they think we would murder them? *We* are not fascists."

Praeger, who had been motionless in the shadows, sitting on a desk, now stirred. "Arturo, I think what Mary wants to say is—if I may presume—that there are people in the embassy who will suspect the worst unless they know otherwise."

"That's it," said Mary.

Barea looked at the paper once more, and handed it back to her. "I don't know which ministry is dealing with this. But I don't know which damned ministry is dealing with anything. It isn't my territory, of course. But I'll see what I can do."

"Thank you," she said.

But he was looking at her vigilantly. "Miss Byrnes," he said, with a hint of formality, "you are not only a reporter. You take photographs?"

"That's right."

"I see your copy, but I do not see any photographs. Since the battle began. But you have been at the front line."

"I'm not filing any pictures."

"You know the policy on photographs? The military has to clear every print."

"I know."

"Things that might seem harmless to you could be very useful to our enemy—equipment, dispositions. You understand?"

"Yes."

Praeger broke in, repeating Barea's phrase, "The military has to clear every print," and then added, "Who *is* the military?"

Barea was exasperated. "I send it to headquarters."

"Have you heard," said Praeger, "of a Russian, a general called Goriev—Vladimir Goriev?"

"Russians!" Barea exploded. "Always you ask about Russians. *Why?* I tell you, I don't know this general. But I know, if we have friends in the world, it is the Russians. What is wrong about that? The Russians know what we are fighting—what we are fighting for."

Before he had finished—but not diverting him—the whine of a

shell passed overhead. They waited for the explosion. Instead, there was a thud followed by the sound of falling masonry.

"Another dud shell," said Barea, his anger gone. "There are sometimes messages in the shells, instead of explosive, from the workers who have sabotaged them, in Germany." He looked at Mary. "Everywhere, the ordinary people are with us, you see. They understand, that this is their fight." He went back to his desk. "You will understand that, too, I think."

They left him trying, vainly, to get Valencia on the phone.

In the elevator Mary said, "Thanks, Max."

"You looked uncomfortable."

"I was. I hate to have to cheat him, on the pictures."

"He's living on the edge."

"Aren't we all?" she said, but then looking at Praeger she wondered. He seemed to go from one drink to the next without any sign of cracking up—without, she realized, any hint of commitment. "Max, where did you get that name from, the Russian?"

"Oh, a source."

The elevator opened to a lobby that echoed with emptiness as she laughed. "And you're not sharing it."

"No."

"Why *are* you so interested in the Russians?"

As they went out into the street he put on his paternal tone. "It should interest everybody."

"You think I'm green, don't you, Max? About things like that."

But he shook his head benignly. "Oh, I wouldn't say that. You seem to learn very quickly."

She saw that his eye was already on the Miami Bar, across the street. He seemed to be steering her toward it, taking her by an arm.

"Max, I think I'm going back down to the river, to the Segovia Bridge. Why don't you come?"

"You know I don't do that kind of thing." He looked up. "This cloud is breaking. The bombers will be back."

"Is the Miami Bar any safer than the bridge?"

He let her arm slip. "It's all a question of atmosphere."

"God, you are—"

"What?"

□

appeared, belching black smoke, turned to the line of the river going south, and looked crippled. Two of the pursuit planes were closing on it. Their machine guns overrode the din of the engines. The women were jumping in the air, waving their arms and rifles. After the second bomber had disappeared behind trees, there was a huge explosion and a column of thick, oily smoke. The two pursuit planes pulled up and went into a kind of sky dance, wings flashing as they twisted. There was no sight of the other bomber or, then, of the other three pursuit planes. The women were running onto the bridge, with the men who had been below; they began their own dance.

"You see," said the woman in the greatcoat, suddenly next to Mary again. "The Russians. The Russians have come." She looked quickly away from Mary. A car was coming from the north to the bridge, flying the black and red anarchist pennant on its hood. The woman ran a hand through her tangled black hair, an unconscious vanity at odds with all else in her manner.

Mary knew him even before he stepped out of the car. She hung back; the woman went to him and they talked, out of earshot. They never touched, but Mary knew now why the woman had run her hand through her hair. They were talking about her, because the man, solemn and yet more animated than the woman, gave her a glance that turned into a surreptitious acknowledgment. He was taller by a head than the woman. He seemed to persuade her of something, then broke away to come to Mary.

She hadn't recalled him being so slim. His battle tunic was open and revealed a narrow waist and hips; he moved lightly and arrogantly, thick hair slicked back from a high, tanned forehead.

"You are recovered," he said, offering a hand with courtly formality.

"Yes—you left before I could thank you."

"You seem to have an attraction for bombers."

His hand gripped tightly and then let her go.

"My name is Mary Byrnes."

"Nicolás Cordón."

The woman had appeared at his left side, and he touched her for the first time, lightly at her elbow, as though giving her an unwanted encouragement. "May I introduce Aneta Ferrer," he said.

"We have met," said Mary, smiling in spite of the woman's stance, "and we have talked."

To Ferrer he said, "We met in the Plaza Mayor, between falling bombs."

"Yes," said Ferrer, "a reporter."

Still Mary smiled, and said, "Bombs don't distinguish between reporters and other people."

Cordón laughed, and she was surprised by the open warmth in it.

She said, "It was good of you, to do what you did."

This checked him, and he said, with a shrug, "It was all so fast. But now—" He looked at Ferrer. "—but now we have the Russian planes to defend us, as Aneta has always said they would." And then, with a hint of sarcasm, he said, "Aneta has always believed in the Russians."

"Do you?" said Mary.

"I do not argue with Aneta."

The dancing on the bridge had broken up. Militiawomen came back to the barricade, and with them one of the men who had removed the detonator from the bridge; on his arm was the girl who had sat with Ferrer. They came up to Cordón.

"Captain," said the man, who at close hand was revealed to be younger than Mary had thought.

"Álvaro, you were a hero today," said Cordón.

The girl said, "Álvaro is crazy. He wants too much to be old. He will not live to be old."

"María," said Cordón, "Álvaro is a good man."

She succumbed to Cordón's charm and said, almost blushing, "I know that. I know that, Captain. But I love him."

"Captain," said Álvaro, in a rush, "I love María, and we want to marry."

"Marry?" said Cordón, as though dealing with children.

"Yes, Captain," said María, "we want you to marry us, officially."

Ferrer broke in. "If you want to have a marriage, you should find a bishop."

But Cordón turned on her. "If they want to marry, I will marry them. Today. We have our way of doing it. It may not be made in heaven, but it serves a need."

"Anarchists!" snapped Ferrer. "Petit bourgeois nonsense." She turned to Álvaro and María. "You have each other. You live together. You are *free.* Marriage is prostitution."

María looked at her with cool and resolved eyes. "There has to be more. Something that people will know."

Cordón turned to Mary. "Miss Byrnes, will you consent to be the official photographer, to record our ceremony for us?"

"Of course."

"Good," he said.

Ferrer had walked away.

"Why are you called Captain?" asked Mary.

"Álvaro followed me from Aragón to Barcelona, and from Barcelona to here. Somewhere he decided to call me that. Of course, we have no ranks, as anarchists. It is a joke."

"It is not a joke, Captain," said Álvaro. "I follow you."

Cordón delivered a mock punch to Álvaro's arm. And he looked at María. "Take him away, this man. And come to the headquarters, at six."

As they went, arm in arm, Cordón said, "He seems to have no fear. That is dangerous."

Mary sensed his concern—it was almost paternal. "What kind of a marriage will this be?"

Cordón's gaze lingered on the retreating figures of Álvaro and María before he turned to answer. "We call them precipice weddings. You can imagine why."

"Yes," she said, suddenly as grave as he. "Yes—I can."

■

Praeger poured more brandy into his coffee; he liked the vapor that came from the mingling, a result more appealing than its parts, and he inhaled it before he raised the cup. Where had that habit begun? With bad coffee, ersatz coffee, Budapest or Petrograd? Too long ago to remember, or did he lack the will to remember, the *desire?* There was a word; the whole of life in memory cleansed of it, of desire. Faces overlapped. Voices lost clarity, most voices. Perversely, only the most distant were clear.

Perot came into the bar and saw Praeger before Praeger saw him, through his aromatic veil. Perot came mincing through the tables, not minding the crush, liking contact.

"*Well!*" he squeaked as he sat down.

Praeger brought him into focus. "You resemble a canary out of its cage," he said.

"Well! And why not, Maxie? What's stuck in *your* throat today?"

Perot broke off to smile familiarly at a waiter and then leaned across the table so that Praeger caught his honeyed scent. "I've something for you, Maxie. Do you have a cigarette?"

Praeger pushed a packet of Gitanes across the table. "Take them."

Perot took one and pocketed the pack. The waiter returned with Perot's glass of Madeira, earning another familiar smile, which remained fixed until the waiter left; then Perot lit the cigarette and nosed toward Praeger again. "The reason why Franco has been stopped in his tracks, Maxie, is that they were forewarned; they knew that the attack in the south was a feint, that Franco's main attack would come in the Casa de Campo. They knew."

"How?"

"Luck. Some would say divine intervention, though of course not me." Perot smiled with pleasure in the irreverence, and with the satisfaction of making Praeger wait. "Luck. A few days ago they knocked out an Italian tank. On the body of the tank commander were papers, the whole order of battle. Simple as that."

"I see."

"What's it worth to you, Maxie? More than a packet of Gitanes, surely?"

Praeger drained his cup. "I'm getting very tired of Spain."

"It's just getting to be fun."

Praeger allowed him a jaded smile, and then said, "You've got something else, haven't you?"

"Oh, Maxie, you're so fucking shrewd. Yes, I have—but I wanted a price for each piece; otherwise you'll cheat me." He got no reaction, and so continued. "Yes. The Russian you asked about."

□

"Goriev."

"That's not his real name, but it doesn't matter. He calls himself Goriev while he's here, he—apparently he is as smooth as silk, a dandy, speaks beautiful, beautiful English."

"What does he do?" said Praeger with mounting impatience.

"Well, Maxie. They say the defense of Madrid is the work of General Miaja, don't they?"

Praeger waited.

"Goriev decides everthing: deployments, weapons, artillery support, everything. My friend doesn't like it. He's *quite* upset."

"That's a nice watch."

"You like it?"

"Expensive. Your friend is generous."

"Aren't you pleased? I mean, this is what you wanted, isn't it?"

"See if you can catch that waiter of yours. You have his eye. Yes, it is what I wanted. But I want more."

With one craned glance Perot captured the waiter, pointed to Praeger's cup and his own glass, was acknowledged, and—as a flourish to these services—smiled at Praeger and said, "I'll try. But it's not easy to see him, just now; he's at headquarters at all hours of the day and night. But I'll try."

Praeger slumped a little and said, "That's good, Perot. I can give it to you in francs this time."

Perot lit another Gitane. "I'll *never* go back there, *never.* No matter what happens here."

"No. I can see that."

■

With a note from Cordón to guide her, Mary found the anarchist headquarters, and the note was effective as a pass; the guards were, in any case, amiable to the point of casualness. And they knew about the wedding; they treated it as a joke. But Cordón did not. She found him standing at the table in a conference room bringing the assembly to order—many militiawomen from the bridge were there, but not, Mary noted, Aneta Ferrer.

Cordón put three sheets of paper on the table and brought María and Álvaro to his side. Álvaro, cleaned up and in an oversize alpaca jacket, was the more nervous of the two. María remained in her *mono,* but had conceded a white silk head scarf.

"Some people . . ." said Cordón, casting his gravity at the room, ". . . some people believe that marriage is an outdated institution. Well, I do not argue with that. But I do believe that if two people are very much in love, and if they want some formal recognition of that love from society, without having it corrupted by the embrace of the church—then, in that case, they should have it."

He looked at Álvaro. "This is a simple ceremony. But do not make the mistake, Álvaro Ortiz, of thinking that it is something you can do one day and undo the next."

María squeezed Álvaro's hand; Álvaro looked dutifully at Cordón.

Cordón directed them to sit and to sign each of the three sheets of paper; then he signed them himself. He kept a copy and handed one each to Álvaro and María.

"In theory," he said, beginning to enjoy himself, "according to the rules, you can have it—the paper—destroyed, if you wish to separate, to abandon the whole venture."

Suddenly María was in tears.

"But let me tell you, if you come to me with that idea, I'll send you back over the Segovia Bridge with a kick to help you. *Long live the revolution!*"

"*Long live the revolution!*" rang out, followed by pent-up applause.

Cordón bent to kiss María.

Mary took a picture with the flash.

María embraced Álvaro, who finally grinned.

Then each of them was, in turn, kissed by everyone in the room.

Mary went to Cordón. "That was a nice speech."

"I hope it sticks."

"They are wonderful, aren't they? I'm glad you asked me. You know, it's the first time I've really been able to feel in touch with the real people since I came here. I like it."

Cordón seemed about to ask something, but then he held up a hand to silence the babble.

□

"Please. We have a photographer. Álvaro, María. Arrange yourselves at the end of the table. Everyone else, gather around them."

"You, Captain," said María, "you must be with us."

"Yes," insisted Álvaro, "next to us, Captain."

Mary waited for them to settle and squatted to steady the camera on the table, taking a slightly upward angle that brought out, as she found him in the viewfinder, the arrogant line of Cordón's face—something indelibly feudal in it, she thought. Then she had to wait for María to dry her eyes. In the reflex from the flash they all, momentarily, seemed to freeze. What the light had caught, she felt, would never exist again—she had caught not a wedding group but, unbeckoned by the faces, mortality.

There was champagne, but no glasses. The first bottle, and then the others, was drunk from by María and Álvaro and then passed around. Foamed lips and chins introduced a more open surface of revelry.

Cordón gave a bottle to Mary before he took his own draft. The champagne was Spanish, not French, and sweet. But it was cold, and it dispelled morbid reflection.

"Where is your friend, Aneta?" she asked him as he took the bottle.

He drank, then wiped his mouth on the back of a hand, passed the bottle, and said, "You heard her, at the bridge. She doesn't approve of this."

"But you do?"

"In this case. Yes." He leaned on the table. "I listen to you and I wonder—you cannot speak Spanish as you do without being a long time in Spain; you even have a *madrileño* accent."

"Three years ago I came here to do research at the Prado. I was studying Goya, for a graduation paper. Strange—it seems now as though those Goya etchings, the *Disasters of War,* were a premonition; the horror was all there. But I came late to the war, only weeks ago. The chance came, I took it."

"You care about Spain so much, to leave America for this?"

"Well—you want the truth?"

He was supercilious. "Can I expect it?"

"What I care about is reputation. This was a quick way to get one."

The hauteur remained in his body but not any longer in his eyes. He said, "That is the truth; I see it."

"But you don't like it."

"I appreciate the candor."

Some of the women had formed a chain and begun dancing around the table while María and Álvaro drank more champagne and looked desperate to escape. Álvaro raised the bottle and cried out, "Hey, Captain! We fight together. *Always!*"

Cordón laughed. "Not tonight, Álvaro."

They all laughed.

Álvaro waved the bottle so that champagne spilled on María's *mono* and laughed. "No. Not *tonight!*" Then he put the bottle on the table and gathered up María and they went unsteadily out, followed by ribald instructions.

Cordón turned back to Mary, who was packing her camera and equipment in her bag. "Thank you, *Yanqui.*"

"A pleasure. You can pick up the prints tomorrow. I'm at the Gran Vía."

"Thank you. I will get them—when I can."

"I could drop them off here."

No," he said, suddenly firm. "No. That is not necessary."

She pointed to a large photograph hanging at one end of the conference room; it was of a man in a black leather trench coat with a face that would have made a Mongol look cultured. "Who is that?"

"Ah, that. That, my *yanqui* friend, is Buenaventura Durruti. That is the man who is going to make the revolution, our revolution. That is a man."

She was surprised at the sudden burst of reverence. "Where is he—this Durruti?"

"Fighting. At Zaragoza."

"Well," she said, "I have to go. Thank you. For a lovely wedding."

"I hope you get it—your reputation," he said, stepping back for her to pass.

"The way I see it," she said, smiling nonchalantly, "is that I'll either get a reputation or I'll get killed." And she swept out.

□

■

At the hotel Praeger came skidding from the bar to intercept her.

"Aha, Mary."

"Aha, Max."

"Mary, a message from Barea. He will collect us from here at eight in the morning. To take us to the Model."

"Us?"

"Oh, he rather expected me to be there, also. You don't mind?"

"Well—no. Of course not."

"Something has annoyed you, I think."

"Yes. It has. As a matter of fact. I went to a wedding, and something got up my nose. Not only the champagne."

"A wedding, you say?"

"Improbably, yes. Look. Let me put this stuff in my room, and you can set up a cognac, or two, for me. Okay?"

"Certainly."

In the elevator she thought, this wasn't supposed to happen, not here, and certainly not with an arrogant bastard like that.

3

The eyes of Joseph Stalin followed Nicolás Cordón as he crossed the square. A cold northern wind inflated the banner, draped from a balcony, and filled out Stalin's cheeks, giving the illusion of breath: a face looking down not, as usual, imperviously on a subject people but watchfully on alien heads. To Cordón it offered no inspiration, nothing remotely uplifting of heart, spirit, nor even of political will. He dipped his head deeper within his shearling collar and felt, unreasonably, fugitive. At the anarchist headquarters two guards huddled in the wind.

It was not much warmer inside. In the conference room, where the nuptials had been performed the night before, there was the smell of stale clothes and coffee. Everybody was there. Everybody was arguing. And waiting for him.

He poured himself coffee from the large urn and took the seat left for him at the center of the table. Younger than many of them, he nonetheless had to be the elder.

"Where is Durruti?" said one of them, immediately.

"He is coming," said Cordón.

They were shuffling chairs in their rush to take aim.

"How many—how many men will be with him?"

"I am not yet certain. Four thousand, perhaps. Yes. I hope for four thousand. At least that."

The man who had spoken first, a schoolteacher Cordón knew from

Barcelona, was on his feet. "*Four thousand!* The Communists have *four* times that, already in the field!"

Other voices rose. Cordón waited for them to subside. "Durruti was on the edge of Zaragoza. So close he could see the streetcars. Do you think he wanted to leave? Only the appeal we made could have brought him here. It would be madness to commit all our men to Madrid. That would leave Cataluña naked." He paused to gather more force. "We should remember—Durruti can do more with four thousand men than the reds with twenty. Isn't that the point? What we want to show them?"

"We should be making the revolution. Not war." This was from the end of the table, from an old but bellicose voice.

"León." Cordón looked down the table, with patience and affection. "León. What good is revolution if we lose Madrid?"

"Durruti is taking too long," said the schoolteacher, but León had been forced to think, and most of the others were thinking with him; Cordón had, he saw, a chance to isolate the persisting critic.

"Yes," he said, "it may seem so. But we can make ourselves more useful. We must be more visible, more in the streets. I want our people on every local defense committee. We must match the reds, committee for committee. We have enough people—if you can get them out."

"Yes," said the teacher, "we have enough people. But how do we explain to them—how do we explain that we, who do not believe in central government, now have four ministers in the junta? How do we explain that? It seems like a betrayal of everything we have ever stood for."

Heads nodded with him.

"Then—" said Cordón, "—then you have to explain. It is simple. If we had not taken those places the reds would have. What voice would that leave us with?" He stopped; none was prepared, any longer, to argue. "There is no betrayal. This is war. War imposes its own logic. We have to win the war first, and then we shall make the revolution. With Durruti."

For seconds it seemed still to be in the balance, and then fists were banging on the table.

"Durruti! Durruti! Durruti!"

□

■

Mary settled back into the car, glad of its warmth, and spoke to Barea, who was riding in the front with the driver. "This is good of you, Arturo, to do this."

"At the prison you will see what kind of men these are."

"Fifth column," said Praeger, mildly. He sat beside Mary in a threadbare tweed topcoat that was already steaming from the heat in the car.

"We did not invent that term," said Barea. "You should remember that."

"How did that happen?" asked Mary. "All I know is that anyone at all who is suspected of fascist sympathy has become a fifth columnist."

Praeger said, "Before the first attack on Madrid. One of Franco's generals was asked by a reporter, how many columns have you for the attack on Madrid. He said, four—but there is a fifth, already in Madrid, waiting."

"You'll see what he meant," said Barea, "when we get to the prison."

Out of the window she saw the banner flapping in the wind. Stalin. But—inexplicably—the eyes seemed not secular but papal. The same kind of omniscience, she supposed—and nearly the same colors.

"What is it?" said Praeger.

"Nothing. A private joke."

"Ah. yes."

Praeger, when shabby, was at his most benign.

They were there in five minutes. The Model Prison was circular, four stories of cells radiating from a courtyard. The car pulled into a vaulted passageway and stopped. Barea showed a pass, and they were waved through by soldiers.

Barea led them into an office so cold that its single occupant, a young officer, wore a greatcoat.

"Señor Barea," he said, "and—?"

Barea introduced Mary and Praeger.

"Well," said the officer, very young to be a captain, "My name is Amposta. Señor Carillo told me to give you every assistance."

□

"Miss Byrnes has a list of men she would like to see."

Barea gave the paper to the captain.

"All in the same block," said the captain, ". . . that is curious. We have a thousand of them, their kind, here." He coughed and his eyes watered. "At least they keep warm; it's so crowded they can—" He hesitated and, making a judgment about Mary, said, "—they can piss in each other's pockets." He led them out.

In the courtyard a white horse was being ridden slowly and with absurd precision by an officer equipped for dressage. He rode by them without taking his eyes from his course, rigid and impeccable but for one detail: his tricorn was askew.

The captain said, indifferently, "Major Prada."

"Who is he?" said Mary.

"Commander of the prison."

"He looks crazy."

"No. Shell-shocked."

"They should put him away," said Barea.

"He *is* put away," said the captain.

Major Prada broke into a measured canter.

They found that Manuel del Olmo shared a cell with four others; they had been there long enough to add personal touches, a small icon on a wall, a shelf of books, some family photographs. Though cramped, they seemed comfortable and well-fed. More than that, Mary felt at once, they could not suppress their arrogance, as though confident that liberation was at hand. Del Olmo's suit must have been expensive; even crumpled it gave the aura of a man served by others—not, like his wife, an aristocrat, but an autocrat. In voice and eye he was direct; he had force, and he repulsed any suggestion of offered sympathy.

He spoke to Mary in American-accented English. "You can say we are all fine—okay. Tell Mr. Esposito that, please."

"Don't you get any mail?" she said.

He shrugged. "No. No newspapers. But we know how things are going."

The captain lounged at the door of the cell, rubbing his hands. Barea took more notice. Praeger had made himself almost invisible.

"My wife," he said, "she is well?"

"Oh yes." She looked at the other four men, striking their various poses of superiority, their collective colognes countering the air soured by concrete. "May I give your wife any message?"

"To keep the Christmas arrangements."

Barea seemed to be more alert at this.

"Paris for Christmas." Del Olmo smiled. "Every year."

Suddenly, with his trick of materializing from a void, Praeger said, "Is it so, that there are thousands of you here?"

"All collected in one night," said del Olmo, "for our own safety."

Barea whispered to the captain.

The capitan said, "That is enough."

Del Olmo put out a hand to Mary, squeezed her hand. "Thank you. We shall meet again. Soon."

As they turned to leave she understood, in one glance, the contempt that Barea felt; it was in the set of his mouth, a gentle man discovered, in that moment, to have a grudge.

In the courtyard Major Prada used his spurs. The horse lifted its head and gave a snort of obedience and pleasure that echoed around the tiers of the prison above.

They had not spoken until they got into the car. Then Barea, settling next to the driver, said, "I would push them across a bridge, to Franco. Where they belong."

Praeger sighed. "Their faith is quite touching."

"Faith?" said Mary, as the car pulled away.

"Oh, certainly," he said.

Barea took a last look at Major Prada, who cantered across an archway. Barea shook his head, and directed the driver to the Telefónica. "All your colleagues are coming back," he said. "Already, they have had enough of Valencia. A rare case of the rats joining the sinking ship."

"Then we'll all go down together," said Praeger.

"I don't think so," said Barea. "You're very quiet, Miss Byrnes."

"I was thinking about faith," she said.

"One of the curses of Spain," said Barea. "It took me many years to see that."

It was enough to make them all silent. Praeger absorbed it with the meditative focus of a monk.

□

■

Ferrer sat hunched on the bed with a greatcoat draped around her shoulders, talking to the floor as Cordón slipped a sweater over his head. "So," she said, "the end of this—this billet, this experiment in collective living."

"When Durruti comes."

She looked up at him. "It is pathetic, the faith you have in that bandit."

"I don't want that argument again."

Slowly her face conceded to him. "Nicolás, it has been good for us, here."

There was a small, cracked mirror hanging from a nail. He began to comb his hair, tilting his head to the glass.

"Nicolás, I feel stronger for it."

"You were always that."

"It was a compliment."

He stopped combing and held her image in the mirror. "Yes," he said, with more affection, "it has been good for us." He turned to face her. "I respect your convictions. But they follow a different flag."

She let the greatcoat slip from her shoulders to the bed; her deep gypsy eyes held him; her thin shirt was rucked at her nipples. "Come here, Nicolás. While there is still time. Come."

■

"My name is Koltzov, Mikhail Koltzov. How do you do?"

He was a good two inches shorter than Mary, and peered up through lenses that deflected her immediate instinct to find his eyes. The voice was almost a comic English, the "How do you do?" like mimicry.

She put out a hand. "Mary Byrnes."

"Yes, I know."

"I'm sorry—"

"Arturo talked about you, and when I saw you, crossing the lobby, I knew it could not be anyone else."

His thick, dark hair was shaped and cut carefully to make him look fuller in the face than he really was; his vanity was apparent in every detail. Among the increasingly shabby press corps he appeared like a boulevardier; even his shoes were brogues with a hard English shine.

"I am the correspondent of *Pravda.*"

"Russian?"

He laughed. "You make it sound exotic."

He had the knack of seeming immediately to be on close terms; she laughed with him, and said, "Well—to me, it is exotic. Russia."

"While to me, it is America, New York—the great adventure of capitalism. Miss Byrnes, I have read some of your pieces. You write for an agency, do you not? I saw the pieces in several papers."

"You're remarkably well-informed. I've never met anyone here who has seen any of my stuff. Or, if they have, they haven't felt like telling me."

"Ah!" he exploded, with an enveloping familiarity, "then we must have a drink. You have found a fan, and I have found the most beautiful woman in Madrid."

She found herself following Koltzov to the bar without having made a conscious surrender to him.

Waiting for attention—the bar had recovered its old population—Koltzov said, "You're a friend of Max Praeger's."

Statement, question, or innuendo—it could have been taken as any, or all. She was more than ever confused by the elusiveness of his eyes. "Yes," she said, feeling unreasonably defensive.

The barman came in response to a quick flick from Koltzov's hand, and when he had ordered Koltzov said, "Arturo was impressed, that you did not go to Valencia, with the rest of them."

She took the cognac and raised it to him. "That wasn't courage, it was ignorance."

"Really?" He put soda into his whiskey. "Well, cheers!"

"Cheers!"

"Miss Byrnes, look around you. What do you see?"

She took in the familiar faces. "Reporters."

"Yes." Koltzov motioned his glass toward them. "The world's eyes. And what do they see, do you think? Can the world be happy with these eyes to serve them?"

Then she finally did get a glimpse of his eyes, from the side as he turned. They were larger than the lenses made them appear, and heavy lashed.

"I guess we all do the best job we can—under the circumstances."

"Under the circumstances," he repeated, reflectively, and then turned the glasses on her again. "Let me give you a thought. When you look at the sun, you cannot see the stars."

"I don't know how to take that."

He raised his whiskey to her again. "You will, Miss Byrnes. Sooner or later, you will."

■

Somewhere above in an apartment a child had been crying and then, abruptly, stopped. Praeger wondered how that had been achieved. He was left alone, now, with a dead street, and—from the other side of the river—the sound of intermittent gunfire. He felt the cold through the soles of his shoes and began trying to revive his circulation by a soft-shoe dance, not wanting to make a noise.

This was how he was apprehended by the lights of Perot's car: a lone figure swaying like a drunk in a doorway.

"You're late," said Praeger, getting in beside Perot.

"My fault," said a voice from the backseat. Praeger hadn't taken the trouble to see the other passenger.

As Perot pulled away he said, "This is Francisco, Francisco Rey."

Praeger, still annoyed by his carelessness, saw a young man in a black coat and a black beret, little more than an outline. Praeger nodded perfunctorily. "Where are we going?"

"The Plaza de Cibeles." Perot was an inattentive driver; he looked at Praeger rather than the road. "This is a big one for you, Maxie. The biggest."

The car had strayed wide and hit a curb as it turned into the next street, a wider street with chestnut trees being stripped of their last leaves by a wind coming directly from the north. Perot overcorrected, but they were the only car on the street and the wild driving pleased him. He giggled. Praeger steadied himself with a hand on the dashboard and said, "The Plaza de Cibeles, that's the Bank of Spain?"

Rey said, "Yes. That is where I work, as a clerk."

"We are going to drive through the square," said Perot. "We cannot stop."

"It seems rather theatrical," said Praeger.

"My, my, Maxie. You are in a bad mood. Theatrical? No. You'll understand."

He managed to avoid the next curb as they turned into the plaza. Rey leaned forward to put his head next to Praeger's. "You see the bank?"

"Of course."

"As we pass, look through the gates, into the courtyard, on the right. We have only one chance for you to see it."

Perot slowed slightly, gnashing gears.

There were no streetlights in the plaza, but in the bank's courtyard there were two weak lights flanking a door and several more along a wall.

"There," said Rey, "you see, under the lights?"

"Trucks," said Praeger.

Perot picked up speed again as Praeger realized that in the shadows outside the bank there were troops; it was a rare sight of the regular army.

No one spoke until Perot had left the plaza and they were back in a side street. Rey, now leaning back in his seat, said, "The trucks have been there every night for a week. They come and they go in the night. They go to Cartagena."

"So?" said Praeger.

"So," said Perot. "Tell him everything."

"They are taking the gold. Nearly nine hundred million dollars in gold. Some in bars, but millions of coins, every kind of coin, from gold louis to dollars, the loot of history. All the gold, all the wealth of Spain, all the gold reserves."

□

Praeger, at last fully engaged, turned to look at him. "Where—where is it going?"

"At Cartagena it is being stored in caves. Only a handful of people at the bank know what will happen to it after that. All we were told—the rest of the staff—is that the vaults are being moved to Cartagena for safety. But that is not true. There are ships coming to Cartagena. To take the gold to Russia."

"You see—" said Perot, "—you see, Maxie. A big one. The biggest."

"It's hard to believe," said Praeger.

"You saw it happening," said Rey sharply.

"All I saw was some trucks at the bank." Praeger put an arm over the back of his seat as he tried to get a better view of Rey. "For example, how could it be done without it getting out? How come *you* know?"

Perot tried to answer, but Rey cut in.

"At first," said Rey, "they said that Durruti and his gang were planning to steal it, to take it to Barcelona to finance the anarchist revolution. They are always expecting trouble from Durruti, but that didn't fool anybody. So then they said it was being done in case the city fell to the fascists. That did make sense."

"That still does not explain how you can know it's going to Russia."

In his excitement Perot was more erratic at the wheel than ever; they careened around a corner and nearly crashed head-on into a black limousine.

"For God's sake!" said Praeger, grabbing one of Perot's flailing arms.

"A Russian general, in that car," said Rey, craning to look through the rear window at the disappearing limousine.

"You—you haven't explained," persisted Praeger.

"I know one of the key men. The key men, there are four of them, are the only ones with keys to the vaults. He's an uncle of mine. He found out where it was going. One night a Russian came. His name was Yanin. I. Yanin. There was a discrepancy in the counting of the coins. He checked it. Two days ago the key men disappeared. All of them. I think they will go to Russia, also."

"You *see?*" screeched Perot.

Praeger turned away from Rey and slumped into his seat. Perot was waiting, and driving more prudently. "Well," said Praeger, "Yanin, you say? I. Yanin?"

"Yes."

"It's something. Something to go on."

But Perot seemed still to be annoyed that Praeger had not reached his own pitch of enthusiasm. "You're very hard to please, Maxie."

Praeger slowly turned to survey Perot. "Yes. Yes, I am."

■

The sound of tank treads spitting stone on the bridge—a sound that ran up the spine into the brain. Then another sound, distinct and opposed: of a galloping horse. The horse closed fast on the barricade at the bridge, leapt it, and went headlong over the bridge toward the tank, a single horseman, tricorn askew, digging in his spurs. Against the gray the horse was translucently white and blurred with speed.

The tank stopped.

Major Prada reined in the horse for a second, to steady himself enough to draw his sword and level it at the tank. "*No pasarán!*" he cried out.

The horse raised its head, and Prada leaned into his line of thrust. They were nearly on top of the tank when its machine gun opened up. Too late. Even as the bullets cut into the horse's chest it leaped and struck the angled armor below the turret, legs folding beneath it. Prada, unseated, seemed to keep his posture. He was thrown at the machine gun with such force that he was impaled on its barrel; it was firing through him. His sword rose and flew over the turret to fall behind it with a vibrant, dominant timbre, like that of a bell ringing out. The horse slid slowly from the armor plate, leaving a scarlet streak behind it. Prada's tricorn fell where the horse lay. His body began to smoke.

Mary woke with a spasm in her legs, a reflex, part of the effort of trying to run across the bridge. She kicked off the sheet and blanket and gulped for air. The snatching for breath sounded like a sob. She reached for the light. Her whole body glistened with sweat. She began to shiver. She drew the blanket around her, sitting up and then getting up, pulling the window open for air. Below, in the Gran Vía, a car—the only thing moving—made a U-turn toward the hotel, sliding on ice. She saw it pull up like a badly moored boat, and Praeger got out. He pulled himself together, leaned into the car for a minute, and then came into the hotel. The cold air cleared her head. She left the window open and turned back into the room. The prints, wet when she had laid them out on the floor, were dry. She sat on the bed and moved them around with her feet, looking at them.

The printing had been a bit careless—too much brandy with Koltzov. The faces were polarized, whites washed out and blacks too emphatic. It heightened the feeling she had had at the time: of something immanent, a truth of their condition not normally apparent. And she saw what she had not seen then—Cordón, with María and Álvaro but not with them: looking the camera hard in the eye, looking at her with arrogance and—she saw it now—with challenge. She pushed the prints away with her foot and lay back in the bed, still moist from the nightmare.

■

Koltzov put down the phone and walked over to a window. There was a weak light in the dawn. He cleared a section of the misted, cold glass. Goriev's limousine was just coming through the gate. Koltzov's voice was raw from the phone; he could never understand why, when he had to shout every word, Stalin's voice remained clear and soft.

When Goriev walked in he had the air of a man refreshed rather than depleted by the night.

There were just the two of them in the gilded ballroom, now lined with typists' desks.

"You look terrible, comrade Koltzov," said Goriev without evident sympathy.

"Spanish nights."

Goriev pulled off his gloves and nodded at the flickering chandeliers. "It is like Petrograd, such a place. We should have those things taken down. All that glass, they could be lethal." He looked more closely at Koltzov. "Your shoes—my God!"

"First drizzle. Then mud. Then it froze, in the field."

It is done, then?" said Goriev with a slight nervousness.

"Yes. All of them. Without trace."

"Then pull yourself together."

The chandeliers dimmed and began to rattle.

Goriev looked up, and then out the window. "Another dawn barrage. One more attempt to cross the river, and they have found our weak point. The university campus. It's a gamble. I want to draw them over—but then, can I hold them? The International Brigade, can I risk them?" He sat on a desk, swinging a leg. "You talked to Moscow?"

"Moscow is in love with Dolores."

"La Pasionaria! She is worth five divisions, that woman."

"However," said Koltzov, in a different tone, "Moscow is worried about Durruti."

Goriev did not at first respond. The leg continued to swing like a pendulum, the heel of his boot hitting the desk. Finally he said, "The answer is, comrade Koltzov, to find Durruti something that will appeal to his own estimate of himself. After all, he calls himself the finest general in Spain. I am sure we can find him a battle." He looked over the ballroom. The barrage continued, the chandelier chains groaned, and the glass set up a faint chorus; it all seemed part of a tentative symphony. "What *was* this place?"

"It belonged to a man called Juan March. The kind of man even a capitalist would be wary of. Smuggler, pirate, banker. It was his money that financed Franco's insurrection."

"All property is theft, comrade."

Koltzov could not tell if Goriev was serious; he did not yet know him well enough, could not reconcile Goriev's dandyism with a mind that chose which battalions should be sacrificed on any given morning. They both disposed of lives, professionally, but they had no shared principle for doing it.

■

One window of the store still displayed evening gowns, complete with elbow-length black gloves. Mary saw a cat there, sleeping between the feet of a mannequin. The next window was a patriotic tableau: a mannequin in the zippered *mono,* with her right arm pivoted unnaturally into the radical salute, against a backdrop of posters. She went in. There were few customers, and the place was so cold that the assistants wore coats. A tall, sour woman of a dark, southern color served her. The problem was height: the *monos* were cut without shape, she could just get into the largest, and it clung more tightly than intended. The sour woman disapproved of the fit, clacking disparagingly while Mary stood at the mirror. Other assistants were watching. Some kind of internal war was involved, a civil war of the genteel, black gloves versus the *monos.* The other assistants were unpainted, the sour woman groomed and manicured.

Flattered by the mirror, Mary bought three *monos.* She kept one on and had her old clothes put in a bag. She felt good. Her red hair, uncut for weeks, looked wild and as warlike as the *mono.* And, at last, she was warm.

Only going back into the hotel did she feel suddenly self-conscious and aware of having made a costume change that some would think too showy. But before facing up to that she found herself intercepted—by Nicolás Cordón.

He showed no sign of surprise. He came forward from a seat, nodded graciously, and said, "Miss Byrnes."

"You came—you came for the pictures?"

"Yes, for the pictures. And for another reason." He looked around as though checking to be sure that they were not overheard. "Durruti is coming to Madrid. You remember, you were interested in his photograph?"

"Oh yes. Who could forget a face like that?"

"I could arrange for you to be there, when he arrives. Would you find that interesting?"

"Oh yes—oh yes. That *would* be a story. But why me? Why are you asking me?"

This directness momentarily unsettled him; then he said, "To return the favor, of taking the wedding pictures."

□

Not very convincing, she thought, but she smiled. "You didn't owe me any favor. But it's good of you."

"How are the pictures?"

"The pictures? Oh, the pictures are fine. Just fine. But about Durruti. How many people know about his arrival, when and where?"

"It is better that not too many people know. I cannot tell you; you will just have to come with me, when we go."

Out of the corner of an eye she could see first one and then another of the journalists in the bar appraising her in the *mono.* She was aware of a vague annoyance that Cordón had not himself commented on it. "That's swell," she said. "I'll go get the pictures, but before I do, let me buy you a drink."

He looked across to the bar.

"I do not think—"

"Oh, come *on.* You look as though you need one."

Though he surrendered to her, she knew that it was at a price—that she was not in step with him, not on easy terms. He was as prickly as he was handsome, and more of a mystery than ever.

□

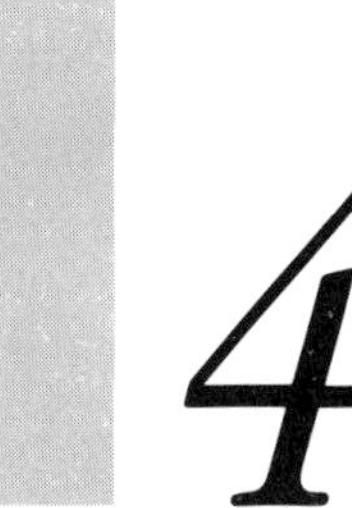

BIARRITZ

A full-blooded Biscay storm shook every pane of glass in the hotel; but for the absence of motion it was like being on a great ocean liner making the last crossing of the season with only a handful of unfashionable passengers. The fashionable would be at the Côte d'Azur by now, not within the grasp of the Atlantic. The windows of the lounge were salted by blown spray. Liam Casey was trying to see through them. Gulls were taking shelter in the palm-lined garden. Liam had not slept well. The bedrooms of this colossus were unheated: the place would be closed in a week and had obviously been chosen for its discretion rather than its comfort. The lounge was closed off to all but a few guests, and a table was laid for six breakfasts.

"Good day, Mr. Casey."

"Miss Eichberg, good morning."

"Well—it is not."

"No, no it isn't." He liked this direct and sharp woman.

She crossed her arms over her gray jacket, compressing shoulders and breasts. "I wear all wool today, and still I am cold."

"Coffee would help."

"I have organized it."

"There is not much you do not organize."

"Mr. Casey. That is a compliment—or not? I cannot tell."

"Miss Eichberg, it is a compliment."

□

"Good. We finish today, perhaps."

"I hope so. I sure hope so."

"And then you can go home. I would like to go to America."

"You should."

"Oh—" She was suddenly solemn. "It is not very likely."

A waitress wheeled in a trolley and poured two cups of filtered coffee.

"At least the kitchen is French," said Liam, gulping the coffee. "That helps."

Before she could answer two men joined them, both, like Liam, dressed in banker's serge.

"Good morning, Freda, Mr. Casey," said one.

"Good morning, Otto," said Liam.

"Hell of a day, Liam," said the other. "Miss Eichberg warned us that these storms go with the territory. You were right, Freda."

"Shall we sit down?" said Liam.

Otto Heidel looked at his watch. "Yes. They will, as usual, be late." As he went to the table he said, "Liam, I think Mr. Byrnes and I have the Hamburg arrangements all agreed."

"That right, Pat?" said Liam.

"Yes. Perhaps Miss Eichberg could give us the papers."

She put a folder by each of the six places, and Liam opened his while the others waited.

"The holding company is okay under Swiss law?" said Liam.

"Perfectly," said Heidel.

Liam took more time to read the papers. Byrnes watched him more closely than the others.

"Pat," said Liam, finally looking up, "are you sure there's no problem on the export licenses? It looks tricky."

Byrnes, older by twenty years, had to make an effort to be deferential. "Not with our connections."

Liam drummed fingers on the file, but let the doubt drop. There were approaching voices. They all stood up.

Juan March, a man with a face the texture of buckskin, never apologized for being late. He went to the table in the style of a monarch, followed one step behind by his courtier, Ettore Fumagali.

□

"Gentlemen—and Miss Eichberg—to business."

Two more waitresses appeared with breakfast salvers of scrambled eggs and mushrooms. Until they had gone there was total silence, like the prelude to prayers.

March opened his file, followed to the second by Fumagali. March glanced at the material only briefly, then looked across the table to Liam.

"Mr. Casey, you want my business."

"I thought that was clear."

"At five percent?"

"On a line of credit as large as this, five percent is normal."

"But I am not normal, Mr. Casey. I am Juan March, and for me this is not normal."

"We agreed on five percent."

"That was yesterday."

Liam looked at him steadily. "Señor March. The Banco March knows the going rate as well as we do."

"What do I give you? I give you everything you ask. In exchange for this line of credit I give you contracts for American oil, American trucks, American munitions. All these things I give you."

"The risks are high. These are not *at all* assured contracts. I read the newspapers."

March's mouth tightened. "What do you mean?"

"Franco is not in Madrid."

"This morning I talk to Franco. A temporary setback. We did not know about the Russian tanks and the Russian planes."

"All I'm saying, Señor March," said Liam quietly, "is that the value of the contracts is going to be determined by how long the war lasts, and that isn't decided."

Byrnes spoke. "Liam is being fair. We can't confuse the value of these contracts with the funding of the credit. Five percent is equitable."

March turned to fix Byrnes with a sustained and antagonistic glare, but said nothing.

Heidel said, "Gentlemen, we must be realistic. These things cannot wait. The Führer is providing more assistance than Germany can really afford—he has had no easy task in persuading Göring to commit our best men and machines to Spain. The time to decide the war is now."

During the course of this March had, like a chameleon, changed color and even, it seemed, shape. His stomach, which had been as firm as if held in a corset, now slackened into an overhanging paunch, a muscular trick more common in a wrestler. His face, assuming sweet reason, had blanched. He pointed at the eggs in their salver, and Fumagali replenished his plate.

"In Rome," he said, "I have one and a half billion dollars in gold. That is more gold than in the reserves of most countries." He dug a fork into the egg and, before eating, soaked it in salt. "Some collateral," he said, accurately mimicking Byrnes's accent.

"The securities are enough," said Liam.

March swallowed the egg. His face offered a smile that would have chilled a baby. "Mr. Casey, any time your father becomes too ungrateful, you can have a job at the Banco March."

Fumagali put a spoonful of mushrooms onto his master's plate.

Heidel sat back and said, "I congratulate you, gentlemen."

But it took most of the day to satisfy March on paper. Successive drafts of agreement were produced by Freda and each time, until the fifth, March found clauses to change.

When it was done, Liam needed air—even the saturated air of the storm. He put on a trench coat and walked to the casino. The bar was the best place he had seen in a week. A pianist played Cole Porter, there were attractive women, and the barman made a powerful Manhattan. It was not exactly chic, but it was not drab. He sat on a stool at the bar and let the day sink into his feet.

Calling for his third Manhattan, he attracted the notice of a couple at a table. The man came over.

"American?"

"That's right."

"I'm Drexel King. Solitary drinking is bad for the brain. Would you join us, please?"

"Sure. Liam Casey. Pleased to know you."

"This is Serena," said King, introducing Liam to the girl.

□

"Serena Pollard, actually," she said, in an English voice that Liam would have robbed for.

"You look a bit beaten, sport," said King.

"Yes. Guess so."

"Oh, I don't know," said Serena. "Not everybody is at their best when at their best—if you understand."

"Serena has a funny way with words, sport."

King, thought Liam, had read too much Fitzgerald—he was dressed in a loud jazz-age style with a flashing diamond tiepin, a style that was already a curiosity. Liam thought Serena deserved better, but it was going to take too much of an effort to compete with King.

"Bit of a backwater these days, Biarritz," said King. "You on vacation?"

"No. Business trip."

"What business would that be?"

Serena managed with only an eyebrow to signal to Liam that King's curiosity was, to her, impertinent.

"Finance."

"Ah. Well, anything I can do to help, just ask. I'm at the U.S. embassy, in exile. We moved from Madrid when it got too hot."

Liam's interest in King increased. "Then you would know Esposito—Tom Esposito?"

"Of course. Matter of fact, Tom is one of the wild ones. He elected to stay on in Madrid. You know him?"

"I've dealt with him."

"I think," said Serena, drinking a cocktail that looked like a blue flame, "that you've all backed the wrong horse in Spain. I think that fat little general is pissing in the wind. Historically, that is." She smiled with the delicacy of a nun.

"Serena is a tad pink," said King.

"Only to a reactionary like you, darling."

"Her brother is in the International Brigade," persisted King happily. "He deserted the family castle for the great red brotherhood of man."

"Let's have champagne," said Liam, deciding that perhaps Serena was detachable after all.

□

"What a super idea," she said.
King looked hesitant, but then remembered his role.
"Why not, sport?"

"The most refined lady bugs do it,
When a gentleman calls.
Moths in your rugs do it;
What's the use of mothballs?"

The pianist nodded toward them as he sang. Liam sent him a glass of champagne.

"Let's dance—Mr. Casey?" said Serena.

When she stood she unfolded into more height than Liam had anticipated. Tall women were one of his weaknesses. She danced with a sobriety remarkable in one who had drunk so much. She looked over his shoulder at King, who had sagged.

"Poor Drexel," she said. "What you see now is the lesser scaffolding on which the larger ego is insecurely draped."

Liam laughed.

"Drexel thinks he's Jay Gatsby," she said. "I think it was seeing the light at the end of the pier, when he was very young."

"Can we lose him?"

With her tulip lips she picked up the words of the pianist—

". . . you're the top!
You're the Louvre Museum . . ."

And then, "Leave it to me, darling."

She excused herself after the dance.

Liam returned to the table. King looked at him with exaggerated belligerence. "You make a swell couple on the floor. She's quite a lady, don't you think?"

"She has class."

"Kind of class money can't buy, sport."

She returned and invited King to dance. He straightened himself and, going to the floor, put an arm around her waist possessively. But before the dance was over a waiter called him off the floor.

□

She came back to the table. "Urgent phone call." Her smile was as good as a wink.

"You're very deft," said Liam.

"Oh yes. Absolutely. Very."

King had visibly sobered when he returned, to explain that he was needed at the embassy "for some damn fool cable work." He became obliging. "Why don't you stay, Serena? No point breaking up the party. I'll catch up with you later. Mr. Casey. Hope to see you again."

"Would you like dinner?" said Liam, when King had gone.

"First?"

He tried not to seem dumb.

"I always think it's better on an empty stomach," she said, picking up her purse.

"Anything you say."

At the hotel she said, "Who are you trying to avoid?"

"Is it that obvious?"

"Well, darling, it makes me feel like a tart. I mean, coming in the garden entrance."

"It's not what you think."

"What is it, then?"

He led her up a rear staircase.

"I'm with some very disagreeable people."

"That's odd. You seem very agreeable."

"Business is business."

"Then you shouldn't be in it."

He laughed nervously and opened the door to his suite. "It's freezing in here. Like a meat locker."

"Oh, never mind that. I'm English. Cold bedrooms are an essential part of the national character."

She looked younger when naked; shedding the black silk dress and, finally, the single string of pearls, suggested the removal of a subtle mask. Sophistication, worldliness, the finishing school movements, and the sharpness of mind and speech did not belong to this body. It was unblemished ivory—only the lightest brush of pubic hair prevented it from being a virgin from a Titian panel. The name, Serena, was the name of the body. Her long legs had the springiness of a fawn's: she leapt into the frigid linen and snared him as he joined her. And the body had wit. It slid and turned and teased and then duly collaborated. From beginning to end it was well-humored, and her playful eyes, even in orgasm, were those of a fresh and unclaiming spirit. It was the least emotional and yet the most physically replete lovemaking he had ever had. It left, he knew, no obligation. Yet to have called it promiscuous would demean it.

And she slept serenely.

In the morning, when he moved to get up, she claimed him again, and then she said, "Don't disturb me before noon, there's a pet."

Freda, hair plaited and parted with a symmetry that caught perfectly the spirit of a Wagnerian Rheinmaiden, was eating breakfast alone. Liam joined her.

"I thought you would be on your way back to Berlin," he said.

"I hoped so. But, instead, we go to Spain, to Algeciras. We have to wait here for a plane from Germany."

"Algeciras?"

She gave him one of her steady and unself-conscious scrutinies. "Mr. Casey, you have a very hearty appetite this morning. Not like yesterday."

"Algeciras?"

"At least it will be warmer than Biarritz." She was going to offer no more.

"Has March gone?"

She nodded.

"I do business with all kinds of people, but *that* man . . ."

"He's a pirate."

It was the first time he had known her to speak her mind. He nodded, and wanted to push her further. "That's exactly what he is. That was how he made his money. At the beginning. But then I guess you know others like that."

She did not take the bait. Instead, she watched him eat, and he felt that she had divined him only too well.

"Have you finished with that newspaper?" he said.

"Yes. Yes—please take it."

"Don't like the French newspapers. Too hysterical. The *Paris Herald Tribune* is more my speed."

"But you have some terrible newspapers in America. How can you call the French press hysterical? Look at what your papers have done to poor Charles Lindbergh when his baby was kidnapped."

"The price of a free press is to have all kinds. I like it that way." He unfolded the *Herald Tribune* and gave it half his attention, watching her at the same time, but she again failed to react. Then he registered what was on the front page.

"*Jesus!* Jesus Christ! Has anyone else seen this?"

"What is it?"

"You see this?"

She peered over. "Yes. It is interesting. But—"

"It sure is interesting. Jesus Christ! You see the name on that piece?"

"It is not related to . . ."

"Sure as hell is. Forgive me. It's Pat's daughter."

"I see." She was like an interpreter, pausing before translating. "I see. Yes. It must be embarrassing for him."

"For him? For us." He began to read the story. After a minute he said, "She always could write like a dream."

"You know her well?"

"She was at Radcliffe when I was at Harvard. We sort of . . . we sort of grew up together. You know—with Pat working for my father. Not close. But, well, Mary was always a handful. She has this red hair and—"

"And?"

"And she's trouble. Always kicking the hand that feeds her."

"But you admire that?"

"I didn't say that."

"No. You did not say it."

This time there was a hint of humor in her perception, even the suggestion of a smile in the eyes. What annoyed him about Freda Eichberg was that she could not have been much older than he was, but she had the wisdom of the ages. A wisdom with a knowledge of some pain, he suspected. Some hurt had given her a maturity and a moral advantage that, nonetheless, she was reluctant to reveal or to use.

Mary's story was played as a box beside the news from Spain and was headlined THE SPIRIT OF MADRID: SURPRISE FACTOR IN FRANCO'S MILITARY REVERSE.

He read the first paragraph again, this time aloud:

"In one sense the Battle of Madrid seems complex. It is not being fought between armies. On the Nationalist side there is an army, but it is an army risen against the state. On the other side there is no simple army, and many factions. But what in the end is prevailing here is not the force of arms alone. It is a spirit."

He stopped and looked up. "You have to admit—she has a touch."

The story went on to describe the Battle of the Segovia Bridge and ended with conversations with men riding to the front on a tram.

Patrick Byrnes appeared.

"Liam, I was looking for you last night," he said, with a touch of exhausted patience. "There was no reply from your suite."

He sat down. "March gave us a little party." He saw the newspaper. "What's the latest?"

Liam gave him the paper and said, "You'd better read this, Pat."

Byrnes pulled out his glasses, slightly puzzled by the pregnant silence. His eyes moved from the main story to the box. His expression barely registered any change. He broke off to order his breakfast, looked at Liam, and resumed reading.

When he had finished he said, "I see. I'm thankful at least that March has gone. I would not have enjoyed explaining the connection. I can't say I am as awed by it as the editor of the newspaper seems to have been, judging by the prominence he has given it. It's what I would have expected. Impressionable, jejune, and—most predictably—politically sophomoric."

Freda had listened with neutral attention.

Liam, however, was more aroused. "*Come on,* Pat. It's going to make her name."

"I would prefer it was another name. She is a liability."

"She's your daughter, not a balance sheet."

Byrnes fixed Liam with a look that abandoned all deference. "Do you think your father will be more forgiving?"

Liam looked from Byrnes to Freda, who offered no help, and back to Byrnes. "I tell you what I think. I think, if you want to make it a professional issue, that this story of Mary's could have a bearing—a lot of bearing—on our investment. I think we should take it seriously."

"What does taking it seriously mean?"

"She's a lot closer to it than we are. March has been boosting Franco like he's the only game in town, because he's put all his chips on him. What arrangements have you made for getting out of here?"

"Car this afternoon to Cherbourg. There's a boat tomorrow."

"You take the boat. I'm going to Madrid."

Byrnes leaned back and pulled off his glasses. "*What?* Are you out of your mind?"

"I'm going to Madrid. Call it checking out the investment. You don't need me in Boston. You have everything to get the deal rolling."

"What am I supposed to tell your father?"

"I'll give you a note."

"This is preposterous."

"I've considered it carefully for the last sixty seconds. It makes a lot of sense."

"You'll need a visa. There will be all sorts of—" He stopped and reexamined Liam. Then said, "Dammit, Liam, I can't stop you. But it's a damn fool thing to do."

Freda said, "We will be on different sides, then, Mr. Casey."

"That's right," said Liam, "but at least not as combatants." He reached for the newspaper. "I'd like to clip this. That is, unless you want it, Pat?"

"Don't be facetious."

Liam's grin was implacable. He nodded to Freda. "Sometime, somewhere, perhaps."

"I hope so, Mr. Casey."

She may have meant it, he thought, as he went back to his suite, with a spring in his step that had not shown itself for a while.

But Serena was gone.

In cerise lipstick on the bathroom mirror she had written, "Bye-bye. You're the top."

The script was exuberant and devoid of apology. He adored her.

5

A road at first empty, but for one woman in black walking away from the city with a peasant's broad strides. The weight of a rolled bag strapped to her back did not bend her. She was done with the city; it showed in every step. Where to, as the wind pressed one side of her and flared her skirts on the other? The wind had cleared the last of the low dark clouds, and the road was drying fast as the sun put the flint sheen back into the Castilian earth. The wind was from the south. The men at the barricade had taken off their coats, heavy from the days of rain, and draped them over a wall. The coats looked as bodies often looked when they were left at the walls.

A sudden clearing like this was dangerous. The fascists were learning not to fly until the sun was behind them, making interception more difficult, and the sun was passing from one Spain to another, from the Republican east to the Nationalist west. The woman walked on and disappeared. One man kept his field glasses on the horizon. The foreshortened road in his lenses became molten in the glare. Nothing came.

It was an emptiness that was not empty to Cordón: the city was at his back, and this was Spain, for a moment left in peace. All the covert life in the earth could be sensed again as he had encountered it as a child; it was possible to recover a wisdom lost in the later wisdoms. Perhaps in their different ways all of them knew it. Like the crew of a ship released from a storm into the doldrums, they had all become silent and inert, not trusting the respite but succumbing to it.

Then Durruti came.

They heard him first. The convoy was over the horizon before the man with the field glasses picked them out. Ahead of the trucks a black sedan was accelerating toward the barricade. Durruti's Packard.

"*Make way for Durruti!*" cried the man with the glasses, and the rest of them, anarchists and communists alike, took up the chant even while the Packard was half a mile away.

Mary had been asleep under a tree and was wakened by the shouts. She picked up her camera and followed Cordón as he joined two other anarchist union men delegated to meet Durruti. Others jumped from walls and came out of the old farmhouse that served as canteen.

"*Durruti! Durruti!* Make way for the Durruti column!"

The bandit king of Barcelona slowed to the threshold of the *madrileños.*

The Packard's whitewall tires were freshly scrubbed. Chrome flashed in the sun. Durruti was beside the driver.

One of the union men opened the door for him before the car had stopped. Mary found a gap through which to focus on the man as he emerged.

Like a poster tyrant, Durruti had the intensity that appeared able to appraise everyone at the same time. In the camera he was framed from the waist up, and his dark, hard eyes subsumed everything else. Unusually big for a Spaniard. Made more bulky by a double-breasted black leather trench coat. A face that rammed itself into any obstructing object. Wide mouth. Full flat lips, high cheekbones, and thick brows.

He let the chants of his name continue and then held up a gloved hand.

"Yes," he rasped, "Durruti is here. *Revolution*—and *victory!*"

"*Revolution and victory,*" they echoed.

The trucks carrying his men reached the barricade and filled the road to the horizon.

"We are one people in the revolution and we will be one Spain," said Durruti, subjecting the communists to the embracing eyes.

□

"One people!"

The union men spoke to him.

Mary crouched for a low shot. The holstered pistol at his waist looked like the accessory of his voice—not for decoration, but to be frequently used. Everything about him was brutish. She wondered how Cordón with his seigneurial grace could have fallen in with such a man. And, as she took the picture, Durruti broke from the men and reached out to Cordón.

Cordón stepped forward. "We have needed you," he said.

"And we have needed you, my friend." Cordón was engulfed in a bear hug, and held in it while Durruti said to the union men, "In Barcelona they call this one Captain. We have no captains, but if we did he would be the captain general. He saved my life at the Atarazanas barracks, when Ascaso was killed by my side." He partly released Cordón but gripped his shoulders. "You will come in the car with Durruti!"

The union men looked uneasy, but Durruti intimidated them too much for complaint.

As Cordón was released, Durruti's eyes fixed on Mary. "Who is this with hair as red as a Bolshevik's heart?"

Cordón introduced her.

"Any friend of the captain is a friend of Durruti's—even a *yanqui*." He laughed. "You will avoid my profile. I look like an old bull."

Others laughed.

"You see—they know this bull is not so old." He played to the crowd again. "*Revolution! Victory!*" And while they responded he took Mary by the arm. "You come in my *yanqui* car, too."

He smelled of leather and garlic.

On the ride into the city Durruti and Cordón were together in the back; Mary sat with the driver, Julio. Although she could not hear what was said between them—they were followed by the noise of the trucks and hailed in the streets—she could see enough to understand the unlikely attraction of one for the other. Durruti had only one volume, even in the car: bombast. But Cordón remained himself, listening to it with little reaction except for an occasional nod and, given the chance, responding with pointed brevity. Durruti's eyes began to show more reflection than his voice. By the time the car reached the Calle de Miguel Ángel and the anarchist headquarters, the tyrant was too lapsed in thought even to wave to the crowds.

She took a final picture and they disappeared into the building, still ignoring the crowd.

■

Álvaro had been waiting hours for Cordón. The house they used as a militia billet was the first place he had ever known with a flushing toilet. He had taken to sitting there and reading—María was out and it was the only privacy. Now someone was banging on the door.

He came out, pulling up his trousers.

"What is the matter with you? You shit all day?"

Álvaro concealed the book. "You know how it is."

"Your captain is here," said the Marxist, going in.

Cordón was getting coffee and looking around the room.

"Where is everyone?" he said, as Álvaro appeared.

"The communists are going."

"Already?"

"A new central command, Captain. How—how is Durruti?"

"Álvaro, Durruti is Durruti. Now I know how much we need him."

"Are we moving out, too, Captain?"

"Yes. Durruti does not want to waste a minute. How is María?"

"She is good. She works in the field kitchen."

"The war is different now," said Cordón, patting Álvaro on the back and going upstairs with more vigor than Álvaro had seen in him in weeks.

In their room he found that Ferrer's things were already packed.

Her books were strung together and stacked by her canvas duffel. Books that they had argued over all night—always at night. The best and the worst of her was in that bundle of books. And there was pain in seeing it suddenly gathered up like this.

She had not touched any of his things. Where she had taken her dresses (not worn since the war) from the cupboard, she had uncovered his guitar; like the dresses, it was too romantic for war. Why had she bothered with the dresses? What would he do with the guitar? He pulled out his suitcase.

He didn't hear her on the stairs. She was in the room before he knew it. He was folding a suit with the deftness of a valet, lining outermost.

"A man's background always comes out when he packs," she said.

"You took the dresses," he said.

She laughed in a brittle way. "Clearing out, that is all."

For a moment the days of dresses and suits came back to both of them, and Cordón wanted to hold her. But the moment slipped away.

"Álvaro is behaving like a child," she said.

"He will be with me." For the first time he noticed that she was, under her heavy man's greatcoat, shaking. "Are you all right?"

She stiffened. "Of course."

"I will miss it, this house."

"Only the house?"

"No. Not only that."

Before he could fully realize what was happening she had pulled a gun from the coat—an old hammer-lock pistol, so heavy that she had to steady it with both hands pulled into her chest. Antique though it was, it was lethal.

"How many lovers do you want, eh?" she said, on the edge of shouting.

"How many lovers do you want, eh?" again.

She lowered the aim slightly but kept her grip on the trigger.

"I shoot your balls off. Then you sing like a choirboy."

He kept perfectly still. "What are you talking about?"

"How is she, the American bitch?"

He remained still. "This is ridiculous."

"I shoot your balls off. You should fuck your own kind; plenty of anarchist girls need fucking. That I would not mind. But you want to fuck someone who works for the capitalist lie-mongers, someone who sells the war for profit."

The pistol was constant in purpose. But Cordón was now more angry than cautious. He moved toward her.

"I shoot your balls off."

"You would not—" He lunged at the pistol.

□

The trigger needed more effort than she realized, and the delay was just enough for Cordón to deflect the barrel. The recoil tore the weapon out of her hands. The bullet went through the floor within a hair of Cordón's feet. Flame, smoke, and detonation dazed them both.

Before the smoke cleared she was screaming at him. "*You idiot!* Did you think I was going to do it? *You idiot!*"

"What did you want to prove?" he shouted.

Álvaro had bounded up the stairs and stood at the door. "What is happening?" He looked at the hole in the floor and then saw the pistol lying by the bed.

"An accident," said Ferrer.

Álvaro looked from her to Cordón.

"Yes, an accident," said Cordón.

Álvaro tried a nervous smile. "That's an old gun."

Cordón looked down at the singed gap by his feet. "Old guns make large holes." He looked up at her and realized that already she believed that she had not meant to shoot him. He knew this trick of her mind: the new conviction had eradicated the contrary truth.

She said, quite calmly, to Álvaro, "Could you take down my case, please?"

She picked up the books, letting them swing lightly on the loop of string. She had done the same with the satchel of books in Paris. But she had looked at him differently in those days. He wondered as he fell under her half-mad smile where the seed of this had been planted, or if it had always been there. She was mad in a way that could find employment; the world was opening up for people like her. She frightened him much more with the smile than she had with the gun.

"Good-bye," she said, and followed Álvaro down the stairs, the hem of her greatcoat brushing the steps behind her.

■

The Russians came late at night to the Calle de Miguel Ángel, two men used to the work of the night, Koltzov and I. Yanin, and one who preferred the day, General Vladimir Goriev. None of them relished this encounter, but they disliked it in different ways: Koltzov had met Durruti in the first anarchist offensive—the making of the Durruti legend—and Koltzov had been sure that if the legend were given its run it would burn out quickly; Goriev knew Durruti only from the noise and held him in contempt for his tactics on the field; Yanin, as a man who had to live with low, constant pain, felt that Durruti would be a minor aggravation, swiftly extinguished.

"They are all the same," said Koltzov as the Buick pulled up. "Bandits pretending to be libertarians."

Inside, the bandits were ranged around one side of a long table, waiting.

Durruti, grenades dangling from his belt, stepped forward to crush Koltzov's outstretched hand. "You see, comrade! They have not made a Bolshevik of me yet!"

Koltzov did not give him the satisfaction of registering pain. "That was a joke."

Durruti was introduced to the others by Koltzov and then, making an effort to be procedural, he brought forward his own staff, the last of whom was Cordón.

The three Russians sat down to face seven anarchists, with bottled water between them.

"When will you be ready to fight?" said Goriev.

"We *are* ready," said Durruti.

"Good. Good. We need you." Goriev pulled a field map from his portfolio. "Here is where we need you. University City. A counterattack in the line of the Casa de Velázquez."

Durruti spun the map around and gave it a cursory look. The man beside him, the only anarchist who had recently shaved, looked at it more carefully.

"Tomorrow," said Durruti.

"One moment," said his companion.

Durruti was annoyed, but checked himself. "It is simple enough, Cipriano."

But Cipriano Mera looked across to Goriev. "Franco has his best units on that line. They have artillery. And Germans directing the artillery."

□

Goriev was untroubled. "We will give you artillery support. And air support. If the weather allows."

Durruti settled both elbows on the table as though it was decided. "There! The Bolsheviks will give us air support and we will blast the fascists until the shits turn and run."

Mera spoke again. "A frontal assault against such well-prepared positions is a great risk. Even with artillery and planes."

Goriev was now showing as much impatience as Durruti. "I would remind the delegate general that we have already deployed the International Brigade in the sector and they have held their positions."

Durruti smashed a fist on the table, rattling the water. "The delegate general has been too long in Madrid. The Durruti column has never sat on its arse."

"How many men has the Durruti column?" said Yanin in a listless voice.

Durruti was as casual as the question. "We have brought more than four thousand from the Aragón front."

"*Four thousand?*" said Goriev. "But I thought—"

Yanin cut in. "Four thousand men of such reputation should be more than enough."

Durruti looked at Yanin with a new interest. "Every one of them is ready to die."

Goriev recovered himself. "We are agreed, then?"

Mera had subsided to join the mutes on each flank of Durruti. But Durruti was not yet done. He leaned across the table and stabbed a blackened finger at Koltzov. "We will teach you Bolsheviks how to make a revolution!"

"In August," said Koltzov agreeably, "if I remember, you were saying, 'We renounce everything except victory.' "

Durruti was uncomfortable. "We are carrying on the war and the revolution at the same time."

Yanin, almost in a whisper, said, "The revolution will wait."

Durruti suddenly leapt out of his seat, sending it spinning. Yanin recoiled, but Durruti was already marching across the room. He went to a window, a large double window running virtually from the floor to a heavy lintel under the ceiling. He pulled aside the blue velvet curtains, tearing at them and breaking a sash.

Cordón wondered if Durruti was about to throw a grenade into the street—he had seen Durruti fire his pistol out of a window with far less provocation.

The others remained fixed in their places.

Durruti stood outlined against the dark city, a raging man jabbing a fist at the night. "There!" he shouted. "*There* is where revolution begins—in the streets. I have a nose for revolution." He turned on them all. "I *smell* revolution in these streets. I know that smell. I knew it in Barcelona, and I know it now in Madrid. So do not play your Bolshevik games." He leveled a deadly eye on Yanin. "*The conditions for revolution exist!* We want the revolution here, in Spain, now and not tomorrow."

Still nobody spoke or moved.

He strode back to the table, poured a glass of water, and downed it in a gulp. To Goriev he said, "We will be in position by dawn."

As Cordón watched the troika leave the room he was struck by how mismatched they were: the vain general, the urbane Koltzov, and the nebulous Yanin. They did not seem to have a country in common. What was this Soviet Russia that sprawled so large on maps and gave men like this a common cause? Cordón could not grasp it as a matter either of scale or of mission; what he did understand, what they all understood now, was that their war was in alien hands.

"Nicolás," said Durruti, putting a hold of custody on his shoulder. "You know this terrain. Explain it to me."

In an assembly free of hierarchy, the delegate-general should not have felt slighted, but he was. Mera stood darkly by as Cordón went over the positions on the map.

■

Purple-gray carbon paper shrouded the bulb over Barea's desk. He was groping through a dispatch filed in English, needing a dictionary to check something in almost every line. Predictions of Madrid's fall were being revised; it gave him wry comfort in the night. In the background, beyond the reach of the single light, Luis snored to a regular beat on a couch, still in his uniform. Barea hardly heard the sound of the swinging door, or her steps, until she stood at his desk.

"Arturo."

He looked up, but her face was in shadow.

She spoke in French. "Arturo, you still work all through the night."

As he leaned back he got a glimpse of the familiar mass of dark hair. "Well," he said, "can I help you, *camarade* Poldi?"

It was an old joke, the political word concealing the term of endearment, and he said it with a half-smile.

"I've had enough of Valencia," she said, moving slowly around the desk to put a hand on his shoulder. "Are you happy to see me, Arturo?"

"Ilsa Poldi. I have a wife. I have a mistress. I have the worst job in Madrid. Of course I'm happy to see you."

"I have a proposition." She glanced at the snoring Luis and back again, looking over his marks on the typescript. "Arturo, I have not six words of Spanish. You cannot handle English. We speak in French, I help you with the English, the French, the German, the Russian. How is that?"

"And you are Austrian."

"Who can be Austrian today? I have no country."

He took her hand from his shoulder and held it. "I need help."

"Good." She looked over to Luis again. "Good. I sleep here, with you." He pulled the hand to his mouth and kissed it. "Arturo." He released the hand. She pulled something from her bag and put it under the light. It was a copy of the *Paris Herald Tribune.* "Arturo. You should read this—I read it to you. I found the paper in Valencia. It is a wonderful story, by the American girl, Mary Byrnes."

But Barea scowled—he saw the photograph before she read anything. "She did not clear the pictures," he said.

"Don't worry. It doesn't matter. Arturo, that smell—"

"I know. It's the carbon paper, on the lamp." He pushed away the lamp. "The wax, in the carbon paper. Like the smell in a church, when the big candles of the main altar have just been put out. I hate that smell."

"Poor Arturo." Moving away the light had drained the last vestige of his authority. He opened his arms to her.

□

■

The basement of the Gran Vía Hotel had been turned into a canteen for the journalists, who were now its only guests.

"Irregularities of supply," said Praeger, looking without enthusiasm at what was offered for breakfast. "To be charitable, to make allowances . . . stale bread, no milk, and those filthy sausages. But, thank God, coffee."

Mary saw the bulge in his jacket where he kept the flask of cognac. "I like the sausages," she said.

"Your stomach must be lined with steel."

They had just settled at a table when Praeger groaned, "Oh no, not him."

She followed his eyes. Bearing down on them, with his tray, was a man she had seen before but only in the gloom of the bar. This morning he was in green tweeds—a suit that retained no shape at any angle and was more or less suspended on him—jacket from the shoulders and trousers from braces, the waist of the trousers hoisted nearly to his chest, and a soiled silk tie disappearing inside the trousers. His pockets were stuffed with newspapers.

"Barrington-Taylor," hissed Praeger and then, simulating an entirely different tone, "Barrington-Taylor, good morning."

It was surrender to the inevitable; the man had already settled his tray before them.

"Praeger, mornin' to you. And—Miss Byrnes, is it not? Miss *Mary* Byrnes?"

"Yes."

"Barrington-Taylor. *Daily Chronicle.* London. I say—" He pulled one of the papers from his jacket. "Been reading this. Your stuff."

He spread the *Herald Tribune.* Praeger gaped at it; Mary nodded. "Yes. That's mine."

"Well, Miss Byrnes. I'll be frank. Always am, frank." His several chins rippled. "What you have done in this extraordinary piece is to sentimentalize the war. What do you *mean,* if I may ask, by the spirit of Madrid?"

"I think that's obvious."

"Oh, is it? Is it? It's just a phrase, darling. Nothing more. Quite a clever phrase." He took and swallowed in one movement an entire stale bread roll. "You're a pretty thing—" he said, reaching for his coffee and smiling at Praeger companionably, "—and intelligent. One senses the *raw* intelligence. I'll give you that. But you don't seem to understand one thing."

"What's that?" she said, wanting to push the coffee into his lap.

"Oh, look around you." He smiled at Praeger again. "War reporting is hackwork, darling. The best people don't do it. The best people come here and make extensive notes and go away and write something awfully profound, a novel, something like that. That's so, isn't it Praeger?"

"I don't know the best people," said Praeger.

"Don't you?" Barrington-Taylor laughed. "No. I suppose you don't." He looked at Mary again. "So you see, while you're with us, darling, play the game. There's a sport. Don't try to be clever." Coffee dribbled from his lip as he waved the cup. "If you win the censor's enthusiasm it's apt to be used against the rest of us, and that could put you in a rather uncomfortable position, couldn't it, Praeger?"

Praeger, who had been absorbing the front page of the *Herald Tribune,* looked at Mary rather than at Barrington-Taylor and said, "You'll make Barea a happy man."

God!" she exploded, glaring at him and then at Barrington-Taylor. "You don't have *any* damned convictions, do you?"

The word seemed to sweeten Barrington-Taylor's coffee as he drained it. Then he said, "Convictions? Oh dear me, is *that* what we need?"

Mary sprang up and walked out.

Barrington-Taylor looked at Praeger rather than at her. "Well, *well.* Are you—are you in any way close, you two, old boy? Forgive my asking."

"No," said Praeger flatly.

"Just as well, if you ask me. Such conceit, those damned Americans. What do they understand?"

"She's surprising," said Praeger, picking up the *Herald Tribune* for closer scrutiny. "I didn't have any inkling of this."

"There you are," said Barrington-Taylor, "there you have it."

"Yes." Praeger looked up from the paper, but Mary had gone. "I think she's up to something else. She came down with a pile of new stuff in her hands this morning, stuffing it into her bag when she saw me."

"Oh, don't worry. She won't pull another one, not today."

"Oh?"

"There's a total embargo, put on by the military this morning. Nothing is going out, for at least twenty-four hours. Something is up. Something big. Nothing to do but sit it out. I say, Praeger, do you think you could spare just a drop of that cognac for my coffee? There's a good chap."

□

An outbreak of laughter drew Cordón. He put down the field glasses and walked over to where some of his men had gathered.

"Look, Captain," one of them said, pointing beyond him. "They dig their own graves before they fight, these Bolsheviks."

Cordón saw a mud-smeared face staring from the ground like a surfaced mole. The face was topped by an old French helmet and looked up at the anarchists with annoyance.

"Can't you buggers shut up?" said the face. "You'll get the whole bloody fascist army down on us with that racket."

Cordón's men could understand the tone but not the words. Cordón said, "They have never seen a foxhole before."

"Sod me," said the face. "Where have you buggers been?"

Cordón told his men to keep their voices down and tried to explain the rudiments of trench warfare.

"We don't live like that in our own shit," said one of them.

Cordón led them back to his lines. "That is the way they have been trained," he said. "That is how it was in the last war. They stayed in the trenches for years." At this moment, with half an hour to go before their first assault, he needed to encourage them. "No advance and no retreat, and millions of them died. We are not fighting that kind of war. We do not have the time."

"They look like rats, Captain."

□

But Cordón had been disturbed to discover how thorough the International Brigade had been in preparing the rear defenses: if this was the work of the commissars, they seemed to be resisting the idea of any attack, preferring to win by attrition, or at least to wait for more equipment. They had poor weapons, but good organization. He had seen the field telephones and ammunition held in reserve. If it had not been for Goriev's commitment of artillery and air support, Cordón would have agreed with Mera. Through his glasses he had seen that his line of attack was thinly covered and that the fascists had the high ground to the Casa de Velázquez. The weapons so willfully brandished by his men were nineteenth-century Swiss carbines. The only concession they made to caution was to wear steel helmets distributed just an hour ago; many of the men were already out of them. One, surrounded by others, had defecated in his.

The attack had three prongs. Cordón was on the right flank. He looked through the glasses again. After showing a brief rim of weak blue at dawn, the sky had become darker rather than lighter. Nothing seemed to move around the Casa de Velázquez, but visibility was too poor for the glasses to be reliable. The cloud cover probably ruled out air support. The International Brigade lines were to his right. They had machine-gun emplacements, but they were positioned to meet an attack, not to support an assault.

The coldest part of him was his feet. The ground was sodden and held to their boots with every step, sucking at them and then releasing a spurt of mud to the knees. The effort of walking made the men look like apes loping through a swamp. Some of the men, peasants rather than city anarchists, had not worn and would never wear boots. In their rope-soled sandals, they were the only ones who moved easily. Cordón's men still clung together in the small groups that had formed at the beginning in Barcelona.

There was five minutes to go. He called for a passing of the word. As it traveled, the men, still not properly spread out for an assault, gave final attention to their rifles.

Cordón raised his pistol and checked his watch. The final minute crawled around the dial. *"Forward, Durruti column!"* he cried, and fired the pistol. The men echoed him and began the charge.

□

Slight though the gradient was, they were slowed by the mud. The unit on their left, where the ground had drained better, was a little forward of them; Cordón saw them as a thin wave of dark forms, and it was exhilarating to watch and feel the lung-filling aggression of thousands of men.

The first objective was to get within range of the Casa de Velázquez—the range of the Swiss carbines was only five hundred yards. A low stone wall and intermittent bushes promised some cover at the right point.

Some of the wilder men were firing in the air as they ran.

There was no opposing fire, and in two minutes they were halfway there—not simultaneously, because some of the clusters of men were still held back by the mud.

The men on Cordón's left were within several hundred feet of the wall when the fascist machine guns opened up. A group of eight men ran straight into the fire—seven crumpled and the eighth, either not knowing what had happened or crazed by it, went running on to the wall, raising his rifle. The rifle was knocked out of his hands, and in the same instant he seemed to give off smoke and disintegrate. All along the left flank the same thing happened.

Cordón called out to his men to fall. Some ignored him and ran on. Other machine guns cut them down.

Within thirty seconds the entire line of assault had been stopped, well short of the wall. They looked for what cover there was; in many places there was none. They were getting no artillery support. Cordón had fallen within the cover of two bushes. He could see, from the blue-red cones of flame, where the machine guns were—the light machine guns used by the Moors, dug in and placed so that their enfilading fire overlapped. As one gun swiveled it met the arc of another. It was murderous and impossible to penetrate with only rifles. Only six machine guns could pin down the whole assault.

Men caught in the open were trying to crawl back. Some tried to run, but as each rose he was eviscerated. Then Cordón saw something else: there was sniper fire. The machine guns were not able, with the gradient and their angle of fire, to hit the prone men. But the crawling men were systematically being picked off.

Those with cover lay, still in their groups, comprehending the trap for the first time. None had ever faced entrenched machine guns. All the bravura had drained from them.

A man rolled close to Cordón.

"Captain, we cannot stay here."

"We cannot go back. They will get us on the open ground."

The man looked back, and then forward. "The bastards. They led us into this."

No, thought Cordón, someone else did that. He looked at the huddled and prone survivors. "We have to stay. We should have artillery cover." Then he pulled up his rifle. "We must give covering fire to the men still out there."

The two of them began firing—it was impossible to know if it had any result. The sniping continued, but one or two men reached cover. As Cordón reloaded, there was a stunning roar. For a second it felt like his head was blown sideways. All his hearing was gone. He rolled over, expecting to see either blood on his body or pitted ground where the shot had hit. Instead he found another of his men with a smoking carbine: the man had fired with the muzzle next to Cordón's head. The moronic face grinned at him.

"We show them, Captain," he said.

But Cordón saw only the moving mouth. "For pity's sake," he shouted, "get that rifle away from my head."

Cordón knew his lack of experience was as great as theirs. Guerrilla and street fighting were the Durruti strengths; textbook assaults were not. Yet he had to give the impression of experience; this idiot's eyes already expected that Cordón knew what to do next. It was to do nothing—and that was against the nature of these men.

The Swiss carbines were useless, and trying to employ them fatal. A prone man raised himself to fire and before he could aim was shot through the head. The snipers went for the head. They did not waste bullets.

The surviving men were spread in a broken line across the entire front. It was sometimes impossible to tell, from where Cordón lay, who were the living and who the dead. The wounded were the only ones trying to move. Cordón realized that soon anyone who was not hit would be covered from both the machine guns and the snipers.

But the cover was perilously sparse—like the bushes and stones that covered him and the two men with him.

The firing eased off—the fascists had come to the same realization. Men died audibly. What were first heard as cries or groans would gradually ebb away with their strength. Cordón saw one of the wounded burst into flame. A sniper had finished him off with an incendiary bullet. Flame fed by the phosphorus rippled over him, and the smell of burning flesh came down the hill on the same wind that carried the fascist voices, no longer concealed. Cordón also heard the throaty cackle of the Moors. The question now was whether they would be left pinned down or whether the Moors would, under cover of their machine guns, come down the hill for them. It began to rain.

■

"You should not take me for a fool, Miss Byrnes."

Barea held his copy of the *Herald Tribune* rolled like a baton and hit his desk with it.

"I could take your cameras, confiscate them, stop you having any more photographs."

"I'm sorry—" said Mary, "—but without the pictures, the story would not have had the same play."

"I am not a fool," said Barea, a little less aggressively, "and I will not forget." He put down the paper. "The story is—"

She looked at the door as he did: Koltzov came in.

"Miss Byrnes, good morning. Arturo, good morning."

"Mikhail—" said Barea, but again stopped.

Koltzov was nodding at the *Herald Tribune.* "Everybody in the Gran Vía is talking about that story," he said, fixing Mary with the masking glasses.

"I'll bet."

"Now you will find out who your friends are," said Koltzov.

She still had no sense of his mood.

He looked at Barea. "Is that not right, Arturo?"

Mary realized with surprise that Barea was nervous with Koltzov. He nodded perfunctorily.

"Well—I tell you, Miss Byrnes," said Koltzov, picking up the *Herald Tribune,* "you are a fine writer."

"Thank you."

"Yes," he said, more thoughtfully, "a good writer. But today, Miss Byrnes, we are all spectators, today we cannot file anything. So, you will be my guest, perhaps? We go to the ninth floor, and we watch the war from there."

"The ninth floor? I thought that was off-limits."

"Not today." Koltzov looked at Barea. "Arturo, I take Miss Byrnes to the gallery."

Barea seemed relieved to see them go.

Koltzov, she discovered, had his own key to a small, private elevator.

In the elevator he said, "So, you have seen Durruti."

"How did you know that?"

"Durruti is all mouth," said Koltzov, ignoring the question. "Soon, you will see."

■

Slowly, covering only one or two feet with every effort, four men dragged the two pieces of the gun through the mud while a fifth pulled the case of ammunition. They had left their prepared emplacement on the anarchists' right flank and had thirty or so yards to cross to reach a depression, little more than a shallow gulley with a low brick wall on its left, which would give them better cover. The man clawing for a grip on rocks and grass at the head of the others was more anxious about noise than speed; at least the mud muffled sound as much as it held them back. It had taken them half an hour to dismantle the old Maxim and secure it with ropes wound around their waists. In that time the fascists had continued a sporadic fire on the anarchists. Snipers mostly, picking off anything that moved.

"Poor bastards," said Taffy, the man with the ammunition, as he wrapped the case in oilskin.

Pollard thought, Taffy always knows somebody in deeper trouble than himself, but they were in enough trouble anyway. He hoped the Moors kept their eyes on the anarchists.

They didn't talk again until they reached the depression. Water was pouring down it.

"Keep the ammo dry," said Pollard.

"Don't worry," said Taffy.

"Let's move it, then," said Pollard, and with the better cover they were able to crawl. Now only their legs got soaked.

■

One of the Moors' machine guns had been elevated. Cordón realized this when the top halves of the bushes were stripped of foliage in the first burst—the crisp leaves were turned to a powdered mist, and those branches not severed were chipped white. They had spotted Cordón's position, and if the gun were realigned only slightly Cordón and his two men would be as pulverized as the bushes. Some ten yards below them was a crumbling wall of flint, just high enough to cover a prone man. They had to reach it.

"Forget the rifles. They are useless. Roll down," said Cordón, "and keep your heads down."

"What about our balls?" said one.

"Keep everything down. When I nod, roll down." He knew the gunners would rake the bushes again and waited until that burst came and went—the bullets went through the bushes and left a line of small, steaming craters below them. He nodded.

Against the drag of mud he had to roll with feet and hands kept low, pushing on the spin of the body. He and the man so concerned about his balls got up enough momentum to cover the ground like loosed logs. But the idiot began to spin away from their line. He kicked wildly to right himself but was yards behind as the other two topped the wall and fell behind. He came rolling on with a bellow of a curse and then, just as Cordón thought he would come over the wall on top of them, there was a single sniper shot.

An arm reached over the wall. Cordón saw it appear within inches of his face. The hand jerked and tightened into a clasp then was still. Both of them heard the gurgling of blood in the throat, but they could see only the arm and hand. In a few seconds the blood began to drip over the wall, coloring the mud.

Cordón's companion, back against the wall, stretched himself to see his sandals, as if to be sure that his feet were intact. "He was a pain in the arse, Captain. He could not even fuck a goat." Assured that his feet were sound, he pulled out something wrapped in rags, three *butifarra* sausages. "Here," he said, passing one to Cordón, "if you have not already shit yourself, this will do it."

He watched Cordón take the first bite. "Okay, eh? Good Catalán sausage. These *madrileños*—they look like they drink milk." He severed a sausage with one of his two visible teeth.

■

At the head of the gulley they crawled around collecting stones washed down from the old walls above. They had to gouge out three holes so that the Maxim's mount could be set low enough to line up the barrel with the wall. When the gun was mounted, and only at the last second when it was loaded and aligned, would they risk the noise of knocking out enough of the wall to fire through it.

Pollard thought it odd that they had not already been spotted. He could see the Casa de Velázquez without his glasses, and the Moors in their emplacement, not firing anymore but sitting back while the snipers had their sport. The snipers were somewhere above. They must have had telescopic sights. Their use of incendiary bullets was, of all the barbarisms that Pollard had seen, the most sickening. He had watched the three men roll down from the bushes and seen the third hit. Now a sniper had put an incendiary into the corpse, and it was smoldering so that the smoke and the stench of it covered the two survivors under the wall.

"Now, gentlemen, your cocks," said one of Pollard's men. He passed a can. Squatting against the wall, each of them urinated into the can.

"Quick—otherwise it will drop off," said Taffy.

"Yours might, mate. Mine's been taken better care of."

"Keep your voices down," said Pollard.

The can was emptied into the cooling jacket of the Maxim.

Pollard made a final check of the belt of ammunition. "Enough for fifteen minutes—or twenty, if we use it sparingly. We can't do a lot of damage. You know what these cartridges are like. It will be enough to draw their fire." He nodded to Taffy.

Taffy pushed at the wall where they had already loosened stones. He had to push harder, and more of the wall fell away than Pollard had wanted.

"Shit," said Taffy.

"It's the rain," said Pollard. "Right you are, lads. You know where the bastards are."

■

The body had almost burned itself out, leaving a bundle of bone, rags, and the pervasive stench. The hand over the wall had, because of its position and the rain, remained intact. Flame had flickered at the cuff of the coat and then died away.

Cordón wished he had not eaten the sausage. He wanted water. He was surrounded by mud and soaked to the skin; his mouth was raw and dry, and tasted of paprika and incipient vomit. His companion was untroubled. He had moved clear of the overshadowing hand and lay looking down the gradient, counting off the men he thought still alive.

"It's not so bad," he said. "If we can hold out until dark."

Cordón was surprised that the Moors had not come down the hill. "We have to," he said. And then the Maxim opened up. For an instant he thought they had been outflanked and would be finished off. Then he realized that it was friendly fire.

The desultory battlefield came alive again. Before the Moors had recovered their attention, the Maxim was ripping into their emplacement. Cordón picked out the Maxim's position. It was well-covered, but on its own. He knew there was very little time.

"Pass the word to pull back," he said. "Make it quick."

□

"What about you, Captain?"

"I'll make sure everyone who can get away does."

There was nothing redeeming in flight, he thought. He waited to see that the word was passing and the small clusters of men had begun running. More of them appeared than he had been able to see.

Instead of following them down the hill, Cordón ran in a crouch across to the right flank.

A Moorish machine gun to the left, out of range of the Maxim, opened up again, but most of the men in its field of fire were already clear. Some of the snipers also, at first diverted by the Maxim, started trying to pick off running men. Stragglers began to fall. Shots fell in front of and behind Cordón. He changed pace and zigzagged. A third shot went by his head close enough to be felt. The wall was suddenly there, and he virtually fell over it, into the gulley, with another bullet deflecting off the flint and spitting up mud beside him. When he had gathered himself, he realized that changing course had brought him farther down the gulley than he had intended. He could see the five men with the Maxim higher up—about fifty feet away. One of them had seen him come over the wall and was urging him with hand signals to go back down the gulley.

But Cordón went up, keeping close to the wall.

Pollard was still directing the fire. One belt was nearly exhausted and Taffy had the next ready.

As Pollard had foreseen, they hadn't been able to knock out a gun, but some of the Moors had been hit. Others had been redirecting the guns to search out the Maxim. Sniper fire began to come in.

"Steady does it," said Pollard, as Taffy clipped in the new belt. Pollard saw Cordón reach them but concentrated on the gun. "Right—this time creep a bit, to the left. There are snipers there."

The Moors began to find the Maxim's range. The gap in the wall forced all but the gunner down, but all the time the concentrating fire was eating away at the wall.

"Easy, down a bit," said Pollard.

The gunner dipped the barrel. A bullet hit the cooling jacket and deflected. The gunner's face was blown off, but his hand still held the trigger, and the Maxim swung as he blindly kept firing until, with one spasm, he fell away into the mud.

"Christ!" said Taffy.

"He's had it," said Pollard. "Get him out of the way."

Pollard took over the gun.

Cordón helped pull the gunner away, while Taffy joined Pollard and fed the belt.

The cooling jacket had cracked where the bullet had struck, and the gun was beginning to leak a jet of steam. Then the belt jammed. Taffy struggled with it but to no effect.

"That's it," said Pollard.

Sustained fire was beginning to shatter the wall.

"Dismantle," he said.

They pulled the gun down. Cordón helped with the mount.

"Can't leave the ammo," said Pollard. "Worth its weight in gold."

"I will take it," said Cordón.

"Oh, you speak our lingo, do you?" said Pollard. "I just want you to know that that was a bloody crazy thing you people did today."

Taffy broke in. "Palmer is still alive."

Pollard went to the man without a face and held his wrist. "You're right."

They were all crouching to keep below the wall. Cordón took the oilskin that had wrapped the ammunition. "Lift his head," he said.

Pollard and another man got Palmer's shoulders up. Cordón pulled the oilskin under his trunk. Taffy helped the others raise the body as Cordón pulled the oilskin as far as it would go, to the knees. Then he gathered each side and pulled it over like a shroud. "One at the feet. I take the head. We slide him down."

"You've done this before, comrade," said Pollard grimly.

Taffy took the feet. The other three took the gun. Pollard abandoned the ammunition. Going down the slope was as slow as coming up. As they slithered down there was little cover. Snipers were firing incendiaries to supplement the machine guns.

They rested at the foot of the gulley. Cordón felt Palmer's pulse and put a hand to what remained of his mouth. "Still alive." He looked up at Pollard, who was crouching at Palmer's feet. "A man can live without eyes and without a face. The brain, the heart, other things—a man cannot live without those. It is now a question of how much blood he loses, how the heart takes the shock." He pressed an ear to Palmer's chest. "The lungs are still clear. That is good."

Taffy said, "Let's for Christ's sake get him back, then."

They were two-thirds of the way to their lines when the sniping became more accurate. A shot hit the Maxim mount. Pollard called out to Cordón, "Get moving!"

But just as Cordón and Taffy made an extra effort with the body, two shots found targets: one of the men with the Maxim was shot through the throat, and Taffy went spiraling into the mud with a low howl. Cordón kept pulling at Palmer's body.

Pollard shouted, "Keep moving if you can," and went sprinting to Taffy.

Palmer's feet were dragging in the mud. Cordón pulled the oilskin into a sling under Palmer's arms to put the stress where it did the least harm, under the armpits, and went on downward in a backward crouch.

The man shot through the throat was already dead. Pollard left him and with the others managed to get Taffy up and moving. Men were coming up from the foxholes to help them. The sniping was now falling short.

Back at the lines Pollard could see that Taffy had been hit in the ankle by an explosive bullet. When they cut away the clothes, they could see that the lower leg was a mess of blood, sinew, and shattered bone. Stretcher-bearers came, and Pollard went over to Cordón, who was helping to put Palmer on a litter. Palmer's blood had soaked Cordón's arms to the elbow.

When Palmer was carried off Pollard said, "I'm sorry about what I said up there. What I said about you being crazy."

Cordón put out a hand. "Nicolás Cordón."

"Giles Pollard."

"It *was* crazy. We were promised artillery."

"Were you, indeed? We've been promised all kinds of things, but never artillery. The commissars do what they can, but it's pitifully little." He nodded toward the hill. "Those bastards know what they are doing. I hope we do."

□

■

The ninth-floor gallery was much warmer than the fourth floor of the Telefónica, and it had panoramic views. One man was already there, bent over the largest field glasses Mary had ever seen, fixed to a tripod. He broke away as they came in.

"Miss Byrnes, I would like to introduce you to comrade Goriev," said Koltzov, leading her to the man, who was in a well-cut brown suit. "Vladimir, may I introduce the brightest star of the press corps, Miss Mary Byrnes."

"Ah," said Goriev, giving a slight bow as he took her hand, "a pleasure."

"Goriev?" said Mary.

"Vladimir Goriev," confirmed Goriev.

Koltzov, curious, said, "You have heard the name?"

"I—it seemed familiar."

"Comrade Goriev is a military adviser," said Koltzov with a quick glance at Goriev, "simply an adviser."

Mary now saw that spread on a table beside the field glasses was a map that had crayon strokes on it.

Goriev said, "Yes, let me explain, on the map, before you use the glasses. The battle has reached a very interesting point."

In the poor visibility outside she could see constant flashes of gunfire, to the north.

Goriev put a finger on the map, waiting for her to turn from the window. "Today the fighting is concentrated on the Casa de Velázquez, here." He looked across to Koltzov, who was standing at the window. "It is not going well. Durruti is learning the hard way."

Koltzov nodded.

"Durruti?" said Mary, looking up, trying to relate the map to the landscape.

"Yes," said Koltzov. "The anarchists went into battle this morning, for the first time."

Goriev offered her the glasses. "I am afraid that the anarchists are dissolving—dissolving like sugar in the rain."

In spite of the warmth, she felt a sudden chill and had to use the glasses to steady herself.

□

■

Dissillusioned men carried their mood in their feet—some feet were bare, some in rope sandals, some in boots, but they had the common tread of broken spirit. In the rain the sandals made more noise than the boots, slip-slop, slip-slop across the deluged paths. The mud of the hill ran off their legs and left the column's mark trailing through the West Park, the stain of retreat. The walking wounded were helped along. White bandages in the pall of dusk; bright, bandaged heads called the Spanish turban. Limp from the knees down but heads trying to keep the pride.

Pride, the deadly sin: watching the last of them come through the park, Cordón cursed their pride and yet loved them as kin. Madrid it was that had betrayed them all.

Durruti turned from the balcony and went inside, his shoulders and cap dark with rain but no darker than his mood.

"They are not anarchists—they are shit."

Cordón closed the door on the foot beats.

"And you—you they call the Captain! You are shit, too! You have to be saved by the Bolsheviks." Durruti lunged at Cordón's blood-crusted sleeve. "You wear the people's uniform. Not the Bolsheviks'." Only as Durruti's fingers pinched the cloth did he realize why it was so stiff. Then he was wilder still, pulling Cordón's arm and half-lifting him to his face. "Did you shit yourself out there? Like the rest of them? You are not fit for the people's uniform. You are a disgrace."

Somewhere in the shadows of the room Cipriano Mera stood watching.

Cordón's blanched face was pulled closer to the breath and the eyes.

"*Answer me,* shit."

But Cordón kept as composed as a death mask.

"*Answer me!*" Durruti pulled him an inch closer and then threw him away.

Cordón regained balance and said, as though having come freshly into the room, "There will be no anarchists left if you send us back."

"It speaks!" snarled Durruti. "It speaks and it speaks like a whipped dog."

"No victory, no revolution."

"*What?*"

"We renounced everything except victory, that is what you said. This way we get no victory and we have no revolution."

Durruti seemed set to lunge again at Cordón, but at the last second held back.

"It was a trap," said Cordón, "and you know it was. You *know* it," he said, for the first and last time raising his voice on the one word.

One of Durruti's fat fingers drummed at the leather of his pistol holster. He kept every part of himself braced, but his eyes conceded slowly.

"Yes," he hissed finally. "Yes. I know."

Cordón thought, pride from the bottom to the top. Deadly.

"They had excuses," said Durruti, "and one of them was plausible. No planes could fly today. But the artillery—"

Mera spoke. "They never commit artillery unless it is under their own commissars. They never do anything that they cannot control."

"But I have to have a victory," said Durruti. "I came here to show them all what anarchism can do. I *have* to have a victory. If we do not show them, the reds will be able to go on saying that they saved Madrid. That black bitch of a woman."

"We have lost a thousand men today," said Mera.

"We had no count to begin with," said Cordón. "We do not know how many are left because we did not know how many there were."

Detail disinterested Durruti. "We will choose our own target," he said. "No more maps from that Russian reptile. Our own battle, in our own place, at our own time."

■

A man with very few teeth smiled at Mary. "I remember," he said, "you were at the wedding."

"Yes."

The man was the only guard at the entrance of the anarchist building, but he was festooned with enough weapons for three.

"I remember you," he said. "You do not have your camera, today."

"No. I am looking for Nicolás Cordón."

"He is here," the man said, but did not move. The butt of his automatic rifle was between her and the door.

Then she saw Álvaro. He saw her, and opened the door. He looked ten years older.

"I am looking for Nicolás," she said.

He held open the door; the guard moved aside.

The vestibule was crowded with men, all talking.

"The captain is with Durruti," said Álvaro.

"Can I wait here?"

Álvaro seemed about to ask a question, but swallowed it and, instead, said, "I do not know how long he will be up there." He looked toward the staircase and then back at her. "But you can stay here."

"Álvaro—"

"Yes?"

"What happened today?"

"They left us without artillery, the red bastards."

Then she saw Cordón, coming down the stairs. All the men stopped talking and looked to him. Three steps from the bottom he stopped and said, "Durruti will not come down tonight."

There were a few murmurs.

Cordón said, "We will run our own war now. We meet at the barracks, eight o'clock tomorrow morning. All unit commanders."

"All who are left," muttered someone.

But they filed away, not giving Cordón another glance. It was then that he saw her. He walked toward her in a hunched, dispirited way. The ego had gone from him.

"Álvaro," he said, "I want you at the barracks in the morning."

"Yes, Captain," said Álvaro with suddenly renewed life.

"Tomorrow, then," said Cordón.

Álvaro looked from Cordón to Mary and back to Cordón, nodded, and went.

"He was lucky today," said Cordón to Mary. "Two promotions in an hour. Dead men's shoes."

"It was terrible to see," she said.

"You saw it?" he said, with a trace of disbelief.

"From a safe distance. From the Telefónica."

"Ah."

"I am glad you are safe."

"Is that why you came here?"

"Yes."

He reassessed her. "Why are you so concerned about me?"

"Don't you know?"

This time he took longer to study her face. "I am tired, very, very tired."

"And hungry?"

"Yes, hungry."

"There is a place, near my hotel. Will you have dinner with me?"

He laughed with a suggestion of his old arrogance. "You watch the war from the Telefónica. You come here and ask me to have dinner, in a restaurant. You want to remind me how crazy this city is—one part of it eats, another dies. I hate it. *I hate Madrid.*"

"I can understand that."

"Oh, can you?" He began to pull his thin overcoat around him. "Can you? Well, I tell you something. You will have dinner with me. In a different place. Not on the Gran Vía."

He took her by an arm and propelled her into the street.

The place he took her to was a five-minute walk, and neither of them spoke. He led her down steps, opened the door, and she was in a bodega. There was a picture of Durruti above the bar, and about five hundred people inside. He renewed his grip on her arm and led her through; men nodded to him, the crush opened for him like the Red Sea for Moses. In a far and shadowed corner an old waiter saw them coming and pulled the collar of a young man sitting with another at a table; they looked up, saw Cordón, and removed themselves. The waiter flicked the table with his cloth, smiled, and pulled out a chair for Mary.

"Well!" she said, "thank you." And, as Cordón sat opposite, she said, "I realize now how renowned you must be."

Cordón ignored her and looked up at the waiter. "A bottle of Osborne, two omelettes."

"Omelettes?" she said. "I haven't seen an egg in a week."

"The communists are in charge of the chickens."

"Who is in charge of your chickens? Durruti?"

He scowled. "Durruti is the only man I trust."

"I don't understand that. I don't understand this worship of Durruti. I thought anarchism doesn't permit leaders."

The waiter dropped the bottle of cognac between them, already opened, and two glasses. Cordón poured. He said, "Have you ever seen a flight of birds, migrating?"

"Yes," she said, puzzled. "Every fall, on the Cape. Geese going south."

"And what do you see?" He drained his glass in one swig, and waited.

"They fly in formation, a V-formation."

"Exactly. At the point of the V, there is one bird. Every goose knows where he is going, but one of them goes in front. That does not make the rest of them any less free, and it does not give the leader any more rights than they have."

She followed his example and drained her glass. "With geese," she said, swallowing hard and trying to keep her composure, "it's instinctive."

"With anarchists also."

She smiled and looked around her. "I like this place." Then she examined him. "Is this where you bring the dark lady? Aneta?"

"Sometimes."

"Is—is she as serious as she looks?"

He refilled her glass and his own, and again downed his in one swallow. "Aneta is a Marxist. A peasant's daughter. From the very bottom of the system that was Spain. The class war is in her blood."

"And yours?"

"You ask too many questions."

The waiter brought the omelettes, thick, crusty, and smelling of peppers.

She didn't argue. In the badly lit alcove he seemed to have found some ground he could hold, and yet share with her—he was apart, *they* were suddenly apart, from the crush of people, from the city, from the war, and it would have been crass to have argued. She would try to drink him under the table.

□

7

SOUTHERN SPAIN

The Biscay storm had delayed them for three days; not until the plane was south of Lisbon did the clouds thin and then break up. Now they were flying east over the Strait of Gibraltar and descending. On her right Freda Eichberg could see the coast of North Africa. As they banked left she could see, through the opposite window, the Spanish hills. Everything was clear. Atlantic water lapped at the mouth of the Mediterranean. Gibraltar's rock loomed sharply on the right with light blue water beyond it.

Heidel did not fly well. The lower they got the more rigid he was in his seat. The journey had been purgatory for him. She had warmed to the young Luftwaffe pilot when, in Lisbon, he had told Heidel to stop drinking—"It only makes it worse." Heidel was unused to taking orders. The pilot was one of a new breed, one of the clever men from a working-class background. Heidel had no way of dealing with him, with anyone whom he thought unfit for his dining room. The pilot's rank lay in his skill; he was glacially indifferent to the rank of class, a professional having to suffer an aristocrat who had jumped aboard Hitler's bandwagon.

So it was a grateful Heidel who put his feet on the ground at Algeciras; grateful to be done with the plane, the pilot, and the delay. It was warm and the air pleasantly salty, good for his blood. He hoped there would be time to drive up to Jerez to select some decent sherry to take back to Berlin. And he was relieved to see Leissner again. Leissner knew how to live, whatever the station. But Leissner was not called Leissner here, he was Colonel Gustav Lenz, and the station at Algeciras was the Büro Lenz. For the moment, in front of Freda Eichberg and the pilot, he would have to observe this masquerade, tiresome though it was.

From the airstrip to the port the view was dominated by Gibraltar. Leissner alias Lenz pointed out a British warship anchored in the bay. "They watch us, we watch them. Nothing comes of it."

Heidel smiled. "Their interest is identical with ours." In the rear seat with Lenz he began to sense some uneasiness in his old friend. Nothing was said, but the expected bonhomie was missing. Was it Freda Eichberg's presence in the car? In cars, he noticed, her head was like a duck's. It swiveled on a slender neck, and her eyes were everywhere at once. He would have to reassure Lenz about her.

"We've put you in the Reina Cristina," said Lenz. "It has the best view and it's in its own park. More discreet."

Discretion seemed to be a plague. Lenz said not another word until they reached the hotel and were alone in Heidel's suite. He opened a window to freshen the room, which seemed not to have been occupied for some time.

"Algeciras is a hole," he said. "The rectum of Spain."

"My dear Leissner—" Heidel saw that this was a mistake. "My dear Gustav, what is the problem? Where is the old—the old roving eye?"

"In one word, Gestapo. I was assured that this would be exclusively an Abwehr operation. It has gone well, at least it had gone well until about a month ago. I lost one agent, then a second, now a third. The best men in Valencia and Barcelona. All since the Russians arrived. The NKVD."

"You said Gestapo."

"Yes. We have a house cleaner from Berlin called Rohleder, Major Joachim Rohleder."

"Rohleder? I think I knew him in Buenos Aires."

Lenz looked nervous.

"Yes," said Heidel, "it must be the same man. A fanatic. Always."

"My main worry is Madrid. We have small fish, Falangists mostly, in useful places. But our own man is the one indispensable part of the network. Rohleder wants to pull him out until we know how the Russians have penetrated us. I cannot do that. He is too productive, and without him we would be blind."

"'Who is this indispensable man?"

Lenz shook his head. "Even I do not know his name. Only Canaris in the Abwehr knows it. He was Canaris's creation. In the code book he is simply V-Mann one-ten."

A door closed nearby. Lenz was on edge again.

"I should tell you," said Heidel, "that Fräulein Eichberg is absolutely dependable. She handles all my papers. Even the Gestapo could find no blemish."

"She could *be* Gestapo."

"I can assure you—" said Heidel, but he tapered off. "Gustav, you are bad for my nerves."

Lenz forced an injured smile. "*Everything* is bad for the nerves. It's good to see you again. We must make the time to have some pleasure while you are here. Is Fräulein Eichberg . . .?"

"No," said Heidel adamantly. "Not to be confused with pleasure."

"I thought so. It does not matter. There are several Spanish ladies whom you might remember."

■

To be in a warm place in November was itself a luxury to Freda. She had so far always been a prisoner of the northern European seasons. The tan of a Bavarian summer faded quickly in the Berlin autumn. To be able to shed the Berlin clothes gave a reprieve to the spirit. She lay in the garden of the hotel on a sun mattress and hoped that Heidel would be a long while in Algeciras.

"Your hair is better so, I think."

She looked around with sharp annoyance at having been taken by surprise.

"I am sorry—"

"You startled me," she said, relenting when she saw that it was the Luftwaffe pilot. He, too, looked better for being out of uniform. "Are you staying here, too?"

"Yes. It was lucky."

"Lucky?"

"I did not know that you would be here."

She was not susceptible to this. She looked at him as though he were a gauche adolescent.

"Can I get you a drink?" he said.

"I have some Vichy water, thank you."

"Something stronger, perhaps?"

"I do not drink anything stronger."

He was poised there not knowing what to say next.

"Do not let me stop you," she said.

His awkwardness dissolved. "No. I will not." And he went.

Perhaps, she thought, I should be more agreeable. The scents of flowers, herbs, and fruit mingled in the garden. It would be easy, too easy, to become careless in a place like this. She stretched her legs to take the sun and arched her back with a sigh of pandered senses.

When he returned the idle flattery was gone. He brought a silver ice bucket bearing champagne. And two glasses.

"You have a choice," he said, sitting on the next sun mattress and putting the bucket between them. "You can watch me drink the whole bottle. Or you can start to be a little human, show some human weakness." He poured into both glasses twice to fill them without spilling, and held out one.

"I do not drink."

"This is not a drink. It is Krug. And it is nectar."

She took the glass and felt the effervescence on her skin. There was an affinity between the drink and the scents of the garden. She raised the glass to him.

■

Heidel saw what Lenz meant about the town. The harbor had the look of a place where too many currents mixed. The *salero* sparkle of Andalusian women, all the sexual vivacity of Figaro, drained to an oily, mercenary face in Algeciras. By the time he had climbed the long stairs to Lenz's sanctum, he was sweaty and dispirited. Only here, it seemed, was Lenz at ease. Recognizing Heidel's condition, Lenz gave him a cigar, and the two of them sat back and smoked a little before getting to business.

Heidel gave Lenz some papers. "Tangier is the gateway," he said.

Lenz nodded as he read, then said, "It is quite an achievement, Otto. Frankly, knowing Roosevelt's stated views on neutrality, I did not expect you to get anywhere with the Americans."

"It is not done yet. Not yet. You know the Americans. They drive a hard bargain. Before the bank was prepared to handle this they made sure of their slice."

Lenz nodded. "Bankers are above neutrality. They are the only truly disinterested parties in any war. They have no allegiance except profit."

"You sound like the Führer."

"The Führer knows bankers."

"Yes. I can never quite—"

Lenz waited, but Heidel did not choose to complete the thought.

"So. Tangier."

"The importing company will be called Vacuum Oil. In fact, an agent for Texaco."

"Oil is always our greatest worry."

"There will be no direct transactions at any time. The American State Department will see only shipments to Italy. From there it will go to Tangier."

They were interrupted by a desk buzzer.

Lenz spoke on the intercom.

"I'm sorry," he said to Heidel, "I have to take this. You will be interested, I think."

An orderly brought in a decoded cable.

"Here, you see. This is V-Mann one-ten."

Heidel read the cable. "Astonishing! Can it be true? *All* the gold, gone?"

"Read the last paragraph."

When Heidel had finished he said, "I can see why you need to keep this agent in Madrid."

□

"As I said, indispensable." Lenz took the cable. "Fortunately, there seems to be time for us to take steps. A job for the Luftwaffe, I think."

■

"You had only one glass," said the pilot.

"If I am on the path to corruption, I should like to take it one step at a time. It was very pleasant, thank you. But enough."

He smiled. "You are a stranger to the path of corruption, I think."

"It seems to create an appetite. I suppose my stomach is recovering from the flight."

"Well, at least you will allow me to take you to dinner?"

"Yes. I think so. Thank you."

■

With the eroticism of the dancers to distract him, Heidel began to relax. The wine also helped. Not that Rohleder had been disagreeable. He sat between Lenz and Heidel and drank as much as they did—a webbed flush on his cheek suggested a heavy drinker. There remained, however, a sharpness of the eye that had not yet come to its point in anything he said. And he was clearly not as much in the spell of the dancers as they were.

Scarlet and black silk and stiff white lace beneath—she swirled with color and her face had an aristocratic cast—but there was an animal force in her too. Perhaps a trace of the gypsy in the looks. High heels smacked into the floor. The heels lifted her muscularly from calf to the arch of her back and, although masked by the silk and lace, the hinge of her sex was the whole focus of the dance and what Heidel remembered from ten years ago.

He muttered, "Not the ersatz flamenco of a Weimar bordello. This is the authentic article."

Rohleder said, "I am afraid, my dear Heidel, I would have no means of comparison."

Heidel was not going to be cowed by this latter-day Puritan in an ill-fitting suit. "Just a memory. Wild oats."

"Would you consider yourself an aficionado of things Spanish?" said Rohleder casually.

"I have had good times here."

"A very mixed race, I find," said Rohleder, as though the flamenco offered a commentary on his views. "Mixed blood and mixed ideas. Even now I am not sure that we are wise in being here."

"Being here?" said Heidel.

"Being involved in such an imbroglio. The Führer was of two minds about recognizing Franco as head of state—in view of his failures in the last week. However, he has been prevailed upon to do so. Tell me, as a Spanish expert—the name Franco. It is not the family name."

Lenz nodded. "Bahamonde y Bahamonde," he said with pedantic Spanish pronunciation.

Heidel was annoyed that Lenz wanted to prove his own expertise.

"Bahamonde," repeated Rohleder. He looked like a man uncertain of the taste of a dish. "Bahamonde. Tell me, Heidel, there is Jewish blood, is that not so?"

"I could not swear to it."

"I think so," said Rohleder. "I think so. One can see it in the face. One can always see it. They have been far too lenient on the Jewish question."

"There *was* the Inquisition," said Heidel sharply.

The dancers were taking their bow. Heidel tried to catch her eye as she glided from the floor.

"The Jews and the Gypsies," said Rohleder. "All trash."

■

There were four names, *Jruso, Kim, Volgores,* and *Neva.* With names like that the ships could have been of almost any origin. Heidel wanted them checked. He sent Freda to find a *Lloyd's Register of Shipping.*

Lenz's car took her to the quayside. A British shipper happened to be the first she saw. From the pleasant oak-sweet smell of the building it was clear they were sherry shippers. The clerk was alone in a cool, whitewashed office. He was young but had the nose of a sherry man—if there were such a nose, which might just have been whimsy on her part.

He was very English. "Of course, it's a pleasure, madam."

She leafed through the register. And found them. Varied owners but a common port: Odessa. The clerk kept a respectful distance but was interested.

"Thank you," she said.

He looked at his watch. "Would you like to try one of our sherries? It's about that hour. We have all styles, from the sweetest—not *my* style, I may say, but much favored by the ladies—to something as dry as a bone."

"You are a dry man, I can see."

He blushed slowly from the neck upward. "Yes. Quite right."

"Then I will try the dry."

Not quite regaining his poise, he produced two fluted glasses and a bottle without a label. The sherry had almost no color.

"Do you drink sherry?" he said.

"I do not drink at all. Usually."

"Oh. I see." He was flustered again. He suspected he was being teased.

There might never be a better moment, she knew. Although the sherry was awful she drank it with the same delicacy that he did.

"What do you think?"

"Unusual. That is, I suppose it is an acquired taste."

He seemed disappointed. "Well, of course, it's young."

"I wonder, may I ask a favor of you?"

"Of course."

"I am very short of time and I was going to the telegraph office, but you know how these places are in Spain, and I see that you have your own telegraph."

"Essential in our business," he said, rather grandly.

"If I write out the message, to a London address, could you send it for me? I will cover the cost, of course."

"Oh, please, don't worry about the expense. Here, here's the pad."

As she wrote out the two sentences she wondered what he would make of them, though he was far too well-bred to look at the message in her presence. She felt something near to contempt for him and his kind: the world was full of people complacent in their unguarded freedoms. The new order came through that door, and it came easily and quickly, as easily as sipping sherry. In three years she had seen it close around her with its tasseled banners, bright morning faces, and upraised arms. What did the young sherry clerk know of that? The Americans in Biarritz were the same, especially Liam Casey, with his green Irish eyes dancing between the calculations of credit and calculations of her.

Going back in Lenz's car she thought of the pilot. She had misjudged him. She had thought him merely an artifact of the machine. But under his flirtatious patter was a darker propulsion, like that of a man who had accepted a doctor's prediction of limited life span.

When she got back to the hotel she was puzzled by Heidel's behavior. Something more than a hangover was souring his manner. He was usually difficult to work with, but this was a new and more churlish Heidel. He had no thanks for the information on the freighters, which he incorporated into a long memorandum he found hard to compose, and which was to be sent to the unit called "Sonderstab W" at the Reich Ministry of Aviation. He then became worse after a telephone call from Berlin.

"We have to leave," he said, trying to check and sign the memorandum. "I have hardly had time to breathe the change of air." He glowered over the silver-rimmed glasses he used for reading. "Please arrange for everything to be packed by two."

"For Berlin?"

"For you, yes. For me, no."

She waited for more information, but he seemed to be surveying her in a new way, before elaborating. "I leave you at Lisbon. I am sailing from there to New York."

That was the first surprise of the day. The second was that the same pilot was not flying them back.

"For me, it was the last of the meat box run," he told her.

"Meat box?"

"People. Flying people."

□

"I do not think I like being thought of as meat."

"Luftwaffe humor," he said. Her hair was plaited, and not a lascivious thought seemed possible in her head. The governess had gone back to work.

"Where, then?" she said.

"Bombers. No more mock wars. The real thing. Legion Kondor. At last."

It was probably just as well, she thought, if she never saw him again. They parted with a formal handshake.

They turned from the street into a small, arcaded courtyard. There were no lights, but Cordón knew where he was going. Rain cascaded from a broken gutter, but under the arcade, where it was dry, a cat lay against a grilled basement window. The short walk from the bodega in the rain had partly sobered her, but Mary felt interrogated by the cat's eyes, the salient things in the gloom. Cordón led her through the courtyard to a wooden staircase. He had matched her drink for drink but seemed more jaded than drunk.

She stopped at the foot of the stairs. "What is this place?"

"Are you coming?"

Rain ran from her hair down the back of her neck, and she realized how cold she was. She went up the staircase with him.

He opened the door at the top and put on a light—a single, bare bulb. It was spartan: one room, a mattress on the floor, a suitcase, and a few books. She picked up a smell.

"Coffee," she said, "I smell coffee."

"Until recently it was a coffee warehouse, below. I moved here only yesterday."

"*God.* Coffee. Coffee would be nice."

"Please, sit on the bed. I will get coffee."

"Are you serious?"

"Below, there is a kitchen. I get coffee."

He thought, when he returned, that she was asleep. She lay full-length on the mattress, red hair splayed on a pillow, her black *mono* stood out against a white blanket. He put down a tin mug of coffee by her head, and she stirred, looking up.

"Mmmm," she said.

He sat on the floor, cross-legged, sipping his coffee.

She sat up slowly, shaking her hair. "*God.* How do you manage to look so sober?"

"You—I have never seen a woman drink like you."

"You haven't?" She laughed. "I was a convent girl." She drank the coffee in several gulps. "Does that surprise you? Don't answer. I can see it does. You just moved in here? It's bare. But there's something about it. It fits—I mean, it fits you. Am I making sense? I'm trying to figure you out. Canvas shirts, hair shirts. Young, but older men look up to you. I saw that. When you came down from Durruti. They looked up to you. Not just Álvaro. All those men. It comes naturally to you, you have the habit. The manner. It was —it was like that when you fell on top of me, in the square. I think I've figured it out, now." She broke the eye contact and looked around the room, lying back slightly on the pillow. "Yes. This all fits. You're divesting. Divesting yourself of the worldy goods." She fixed her eyes on him again. "This wasn't how it was, was it? The way things were? You speak English English. Money bought that."

He didn't answer, he didn't seem to blink, he just considered her.

"Are we playing secrets?" she said, leaning back on both elbows. "I have no secrets. Try me."

"Tomorrow—" he said, putting down his coffee, "—no, this morning. This morning the war continues. There is something you can tell me. I am alive because someone else saved me, but he was not Spanish. He was English. And a Bolshevik. An English Bolshevik. I wonder, what would make me go to England and fight for them, supposing there was a revolution in England? What would make me do that? What is the obligation? The *obligation?* Why do they come here to Spain? It cannot be for the sake of Spain. I do not *want* to be saved by these people. I want to know why they are here."

□

"I can't answer that question." She lay back on the mattress. "For me, it would be enough that I was alive."

He remained Buddhalike on the floor.

She turned more to his side, to look at him. "I need you, but I'm not sure you need me."

For the first time since they had been in the room there was a response in his eyes, first a curiosity, and then, slowly, a resolve. He moved to the bed and knelt over her and unzipped the *mono,* all the way, in one movement. He pulled it from her shoulders, and unbuttoned the woolen vest beneath it.

"It's easier if I help," she said, taking his head in her hands and pulling it down to her breasts. He was avid, suddenly avid, and the avidity rendered him vulnerable. She felt as she held his head there that at last need had overcome pride. His pride fell, like his clothes, to the bare boards.

There was an odor in his hair, smoky and suggestive of something that she couldn't place. His lips were blistered, his tongue came dry and bitter into her mouth. Her strength and her height seemed to surprise him; he stretched as though trying to absorb her and found that, instead, she could lock his legs in hers. His hands came around her haunch, cold and gripping. She stopped fighting him.

Afterward he fell asleep in her arms. She could not sleep. She held him and listened to the night, water still cascading from the broken gutter, occasionally tires in the rain, one distant burst of gunfire and what must have been the limb of a tree moving against the roof as a wind came up. Then she realized that he was awake and looking at her.

"What are you thinking?" he said.

"I was thinking that we are making love in the precinct of death. This whole city is making love in the precinct of death, defying death."

"Not the whole city."

She smiled. "No. But as I imagined it, many people. War and death do concentrate the mind."

"Death seems to draw you."

"It seems like that, to you?" She was insistently pensive. "It's something I try hard to adjust to, as a reality. Sudden death, you see, is something new to me. It *is* so sudden. Quicker than the shutter of my camera."

He made as if to move away, reaching for his clothes.

"No. No. Not yet," she said.

He allowed her to restrain him.

"Nicolás. This doesn't lead anywhere. We must take it, while we can."

She cleared hair from his brow.

"Nicolás. When I took those wedding photographs I had the feeling that—that you wanted María and Álvaro to have more than you could have for yourself. That was very fine of you. But you can't bear being thought sentimental, can you?"

"You don't understand."

"Understand what?"

"People I loved have died. People I love are going to die."

Without being able to help herself she began to cry, slowly, with at first just a moistness of the eye. She held on to him and said, "I'm sorry. How could I not see that? Oh God, why didn't I see that? You must think I'm awful. I only wanted to . . ."

He ran a hand through her hair. "I know. I know. It is not good always to say what you are thinking—even if you are asked." Gently he slipped from her and began to dress. "You can stay, I must go," he said. "There is no lock on the door. Nothing worth taking."

She pulled the blanket around her. "There is a difference—" she said, "—between saying what you are thinking and saying what you are feeling."

"Yes," he said. But he pulled on his coat and went without looking at her again.

She slept beyond dawn. It had stopped raining. The cat she had seen in the arcade below was now lying curled up on the end of the mattress. The light was still on, and the cat looked orange in it.

"Do you have a name, cat?"

The cat blinked in a sanguine way.

"All cats must have names," she said, trying to retrieve her *mono* without losing the cover of the blanket.

■

Perot was usually underdressed for the climate, but today he was wrapped in an ankle-length fur coat. He hadn't sat down. He was waiting for Praeger by the cigar counter of the bar and, as soon as Praeger appeared, Perot pulled him out again into the street.

Irritated, Praeger said, "What's the matter?"

"Let's walk."

The wind caught the yellowing fur in the collar of Perot's coat and it fanned around his face. Praeger felt more conspicuous with this apparition in the street than they would have been in the café.

Perot hissed through the wisps of fur. "The head cashier of the bank has committed suicide."

"The Bank of Spain?"

"Of course. Of course."

"How do you know?"

"Rey. So you see, Maxie, he must have known about the gold."

"Why are you behaving like this?"

"You remember Rey mentioned a Russian, Yanin, I. Yanin?"

"Yes."

"My friend knows about him. My friend calls him a *sopo.*"

"Sopo?"

"That's the part of the donkey's tail that wipes the arse. He doesn't know what the *I* stands for. Not idiot, that's for certain. My friend is worried about him."

"Yanin?"

"He says he's young. One of the new gang. The nastiest. A butcher's boy from the NKVD." Perot gave Praeger a sidelong glance over the fur. "We'd better be careful. I wish we'd never heard about the gold."

"It's too late for that."

"That doesn't stop me wishing."

Praeger left him on a street corner, glad to be rid of him and worried that an asset might be turning into a liability. Preoccupied with this problem, he was putting the key into the door of his suite before he realized he was even in the hotel.

□

"Max!"

Mary, having heard the key, was coming out of her room.

"What is it, Max? You look as if you've seen a ghost."

"A new one every day," he said, and forced himself to brighten; he saw how jaded she looked. "What can I do for you?"

"Soap. There's no soap. The latest famine. Max, I know you saw all this coming. You must have laid some in. Right?"

"You look rather pale."

"Bad night. Max. Soap? I could kill for it."

"That won't be necessary." He opened the door and waved her in.

A single light was on over his desk.

"You do like gloom, don't you, Max?"

He disappeared into the bathroom and came out with a cake of soap wrapped in brown paper. "There. You're not to—"

"I won't tell a soul. Thanks." She bent to kiss him, on the brow.

"What kind of bad night?" he said.

She hovered over him. "I must reek of the cognac."

"Let us hope that cognac will not be subject to famine."

"Max—don't you ever—don't you ever *let go?*"

"Let go?"

"Really let go. Have a fling."

"You mean, of a romantic kind?"

She laughed and patted his cheek. "Well, that's one way of putting it." Then she became more solemn. "You're still a mystery to me, Max. But thanks for the soap."

It was only later that she paused to see the whole scene again, of Praeger with the key in the door, of the one light in the room, of the way he had said "Let go?" and realized what she had missed. The fear. Was he cracking up? Was she? The questions heightened her fatigue, and she was asleep within five minutes.

She awoke hungry. She looked out. It was dark. She dressed in a *mono* and went down to the canteen. There were only a few people there; she ate by herself. She was crossing the lobby on her way back to her room when a man in a leather trench coat intercepted her.

"Miss Byrnes. Captain Amposta. Perhaps you remember. From the Model Prison?"

The captain who had mocked Major Prada; there was no mockery in him now: something furtive.

"Yes. I remember."

He looked nervously around the lobby. "I have been waiting for you. I thought you should know, what has been done to those prisoners."

"You mean—the men I saw? Del Olmo?"

"To all the prisoners. They have been shot."

"*All?* Shot?"

"More than a thousand, in one night. I see you find it hard to believe. I, too. I did not believe it was being done. They were fascist scum, but this makes us scum too."

Under his coat he wore a rough sweater; he had made an effort to cover his military bearing by dressing seedily, but two things—the shine on his boots and the cropping of his hair—gave him away.

"Where was this done?"

"I show you. Now."

"Now?"

"Outside, there is a man who will take us. He is waiting."

For a moment she thought of first trying to find Praeger, but an instinct told her that Amposta could be trusted; there was a newly pathetic quality in him that invited sympathy. "Okay," she said.

An ancient Citroen was parked by the kitchen yard.

"This man," said Amposta, implying that no name could be given, "is a bus driver." The man made no response as they got into the backseat. "He drives city buses. On the morning of November seven he was one of three drivers who were ordered to a special assignment."

The driver had a professional's knowledge of the city's labyrinths. He avoided all the main streets and the bombed districts, going through—it seemed—an unscathed city of elegant houses and apartments until she recognized one building looming in the night, the Monumental Theater. They were leaving the city at the northeast corner. Amposta was silent. Eventually they were on a country road that began to climb into low hills.

The driver pulled into a grove of pines and switched the motor off.

"We walk," said Amposta.

His boots were an advantage; her shoes sank into clay. The driver led them from the trees into a field. They were on some kind of plateau and she could pick out the form of a ridge; the cloud was broken enough for there to be a gray-cast light. Looking at her feet she realized that the clay had been pressed by many other feet; it was embossed like a complex mosaic—prints of assorted pattern and size. The driver stepped down a shallow grassy embankment. She was about to follow, but Amposta restrained her.

The man pulled a shovel from the grass and went to a corner of the field that look freshly tilled. He tapped the ground several times until the metal hit what sounded like stone. Then he began to dig—with careful raking movements, pushing the topsoil to one side.

He signaled to Amposta.

"Come now, please."

The wind had the iced edge of winter in it, but this was not enough to mask the stench that came from the earth as she went down to where the man stood, shovel still.

Amposta had an insistence bordering on the brusqueness of a jailer. He marched her down the embankment and pulled her to the edge of the small trench, making sure that she could see.

The sight was almost as bad as the smell. She saw, cleared from the waist up, three bodies—or, more precisely, three faces. In the gray light they had a pale, moist sheen. One had thick hair matted into a skullcap by the clay. Another was bald and had its mouth wide open. The third was partly hidden, just closed eyes and a clay-streaked forehead. They all wore suits.

Amposta said, "There are four pits. It took three double-decker buses, jammed full, to bring them."

She stepped back. He went on talking as the bus driver began covering the bodies.

"It took thirty men to bury them. It takes some time to bury a thousand men. It takes some time to shoot a thousand men."

"Who did this?"

The bus driver said something that, in the wind, Mary failed to catch.

□

"He says," said Amposta, "that there were two trucks, carrying the men with the guns. And a car, with a Russian. His name was Miguel Martínez. At least, that is what he calls himself. That was the name on the order. But he is a Russian. This was not the work of Spaniards. How can we uphold our cause if we act the way they act? Matching atrocity for atrocity is the way of the dark ages."

The shovel strokes had the look of a rite performed sacrificially in some far distant pagan night. She turned away and hunched over and vomited until there was nothing left in her stomach.

■

Ferrer's commissar had been unusually nervous. He gave her a slip of paper and said, "You will not disclose this address to anyone, at any time." Was there a trace of resentment? He murmured, "You are privileged, comrade," and then added, "Central Committee business."

The address was not the kind that she would have associated with the Central Committee: a block of apartments more suited to prewar luxury. She checked the slip of paper again to make sure it was the right place, the corner of Vergara and Lista; and that was where she stood, reading the note in the light of a lamp over the bell. She was soaked. The rain ran off her hair to the paper and the ink began to smear. She rang.

The automatic lock clicked open. There was no doorman, no concierge inside, just a weak light at the foot of the marble staircase. She had the number of an apartment on the second floor. The stairs had been recently washed with something smelling of ammonia, and the brass rail was polished. Her dripping coat left a trail and her boots some of the street's slime. Anyone who lived like this should have a mess to clear up, she thought.

Once again, at the pressing of a bell, a door clicked ajar, but this time someone was there. The light was still poor, and at first she could not see a face—she got just an impression of oiled hair, cologne strong enough to supplant the ammonia, and a uniform. Some long-buried reflex made her hesitate, as though intimidated, but she collected herself and strode through the door and onto the carpet.

"Comrade Ferrer," said the uniform, not as a question but more like a command.

She thought he was an unusually well-turned-out janitor.

"Yes."

"Let me take that coat. I am Francisco Antón of the Central Committee."

His hands, as he took the coat, were strong and yet manicured—a paradox that extended to him as a whole. Inside the party uniform was a Casanova. He anticipated her.

"It is safer, comrade, for us to be where people would least expect us." He shook the coat as he might have shaken a dishcloth and then noticed her boots. "Let me have those, too," he said.

She sat on a gilt chair and took them off, all the while still bemused by the place—and its custodian. He disappeared, to return with a pair of red suede moccasins.

"I think they might fit."

They slipped on like gloves over the damp socks.

"Good," he said. "Please. This way."

They went from the vestibule through a sitting room—no sign there of any political identity—and into a study. At last there was something congruous, a wall of political literature in at least three languages, Spanish, French, and Russian.

"Please." He indicated a chair. It had its back to a curtained window and faced a sofa. Strewn across the sofa were papers and a file. The file was—she saw as she sat down—marked "Ferrer, Aneta." It looked as though the sofa had been occupied in one corner by whomever had access to her party history, someone other than Antón, because Antón was too large for the space and was already leaving her.

"Please wait."

She heard the cough first. It came from somewhere beyond the study and, though partly muffled by a closed door, was enough to be disturbing. It was almost like retching. Then, with a deeper surge, it was over.

It was another minute before a man appeared.

□

"Comrade Ferrer."

He was virtually bald, but young, and resumed the place on the sofa as she sat down. "Yanin. I. Yanin."

She could see the effort he made to be disassociated from what she had heard. One hand tightened on an already tight watch strap. The other gripped paper hard enough to show bone at the knuckles. He was all bone.

"I asked comrade Ibarruri who was the most promising of her protégées. She gave me your name."

What was expected? She felt the rainwater still dripping down inside the collar of her tunic. She blushed.

"Yes. In itself a considerable compliment. But, of course, I had to check for myself. Your file supports this view, of course. But a file is a file." He stopped pulling at the watch strap and the freed hand went by reflex to the handkerchief in his breast pocket. He dabbed his lips but, throughout, his eyes remained steadily on hers.

She met them with equal steadiness. His weakness was merely physical; beyond that his was the most powerful presence she had ever felt.

He broke the contact first.

"An exemplary academic record," he said, referring to his notes. "Even by the standards of the Sorbonne." A moment of whimsy claimed him. "I would once have chosen Paris rather than Moscow. There was a time—" Then the scrutiny resumed. "Have you ever considered political work? That is, not the kind of routine party work that you will already have seen, but political work in the inner—" He stopped and coughed lightly under cover of the handkerchief. "Work of the most confidential kind."

"I—I have no suitable experience for it."

"I hoped you would say that. It is true. A pity that you were not sent to Moscow earlier. As it is, I have an instinct in these things." He searched among the mess on the sofa and found a newspaper. For the moment he kept it on his lap.

"Poom!" he said. "It sounds like a small, a very weak gun."

She found this momentarily puzzling.

"Or, POUM. That way, a troublesome sound. A noisy gun."

□

"Marxists," she said.

"Oh," he said in lament. "Oh, if only they *were,* were Marxists. They may call themselves that. I am a Marxist. You are a Marxist. In the same sense that the pope is the vicar of Christ. But these people." He unfolded the newspaper. "These people are Trotskyists. The worst kind. Look at what they write." He threw the paper to her. "They choose this of all times to write seditious poison."

It was a copy of *La Batalla.*

"I can save you the trouble of reading it," he said. "The article states, and I quote, Stalin's concern is not really the fate of the Spanish and the international proletariat but the protection of the Soviet government unquote et cetera et cetera ad nauseam."

"They are reactionaries."

"Certainly, comrade. Agents of the right determined to undermine the brotherhood of the Soviet and Spanish peoples." He looked at her more reflectively. "I saw him, once. Trotsky. Before he went into exile. I was not more than a boy. It was clear to me, though. He was a man in love with himself. It had all come to that. With women, you know, he was a predator."

She felt in a world alone with this man—a man who saw the sharp lessons of history as she did and also the imperatives of the world to come.

"I have always wanted to see Moscow," she said.

His smile was encouraging. "You shall. You shall; I know it." More briskly he said, "Your assignment, meanwhile, is to identify for me the principal agitators behind that rag. I find that the party here has not even the rudimentary skills of counterespionage. The security services are a joke, a travesty. I am afraid that comrade Ibarruri has no grasp of such things. As for her paramour—"

She failed to mask her surprise.

Yanin pointed to the moccasins. "La Pasionaria," he said mockingly, "whom did you suppose they belonged to?"

"You mean—?" she said, looking at the door.

"Yes. *Him.*" He allowed her time to recover. "You can see how lax it has become. The Central Committee. You are fortunate, comrade. This is the beginning of a new regime. If you—as I am sure you will—if you help me you will be well placed when finally we have the organization that such work requires." He got up and took the newspaper from her.

She wanted to do more; she was so physically empowered that she felt, against his emaciation, unfairly favored. But there was no appeal from him. He was severe and without a vestige of self-pity, or self-regard.

□

After seeing the state of Cordón's clothes, someone had given him a leather hunting jacket. A dead man's jacket. They didn't tell him that but he knew—you always knew, though there was not a mark on it. He did not mind; it kept the insidious dampness at bay. They were standing, the three of them, on the open balcony of a tower above the Civil Guard barracks and it was still raining. There was just enough light, two hours after dawn, to see through field glasses the weakest point of the front.

Durruti had been studying one building.

"It is taking too long," he said.

"The basement is the problem," said Mera. "It's the best position in the whole city. Until we get them out of there we cannot turn them back."

Durruti lowered his glasses and turned to Cordón. "Find out why it is taking so long. And do not get yourself shot."

The object of concern was the Clinical Hospital, strategically placed at the edge of the University City. The fascists had crossed the river in significant numbers and driven to this point. Durruti's men had gone in to root them out. Cordón had wanted to go in with them, but Durruti had ordered otherwise.

"Take my car," called Durruti.

Cordón would have felt safer in something less conspicuous than the Packard. The driver kept to side streets and came to a junction where the anarchists had set up a field telephone linked to the Clinical Hospital. Cordón stopped the driver short of the position to keep the car out of view.

Opposing fire was so intense that Cordón had to press against a wall and judge the moment to dash across the intersection. The men with the telephone were sheltered behind some wooden shacks, about five hundred meters from the hospital.

He found that the lines had been cut.

"We lost contact ten minutes ago," said the operator. Chips of wood flew off the wall of the shack as it was raked by machine-gun fire.

"Where were they then?" said Cordón.

"The idiots have lost contact with each other. We never heard from the men on the upper floors. The men on the gound floor are tied down by the Moors in the basement." More wood showered them. "They have two machine guns in the basement with a field of fire that is murdering us. They got the telephone line and they got the two men I sent out to repair it. We're tied down like mules in a swamp."

"How many men have you left."

"Not enough for what you have in mind, Captain."

"We have to take care of those machine guns." Cordón squatted against the shack and looked around the intersection. There was a small hotel across the street, untouched by fire. "If we could get a heavy machine gun up there, on the upper floor, that would do it."

"Where would we get something like that? We don't have anything like that. If we did we would not be in this shit."

"Give me time," said Cordón.

As he sprinted across the street he was followed far too closely by a ribbon of fire.

Durruti's driver was asleep. Cordón shook him awake.

Back at the barracks Durruti was eating breakfast. He listened to Cordón and then, chewing bread and drinking coffee at the same time, spread his legs and rocked back on his chair. Cordón knew this as the prelude to an eruption. Swallowing the last of the bread, Durruti crashed his tin mug on the table. "Is it Durruti who is simple—

or is it something that I cannot understand? They are in the building. We outnumber them. We are above them. We have the advantage. And you say we need a heavy machine gun?"

Cordón saw Durruti's boots kicking as though spurring a horse. "It should be simple. The problem is that they have lost contact with each other and we have lost contact with them."

The chair scraped back and Durruti stood up. "Let me see this fiasco for myself." He picked up a submachine gun.

Cordón was not given a chance even to take a gulp of coffee, and he was ravenous.

Mera was swept up with them.

"Go like the devil, Julio," said Durruti as he climbed into the car beside his driver. The driver obliged. They came swinging and sliding out of the barracks on the slick street and left a spray like a speedboat. The driver began to slow for the intersection, but Durruti waved him on. They drove through the line of fire straight to the wooden shack.

Durruti got out first.

The man in command of the post had recovered his spirits.

"We have made contact again—" he told Durruti, "—and one of the machine guns has been knocked out."

Durruti grabbed the telephone from him. "This is Durruti, do you hear me?" he bellowed. He gave succinct and expletive orders and put down the phone without waiting for an answer. More moderately he said to Mera, "Now we will let them finish off the Moors." He noticed the small hotel across the street. "There," he said, nodding to it, "we'll run things from there."

The three leather-clad men—Durruti, with his submachine gun swinging from the shoulder strap, Mera, and Cordón, the Packard swinging around behind them as they crossed the street—looked like the Capone gang. That was the image in Mary's mind as she took their picture.

She moved from the doorway and Cordón saw her, and then Durruti.

Durruti said, "The *yanqui!*"

"Yes," said Cordón.

Durruti reached her first. "You pick a good place, *yanqui.* Now you see Durruti run those bastards out of Madrid." He looked from her to Cordón. "Tell her what is happening." Then, to Mera, he said, "Upstairs. I want to see the field of fire."

As they went Mary smiled uncertainly at Cordón. "I didn't *know*—I didn't know you would be here. I followed the gunfire. *Really.*"

"Let me see if we can get some food," he said. "I am never surprised to find you in dangerous places."

She followed him inside.

Cordón found the kitchen and a woman who produced sausages and fresh bread.

"How can you eat this stuff?" said Mary. "The sausage is *green.*"

"That means it is mature."

He wolfed it down; she discarded it with a grimace and ate only the bread.

There was a long burst of fire outside, from the Clinical Hospital.

"We are in trouble out there," he said.

"He's crazy. You *know* that."

But this annoyed him. "He's indispensable. They would never take orders from anyone else."

"So—although he's a madman, he's *your* madman. Jesus Christ."

"Who can say who is crazy and who is sane in this war?"

"I don't think that was my point. You *know* that."

He became more testy. "You are lucky he likes you."

"Oh, sure. He's going to get us all killed. But the pictures will be good."

"You came. You are taking pictures."

"So I am. So I am. I'm sorry. What is it?"

He had been distracted by the arrival of some more men.

"What is it?"

"Durruti wasn't expecting reinforcements."

"They're dry. Even their boots."

"They must be from Madrid. Not the men from Barcelona. I don't know any of them."

The squall between them had passed. Someone came and said Durruti wanted Cordón. She stayed on the street level, and when the firing died down she went cautiously to the door. On each side of the intersection, out of sight of the Clinical Hospital, more men were waiting. The rain had eased. But what seemed peaceful ground was dangerous: between the wooden shacks and the building she could see a score or so of bodies.

Durruti came out followed by a phalanx, including Cordón. To her amazement Durruti stood openly by his car, waving his submachine gun angrily at the others. She could not hear what he said. The men in the side streets began to move. Durruti was shouting at them. There was no firing from the hospital. Without any semblance of a formation the attack began. Durruti seemed to have calmed down, and Cordón stayed with him, leaning across the hood of the Packard.

She pushed through toward them, readying her camera.

There was a single shot from somewhere very close. The men around Durruti and Cordón suddenly closed in on the car and blocked her view. There was some wild shouting and then, before she realized what was happening, the car roared away.

"He's been shot! He's been shot!" they shouted.

"Durruti is shot!"

"Murdering bastards!"

"He's not dead yet."

Cordón was gone—with the car.

It took her more than an hour to find out and get to where Durruti had been taken, an improvised hospital at the Ritz Hotel. The anarchist guards would not admit her beyond the lobby. As she argued with them, men arrived from the anarchist headquarters. Nobody seemed to know if Durruti was alive or dead.

Finally Cordón appeared, haggard.

"They are still operating," he said.

"How bad is it?"

"One bullet in the chest. Between the ribs. One of the doctors told me he has a chance. I don't know." He took her arm. "I don't know. If this was a real hospital . . . He needs real surgeons. He's lost so much blood." He raised a hand caked with dried blood. "It took too long to get him here. Twenty minutes, and all the time the blood was pumping out of him, there was nothing I could do."

She saw that he was close to tears.

"How did it happen?" she said.

□

"It came from very close. Someone said Durruti's gun caught on the car and went off by accident. That is not true. I was there. The safety catch was still on. I know. I was *next* to him. It was very close, the shot."

She remembered the cry, "Murdering bastards." She said, "What are you trying to say?"

"I don't know." He was trying to keep control of himself.

"There were so many of you around him. I couldn't see, I was trying to take a picture."

"It was not an accident."

"Are you—that would be an assassination. Why would anyone do that?"

"They're trying to wipe us out."

"They?"

"The Bolsheviks."

"Nicolás, there were no communists there."

He gave her a half-distracted scowl. "Who knows who was there? People I didn't know."

He was called away before she could ask more.

The next person she saw was Barrington-Taylor, arguing with the guards. He spotted her at the same moment.

"Do you have any influence with these people?" he called imperiously.

Having been with Cordón, she was one step closer to the operating theater than he was. "No, I don't," she said.

Barrington-Taylor gave her a lethal look and pulled out a card for the guards. "Look, damn you. I'm an accredited correspondent and I demand—"

He was ambushed by two of the men Mary had seen in Durruti's bodyguard; they were built like Durruti and able to lift him without effort; like a bleating child Barrington-Taylor was levitated to the street.

Cordón reappeared an hour later. "He's still alive," he said. "They can't do anything more. He doesn't have a chance."

"Come on," she said, "you can't stay any longer, you have to rest."

"I have to think," he said, holding back.

"You can't do that here."

□

He went out with her and they walked down the street to the arcaded courtyard that smelled of coffee and up the stairway to his room. The cat was asleep on the mattress.

"I'll make some coffee," she said, and went down to the warehouse.

When she came back Cordón was in bed, sitting up, with the cat on his lap.

"I'm going to call the cat Eleanor," she said, handing him his coffee. "After Eleanor Roosevelt, a fine person."

"How do you know it's a she?"

"It doesn't matter." She sat by him and stroked the cat.

"You will stay?" he said.

"Of course."

■

A portrait of Karl Marx hung over Francisco Rey's bed. It was the younger Marx of Germany, not the older, leonine head of London that became the more common icon of his faithful. Rey had chosen this Marx because, as soon as he saw the portrait, he had seen a more sympathetic quality in it. The great Marx was not yet great. He was still wandering. There was something more Jewish in the face then, more openly curious, less adamantine, less *rabbinical.* Rey believed that Marx had single-handedly led the way from one century to the next. He also believed that Marx had not foreseen that the faith would be hijacked by a gang of murderers led by the Georgian bandit Joseph Stalin, alias Ivan Vasilyevich. There was, to Rey, an inspiring integrity in the portrait of Marx—certainly no hint of anything tyrannical—whereas the portraits of Stalin that were now all over Madrid were indelibly those of a usurper.

Russia was the only fatherland of the oppressed—that was the cry of the mob now. Rey sat on the bed under the portrait making notes with the heightened senses of one who smells burning books. But none of his reading or nightly debates had suggested that the enforcer of the new tyranny might come in the form of Aneta Ferrer.

She flattered him. His mother came to say that a young woman was at the door, carrying a copy of *La Batalla*. She wanted to meet the author of a comment on the Moscow show trials, STALIN'S THEATRICAL DISPATCH OF THE HERETICS, Rey had written. He left the bedroom and the notes and went down to the kitchen. His mother was already making tea and Ferrer was standing with her, looking—it seemed to Rey in one exciting glance—reverential, troubled, and of surpassing beauty.

Very soon the three of them were at the kitchen table drinking lemon tea (in the Russian style) and Ferrer was unburdening a troubled conscience.

"I have always been loyal to the party," she said, "but I cannot accept that what is happening in Moscow is either just or good communism."

A troubled soul of this kind was music to Rey's ears; that it came with such eyes made the encounter almost a spiritual experience. It never occurred to him to ask how she had found his address.

■

They knew, as soon as they got to the Ritz, that Durruti must be dead. There were very few people left waiting, and they were silent and dejected. Mary squeezed Cordón's hand. "It would have made no difference, if you had been here."

"I have to find Cipriano Mera," he said.

He was closing doors to her again; she saw it was inevitable. "Yes. Okay." She gave his hand one last grip. "I'll go back to the hotel."

Cordón found Mera already wearing new authority in manner and words.

"They could do nothing more," said Mera, embracing Cordón, giving a show of condolence and intimacy. "He went two hours ago."

"He must not be buried in Madrid," said Cordón.

"I agree." Mera broke from the embrace. "I have already begun to make the arrangements. The funeral will be in Barcelona. On Sunday."

"I'm sick of Madrid," said Cordón. "*Sick* of this place."

"We have to carry on, Nicolás. More than ever, we have to fight. The fighting is here, not in Barcelona. The war may well be decided here."

"What about the revolution?"

Mera manifested companionship. "We were all of us close to him. I was with him as long as anyone. Longer than you, Nicolás. But Durruti was not Spain. He was Durruti. You know that he could not work with the others. He never made any attempt to work with them."

Cordón examined Mera as though for the first time fully cognizant. "Do you know what he kept saying in the car? When he was dying? He kept saying, 'Too many committees!' *Too many committees.* We are being buried by these committees. We are being buried. *He* knew that. Yes. I know he was not Spain. Not the Spain they are making in these committees."

Mera was not stung; he patted Cordón paternally on a shoulder and said, "You, Nicolás, must go to Barcelona, for the funeral. I have nominated you as a pallbearer. It is your place. And then—and then you should take a few days' rest."

Mera had shaved, and his uniform was pressed and spotless. He might have been, thought Cordón, the Ritz doorman, and Cordón might have been a vagrant who was being patiently reasoned with before being booted out. With this secret thought Cordón smiled amenably and said, "Of course."

■

Before Mary reached her room she was vaguely aware of something different and yet familiar, an aroma, but she was too preoccupied to make the effort to place it. Then she realized that the door of her room was open, and that a light mist of smoke was floating from it.

A second before she saw him the memory of the pipe smoke came back.

"Hello, Tiger."

He was wrapped in a halo of pipe smoke. *That* pipe.

"Liam!"

"Hope you don't mind. A very nice man, name of Praeger, got your key for me, when he understood. My, you look awful, Tiger."

Liam was stretched out on her bed, head against the wall, and impeccable down to the gloss on his brogues.

"What are they doing to you, Tiger?"

"Liam—"

"Look pleased. Try." He didn't move from the bed. "Close the door."

"I can't breathe in here. The door stays open."

"It was the devil's own job to get here at all, at all. There was a Princeton man in Hendaye who decided not to help me get a visa. I found a Yale man. Yale men are much wiser than Princeton men, don't you find? Then I got to San Sebastián—you look a little better in that light—but you can't get to Madrid anymore from San Sebastián so I had to go back into France and drive the whole damn length of the Pyrenees to Perpignan and then there was more trouble with the visa until I called Tom. Tom is a Princeton man, of course, but he fixed it. I read your article and I couldn't stay away. Why are you looking at me like that?"

"I don't give a shit about your visa problems. Esposito is a jerk. The anarchist leader just got shot. People are getting killed here in large numbers every day. You look like a Princeton man to me."

"*Whoa*—now *wait* a minute." He eased away from the wall, sucking on the pipe. "Just like old times. Is that it?"

"*Jesus Christ,* Liam. Why *are* you here?" She pulled off her coat and fell on the bed beside him. "Take off my boots for me, will you? Carefully."

"That's better, Tiger."

Unlacing the boots with a show of servility to her, he looked up. "How's that, Miss Byrnes? Tell me about the anarchist leader."

She told him a lot more. He gradually folded himself into a corner made by the wall and the bed, contracting as she stretched out. He refilled his pipe, said little, and occasionally closed his eyes, a habit that she knew. It meant he was dropping the facade of the freshman joker.

Finally he said, "You've changed. You're different."

She had not so far talked about herself. She was reluctant to do so now. She rolled over onto her stomach and was silent for a minute, thinking of the last time she had seen him. Then she said, "The person I was, the person you knew, couldn't deal with this. It's what changes you—having to deal with it. Nothing had prepared me. But then, how could it have? You people back home have no idea what this is like, no idea. I can't put that in the stories, and I know to them it's just another crazy European war. Yes. I *am* different. You are the first person who could know *how* different. The people here didn't know me before. I've been playing the part they expect of me. You know, bitch reporter. I'm getting good at it. It works. So don't think I don't know how different I am. I'm not doing badly at the reporting racket. I've grown up."

"You're not fooling me. It's not as simple as that. You've gotten involved."

She was about to argue, jutting her chin out to take a better shot at him, but swiftly capitulated.

"More," he said. "There has to be more. You show an uncommon interest in anarchists, I have noticed. When you were telling me the story of the guy, Durruti, it felt like you were leaving things out, editing as you went."

"*Damn* you, Liam."

"Well?"

"I have a lover."

"Are love and lover synonymous?"

"You know better than to ask a chicken-shit question like that."

"Would *I* like him?"

"He—he is just about the most self-sustaining person I've ever known; he has no dependency on anyone. He's brave. Very brave. And I don't think he's going to live a lot longer."

"Then I'd better meet him."

She leaned over the bed and took his face and kissed him lightly, in a filial way.

"Put that pipe out. It's burning the wall."

The door was still open but the fog had thickened.

□

"Where are you staying?" she said, while he tapped out the pipe.

"At the embassy. It's like a refugee camp with chandeliers."

"I know. Did Tom talk about me?"

"He lusts after you."

"Jesus, Liam. Do you think I care?"

"No, Tiger. After all, he *is* a Princeton man."

10

BARCELONA

For as far as Cordón could see the streets were solid with people. They had been assembling since before dawn. And now, looking down from a window, he could hear what seemed like a million voices singing the anarchist hymn, "Sons of the People." They could not all be anarchists. The whole city had come to join the last rites for Buenaventura Durruti. It was not a political demonstration, but a rare upwelling of patriotism without a flag to its name—both a requiem and a pledge of hope.

A man beside Cordón said, "There was never a crowd like this."

"No," said Cordón, "they would not come out for God."

It was Sunday, November 22, and no church bells rang.

"If Durruti alive," said Cordón, "had commanded the unity that Durruti dead has achieved today—then such a column would be invincible."

The man didn't reply. They broke apart and Cordón went down to the basement. The coffin was draped in the black and red anarchist flag, and in that dimness it was the red that caught the light. Cordón remembered Durruti's blood in the car, the heaviness of the strong body as it fell against him and one hand gripped while the head kept falling from one side to the other with the bends of the road.

He joined the other pallbearers and raised the coffin.

□

They could barely get out into the Ramblas or make headway to reach the Plaza de Cataluña. There was supposed to have been a formal parade with two bands. A car attempted to clear the way but was swallowed. The coffin floated without direction above the mass: the flag was all that many people ever saw of it, caught in and bobbing around on competing currents. Fists came up in salute. Wreaths were hung on the streetlamps, in the streets where Durruti had led the revolution. They, the streets, were his real burial place, long before he reached the grave.

That night Cordón had another pilgrimage to make.

Children's voices echoed from the stone stairwell and then stopped as they heard his steps. He never saw them. The apartment was on the second floor. There had been times before when he had come and the door had opened to a world of ideas contested in three or four languages with hardly room to move. The door was opened by a sentinel of a woman. It was a few seconds before she recognized him, then she released the chain and let him in. In this house of words she had never spoken much. She tended from a distance, and now she led him wordlessly through the lobby into the big room with the Florentine paintings and the books—books scattered on every surface as well as packing the shelves. The light in the room was always as much from within as from without. Alabaster and porcelain vases supported lamps and diffused the glare into their own glazed surfaces. A marble table had veins of saffron. Here a political man surrounded himself with random and secular beauty; if there was any design, it was to offset the rigor of his belief with surfaces, rather than opposing ideas.

"Nicolás," he said, "Nicolás."

"Camillo."

"You carry a gun now?"

"For Madrid."

"Oh, not only for Madrid. Do not apologize. Look."

He beckoned Cordón to the lace curtains.

"You see the car?"

Cordón looked down. "Who?"

"Night and day. You seem surprised. It is not paranoia. The funny thing is, in Italy it was the same kind of car." There was a tired contempt in his voice. "Cars in common, minds in common. I see you were surprised."

"Who?"

"Today you thought the whole of Cataluña was anarchist, probably, yes? Well, tomorrow everyone will be back in his place. Who do you think, Nicolás? What is the most reactionary force in Spain? You think Franco?"

"You mean—they are—?"

"The Marxists. Nicolás, you have been too long in Madrid, too long with Durruti, too long away from Berneri. I am an old man who has a good memory. Please, sit down."

The woman brought them coffee.

"It is good to see you, Nicolás. So many of the best are already dead. The best are usually the first. They are the most careless. But Barbieri is still with me. He is good. How long have you carried the gun?"

Cordón told him how Durruti had died.

Berneri listened without interrupting and, after a long silence, said, "It is a death that should not be solved."

"What do you mean?"

"You have already solved it. I see that you think that. I am not so sure. You see, Durruti was ambiguous. What did he mean, 'We renounce everything except victory?' Some people did not understand. If they thought he was betraying the revolution—"

"No. He made that clear."

"Not clear enough."

"He was not killed by an anarchist."

"It is a death that should not be solved. But that is not all that torments you, Nicolás."

Cordón sighed; at last, if he wanted it, he had the opportunity to explain, like a doubting Catholic who could talk only to a Jesuit. "I have made a painful discovery, Camillo. Conviction is not enough. Conviction without artillery leads to slaughter. The problem is, to have artillery you have to have an army. An army requires organization. Centralized power. Command. Structure. Structure is repression—your words."

□

Berneri looked askance. "There can be no confusion on this. Either victory over Franco through a *revolutionary* war, or defeat. I thought you understood. If you enlist democracy as represented by our current government—to fight fascism, you are merely enlisting one kind of capitalism to fight another. Sooner or later the two will be indistinguishable. Unless this war is a revolutionary war it cannot succeed."

"Camillo, what about the artillery?"

"The people can have artillery. Who fires the artillery? Does it make a difference to have an officer to point the gun? The people know which way to point the gun."

"But the people do not have artillery."

"You have had a disturbing time, Nicolás. I can see that. So many have gone. I should remember that." But that was the limit of his tolerance. He smelled heresy and had to stand up to stamp on it. "What seems expedient now will be disaster later. Anarchism *cannot* be militarized. From what you have said, I can see Mera is going that way. He will put on a general's uniform. He will work with the Bolsheviks. He will get you some artillery."

Cordón was spiritually exhausted. He could dispute no more. There might be a pure truth in what Berneri advocated, and it might be immutable on another plane. That had always been his faith. But a rigid hand hanging over the wall from the burning body on the hill had indicated something else to Cordón. Everything around Berneri was fragile, too fragile. He loved the man and loved him devoutly, as pupil does master. He kissed him in the Italian way on each cheek. And, outside, he looked at the car in the rain.

■

Eleanor the cat skidded across the floor in pursuit of a wine cork. Mary and Cordón had drunk the wine before he left. That night the cat had not been there, it had disappeared and had only just reappeared, while Mary was trying to give the room some order. It had hesitated at the threshold, seeing change, and looked around tentatively. The cork had won it back, and Eleanor with the cork was a kitten again. In a while they were both asleep, Eleanor curled up with Mary. It was dark before she awoke, and getting cold. There were voices below in the courtyard.

A door was forced. It sounded like several men were there. They were moving about in the coffee merchant's offices. She could not hear what they were saying, but the voices were getting nearer.

She put on the light and deliberately walked across the room loudly enough to be heard below.

The voices stopped and then, in a rush, they were on the stairs.

She met them at the door. There were three of them, all in *monos* with revolvers at their waists but no badge of allegiance. The youngest came first. He was beardless and had a thin, effeminate voice.

"What are you doing here?" he said. The voice gave him less force than he wanted to suggest, but his two companions were assessing her too, and they were unwholesome.

"Who are you?" said one of them.

"Who are *you?*" she said.

The first of them came closer and looked quickly around the room. "We are from the district *checa.* We had a report that someone was living here. Who are you?"

She explained, but before she had finished one of them was behind her and examining Cordón's clothes in the wardrobe. He pulled out a gray suit and held it up for the others to see.

She explained who the suit belonged to.

The reedy voice said, "There was a fascist living here. This looks more like a fascist's suit than an anarchist's."

She had had enough. Startling him with the quickness of her movement, she went to the wardrobe and pulled out a pair of corduroy trousers and threw them at him. The other two men had come to each side of her.

"There. Look at them. You see blood on them? That is Durruti's blood."

Reedy Voice held the trousers warily. "Why are you here?"

"Why do you think?"

□

The man still holding Cordón's suit laughed. He put the suit back in the wardrobe and said, "Come on, Rico. The *yanqui* is spoken for."

Eleanor was at Mary's feet.

Rico looked at the cat. "The cat eats too well."

The other two, she realized, were nervous with this man. "Come on, Rico. We take someone else for a ride."

His eyes moved up from the cat to her, but he did not speak again. He threw down the trousers and they left.

She realized then how reckless she had been. She remembered stories of the *checas*. But there was nothing to prove that that was what they really were—except the pathological inclinations of Rico. Were they anarchists, communists, or just sadists given guns? They did have a car. She heard it pulling away. What was odd—she realized it as she picked up the cat—was that she had had no fear of them. That was what had most annoyed Rico. There were too many ways to die in Spain to be cowed by thugs.

Pieces of her had moved into the room, in Cordón's absence—a book, a toothbrush, some underclothes. Inching herself over the threshold. Still ambivalent. She lay on the bed, and was nearly asleep when she heard another car outside. It stopped, idled, and then drove away. Then steps on the stairs.

It was Cordón.

"I decided to keep the bed warm for you," she said and then, seeing him more clearly, "*Oh God,* you look terrible."

"I am all right. A long journey. Álvaro drove. But yes—I am tired."

She noticed the gun at his waist.

"I'll make coffee." Eleanor went with her, but slipped away to the street.

When she returned he was lying on the bed, still fully clothed, but his mind somewhere else.

Slight color came back to him with the coffee.

"I read about the funeral," she said.

Quietly, but with purpose, he began to talk. "There is a man in Barcelona called Camillo Berneri. He once taught philosophy, at the

University of Florence. When Mussolini came to power, this man because he was an anarchist as well as a philosopher, was removed from the university. His life was threatened. So, with another, he came to Spain. Spain seemed safe for him then. He came to Barcelona. I met him there."

He sipped more coffee, and she put a hand on his lap.

"He became important in my life. This man would harm nobody. Only if you were frightened of his ideas would you be frightened of this man. Outside his house now there is always a car. I saw it myself. Mussolini was frightened of his ideas. Now somebody else is frightened of his ideas."

He put down the coffee but was tense again.

"There were some men here," she said. "*Checa,* they said."

He looked at the door, as if expecting them to appear.

"They were young thugs," she said.

"Checa," he said.

She moved her hand to his hand. "Nicolás. What is happening? Why are you wearing a gun?"

"I can get the body to sleep but not the mind," he said.

"I know."

He looked at her. "You are the same."

"I have to tell you, Nicolás. I don't know what to do—I have not been able to tell anyone else. I was taken for a ride, the other night I was taken for a ride, somewhere out beyond the airfield at Barajas. I went with two men. One drives a Madrid bus. Two weeks ago he was one of three bus drivers who took prisoners from the Model out to this place, to a field. And then all the prisoners were shot. A *thousand,* Nicolás. A thousand men. Shot. There are four huge pits out there. I saw some of the bodies."

"From the Model? Prisoners?"

"Yes."

"Fascists, then."

"Probably. What difference does that make?"

"Fifth column."

"*No,* Nicolás. We don't know that."

"I am not in mourning for fascists."

□

"You don't want to know about it?"

"What does it matter?"

"*Shit,* Nicolás. The *Russians* did it."

He swung his legs from the mattress to the floor and squatted there, brows dark, beard dark, eyes raw, face pale. "If a man comes and kills all the rats in my house, I do not worry too much what are his politics. It is enough that he kills the rats. It does not mean that suddenly he is my brother. Perhaps he is good at killing rats."

"And who were the men in the car outside your friend's house in Barcelona?"

He got up.

"*Who,* Nicolás?"

"Spaniards. Not Russians."

"What difference?"

"We can deal with them. So—tell me. What are you going to do about this?"

"*Shit.* I don't know." She kicked at the mattress.

"You cannot publish it. One story like that would be worth more than a victory in battle to Franco."

"I know. I *know.*"

"Or is it important for your career, to write it?"

She sat up abruptly. "*Don't—Don't* you dare put it in those terms. How *could* you say that?"

"Is it your conscience, then?" he said, openly sarcastic.

"*Nicolás!*" She was on the verge of screaming, but they heard it at the same time—the sound of someone in the courtyard below, and then of feet on the stairs.

It was an uneven, laboring step. Then a voice.

"Hello. Is anyone there?"

Cordón opened the door.

Giles Pollard stood at the top of the stairs, his face drawn from the effort of having climbed them. One leg was in bandages from calf to knee.

"Ah," he said, "there you are. Had a devil of a job tracking you down. Your people round the corner thought you might still be in Barcelona."

Cordón stepped aside to let him through—and between the two of them Eleanor skated in, straight to Mary.

Pollard was disconcerted. "Oh. Sorry to barge in. Didn't realize—"

"That's okay." She introduced herself.

"Pollard. Giles Pollard. Very pleased to meet you."

Cordón said, "What happened to the leg?"

"Bloody shrapnel. Got in the way of a grenade. Looks worse than it is." He stood awkward and embarrassed between them. "Hope you don't mind, but I'm stuck with sick leave so thought I'd look you up."

"Of course," said Cordón. "I am pleased you came." He turned to Mary. "This is the man who saved us on the hill."

"So—International Brigade," she said.

"You make it sound like a disease," said Pollard.

"Sorry. Not intended."

Cordón tried to straighten the mess of the mattress. "Sit down, please."

Eleanor was brushing Mary's leg.

"Well," said Pollard, easing down, "three makes a bit of a crowd in this room, I . . . But I do apologize too much, don't I? Always being told off for it." He smiled up at Mary. "He was a brave man on that hill, I can tell you. Fact is, they were let down. Badly let down. These bloody Russians are not the military marvels we were led to believe." He tapped his leg. "This is the result of one of their little cock-ups. We got five hundred meters ahead of the Spaniards on our right because the commissar lost touch with them. Took quite a pasting—seven dead and fifteen cut up."

She saw that under this diffident schoolboy language was a tense and troubled man—that in the room were two men more in need of talking to each other than to her. Neither would have said so, but the time had come for her to go. She picked up Eleanor and said, "I'm going to feed this cat. Then I have work to do. So—I hope to see you later, *both* of you." She looked at Cordón. "You know where to find me."

■

□

In the morning there was a cable for her, from New York. It read: COLOR PLENTY BUT TOO PINK STOP. REMEMBER COMPLEXION OUR CLIENTS STOP. SUTTER.

"Damn him," she said. She tore up the cable. New York was a long way away.

The desk clerk watched but did not seem surprised. He was a veteran of cable-induced tantrums.

■

Esposito stood at the window. Columns of smoke rose and merged as the wind caught them, no more than half a mile away. Occasionally there were subsidiary explosions, and in one spot a fire was so extensive that he could see flame above the roofs.

Liam stood slightly behind him. *"Jesus Christ,"* he said, for the third time.

"It's perfectly all right," said Esposito. "The bombing is very selective."

"I've never seen *anything* like that."

Esposito turned from the window. "It looks worse than it is."

"It looks like hell."

"You get used to it." Esposito resumed his seat at his desk. "The Germans are very precise. Thank God the pilots aren't Spanish, eh?" He amused himself more than Liam. "Come on, Liam—what did you expect? It's war."

"They're bombing civilians, Tom, not soldiers."

"Yes. Well—they're getting impatient. This thing has gone on too damn long, too damn long." He waved Liam to a seat. "I don't like it any more than you do, old man. But something has to have an effect. The longer it goes on the stronger the reds will get. I—" He was interrupted by a distant blast.

"I don't like—"

He was interrupted again, this time by the phone. He picked it up irascibly, but as he listened he changed expression. "Yes. Of course." He put the phone down.

"What is it?" said Liam.

"That was the military attaché. *Apparently* they've bombed the Gran Vía. That means that some of our nationals might be involved. *Damn it.* They haven't done that before. We had no warning."

"Very selective, you said."

Esposito was only half-listening.

"Where in the Gran Vía, did he say?"

"The whole damn thing is burning."

"The hotel?"

Esposito shrugged.

"Christ, Tom. *She* could be in there."

"We weren't told. We are supposed to get a warning . . ."

Liam was already on his feet. "For God's sake, man. Let's get over there."

"Yeah." Esposito picked up the phone. "I'll get the car."

The Marine driver spoke in monosyllables and rarely; Liam suspected that his behavior was like that of a butler faced with an employer he didn't much like. The car could not be taken far into the city center. Buildings were burning unchecked, and the heat hit their faces like a summer wind. Smoke and airborne ash mushroomed in the updrafts from buildings suddenly open to the sky. They left the Marine with the car and began to walk. At first it seemed that no effort was being made to deal with the devastation. Liam could see no fire engines, no ambulances, none of the services he was familiar with. But there was something else, in its way more impressive. Nobody was concerned with property. Buildings burned but squads of people—men, women, and children, militia, police, Civil Guards, doctors—concentrated on people, on the wounded and the trapped. Figures came from the smoke with wet cloth wrapped around their faces, carrying others. Children helped carry litters where they were needed. Sometimes mothers would be running without direction calling for children; at others the children would be limp in their arms. Everything came and went through the rolling smoke—people carrying the dead, people saving life, people without hope. The smoke was an acrid veil and the ash was everywhere, wet underfoot and coating heads and faces.

Esposito tried vainly to brush the ash from his striped serge. Some had streaked his hair.

□

"How far?" said Liam.

"Not far."

Neither had spoken until then. Liam searched Esposito's face for a reaction, an opinion, a sentiment. "This is *barbaric,*" he said, finally. "There's no cause on earth that could justify doing this."

Esposito walked on, stepping to avoid a pool of soot-dusted water.

Through a gap in the smoke Liam saw a small plaza. There sat a woman, perfectly composed. with a book in her hands—but she had no head.

Liam stopped.

Esposito saw the woman. "Come on, old man."

But Liam was unable to move. It had all culminated in the one grotesque figure. Nothing else of her was touched, not even a page of the book had been disturbed. He vomited.

Esposito pulled him away. "I know, old man," he said, uneasy with the role of intimate. Music from a radio was playing somewhere nearby. They disappeared into another swirl of smoke. When they emerged they were at the steps of the hotel. Many of its windows were blown out, but otherwise it was remarkably substantial. Liam broke away from Esposito and ran ahead into the lobby. Without windows the place was far less noisy—in any case, there seemed still to be the numbness of aftershock. While staff cleaned up the glass, the guests stood or sat in groups. Liam could not find Mary. He led Esposito up to her floor. Her door was open.

She sat on the bed, making notes, and looked up.

"Thank God," said Liam. "I thought you would be out there."

"I was." She saw Esposito appear behind him. "Liam, you look awful."

"He threw up," said Esposito.

"I've never seen—" Liam broke off. "Jesus, I had no idea. *No idea.*"

"The only thing that's different about today," she said, "is that they've hit the Gran Vía. They must be getting desperate."

"I think it was a mistake," said Esposito.

"Oh, you do?" said Liam, turning on him. "A mistake. It is an outrage. Inexcusable."

Esposito, leaning against the door, surveyed them both.

□

Mary said, "You're beginning to understand."

"I don't think he is," said Esposito. "Matter of fact, both of you seem to know little of what this is really about. Don't interrupt, there's a good girl. You write well. You're smart. But you've gone overboard emotionally. As for you, old man, give it time. A man with your background and your interests has no friends in this town, believe me. You're the kind they want to eliminate from any further human activity. As for me, well, I resent the sullen and unspoken imputation that I can walk through the carnage out there and not mind. I mind. It makes an impression, but it impels me to a different conclusion. These people cannot win. They *can't,* you know. Not in the long run. But they would rather put Madrid, the people of Madrid, through this than accept that. *That* sticks in my gut."

"You're wrong," she said, flatly, without fire.

"We'll see," he said. "I think, if you don't mind, I'll leave you two to carry on the debate. I have other things to do." He bowed with mock grace and left.

Liam went to her and put a hand on her shoulder, which she clasped. "You know," he said, "not an hour ago he told me that the bombing was okay—quote very selective unquote. Selective."

"He is a *bad* person."

"I hadn't seen that side of him before."

"It's only one of his sides."

"Look, Tiger, I need a drink."

The bar was functioning. Liam supervised the making of a martini. "Spain, and no olives." He shrugged, carrying the martini and her cognac to an alcove table.

His parody of a complaint had more humanity, she thought, than the whole of Esposito's philosophy. She was glad to be with him. But she recalled Esposito's phrase, "a man with your background and your interests."

"Liam, why *are* you here?"

"I told you. I saw your story."

"No. Why are you in *Europe?*"

"Business."

"*What* business?"

"Bank business."

□

"You were in Biarritz. What kind of a bank has business in a place like that?"

"Jesus, you *are* the reporter. *Our* kind of business. Look, Tiger—in Biarritz there are rich old men with beautiful young women. They need a good bank."

"The American and British ambassadors are there. They fled from here."

"So?"

"I wondered. You *are* staying at the embassy, remember?"

He took a more devoted gulp of the martini and noticed, as he put it down, that someone was looking around the bar and now was making for their table.

"Do you know this guy?" he said.

She looked up. *"Nicolás!"*

Cordón was very quick, she saw, to discern that this was no casual conversation between strangers. There was a hint of suspicion—of suspicion and his old hauteur—when he reached them.

"Nicolás, this is an old friend from America, Liam Casey. Liam, this is Nicolás Cordón."

Liam's acuity was as swift as Cordón's. Cordón was not what Liam had had in mind as her lover; he was too slim, far too good looking—and far too competitive. As well as being invested with eyes that had aged in ways Liam hoped he would forever escape.

Each was awkward in dealing with the other. She thought for a moment that Cordón would not sit with them, but courtesy got the better of his vanity and he engaged both of them with his sultry presence. The hunting jacket was open and loose on his shoulders. His beard had crept lower, to his Adam's apple. The two of them, she thought, could not have had any habitation in common. But for her, they would not be there, not be talking.

■

Yanin lay on a sofa in Goriev's office; he had taken to the sofa as to a daybed as soon as he arrived and, with his head propped on a leather pillow, leafed through a thick file.

"You believe in coincidence, comrade General?" he said.

Goriev was openly irritated. "The fact that the Luftwaffe bombed Cartagena proves nothing. Cartagena is the republic's main naval base, a natural target, it does not prove that they were trying to stop the gold getting out. In any case, they did not hit one of the freighters."

Koltzov was standing by a window. "We know Berlin received the names of those freighters."

Yanin consulted the file again. "Consider, please. One of our agents intercepted a signal from a German agent here, in Madrid."

Goriev said, "Our agent was one of Krivitsky's people. We have no control over them."

"Krivitsky's agents are not his own property," said Yanin. "Whoever gave Krivitsky that information could lead us to our man."

"No," said Goriev. "Krivitsky cannot jeopardize that source."

Yanin eased up from his pillow. "Comrade General, I am no admirer of personal kingdoms." He stood up. "I wonder, did you ever study the history of the Mongols?"

"No."

"They had a golden rule. One sun in heaven, one Lord on earth."

After Yanin had left them, Koltzov watched him walk across the courtyard to his car. The view from above emphasized the disproportion of Yanin's head to his body; the body was a mere vehicle on which the head traveled.

"One Lord on earth," muttered Goriev. "Does he really believe that shit?"

"Give him time," said Koltzov, "he will push too far."

Goriev sighed. "I did not want this job. As long as I was mediocre I was safe. That was my policy. I realize now that I was not mediocre enough."

Koltzov tapped a lens of his glasses. "You see, everything is dark through these. If they shoot me, I will not need a blindfold."

■

Little was left of the bodega. Most of an apartment building had collapsed on top of it after a direct hit. Its door had been set back within a gothic arch and this had, because of the stonework, survived.

Once the door had opened on a large room with Andalusian murals, mostly scenes of Seville. Now the room and the murals lay powdered at the base of tons of debris. But the door had been cleared of rubble and led down to what had been the bodega's caves. The place was called The Tombs.

Whenever the door opened a banner, stretched the width of the cave, rippled in the draft, the only ventilation. The banner claimed the place for the Partido Obrero de Unificación Marxista, or POUM. Every night it was enveloped by tobacco smoke and oil lamps.

Ferrer put up with it, but Rey mistook the soreness in her eyes for ardor. He was propelled by the urge to recruit this luminous Bolshevik—to recruit, induct, and embrace her if she would allow it. They seemed to be an island of two in a crowd of hundreds, pressed together in a corner.

"The problem," he said, "is not Marxism, but Bolshevism."

"Explain."

He liked her aggression. "There was nothing wrong with Marxism until it fell into the hands of the Russians. Marx thought the revolution would come first in Germany. Not Russia. Bolshevism is just another Russian tyranny, like all the others."

"Without Russia there would be no Marxism."

"No, *no!*" he shouted. "You don't see. Don't you see? Stalin has imprisoned Marxism in his state, the state has swallowed the dream." He moderated himself. "I think we should talk in a quieter place."

She was pleased to leave; heresy was in every face and on every tongue. It was increasingly hard for her to tolerate this hectoring fool with the carnal eyes and eczema under his timorous beard. There was a limit to even this kind of work.

He took her home. His mother had gone to bed, leaving him a note telling him to eat the cabbage soup.

She declined the soup. He declaimed on freedom of thought between spoonfuls, while she appeared to concede. He watched her as she walked around the room.

The smell of metal polish mingled with the sour-sweet smell of the soup. A small copper candelabra lay on a sheet of newspaper. Three of its stems glinted brightly; the remaining six were still dull and flecked with a green crust. She picked up the candelabra and inspected it.

He stopped talking and looked irritated.

"What is this?" she said, turning it in her hand.

"A menorah."

"But you are not practicing Jews."

"Mother pretends not to be, but she always gets that out for Hanukkah. I know it's nonsense, but she has to cling to it, as Christians cling to Christmas."

"It troubles you?"

"*Why?* Why should it?" He noisily drained the last of the soup. "Why should it be harder for a Jew to become an atheist than for a Christian?"

"It was Trotsky's downfall," she said, laying the menorah down on the page from *La Batalla.*

"What do you mean?"

"Jewish sentimentalism."

Rey sprang from the table. "*I am not like that!* I am not one of those Jews who thinks you can be a Marxist and a Jewish nationalist. There is a man—" He put a brake on himself.

"Yes?"

"It's not important. Not what we are here to talk about."

"You must not inhibit yourself like that. You are impressive when you feel so strongly about something."

His smile was grateful. "You are right. Of course. Well, there is this man, his name is Perot. An Austrian Jew. From Vienna. You know what the Nazis are doing to the Jews. Perot came here. He's not a friend of mine, you understand. He wanted some information from me, about the bank. Anyway, he wants to go to Palestine. He cannot understand why I do not. I was tough with him. I can tell you. He seemed—well, I think he's effeminate. I don't think they want his kind in Palestine."

She went closer to him, brushing a breast against him. "*You* are certainly not that kind. I can see that. I am sorry I doubted you, just because you are a Jew. You are a model Marxist. Why did he come to you about the bank?"

"I should not really—" He kept himself close enough to feel the warmth of the breast on his arm. "—but in my position I know everything that is going on. I can trust you?"

"Of course." She could smell the soup on his breath, as repulsive to her as the cold touch of the menorah. But it should not take much more of her time; he was easily checked. "Of course you can," she said, easing away but commanding him with her eyes.

□

11

Koltzov's car was a black Buick. The driver had the size and demeanor of a Tartar. The wipers were louder than the idling engine as Koltzov stood in the rain outside the Gran Vía Hotel, talking to Mary.

"Your scarf," he said, "the red and the black. Anarchist colors."

"Not my colors. Just a gift, from a friend."

"Ah. Well, Miss Byrnes, I am glad I caught you. I would like to invite you— and any of your firends—to a party, at my hotel. It is the nineteenth anniversary of our great Russian Revolution, and, even in war, that calls for celebration."

She had an unsettling perception, of Koltzov and the car as part of an apparatus, a perception at odds with the slick charm of his invitation.

"You will come?"

"Sure. Okay. And—I can bring friends?"

"Of any color," he grinned. The rain was beginning to spot the shoulders of his gray serge suit and the lenses of his glasses. "Max Praeger knows the address. He is coming. Tomorrow, then." And with that he was swept off comfortably in the rain.

But, in a strange and unexpected way, it was Liam who was more unsettling than Koltzov. Liam, whose last line of defense was always the same: flippancy. Quick, clever, beguiling—and yet elusive and unreliable. Coming here now, able to measure her against her past and enjoying the privilege. Coming here for—*what?* A Casey. Was he that? *Now?*

And he was back again, waiting in the hotel lobby and drawing on that pipe as he saw her.

"Hope you know what you're doing, Tiger, with a guy like that."

"Nicolás, you mean?"

"Himself."

"What do you mean?"

"An anarchist. Jesus. This is a wacky town, Tiger. Come on. Have a drink. Esposito introduced me this morning to a guy called Sosthenes—do you believe that?—a guy called Sosthenes."

"Sosthenes Behn," she said, letting him lead her into the bar. "Colonel Behn. Here they call him *Behn malo.* Bad Behn. Big bad Behn."

"That right? Cognac, as usual?"

He called for the drinks.

"Yes," she said, "Behn runs the phone company."

"Father knows him. They did business, once, someplace."

"I'll bet."

"What's eating you, Tiger? Here, let's get us a quiet corner." He ushered her into a seat. "Something's eating you, I can tell."

"He's called Hannibal Sutter. My editor in New York. He thinks my stuff is too pink."

"Ah."

"It's not that Sutter has any political convictions of his own. He doesn't. It's more mercenary than that. Most of the agency's clients are small-town editors."

"The soul of America, and don't you forget it."

"Liam. Don't make light of it."

"Tiger, I've been studying you, carefully. I conclude that you need a little lightening."

She sipped the cognac and found herself succumbing to his charm, but resenting it at the same time. "Well, Liam. I may just have the time and the place for that. How would you like to celebrate the nineteenth anniversary of the Russian Revolution with me?"

"Are you serious?"

"You bet."

□

■

Praeger said, "Oh yes. Koltzov lives at Gaylord's, you know. In grand style. The whole hotel is full of Russians. I wouldn't miss it for worlds."

And so she went to Gaylord's, with Praeger on one arm, Liam on the other, and wondering if Cordón would turn up—she had left a message for him.

Koltzov, having welcomed them, invited her to dance—to Duke Ellington.

Esposito was there. Liam joined him, and they watched Mary and Koltzov kick up their heels.

"What is it about Tiger that gets you so mad?" said Liam.

"You wouldn't understand."

"I think I do," said Liam, tapping a foot to the beat and wondering if Koltzov had any Irish whiskey. He seemed to have everything.

Esposito moved away.

On the floor Mary tried to loosen Koltzov by pulling him into a spin.

"There! You *see!*" She laughed. "*That's* jazz."

Koltzov tried to echo her. "That's *jazz!*" he said, not quite catching the American accent. "I think it is good for me. To be jazzy."

Esposito had joined a circle—the admirers of Barrington-Taylor. They, too, were watching Mary and Koltzov.

"Now I understand how she gets her stuff through the censor so easily," said Barrington-Taylor. "She would kiss Koltzov's ring if he asked her to."

"Pardon?"

Barrington-Taylor turned to see who had spoken.

"What did you say?" said Liam.

"Merely—merely a comment, dear boy. The lady fawns so."

Liam was so quick that Barrington-Taylor was still in the declaiming posture when he was hit by a right jab to the jaw. He reeled backward into his group, sending drinks flying.

The record played on but the dancing stopped.

Barrington-Taylor pulled himself up. "Gentlemen do not do that," he said. "Gentlemen declare their intentions." Though blood trickled from his mouth, he pulled off his jacket. "Raise your guard, sir."

"I don't believe this," said Esposito.

But Liam took off his jacket and circled Barrington-Taylor.

Mary thought they had gone slightly mad, or were drunk.

Barrington-Taylor broke the dance. His right switched with his left, and the left caught Liam off-balance and landed on the side of his temple. Liam fell, without anyone to catch him.

Barrington-Taylor stepped back and allowed Liam to get up.

Mary knew what to expect.

Liam was through with formality. He leapt at Barrington-Taylor with both fists, the first deflecting Barrington-Taylor's defense and the second landing on his jaw. For a moment Barrington-Taylor merely rocked, and seemed to be counterpunching, but slowly he crumpled and then was out cold on the floor.

There was already a blue bloom on Liam's temple. But he seemed disappointed that it was over.

The party resumed nervously.

"How did *that* happen?" said Mary, going to Liam.

"I didn't like something he said."

"What did he say?"

"He implied—" said Esposito, enjoying the opportunity, "—he implied that our host gives you preferential treatment at the hands of the censor."

"Not in those words," said Liam.

"Liam . . ." She looked at his face. "Liam, you're just a mad Irishman in a banker's suit. And sometimes that's okay. *Very* okay."

"Let's get a drink, Tiger."

But at that moment Cordón came through the door.

Liam gaped. "I don't *believe* it. I really don't . . ."

"What is it?" said Mary.

She saw them now, Cordón, Giles Pollard—and the woman.

"Serena!" said Liam. "My God, it's *Serena!*"

She was different: hair bound back with a comb, no makeup, and pale. She saw Liam and stepped ahead of Cordón and her brother.

"Hello again," she said.

"Hello."

"This must be Mary."

Mary looked from Liam to Serena.

"I'm Serena Pollard—you've already met my brother, Giles."

"Oh. Yes."

Cordón and Pollard joined them.

Pollard put out a hand to Liam. "You're Liam Casey, I know. Odd, isn't it, that you have already met Serena."

"The *odd* thing," said Liam, "is to meet her again."

"What *on earth* have you done to your face?" said Serena.

Liam pulled on his jacket again. "A fight."

Cordón stood tentatively on the fringe.

"But where did you two meet?" Mary asked Serena.

"Two weeks ago. In Biarritz."

"She didn't leave a forwarding address," said Liam.

"I think," said Pollard, "that perhaps we should leave these two people to reacquaint themselves."

"That's not—" began Serena, but Pollard swept the others away.

"Look pleased," said Liam.

She studied him. "This is my 'it was wonderful but just one of those things' look."

"We were meant to meet again."

"Let's not be serious, there's a pet." She nodded toward Mary. "She's very dishy. I would give a lot to have hair like that."

"She's in love."

"Yes, I know. He's—well, he's very striking, in a Velázquez sort of way. But so *intense.* Tragic, I suspect. Is she up to that?"

"Let's dance."

She was decorous with him. "I really didn't know you were here, you know," she said.

"No. How could you? For that matter, why are *you* here?"

"I'm driving an ambulance."

"You didn't say anything—"

"It would have been too complicated. I don't like complications."

Mary and Pollard watched them. "You know," said Mary, "I never would have figured you for brother and sister."

"In looks, you mean? Don't be deceived. She was the first."

"The first?"

"The first communist Pollard. It was Serena who had to bear the brunt. Can you imagine—in a family like ours? She went off to Oxford as prim and suitable as any girl from a finishing school and came back with a party card. And a boyfriend from the lower orders. He was killed in July. He hadn't even been recruited. He was in Seville, with the workers in the *barrio.* They were bombarded by cannons and then the Moors went in and finished them off with bayonets." His eyes followed her fondly as she danced. "They never found him. Just as well."

"Liam met her in France."

"She was getting medical supplies. They have to be smuggled over the border. The French are bastards. Two-faced bastards."

Cordón joined them. "So this is how a Bolshevik really lives."

"Yes," said Pollard, "I was thinking the same thing."

"There has to be *some* dancing," said Mary. "I don't care who provides the music."

Pollard said, "With this leg I can't dance."

"Excuse me," she said. She had noticed Praeger with Esposito; no more than a few words were exchanged before Esposito moved on. She went to Praeger.

"You're not dancing, Max."

"I don't. It's a matter of carriage."

"I didn't realize you knew Tom—Tom Esposito."

"I didn't, until this evening. An old friend of yours, he says."

"Acquaintance." She nodded toward Koltzov, who was dancing again, this time without much joy, with a large Russian woman. "Koltzov drinks a lot, but never shows it."

"The ringmaster must never lose control of the circus."

"Ringmaster?"

"Everybody jumps for Koltzov."

"He gives a good party."

"There is another side to him. He has a direct line to Stalin."

"Everyone has another side," she repeated, lingering on it. "You could say that of almost everyone here. Even you, Max."

"Miguel Martínez."

"What?"

"Practically every Russian here has at least two names . . . Pablo . . . Pedro . . . Alfredo . . . A foolish affectation."

□

"Who is Miguel Martínez?"
"Dear girl, you are looking at him."
She was looking at Koltzov.

■

A mouse had been dropped at the top of the staircase. It was unmarked but dead—from the look of its eyes, an untroubled death; it had not been given time to register the deadliness of Eleanor. Cordón found this token of housekeeping when he opened the door. The cat was not there, not downstairs when he washed. He washed and shaved. He was still shaving when the mirror began to swing on its nail. He tried to keep a steady track on his chin, but the blade slipped and cut. The mirror settled but then swung again, and this time the floor creaked as the bombs came closer. Coffee-scented dust was shaken out of the wood. He waited for the mirror to be still again. Then he wiped away the blood and finished. The cold-water lather and the blade gave him a color that was falsely healthy. Without the beard, he thought, he looked like the mouse with the unsuspecting eyes—the mouse had the same pink bloom on white.

On the way back to the room he picked up the mouse by its tail and threw it down to the courtyard, where it sank into sodden leaves.

He felt untypically listless, not from fatigue, not from the party, though he was tired—but from a failure of will. He sat on the bed, pulled on a sweater, and then noticed his hands. The nails were chipped and had developed white fissures like cracked ice. He took stock of what remained in the room from his own past: a pair of boots; more hidden in the wardrobe. And there was the guitar.

It was the music that Mary heard as she came into the courtyard. She found him bent over the guitar, hair falling into his eyes. She watched his fingers: strength and lightness in balance. It was in the music too, harsh chords advancing like a distant storm against the lyrical melody—plaintive melody—a personality and a people at war with themselves. He looked up and saw her, but carried on.

"It's beautiful," she said.

He stopped.

"I didn't know you could play like that."

He inspected his right hand. "It was not so good. My hands are too stiff. You have to practice every day."

"It was beautiful."

"You have done something to your hair."

"I had to cut it."

She pushed the displaced layer of his hair back from his brow, standing over him. "I could cut yours, too. I'm good at that."

He took the hand from his head and held it. "You are shaking."

"I walked here."

"Through the raid?"

"Yes."

"Why?"

She gripped his hand. "Nicolás."

"What is it?"

"I walked here just like I was walking through any city. You know that? As though it was *normal*. Am I *feeling* anything anymore? I went to a party given by a man who probably ordered the deaths of a thousand people. Somebody I thought was a friend lied to me. I don't know why he would do that. It doesn't make sense. Every day the bombs come down, every day, and yet I *feel* less. I came here for the work. *For the bubble reputation*. I take photographs of people dying and I get a byline and I get praised for it. You know? Do you *know* me, Nicolás? *Do you?*"

He pulled her down beside him, putting aside the guitar. "What is it?"

"Every time you go, Nicolás, I feel I have to *let* you go. It's when you go that I realize how much I love you. I can't help myself. I *can't*. It's like—I have to shut out so much. I can't shut *you* out, too." She pulled him closer. "What a *hell* of a time and place to fall in love. Bad judgment."

Her cropped hair suggested a conversion of some kind. It altered her face: without makeup she looked oddly chaste.

"I did not want it to happen," he said. "But I could see that it was happening."

For a few seconds before she cried her eyes were as saintly as a Madonna's. He took her head to his shoulder and said, "If we go on, how long will we have? We will never know. Can you accept that?"

"I cannot accept not to accept it. It would be worse."

"I am not sure it would be worse."

"My love—we must take what we have."

But the struggle within him was as clear as the two selves in his music. He had never trusted the lyrical and he had never, would never, could never use a phrase like hers—"take what we have."

"Please, my love," she said, "you cannot turn me back, not now. It's too late."

But she was asking for a deeper surrender than her own, a surrender not simply of himself but of race and blood.

■

The seat that had been Durruti's was now occupied by Cipriano Mera. There were other differences. Mera consulted a piece of paper and called it an agenda. New faces, his aides, took notes. A pad and pencil were laid out for every delegate. Cordón saw a corridor forming where there had been only an open place: offices off the corridor and, at the end, a larger office with a larger desk and a man who had an agenda. This image closed about him as he stared at his blank pad and listened to them. Then he saw that the woman was silently weeping.

She was large-busted and large-limbed, but there had always been a delicacy in her—a fineness of mind expressed in a precise voice. She sat opposite Cordón at the table. Tears began to moisten her glasses, and she took them off and wiped her eyes.

Mera saw this and stopped his monologue.

"Federica?" he said.

They all looked at her.

She put the glasses back on in a movement that summoned her control. "I am sorry." She surveyed them like a matriarch looking over a family table. "I should not cry. There are too many things to cry for. Too many. Look at me. What do you see? You see the minister of health. Do you also see an anarchist? Look at this table. Are we what we were? Are we? You talk of discipline. You say that the militias are obsolete. You talk of shooting those who desert the front. I tell you, if the success of the war depends on there being a man armed with a pistol behind every seven or eight comrades we can state right away that we have lost."

Mera and his aides looked as uneasy as children caught stealing cakes. "Federica," said Mera, "we are all libertarians, but we cannot fight this war any longer without a military structure."

She seemed to have the innocence of an angel in her eyes, but she said, "You may think that. I see that you may convince yourself. You will not convince me. An ideal is dying here at this table."

Someone said, "We talk of stopping the Bolsheviks but all we are doing is putting on the same uniforms as they wear, giving orders like Bolsheviks, having colonels like Bolsheviks. We are thinking like Bolsheviks and we are talking like Bolsheviks."

Murmurs of agreement came.

Mera let them subside. Then, abandoning the tone of conciliation, he rasped, "The Durruti column is no more. The del Rosal column is no more. I have lost half of my men in one engagement. I will tell you—I will tell you why there must be discipline. Individual willpower, individual bravery, cannot be relied upon in the barrage of artillery, the fire of machine guns, the falling of bombs. There must be discipline."

He waited for more dissent, but they were silent.

With finality he said, "No anarchist division will be led by someone sitting behind a table."

Cordón could not look the woman in the eye, though she was searching him for a response. He knew Mera had won.

They covered their capitulation with detail.

Afterward, Mera singled out Cordón. As the room emptied he said, "I was surprised, Nicolás, not to hear from you."

"What did you want to hear from me?"

Mera paced him away from his aides toward the window—the same window where Durruti had pledged himself to the streets. "You are valuable to us, Nicolás," he said, with a light hand on Cordón's shoulder. "I realize how you feel. I know the sentiment of Barcelona. It is our ark of the covenant, Barcelona. It will not be betrayed."

Cordón stared silently out at the street. There were new gaps in the roofline.

Mera, too, brooded, dissatisfied. Then he said, "I want you to work with me for the junta. There are few people with your experience. In particular, I need someone who is fluent in English."

Cordón looked at him sharply.

"Yes," said Mera, "it would be far more important to us than anything you could do on the battlefield. And it would present no conflict of belief with military reality." He was avuncular. "I have never doubted your loyalty, Nicolás. There is honor in tears—but no future."

■

There was a niche lined with blue tile high in the wall. At its base was the plinth of a plaster figure of which only the feet and lower legs remained. By the arrangement of the legs—feet downcast and giving a sense of the body suspended—Liam knew that the figure must have been Christ on the cross.

Serena explained, "It used to be a convent."

It was a hospital now. Beds were so crammed into it that there was hardly enough space for the doctors to move between them.

"Does it bother you?"

"No."

"You're a Catholic, of course."

There were other traces: one stained glass window too high to have been smashed that was almost secular in the simplicity of its abstract design; a few patches of brighter white on the plaster walls where pictures must have been. The plaster was running with condensation, despite the high, timbered ceiling. There could never have been so many souls at rest here. The air was tepid with the body-breath of the sick.

□

"We could do much more," she said. "Blood transfusion was unknown here. There's a Canadian who is going half-mad trying to do it all on his own. Sanitation is primitive in the extreme. We rely with an almost indiscriminate trust on disinfectant, but you can still smell the foul latrines—as well as all the other usual smells. It's not just medicine we have to introduce, it's basic hygiene. They shit in their trenches, you know. Quite awful."

He was still not used to her way of mixing brutal truths with cocktail jargon. "Why does it matter that I'm a Catholic?"

"It doesn't. To me."

They walked the aisle between the beds without speaking. Many of the bodies were indistinct under the protection of cages covered by sheets. The high ceiling amplified footsteps and the murmurs of nurses to the wounded. He realized why she had brought him here—moral blackmail. She waited for a response.

In a smaller room outside there were stretchers; the room must have been a chapel. It was stripped of the altar, and stretchers were stacked nearly to the ceiling against the leaded windows. The room, though scrubbed, could not suppress the malodor of so much carnage. In the yard beyond, the engine of an ambulance was balking. He heard the curses of whoever was trying to start it, curses in a language he didn't know.

She stopped at the door. "Afraid that's all I have time for. It looks to me as if we are off again. You're very quiet."

"I'd like to think they won't be disillusioned."

She maintained the unflagging voice but there was a moment—and only a moment—of coldness in her eyes. "Your heart is in the right place, darling. It's just a matter of attitude. You're still a little wet behind the ears *politically*. I do have to go."

She gave him a chaste kiss, a kiss that would not have seemed out of place had the altar still been there.

"*Adiós*," she said.

He followed her through the door. It was foggy. The ambulance had just coughed back into life, and its exhaust thickened the yellow with an oily cloud bank of its own. The mechanic closed and clamped the hood and gave her a thumbs-up. She climbed into the cab and turned on the headlights, which picked out the mechanic's great peasant legs as he waved her off with a raised fist salute.

There was, Liam decided, something indelibly holy in Serena Pollard that all her guile could not quite conceal. He, too, gave her a salute.

■

Mary had taken Cordón's shearling-lined hunting jacket and wound his scarf over her head, but she was still cold; the fog penetrated even the car. Cordón was somewhere in the palace that had once been Juan March's. Every window was bright, bright within the shroud of fog—in this weather there was no risk of bombers, and a ball might have been in progress except that there was no music. A score or so cars were parked in the courtyard behind the gates. One was Durruti's Packard. She sat in it beside Durruti's old driver, Julio.

The cars were an assortment of several nationalities: American, French, Italian, Spanish, German—and one Rolls-Royce.

Julio was an aficionado of exotic cars. He knew the vices and virtues of everything from the Hispano-Suiza to the Cadillac.

"It is like a tank, the Cadillac," he said, meaning to please. "You can drive it through a barricade without any trouble."

"Where did they get all these cars?"

"Where do you find the rich in a time of trouble?"

She shrugged.

"In the brothels. In Barcelona on the day of the uprising we go first to the brothels." He patted the ivory wheel of the Packard. "I find her there. At first Durruti had a Hispano-Suiza, a convertible. But this Packard, not so much of a bitch. Sorry—you know what I mean?"

She nodded and smiled. "I think so."

He became solemn. "You make good cars in America. I would like to drive in America. Better there." He made an effort of imagination but gave up and looked at her in search of what he had failed to see. "You like the captain?"

"Yes."

"Durruti said, the captain is my son. It was a joke."

"Nicolás is a long time in there."

"They talk, always talk. Durruti said, too much talk."

"I think they're coming out."

Cordón wore his old wasp-waisted coat. His hair was cut short at the sides and smoothly shaped to his crown. He stepped briskly ahead of the other men. There was more life in him.

Julio switched on the engine and turned on the lights, catching Cordón in the glare.

"Where to, Captain?" he said.

"New York," said Cordón.

□

12

PALM BEACH, FLORIDA

Crossing the inland canal to the island felt like leaving reality for a Hollywood backdrop: behind him Heidel had left a monotonous and often tawdry road, in front of him was this palm-shaded strip with large villas in the Spanish style. The irony of that appealed to Heidel. In this fabricated Spain, a Spain that had never existed outside the sentiment of architects and set designers, he came to take a hand in the fate of the real Spain, which seemed far more than an ocean away. Florida was an anomaly to Heidel: not truly of America, a humid peninsula which the rich had colonized in these coastal sanctuaries, watched from the other side of the canal by all manner of human flotsam. The most degraded of them were not the mulattoes but the whites, with their beggars' faces and soiled children. He was glad to have those faces behind him. He turned into a mimosa-flowered boulevard fresh with Atlantic air.

A pink marble Madonna held out her palms to the heavens at the gates of the Villa Merced. It might indeed rain: as he passed with a nod from the gatekeeper, Heidel saw the thunderheads building from the direction of the Bahamas. Even the clouds kept the theme of pink on their boiling rim. Everything seemed color-coordinated, but despite the Madonna the villa had an immediately erotic feel. Heidel thought of Aryan nymphs cavorting among the palms and fountains and of the pleasures of warm rain on skin.

□

A houseboy took him to his suite, and then waited to lead him back to the garden.

Jack "Oiler" Casey was in the gazebo overlooking a circular pool. He rose to greet Heidel.

"Train late, I suppose? Pleased to meet you, Herr Heidel."

"Mr. Casey. Yes, I am afraid so. More than an hour."

"Damned railroad. Gets worse every year. Have to try the airplane. Did you know you can fly from New York? Take a seat."

Casey had but to rise to be attended by a houseboy.

"What'll it be? This time of day I drink an Irish whiskey and soda."

"That's fine, thank you."

"Really? You sure? Not many of you sophisticated people seem to like the stuff. Me, I was weaned on it."

Casey's laugh had a coarseness that was not in his normal conversation; it alerted Heidel as something truer to the whole man, who reminded Heidel of a Bavarian barroom heavyweight.

"Thought it was a good plan to have you come down here," said Casey. "It's private. It's healthy. And it's the kind of change a man needs from time to time."

"That is true," said Heidel, settling with the drink. He noted the delicate wet footprints beginning to evaporate on the tiles at the edge of the pool. "Change renews the man."

"Saw my boy in Biarritz?"

"Mr. Liam Casey. Yes."

"How did he make out?"

"March is a difficult man. One of the most ruthless men I know. Your son held his own. That was important."

"That so?" Casey was without expression. "He's still a greenhorn. Had to try him with a hard case like March. Byrnes backs up your opinion. But then Byrnes always tells me what he thinks I want to hear." This time the laugh was more brutal. "So I like a second opinion."

The prints on the tiles had gone.

"Business first, Herr Heidel. Then pleasure."

Heidel found that Casey had an appetite for detail: he pressed and hunted Heidel on every point. It was difficult to see how anyone could work for a man like this—he would leave only crumbs. He made no notes but retained all. Heidel, still in his traveling suit and having to check documents, felt slow and overdressed next to Casey, who was in linen trousers and a shirt so fine that his hair-looped nipples showed through. All the while the storm moved closer. The garden became humid. A few petals of a tropical bush floated in the pool, oddly yellow against the leaden water. Finally Casey noticed the change. He looked up and said, "Okay. Okay. It's in good shape. Let's go get ourselves freshened up and then we'll eat. You're the kind of man I can deal with."

Heidel was uneasy with the compliment, but reflected pleasure. He knew Casey had played with him.

Heidel's room was cooler. A ceiling fan helped. Faintly against the first rumbles of the storm he heard voices in the villa. Women, from somewhere close. And then the storm broke and rain drowned all other sounds. He bathed and tried on the seersucker suit he had hurriedly bought in New York. He felt younger in it, but also cheapened. It was not a suit that could be taken back to Germany. It belonged on a salesman.

Four places were set for dinner—pink, again, in theme with boats of flowers of unnatural radiance. Casey stood there alone, in a white suit.

"Champagne?" he said.

A houseboy brought a glass to Heidel.

"Regular as clockwork, the storms. Better than the railroad."

A sound like stirring leaves. A long pink silk dress brushing the marble floor. A face that Heidel knew: a face that in the flesh had the same soft-focus lack of detail that it had on film.

"This is Herr Heidel," said Casey, not touching the vision. "Herr Heidel, this is May Lindt."

"Yes. I recognized you, of course. What a very great pleasure, Miss Lindt."

Hers had been one of the few voices able to make the transition from silent to talking pictures. It sounded like an angel's whisper.

"Herr Heidel, good evening."

The hand was offered for a kiss. The gesture made Heidel's suit feel even cheaper.

Casey looked at her with an unspoken question.

□

"She's coming, Jack."

Lindt took iced water.

Different steps on the marble, sharp and quick, almost in a tumble. A woman in black, and a part of the black was flowing like a cape behind her.

"Sor-rie," she said. Every word ruptured.

"Herr Heidel," said Lindt, "may I introduce Miss Lily Montrose."

"Hel-lo. It used to be Mon-treux, but the studio thought that was too French."

Casey looked like a man who had decided to admit Heidel to an inner chamber. He treated Lindt like a possession, as carefully chosen and placed in the room as a painting or a vase. The table was staged for her, with the light low. Heidel had the inclination to believe that everything, from the manmade Spain outside to the napkins before them, was the work of a studio designer. Casey owned the studio.

As they ate, Lindt asked Heidel about his travels.

"I would love, just *love* to travel," she said.

Heidel thought this an attack of modesty on the part of a woman whose films seemed to move from continent to continent.

"May hates oceans," said Casey. "She won't even step onto my yacht." The coarseness came to his face again. "I'm twice blessed, Herr Heidel. Mrs. Casey doesn't like the tropics, and May doesn't like ocean voyages."

For the first time Heidel saw a flash of steel in Lindt, and said to her, "A pity. We would love to see you in Berlin."

"I was at the Olympics," said Montrose.

"Really?"

But before she could elaborate, Casey said, "That was a good show your people ran. Impressive. The more I see of Hitler the more I feel Europe is on its feet again. I don't want any more American expeditions to sort out European squabbles. We stayed out of Europe until 1917. By the end of 1918 I had lost two brothers in that mess. I'm sure not going to lose a son. To what end? That's why I want to see this trouble in Spain stamped out, and quick. You have to stop these atheistic communists right there. Before they get their roots down."

"That is correct, Mr. Casey," said Heidel. "But I have a question for you. I have found many people here are saying that President Roosevelt should be supporting the Republicans in Spain, because they present themselves as the democratic government. One newspaper says that seventy percent of Americans would approve of that."

"You don't have to worry about FDR." Casey smiled. "Not while Joe Kennedy has his ear. That's a fact. I guess it's hard for you to figure out. After all, what do FDR and Joe have in common? Joe is as far from being a New Dealer as His Holiness the Pope. But Joe delivers the votes and FDR knows that." He shook his head in the only concession to modesty Heidel had seen. "I'm always learning from Joe. We do business. We do business. The ladies are bored. You know anything about horses?"

Heidel happened to be good on bloodstock. It emerged that Casey was buying a racehorse for Lindt. And they were both grateful for Heidel's guidance. Montrose said little, but she interested Heidel more than horses. Casey, however, let the women go to bed while he talked to Heidel about his next port of call, Washington.

The storm had gone without Heidel noticing. It had freshened the air, and when he was finally released by Casey he took a walk in the garden, smoking. Most Americans were offensive to him. This self-made Irish banker had no grace or style and typified the philistine measure of worth that Heidel had found everywhere. At first with Casey there had been the sense of being examined as a potentially dubious partner. Heidel had endured that but harbored the grievance. In Heidel's world—in the world that Heidel wished to preserve—men like Casey would be sent back on the boat they came on.

And so he went secretly disgruntled to his room. No lights were on. There was only the Atlantic moon through the blinds.

"Hel-lo."

Montrose lay on his bed. A pink-ribboned teddy bear sat on the pillow—corpulent like Casey.

"This is Hermann. I named him after that fat man who runs your air force. You don't mind? Hermann likes to watch. *You're* not a watcher, I can tell."

□

NEW YORK

Newspapers were strewn across the bed.

"I have never seen newspapers as fat as this," said Cordón.

Mary shook her head. "Four papers, and between them three paragraphs on the war." She threw a tabloid down with the others. "Full of Christmas advertising. It doesn't take long to see how far away Spain is in this town."

"Everything is fat," said Cordón.

"And you—you have put on weight."

He patted his stomach. "The boat. Too much food."

"It suits you."

He stood by a window looking down on Sixth Avenue. Snow was falling—or, rather, being driven almost horizontally by the wind. "Nothing here seems real to me," he said. "New York is a strange place. It seems so—it seems to be anchored here, like an ocean liner."

"I used to think it was magical." She began to collect the newspapers. "And it is. If you can forget the rest of the world." She put the papers in a wastebasket and looked around the room. "I guess that's as tidy as I can make it. This room hasn't been properly cleaned in a year. Look at the window frames." She ran a finger along wood blistered with layers of yellowing paint. "Dust of ages. I wonder what kind of a man he will be?" She pulled at Cordón's shirtfront. "Definitely becomes you, more flesh. I love you."

The phone rang. Mary took it. "Please send him up."

The man had the build of a bear. With the snow-flecked black coat and the wind-blasted face he could have stepped straight from the woods.

"Dave Backlund," he said.

"Mary Byrnes. This is Nicolás—Nicolás Cordón."

"Glad to see you. Some night out there. Glad to see the both of you. You're late."

"Terrible voyage," she said. "Eight days. I starved. He ate."

"There isn't a lot of time." Backlund already had his coat off and threw it over a chair. Without the coat he was still enormous, and his buckskin boots imprinted great wet pools on the thin rug. He searched for something in his jacket. "We have to move, kids. The forces of reaction are all about." Pulling out a sheaf of papers, he looked at Cordón. "You're the Durruti kid, right?"

Cordón had not yet looked at ease. He nodded.

"I met him, you know. Durruti. In Paris. What a rogue. Loved the guy. I said to myself, here's a guy we can really rob a bank with." He stopped to appraise Cordón. "What's the matter?"

"I have a different memory."

"Yeah. Well, I never saw him in Spain. Look." Backlund unfurled the papers, which in the course of their journey in his jacket had been badly creased. "This is your shopping list."

Cordón took the papers and scrutinized them.

"Ríos has been through it," said Backlund. "He's changed a few things, details, but basically it's three million bucks we're talking here."

"*Three million?*" said Mary.

"That's right. The money isn't our problem. Our problem is—well, to be honest, we have a lot of problems. We'll take them one at a time. The first is called the Neutrality Act of 1936. That's what they *call* it. A better name would be the Partiality Act. They want to stop *anything* going to us, but they don't give a damn about the stuff going to Franco. That's the kind of game this is. It never changes."

"And what are the other problems?" she said.

"Don't worry your pretty head about anything else right now. I read your stuff, by the way. It helped. I'm sorry you're not still doing it. We can use some more help of that kind. We're being killed by neglect."

"Yes, I saw," she said. " 'Tis the Christmas season."

"Depends where you are. Not in the Appalachians. Well, Nick, what do you think?"

Cordón handed back the papers. "Can we get it all on one ship?"

"That's the deal."

"What about the Neutrality Act?" she said.

"We divide forces. I get the stuff to the ship—we have a ship, in Charleston. You go to Washington. There's a man there, Joe Dann. A lawyer. If anyone can shoot a hole in that piece of paper, he can. You handle that one. Leave the bootlegging to me."

□

"We need those planes," said Cordón.

"I know. I know. Everything you're flying comes from Moscow, right?"

"Yes."

"I don't like that any more than you do."

"But—?" said Mary.

"You thought I was a red, eh, kid?"

"Yes. Yes, we did."

"That explains the looks you've been giving me, Nick. You didn't savvy? When I mentioned Durruti? You heard of the Buford gang?"

"Buford?" said Mary.

"December 21, 1919. A date to remember. The SS *Buford* sailed from this very harbor. Yes, ma'am. A ship full of trouble. Communists and anarchists. Teachers. Parlor pinks—it didn't matter in those days. It was a purge. The great American purge. If you weren't a good God-fearing American you must be against them. We were deported, shipped out. Emma Goldman was one. She it was who made me an anarchist. Emma is no sap. She saw Moscow's game faster than any of us. They hate her, now, the reds. People say—oh, Emma Goldman, she went to Moscow and became disillusioned. Well, she didn't. She isn't disillusioned. She knows the difference between freedom and communism."

"Why didn't I *know* about that?" said Mary, as though to herself.

"What, kid?"

"The purge."

"It was a bad time. People were scared—you know, after the Bolshevik revolution. You know, America can sometimes turn ugly, cut off her own at the knees."

"They didn't teach it like that at Radcliffe."

Backlund's smile was not without mockery. "That's okay. You've made up for it. Things are not so bad now. Not so bad—but tricky. Spain is doing funny things to people. The reds are disavowing revolution. The right is calling up a holy crusade. I don't like it." In the warmth of the room he had gained ruddiness, and his physical power suggested an embracing geniality. "Say, why don't you kids come up to my place for dinner? Mrs. Backlund could put some Swedish fire in your bellies. I'd be honored."

BROOKLINE, MASSACHUSETTS

"Why, Liam, that's very thoughtful of you. Very thoughtful. It's quite beautiful. The coloring is very fine."

Wood shavings, in which the vase had been packed, fell to the floor as she raised it to the light—it was not a well-lighted room and she was shortsighted, so she peered closely at the porcelain as though caressing it.

"I thought it might go in your bedroom, Mother."

"The bedroom?" She tilted the vase to read the potter's benchmark. "Yes. Well, perhaps." She lay it back in the pine box among the shavings. "Perhaps." Her hands were as pale as the porcelain and slipped away from it as though relieved of a burden. She looked uncertainly for Liam in the shadows by an unlit fire. "You are very thoughtful, Liam. You must have had an interesting time. Did you visit the Prado? It usually requires more than one visit. It can be *very* tiring."

"Madrid is being bombed, Mother."

"Yes. I read that somewhere. You were gone longer than I expected. Your father was puzzled, I think." She finally focused on him. "Do you find it cold in here? Should I have Andrews light the fire? The trouble is, the smoke bothers my eyes so."

"No, Mother. I'm not cold."

"Well then, you're back."

She sat on a sofa. Liam stood against the oak mantel.

"They bombed a hospital, Mother."

"Where?"

"In Madrid."

She had at some point to give way to his tone; she knew that as well as he did, but she yielded reluctantly, not because she was obtuse but because it was a matter of etiquette. He was developing the rude imperatives of his father. She had hoped for better, worked so long to ensure better.

"An unpleasant war," she said. "Burning churches. Bishop Spellman was here for dinner. He's—he's quite agitated about it." With this admission of the subject she slowly gained asperity. "Weren't you there with Mary Byrnes?"

□

"She was already there."

"Yes. The bishop mentioned that. She is quite an embarrassment to her father. Of course, it's the mother coming out in her. The red hair. Pat had such a terrible time with the mother. Now it's the daughter. It must seem like a curse."

"She's a damned fine reporter, Mother."

"You think so? You surprise me. You do surprise me, Liam. You know the kind of rubbish she used to write when she began on that newspaper. 'Society' they called it. They were not the kind of people I would call society. I suppose she thought she would make a name for herself. It was rubbish."

"She's a good reporter."

"I feel sorry for poor Pat. He's a good man. I think he deserved better. Keep away from that girl, Liam."

"She's—she has a Spanish boyfriend these days."

"Ah. Well, that might be appropriate. You know, Liam, now that I look at you, I can see that you must have had a terrible time. You're very pale. You probably don't like the heat any more than I."

"Madrid isn't—" He stopped himself. "Matter of fact, I couldn't keep anything down on the boat."

A considered silence fell like a mantle over her. Then she pulled her cashmere cardigan more tightly around her. "*I* never have any problems with that. As your father knows, never. Would you get Andrews to light the fire? It's a question of which is worse. The smoke. Or the drafts."

■

The bar on Lexington Avenue was where Hannibal Sutter had christened his business, the Lexington News Service. The bar was used as a second office because the first was a room and a desk and Hannibal Sutter. Business was done in a booth. Sutter drank, alternately, Bushmills and black coffee. He had directed Mary to meet him at the booth at noon.

Her appearance put him off-balance. Having prepared his face for one speech he had to rearrange it for another. His face was like gray clay that had not quite set; all its elements sagged.

"You look different," he said. "Sit down. What'll it be?"

"Cognac."

"It used to be vermouth." He called the order to a waiter and sat down. "You didn't have to come back, you know. That surprised me. I had another story lined up for you."

"I don't want another story."

"Well—" He watched as she took the cognac straight and drained it. "Jesus. I can't take that stuff straight. Well, let me put it to you, Mary. Like I always do. I like you, I like your work. But that story is over. It's over for us. You had the story. The story was Madrid. Our business is paid for by the inch. Column inches. People aren't picking up that story anymore. I don't decide what they print. That story is over. Want another drink?"

"Yes. But I don't want another story."

His inclination was to irritation, but he checked it and called out the order.

"The war isn't over," she said. "In some ways it's only just beginning."

"Meaning?"

"Meaning that it's a different war. A revolution concealed in a civil war that's becoming a world war by proxy—"

"Hold it. That's enough for one paragraph. What d'ya mean, a *world* war?"

"Fascism against communism, for one thing, a kind of trial run. Nazi Germany and Italy against Russia. But it's other things too."

"For instance?"

"It's intensely moral. Pitilessly bloody. Deeply regressive. Hopelessly progressive."

She was more restrained with the second cognac, waiting for his response.

"You know where you are?" he said. "You're in an Irish bar on Lexington and Forty-first. Take a look around you. These people are our readers. Does it seem to you that they would get excited by what you just said? Deeply regressive? Hopelessly progressive? They wouldn't get that. They might go for the pitilessly bloody. If it was local."

"Han, *you're* not like that. You know *exactly* what I mean."

"I do. I do." He gurgled coffee and looked more unhappy as he took the Bushmills. "Sure I do, Mary. And very well it sounded, too. You're a smart kid. They were some smart pieces you filed. Better than anything I saw on the wire, as good as the stuff in the *Times*. But I can't sell it. Not anymore."

"What was the other story?"

"I don't think you'll go for it."

"Tell me."

He shook the ice around in his glass and shook his head at the same time. "Don't scream at me, Mary, but I was going to switch you to London. There's a lady called Mrs. Ernest Simpson and she's marrying the king of England. *That* I can sell."

She sipped the cognac before answering. "I guess that's it, then. No story. No job."

"That's it." He was almost out of character as a sympathetic face. "What'll you do? I could call a few people. You've gotten noticed. There could be somebody who wouldn't worry about the pinko tendency."

"Parlor pink?"

"Pardon?"

"It doesn't matter. No—thanks, but no. If you pay me what you owe me I'll make it through New Year's. It'll give me time. I have a few things to take care of."

"I'll write the check."

He did so before her, on the table. "I'll be generous. Fifty bucks bonus. Danger money."

"That's what you think my life is worth?"

"Listen, kid, you're alive. Dead would be different."

She finally laughed, and took the check. "Some day—some day you'll say, I gave her her first break."

"Yeah. Have another cognac. Yeah. I hope so. Just be careful."

□

BOSTON

Neither Patrick Byrnes nor Liam Casey used Jack Casey's office when the president of First Cape National Bank was away. But the empty office exerted its own kind of presiding aura. It served to remind all the bank's officers of a deliberate vacuum. "Oiler" was the chief, and the only chief. There was no substitute and, as yet, no declared heir.

Liam preferred to go into Byrnes's office rather than have Byrnes in his. Byrnes was a ledger man. Ledgers filled every wall, and there were more on his desk. There were no ledgers in Liam's office, not one.

"I've just spoken to Jack," said Byrnes, as Liam entered. "Heidel has the first shipment already set." He closed a ledger. "Jack wants you to call him. He tried the house."

"I took a long walk."

"It's snowing out."

"I noticed."

"You know, Liam, Jack is very happy about the way you handled March. Heidel told him about that last meeting."

Liam took out his pipe, not answering. He pressed tobacco into the bowl and struck a match on the brick facing of Byrnes's fireplace—a trick that always annoyed Byrnes.

"Why the walk, Liam?"

"This bank is covering a lot of credit. I looked at the figures. More than we ever have. If March defaulted we would be wiped out."

"We're getting a damned good rate. And it's beginning to bring in a lot of new business, corporate business, the kind we've been weak on—not just oil but chemicals, aviation, General Motors, even Jewish money, for Chrissakes."

"It's a big risk."

Byrnes was suddenly sharp. "Your walk hasn't given you cold feet?"

Liam fussed with the pipe until it was glowing. "It's a big risk, Pat. And you know it."

"I didn't hear that from you in Biarritz."

Liam began pacing and drawing on the pipe.

"Listen," said Byrnes. "I've had a letter from the man you saw in

Madrid, Behn. You certainly gave him the impression that you were a March man, one hundred percent."

"I don't recall that. With Behn you don't get a lot of time to say anything."

"He was quite specific."

"Jack is—when is Jack coming back?"

"Not for a week. Why? What is it you want to say to him?"

"I have to look at the figures again."

"What happened in Madrid, Liam? Are you being straight with me?"

"Have you spoken with Mary?"

"We don't talk. You know that."

"Well, I thought that after what she's seen you might want to think about that."

"You did?"

"I guess she won't call you. I have a New York City number."

"Why would I want that?"

"If you change your mind, I have it. That's all. Look, I'm not going to be in the office for the rest of the day. Okay?"

"Is there something I can do? You really ought to be able to discuss this thing with me, before you talk with Jack. I think I'm entitled to that."

Liam stopped pacing and seemed suddenly resolved. "Yes, Pat, you are. You are. Where can I find Tom?"

"Tom?" Byrnes was on the brink of exasperation. "Tom is in the usual place, I imagine."

"Yes, I guess he is. You *do* talk with him?"

"I understand Tom."

"That's good." Liam became light. "You should. He's the family saint. Every family needs one. I'll call you later."

Liam liked driving on snow. It had stopped snowing but the city streets were packed hard and the traffic had a muted quality; snow chains became the salient rhythm of movement and sent splintered ice spitting into sidewalks. He drove with a window partly down to get the sting of the air. The old Cadillac felt solid even on ice. It had been Jack Casey's first Cadillac and was known well in those parts of town where the Irish cabals met. Policemen always saluted it. When it came to cars, nepotism suited Liam. Going out of town it became bleaker, and the parish of Newton Center was Siberian—but this was the seat of the auxiliary bishop of Boston.

The rectory was always kept cold enough to rouge the faces of the two nuns who held the outer bastion. They were ageless faces, unlined, perhaps because of the spartan air. Both had been there for as long as Liam could remember, and they had known him first as someone who could be fed as much chocolate candy as they could slip to him.

"Good morning to you, Mr. Casey," they said in unison.

"Good morning, Sisters."

"It's a sharp morning, Mr. Casey. Very sharp," said the larger of the two. "Do you have an appointment?"

"No. It's not the bishop I'm here to see. Is Father Byrnes about?"

"He is. You can go through."

They seemed still to want to give him candy, but he stood on dignity and kept his gloves on as he went down the corridor.

Father Thomas Aquinas Byrnes, secretary to the bishop, and brother of Mary Byrnes, had jet black hair and no other resemblance either to her or his father; of his mother there was only a gentleness of speech that in her had been defensive and in him was turned to the gift of counseling. He was five years older than Mary and beginning to acquire ecclesiastical girth, the kind of weight that Liam arrogantly assumed to prove that abstinence in one department led to indulgence in another.

"Liam!" he said, with open and instant pleasure.

"Tom."

"Sit down. Please. I'll get Sister Sarah to bring some coffee."

"I think she already is. She would have given me candy, too."

Tom laughed. "Well, you could do with a little filling out in parts. It's a real pleasure to have you back. A real pleasure."

For all Liam's ease with Tom, he felt that within these walls, after the initial small talk, they could not discuss what he really wanted to. As they drank the coffee their old intuitive knowledge of each other made this plain to Tom.

"Liam, you look like you could use something stronger."

"It's a respectable hour for that."

□

"It is. It is." Tom got up. "I'll get my coat. The usual place, then?"

"The usual place."

As he drove back toward the harbor, Liam was led to the point.

"So Mary is back, too," said Tom neutrally.

"She is."

"She didn't call."

"I have a number."

"I saw her reports, of course. Not what most of the people here wanted to hear. I thought—I was surprised, you know. There was a *morality* there, in the people, the way she wrote about their spirit. I thought that was something we should try to understand."

"You did? I thought the church sees them as atheists and reds."

"That's why she surprised me."

"You'd better be careful, Father."

Tom dipped his head and was silent for a few seconds. In this attitude, Liam noticed, there was already a tentative double chin, the onset of the venerable.

"You know, Liam, I've decided that she's not an atheist. I would say she's an agnostic who—I've known others like her—who has to test everything in fire."

"She sure has done that."

"Yes. It takes courage. She has great courage. Greater courage than simple belief. I love her and I pray for her. I pray for her—but I know it needs more. It needs more."

"Another heresy."

"Not at all. She has it within her; I cannot do it for her. She has it within her. I miss her, you know. I don't think she knows that. I miss her."

"Your father doesn't."

"Oh?" The head dipped momentarily again. "Oh—that's what you think, is it?"

Liam nodded to a sergeant who waved them across a snarled intersection where the lights were not working.

"It's going to be a lot of trouble to the church, Spain," said Tom, leaving the unanswered question behind at the intersection. "It mixes the political with the ecclesiastical. That's always meant trouble for us."

□

"Well now, Father Byrnes, you interest me a lot."

"Don't take that line. I don't want that old secular sympathy of yours. If you don't mind."

"Sorry. Sorry."

Tom put a hand on Liam's arm. "No offense. You know what worries me, about this Generalissimo Franco and his holy crusade? Something a very wise old Jesuit once said to me; he was giving me a very painful time on the subject of the Crusades. It was a day rather like this one; it cleared the mind. What he said was, 'I always look particularly hard at the proclaimed allies of God.' "

Liam felt reluctant to reach their destination, a lobster house on the harbor. He slowed down. "I'm glad you told me that. Don't think this is a confessional, Tom—but that's bothering me a lot. Matter of fact, I'm of two minds—maybe three. I'm in the kind of mess I don't think God can fix."

"Oh yes," said Tom, without alarm.

■

During the train ride from New York to Washington the snow turned to sleet and then rain. Cordón had been silent for long stretches, watching the landscapes of New Jersey and Pennsylvania and now of Maryland.

"New York is not America," he said.

"No. I don't know where America is," said Mary. "It always seems someplace else. It's an idea and the idea keeps changing in my mind. I think I know what it is, and then it changes. I guess—I guess it's unfinished. And here we are going to a place where everybody maintains they know America, speaks for it. They're always talking like that, the politicians, the president."

"It seems to me a gentle place." He turned finally away from the window. "Spain is not a gentle place."

"Are you missing it, already?"

"I don't know. Was it right to do this? Should I have agreed to it?"

"You can do far more good here."

"You believe that?"

"Yes, I do. When I meet someone like Dave Backlund, I believe it."

There was no time, when they arrived, for Cordón to do more than glimpse the city—a passing sight of the White House in the rain.

They went straight from the hotel to the office of Joe Dann. It was in a building full of lawyers, and they found Dann in a suite at the end of a marble hall behind expensive veneered doors. In the waiting room it was easy to get an advance sight of Dann: he was the recurrent figure in a score of photographs, with politicians, a general, and a vice-president.

Mary was uncomfortable. As well as this foretaste of a power broker, the luxury of the office itself seemed wrong for the cause they represented.

The Dann of the photographs—ingratiating, slicked hair, gabardine suits with knife-edge creases—came out to meet them, but was somehow not the same. In the flesh he was darker and not, as the camera suggested, silk-voiced.

He spoke with a throaty New York accent.

"Gotta lot to do. You guys left it late."

He had them placed before him on a leather chesterfield but stood and sometimes paced as though addressing a jury.

"Scuttlebutt has it that there'll be a flat embargo by the end of the year. No pious entreaties like the Neutrality Act. I'm talking closed door on anything to Republican Spain. They're at work on that now on the Hill. Maybe you don't yet understand me, or this town. I suspect you don't. So listen. There's a roller coaster of a lobby against us. Some fanatical Irish dame called Aileen O'Brien has called every Catholic bishop in the country, every damned one, and they in turn have mobilized the priests and something like a million—that's right, one million—telegrams have gone to the White House. In their view, sending arms to you is as good as sending them to Satan. Don't look so angry, young lady. That's how things are done in this town. You're gonna tell me it's an outrage, right? That they take notice of people like that? I thought so. Yeah, it is a kind of outrage. It's a violation of the democratic process and it's an offense to any straight-thinking person. I could lose sleep over it, only I don't. It happens too often. You have to move fast because there ain't no way this thing is going to be headed off."

Mary had been checked several times by the way he anticipated her. Now, with him taking breath, she said, somewhat tremulously, "What about the Neutrality Act?"

He was less strident, speaking as he walked back to his desk. "As I said, a pious entreaty. I'm working on it. I have an idea. I'm having drinks tonight with a friendly party from the State Department. I think we can do something. If we can, it's then a question of the manifest. We give the State Department a manifest—everything on that shipment—and if they clear it, Commerce gives us the export license."

Cordón had seemed awed by this marshaling will. Now he said, "Everything? We have to disclose everything?"

"You sure do. If there's so much as a bootstrap on that boat that's not on the manifest, our good friends at U.S. Customs won't let the boat sail. We're not looking for ways to make their job easier."

The two of them were now visibly despondent. Dann came back from the desk. "I didn't want you to be in any doubt about how tough this is going to be."

Mary was impetuously vocal. "It's *so* unfair! So unfair. When you know the issues."

"Can I give you a piece of advice, young lady, personal advice?"

She looked at him guardedly.

"Get rid of that boiler suit you're in—and the leather jacket I saw in the waiting room. The boots are not a good idea, either. Go get yourself a decent dress, maybe two. Some stockings. Suitable shoes. You can't play the battle veteran in this town. Use your head."

He surveyed Cordón.

"This man knows how to dress. Some white shirts. New shoes." His eyes swung back to Mary. "Don't say it. The answer is—yes, you're going to pretend to be a sweet-talking lady. Do you think I work in an office like this out of personal taste? I would be really offended if you thought that. Really offended. Why do you think I'm doing all this? For money?"

□

■

Vincent Farrio was never at ease visiting the State Department: it was a place too peopled with the voice of a comfortable and languid America, not the America in which Farrio had risen and found his vocation. This voice was seldom heard in the Federal Bureau of Investigation, neither among the agents nor their targets—it was a voice with its own self-policed territory, personified by Under Secretary James C. Dutton. Dutton, Farrio felt, could be the reverse image of himself. Dutton looked loftily out from his department windows on Farrio's streets while Farrio looked in at the vested owners of the real estate on the high, wooded ground.

The leather liner of Farrio's hat had left a streak of sweat on his brow. He blew his nose in a movement to cover wiping the brow. But Dutton had given him hardly a glance since taking the file to read. The rain outside and the heat inside conspired to make Farrio sweat a little bit more. It seemed that men like Dutton didn't sweat—J. Edgar Hoover would like that; it was said that if Hoover felt sweat as he took the hand of an agent it could end a career.

"Yes," said Dutton, keeping open the file. "Yes. I see."

"The record on Backlund goes back a way. Seventeen years. He's an old hand at subversion."

"Yes."

"We have a tail on him night and day."

Dutton found the mechanics of surveillance as irrelevant as he would have the mechanics of his car. "I've had a telegram from Madrid. It supports your information. The anarchist Cordón, whom Backlund met in New York, is known to our Madrid people. He was associated there with the worst elements."

"He's here, in Washington. Arrived today."

"Really?"

"With the reporter lady."

"Yes. A ménage, I believe. I'm not too concerned with her. She's a familiar type these days. The fruit of our emancipated campuses. No, Mr. Farrio, the urgent matter is the ship—is it ship or boat? I can never quite be sure." He realized that Farrio did not have that kind of humor and referred again to the file. "The SS *Mar Cantábrico*, contracted by the Vimalert Corporation. At Charleston. Backlund's consignments are all bound for this—this vessel. They seem to be assuming that they can circumvent the Neutrality Act. Under no circumstances must that matériel reach the Madrid regime."

"Is that policy?"

"Policy?" Dutton had not got the measure of Farrio, and thought he might be playing dumb—unless . . . unless he really was as pedestrian as he looked.

"The bureau can't take any action, other than surveillance. We don't have any—"

Dutton snapped at him. "Mr. Farrio, I know the legalistic niceties as well as you do."

"It's not our turf."

"Not your *jurisdiction*, you mean. No. However, since Mr. Hoover regards these people, as we do, as subversives we might perhaps show a little imagination. All we are looking for is a way to—to *impede* them. There must be a way of doing that."

Farrio had more imagination than Dutton suspected—he suddenly saw a door very slightly open to the world of the high, wooded ground. But he snapped like the street dog he really was. "I don't understand you, Mr. Under Secretary."

"Oh, you don't? That surprises me, Mr. Farrio." Dutton closed the file. "Well, all you have to do for the moment is keep track of them. Then we'll see if we can't show a little more ingenuity. I'm much obliged."

If there had been a tradesman's door, Farrio knew, Dutton would have asked him to leave by it.

■

"Would you make love to a woman who looks like this?"

Mary balanced on one leg on a high-heeled shoe while pulling down the hem of a white silk slip.

"Would you?" she said to Cordón's reflection in the mirror.

"Just *look* at me!"

"I think so." He slipped the lace-fringed strap from her shoulder and kissed her neck. "If the woman who looks like this is the same woman who did not look like this."

"Oh, you *tease*!" She pulled up the strap. "Besides, we don't have time."

"No."

"It's the hair I don't really like. Now I look like one of those girls who go hunting for European princes. You're not a European prince, are you?" She enjoyed his scowl in the mirror. "I mean, look at me. *Curls*. I've *never* had *curls*." She waggled her hips to make the slip settle. "And a garter belt. It feels like—like a chastity belt."

"I like the stockings."

"Is that *all*?"

"You—you look very good."

"Hmm." She picked up a black taffeta dress and slipped it over her head. "Button me, please."

They had never made boudoir talk, she thought. He seemed more at home in a boudoir than she would have expected—Cordón with his white shirt and tightly knotted tie of black and red, a coloring that the department store had not suspected of revolutionary meaning. They had laughed at that, to the bafflement of the clerk.

"He's a strange person, Mr. Dann," she said.

"Strange? No. I did not find him strange. We need a man like that."

"But why? Why would he help us?"

"I have stopped asking that question. There, how is that?" He stepped back from the mirror out of her view. "I have stopped asking that question. Every time I meet such people, people like Mr. Dann, Giles Pollard, Dave Backlund. They all have their reasons. It means something to them. Not always the same thing. I think Mr. Dann will approve of you."

"Oh God! I hope so. I look like a Vanderbilt. For God's sake!"

Dann did approve. He looked her over proprietorially, exaggerating the rigor of his eyes. "You did it, lady. And *you* look quite a killer, young sir. Just what I wanted. We're off to a swell affair. Maybe win some friends." Dann had a chauffeured Lincoln at the door.

□

The driveway of the Georgetown mansion was more like the entrance to a park. The Lincoln rolled on gravel that looked, in the rain under the lights, like cascaded pearls.

"God, I can't walk on this stuff in these shoes."

She stumbled to the door, steadied by Cordón, and recovered in time to face the butler. Music and voices—and Mabel Louise Renson advancing, a ship of a woman under full sail.

"Joe," she said.

Dann introduced Mary and Cordón.

"We are *all* so sympathetic to your cause," said Renson, taking Cordón's hand. "And I am so pleased you both were able to come." It was a voice of the South, Mary knew.

Three rooms were connected like galleries, two large rooms that were already dotted with groups of people, and a third smaller one, visible only through an arch framed by orange trees. The walls were covered in lime silk and hung with watercolors in uniform red frames. In a corner of the first room, by a bay window, a trio played Beethoven: a Steinway, a violin, and a cello. Waiters patroled with salvers of canapés and champagne.

"You won't mind, Joe, if I monopolize your friends for a few moments? I do want to explain what this is about."

"Fine," said Dann, moving off to familiar faces.

"I've brought together a few friends on the spur of the moment. Joe didn't give me a lot of notice, I'm afraid. Of course, *everyone* is —" Renson broke off. "Ah, here is someone I hoped would come. You'd better meet him first; he's probably short of time."

The man stood out in one detail: his tie was scarlet against a conservative suit.

"Allow me to introduce Senator Gerald Nye; Senator, these are the two young people, Mary Byrnes and Nicolás Cordón." Without a pause she said, "Senator Nye is a Republican and therefore in a minority in this house and the Senate, but he is a rare voice of reason."

Nye disavowed this as he shook hands. "Why, Mabel, I just happen to think the administration is wrongheaded on Spain." He smiled. "I want you folks to do the talking. I want firsthand information. There's a propaganda racket very well organized by the other side. I represent North Dakota. Many of my people up there are Catholics,

German Catholics. By my estimate no more than forty percent, at most, support the church on Franco. That's not what the bishops represent to us and it's not what goes in the pastoral letters."

This youthful, earnest man had the knack of drawing out Cordón. Mary had not seen Cordón respond so forcefully since he had arrived in the country, and in the course of it he made an impression on Nye.

"That's right," said Nye, having listened, "we're being boondoggled by those double-talkers in London and Paris. When they say nonintervention, they mean nobody but Hitler and Mussolini."

Mary slowly became aware of another presence on the fringe of this conversation, a small dark-haired woman with an arresting Asiatic cast to her face. She said nothing but absorbed everything. Like Nye, she was distinctive in one detail: the brooch that secured her togalike dress at one shoulder was a red star set in black onyx.

"Well," said Nye, "you've confirmed my views. Most valuable. I can tell you I'm going to do what I can for your cause."

As he withdrew the dark woman spoke.

"Miss Byrnes? My name is Nora Stern. I'm an editor at *New Masses*—the communist newspaper. Did you know that we reprinted that piece of yours on the battle for the bridge? It was very inspiring."

"I didn't know." Mary turned to Cordón, but he had been taken off by Renson and she was marooned.

"Yes," said Stern with claimant eyes, "we had a wonderful response to that article. The heroic struggle of the Spanish masses against clerical feudalism."

"I don't recall putting it in those terms."

"I'm talking of the response. We get many letters—did you know the party is winning hundreds of new members every day? Spain is the kind of issue we've been waiting for."

"*Waiting* for?"

"To expose the world conspiracy of monopoly reaction."

"Does your paper take its line from Moscow?"

It was as though she had poured her champagne over Stern.

"Why would we do that? We are the Communist party of the United States. It's our country we're addressing."

"I see." Mary could not decide if this was disingenuous or simply innocent dogma. "You see, in Spain, the Russians have taken over the Communist party—and a good deal else."

"I don't know about that," snapped Stern. "But let me tell you, California is our Spain."

"California?"

"That's where we are building the farm-labor democracy. You've been away. Maybe you should look into what has to be done at home. There's a tide running."

"There's a war to be fought first."

"Here's my card. We should keep in touch."

Renson returned with Cordón.

"Miss Byrnes, Señor Cordón is a real spellbinder. This is doing *so* much good." She glanced at the disappearing Stern. "I don't recall inviting that lady." She frowned and then brightened with renewed euphoria. "But now there's a very special person I would like you both to meet. We will have to go to the orangery, for privacy."

In the orangery, sitting in a peacock-winged rattan chair, was Eleanor Roosevelt. The only other person there was a secretary. After the introduction Renson sat discreetly to one side so that the First Lady could concentrate on Mary and Cordón.

"Please don't be anything less than candid with me," she said. "I am here to learn."

Mary felt instantly able to talk to her, and to be blunt.

"Mrs. Roosevelt, it's a privilege to have such an opportunity. Obviously we are very disappointed that the president will not support the Spanish people and their government."

"Well now," said the First Lady, "that's not strictly fair. We recognize the government in Madrid as the only legitimate government. You're talking of something else. Military support. Isn't that it?"

"Yes," said Cordón.

"The president's concern is to stop all this awful killing. We can hardly do that if we start sending guns and airplanes."

Cordón said, "Germany and Italy supply them to Franco."

"Yes. Yes. We detest these fascist regimes. But if the people of Germany and Italy sign away their freedoms, we cannot stop them."

"With respect," said Mary firmly, "more than half of the Spanish people have not done that. They are fighting."

The gentle intellect before her hardened a little, in the eyes and the voice. "Young lady, I like your spirit. But remember where you are. Our people look to the president to ease the terrible suffering of the poor and the helpless here in America. If the president chose sides in Europe, his numerous detractors would cite this as proof that he's really a covert socialist. Don't seem surprised. That kind of person regards the Tennessee Valley Authority as the advance guard of communism." She smiled at Cordón. "Or worse, anarchism."

Renson rose. "I'm sure we're all very grateful to Mrs. Roosevelt for listening—"

The First Lady put up a restraining hand. "Now then, Mabel. I can look after myself. I think it would be a very nice idea if I gave these two young people a ride back to their hotel."

"Of course," said Renson.

"We would love that," said Mary.

"Well, come along then. By the way, Mabel. You might tell the cellist that her tone in the allegretto is much, *much* too mournful. It's meant to *lift* the spirit, not defeat it."

They left without passing again through the party, by a back entrance.

The secretary sat by the chauffeur; Mary and Cordón rode in the back with Mrs. Roosevelt.

"Señor Cordón, I have read Emma Goldman on anarchism. The word is much misunderstood. If I were Spanish I would be an anarchist."

They all laughed.

"The president might not understand that," she said, with obvious and inclusive pleasure.

Just as quickly, she fell into an apparently melancholy reflection, staring beyond them into the streets, which, though opulent, were also desolate. Mary saw the partly mirrored face on the rain-streaked glass, oddly reduced to the elements of intellect and character, an intellect confined by the car like a bird by a cage. It was a minute or so before Mrs. Roosevelt spoke again.

"Anyone with children," she said, looking at them again, "must pray that there will not be another European war. It is hard for any president to remain indifferent to the fate of what is, for so many Americans, instinctively the cradle of all civilized life."

It seemed to silence all of them for the rest of the ride.

Once they were back in the hotel suite, Mary said, "You see why I called the cat Eleanor."

"Yes."

"What is it? What is it, Nicolás? You're broody. I can tell."

"I do not know you."

"What do you mean?" She was stopped dead in the middle of the room.

"I watched you in that house. The butler. The waiters. The maids."

"What of it?"

"They were all Negroes. Black servants with white gloves, white coats—and white masters."

"This is Washington."

"I watched you. It did not matter to you. You drank the champagne. You showed no feeling. Do you like that—having slaves as your servants?"

"Now *wait* a minute." She stood rigid and isolated in the room as he glowered from the door.

"It is wrong," he said, "that anyone should live like that. And it is wrong that you do not care about it."

"Don't *you*—" She began to flare. "Don't you *ever* dare to talk to me about what I do or do not care about, about my feelings or lack of them. Don't I care enough already about your moral concerns? Now you stand here in this hotel and turn on me because I take champagne from a Negro waiter? What am I supposed to do? We *had* a civil war over that subject, you know that? We *had* a civil war. *We* didn't go begging to others to fight it on our behalf. You conceited—you conceited, arrogant person. How could you choose a time like this to—to make me feel like some Dixie bigot? You bastard. *Bastard*."

She pulled off a shoe and threw it. The black lacquer on the heel powdered on impact with the wall, leaving a mark like a gunshot.

"I'm not two people," she screamed. "Do you *hear* me? I'm not two people—the Mary Byrnes who you *do* know and who you *do* fuck and the Mary Byrnes who takes a drink from a Negro waiter. I'm *one* person, one *whole* person. Don't you dare say you don't know me. You sanctimonious bastard."

The other shoe was better aimed. He had to duck.

She stamped her right foot. "Not two people. *Me.*"

She went to him and gripped him by each lapel and shook him and spat in his eyes. "*Don* Nicolás Cordón."

He gently disengaged himself, leaving her aflame in black taffeta, and went out the door.

□

13

A white bathing cap returned May Lindt's face to its most celebrated role of her silent era: Queen Elizabeth. The bald white skull had been nonsense with the petulant, carnal face (no Virgin Queen she), but historical travesty had made box office millions. Now this capped face coated in the secret cream that preserved it for the lens broke the surface of the pool as a shadow fell over the water.

"Why, Liam!" she said.

"Hello, Miss Lindt."

"Your father is sleeping. He's—he's tired himself."

She came from the water clad in layered lotus leaves. Pink lotus leaves.

"You're looking careworn, honey. Have a cocktail with me."

There was an overexercised tautness to her thighs that betrayed the work of the cream on her face. She was in passage from youth.

"Yes," said Liam, "I could use a drink."

"It's so nice to have you here, and unexpected." She wrapped herself to the ankles in pink terry cloth and took him to the bar in the gazebo. "It's nice to have someone young around. Not that Jack isn't young at heart." She put ice into a glass as though choosing diamonds—one cube at a time, fondled for its chill and then dropped. "I mean the male young. Lily is here someplace. I think she's playing tennis with a Kennedy. I can't do that kind of thing in this climate.

They are so *competitive*, those people. There. That should raise the spirits. *Salud!* as they say where you have been, you lucky man. It must be a thrill, all those crazy Spaniards."

He had no strength to waste on her. "Yes. It was. Crazy."

"Jack had a German down here. Otto something. You know him?"

"He was in Biarritz."

"That's right. Biarritz. That was where the sexy Mrs. Simpson had the king or the prince or whatever. Do you think she's sexy?"

"Not my type."

"What is your type, Liam?"

He found some consolation in the drink. "Redheads."

She pouted as she had pouted a thousand times as the famous gamine. "What a pity. We don't have any."

Much danced before him: the glint of chlorine on tiles; the coloring of tropical foliage stirred by a torpid wind; the vacuous mouth of a movie queen. It was all at a distance. He offered no more than punctuation to her babbling, which was all it wanted, like a script over which she had kept control at the expense of a dummy leading man. Finally he went to the bungalow behind the villa that was kept for him. He bathed and slept until a houseboy woke him with the news that his father was ready to see him. It was dark.

Casey's study was the one place in the villa that made no concession to climate: Boston gothic had been wholly transposed to Florida. In the center of the room, almost aglow against the oak paneling, Casey stood in a pink tuxedo, smoking a cigar.

"You look wasted, son. Why the rush to get here? Cigar?"

"No, thanks."

"No—you still smoke that Yankee pipe. Well?"

"It's not something we could discuss over the telephone."

"Pat says you're cracking up. Are you?"

"No."

"Cold feet, he says."

"He doesn't see it. That's why I came."

"Sit down. Explain."

They sat—Casey reclined with spread-eagled legs, an emperor on a couch of hide. Liam sat hunched forward on a reversed chair, elbows on its back.

□

"In Biarritz, with March, it felt right. In Madrid it didn't."

"Go on."

"Madrid was supposed to be a walkover. They've bombed it—and that's another thing—they've bombed it night and day. It gets them nowhere. In Biarritz I thought we were backing a winner. In Madrid I got to thinking otherwise."

"Heidel doesn't agree. The Germans don't expect a walkover anymore, but they wouldn't be doing what they are if they thought they couldn't win."

"It's one hell of a gamble, Jack. If they don't win, we've never been so exposed on credit as we would be."

"March's collateral is good enough for me."

"You can't be sure of that. The guy is a crook, Jack. That gold is in a place where we couldn't touch it."

There was a silence broken only by Casey sucking on his cigar.

"Yes, son. It's a gamble. It needs nerve." He levered one heavy leg onto the couch, and then the other, and regarded the tips of his white buck shoes. "There was an old man in Texas. A dirt farmer. The shit was in his skin so deep you couldn't have scrubbed it off with a wire brush. He smelled like shit and yet he wore this coat, a fur coat like a woman's. Down to his fucking feet. Maybe he thought the coat would cover his stink. He had a week's growth of beard and his eyes were crazy. He dribbled when he talked. He was shit. He had this fucking drilling rig on his land and he'd put every last cent into it. They were foreclosing on him. I took a look. I had my eyes on that coat. Every dollar I had went into buying off that bank. I took the coat, had it cleaned up. I gave the old man a ticket to Chicago and a piece of paper for five percent of nothing. He died a couple of years later, with a quarter of a million. You know, I don't know what happened to that coat. I think some Texas whore had it."

"Look at the figures again, Jack."

The room was getting darker. The last glow left was from the cigar, flaring to the beat of Casey's breath.

"Don't fool with me, Son. This is nothing to do with figures."

Liam was silent.

□

"What really happened in Madrid? You get laid again by that crazy girl of Pat's? You listening to that pinko shit she peddles?"

The cigar went out. He swung his legs from the sofa and sighed with the weariness of a man encumbered by more than obesity. The pink tuxedo reformed in shape as he stood.

"I spoke with March," he rasped. "That's right. Did you think I would leave it to you and Pat? March knows he would be dead if he defaulted. You'd better get back to Boston. Go get some more sympathy from the other Byrnes kid—the one who keeps himself pure."

But Liam remained adamantly where he sat.

"This is a family business, Jack. It's still a family business. We don't need to do business with people like March."

"*Family* business?" Casey, momentarily nonplussed, then erupted into a noise halfway between derisive laughter and volcanic rage. "*Family?* What *kind* of Catholic family is it that has only one child to show for it? What *kind* of family is that for a man?"

"There was a girl and she died."

Now Casey's body was contorted, and shrinking back into the tuxedo like a hunted thing.

"*That!*" he shouted. "That was a *child*? That *thing*? You come here and—I know, I know. I see it in you—you come here and bridle at the way I live, the women I have. How does it look to you? How does it look?"

Liam left the chair and stood.

"You goddamned Ivy League fancy boy. *Family*. What kind of family business can you have with *one* son? Look at Joe. *That*'s family."

"You're talking dynasty, not family. You *have* family."

"I do?" There was a new note in the question—sarcasm, stripped of rage, a voice suddenly tempered to a controlled and more incisive thrust. "In the eyes of God I have a family. That's my duty. I do my duty, Son. I know my duty. *Do you?* Or are you here as the emissary of those atheistic Bolsheviks that burn the churches and rape the nuns? She got you working for them too, Son?"

"You better get one thing clear, Jack. Nobody, *nobody* tells me what to think. I guess we do have that in common. I'm not going to preach to you about the way you live. That would be cant. You can answer to yourself on that. I *do* know my duty. I have to live with it."

Casey was left silenced—and with the novel and unpleasant feeling that for the first time he had detected something of himself in his son.

■

Cordón came back to find Mary asleep on the bed, still in the black dress: asleep with a kind of cathartic peace on her face. The shoes remained where she had thrown them. Cordón picked them up and smiled and returned them to a demure symmetry at the foot of the bed. He kissed her brow. Though she appeared still to be asleep, one arm came up and held his head above hers.

"Where have you been? Your hair isn't wet."

"The rain stopped."

She opened one eye. "So where have you been?"

"I walked. It was cold but it is a beautiful city at night."

She opened the other eye and let the hand slip from his head.

He sat on the bed beside her. "I came to a memorial—the memorial to President Lincoln. I was there a long time. I read what it says there. You know, there is no memorial like that in my country. No words like that. When you have the freedom to say those things on stone you have freedom. I think I understand a little better now. If that is what the people really believe, what your civil war was fought for, then nothing will stop it in the end."

"Kiss me. You—you strange person."

She sat up to hold him and said, "Next time, I won't miss."

"I am sorry."

"Accepted." She broke the embrace and regarded him solemnly. "I do know—I do know, my love, how hard it must be to get used to how things are here. It's been so fast."

"He was a sad looking man, your President Lincoln. Even in the stone, the face of a man who has had to stand between the past and the future, without belonging to either. I have known men like that."

"He died too soon."

"Maybe not. Maybe he had done what there was for him to do."

"I don't agree." She shook her head. "I don't agree. You're being Spanish again. Americans don't think in fatalistic terms like that."

He loosened his tie and looked at its red and black design wryly, and then at her. "I should know more. There are things to learn."

"If only—if only we had the time. Unbutton me, please. My back is stiff and my legs are cold."

■

Joe Dann's office had woken them at eight, and they were with him at nine.

"My man at State did the trick," said Dann. "The Neutrality Act refers specifically to wars. That no assistance should be rendered to states at war. See the hole? Doesn't apply to civil war. No doubt about it, it won't hold up. State can't block our export license on that."

"Isn't that hairsplitting?" said Mary.

Dann held up two palms virtually together. "All it takes in a law is a hole that wide."

Cordón said, "Are you sure?"

"Yes, I am. Time to divide forces. You're not going to like this. We have to pull out all the stops. You, Señor Cordón, are needed in New York. Backlund could use you. And you, young lady, we're going to need you on the Hill."

"On the Hill?" said Cordón.

"Capitol Hill. Senator Nye wants to have Miss Byrnes sweet-talk a few of his colleagues. The other side are moving. Senator Pittman and Congressman Reynolds, to be specific. They're already lining up the votes in the Senate and the House for an embargo. Yeah, I knew it wouldn't thrill you, Miss Byrnes. We have to make some sacrifices."

"I know," she said.

"Hell," said Dann, "you'll have time for a kiss in the corridor."

"Thanks," she said.

She looked at the pictures of Dann's children on his desk, two girls and a boy. She envied them. She could see that Cordón was happy to have a call to action. Washington was too comfortable for him.

As they were leaving, Dann beckoned her to one side while Cordón went to get the coats.

"Your father is at First Cape National, right?"

"Yes."

Dann was troubled. "I thought so."

"Why?"

"Casey. 'Oiler' Jack. His outfit?"

"Yes."

"You have more guts than I realized."

"I don't understand."

Cordón was returning with her coat.

"Later, maybe. It's not important."

It was a day for lighter hearts than theirs. Sun dried the streets; a southern wind brought a light, sweeter air across the Potomac. Christmas displays in the windows seemed out of season. The streets filled. People looked invigorated. They had not walked streets together since they arrived, and now they had a few minutes in which to do it.

"Come on," she said, with sudden direction.

He followed her across the street.

"Look snappy," she said, dodging a taxi. Her eyes were on a flash of green neon set in a window. She led him through the doors and to the counter stools.

"If you never do it again, you'll do it this once, for me," she said; and to the girl at the counter she said, "Two root beer floats, one scoop of vanilla, one of chocolate."

"Iced water?"

"Please."

Cordón watched as the glasses were filled and topped.

"There's a special way to have this," she said. "First, before the ice cream has dissolved into the root beer, take two spoonfuls of the root beer with the foam on it. Then one spoonful each of the ice cream. Then pause to let the ice cream nearly dissolve. Then suck it all up through the straw. Thus. Just do as I do. You must let the ice cream dissolve, otherwise you'll block the straw."

"What is root beer?"

"Tastes like medicine. This is the only way to take it."

As he followed her directions she patted him on a shoulder. "Everybody should see you now, Nicolás. First corrupting step toward becoming an American."

"Strange taste."

"Give it a chance. It grows on you."

And they were youthful again: she with the debutante's hair and he in the white shirt and tie; they were unremarkable lovers in a soda fountain, disconnected by a simple pleasure from all that pursued them. They were, for the moment, lost among the innocent.

Later, when he watched her waving as his train moved out, she had the set to her shoulders he remembered from the time he had first watched her, the frame of someone alone with a purpose. Even among her own kind she stood out that way.

Backlund was on the track to meet him in New York. Instead of moving off after shaking hands, he took Cordón to a pillar and watched the train empty.

"You have a tail," he said.

Cordón did not understand.

"You were followed. From Washington."

Cordón looked through the crowd but saw nothing.

"It's okay. I can always tell. I'm used to it."

"Who?"

"FBI. They must have picked you up days ago."

"Why—why would they do that?"

Backlund punched him lightly in the chest. "You're a subversive, dummy. Like me. Don't look shocked. Land of the free, right? They can't lay a finger on us. We don't need to lose them. Not yet. I want you to act normal. They'll probably switch tails someplace here. It's better that they keep just one guy on us for now."

Backlund drove to his house in Queens, where Cordón and Mary had gone for the Swedish dinner.

"You're staying with us. At least, that's how it's gonna look."

□

He glanced in the mirror. "Black Ford. Dumb bastards. Always a black Ford. I like your tie. Subversive. What are we going to subvert? Between us? I wonder, why are these guys so worried? It's their *insecurity* that bothers me."

Nina Backlund's sweetness coated an unflagging energy. There were three children upstairs, whom Cordón had heard but not seen, and two men downstairs waiting for him and Backlund. It was a few moments before he saw the roles of "Mike" and "Ted." One was roughly the same build as Backlund, the other about Cordón's size.

"We guessed right," Backlund said to them, as he came in.

Nina nodded. "In the dark, they'll pass. Nicolás, don't they feed people in Washington?"

The five of them sat down to a meal.

"Eat," said Backlund to Cordón. "It may be the last square meal you'll get for a while."

The food, the debris of children, the steamy warmth of the house, the quiet street outside with its identical wood-frame villas, each with a wrought-iron balcony, the bare young birches in the snow, and the one lighted billboard that Cordón could see between a skyline of apartments—this was the only glimpse from inside domesticated America that he had had.

Reading his mind, Nina said, "When this is over, you come stay with us. You and Mary. As long as you like."

Backlund nodded. "Open house." He got up and went to a street window. It was not yet dark, but low clouds gave the billboard an early brilliance; it never did get really dark. "Still there," he said. "Let them get a little colder. Makes them careless."

An hour later Mike and Ted went out to the car—Cordón had exchanged his coat with Ted's, and Mike's was identical to Backlund's. Cordón and Backlund watched the black Ford's lights come on as it pulled out and followed Backlund's car down to the boulevard. The decoys were heading to the East River and then across Manhattan to New Jersey.

"Right," said Backlund.

They walked about a mile through snow. The villas gave way to small industrial buildings, then to a huge railroad yard. Backlund led the way through a paved area where trucks were loaded direct from boxcars, and then across several tracks to a concrete blockhouse on an island with other buildings. There was one man inside, in railroad uniform.

"Abe, this is Nick," said Backlund.

Abe was a sickly, gray-haired man—not as old as he seemed. Rheumy eyes assessed Cordón, but he said nothing.

"Is it all set?" said Backlund.

"It is," said Abe with rationed breath. He pushed a clipboard across his desk.

Backlund studied a buff typewritten sheet.

To Cordón he said, "Things can get lost on a railroad. Happens all the time. This freight is a case in point. It's gonna get lost, and you're gonna get lost with it." He gave Cordón the clipboard. "You keep this. That's an itinerary and timetable. It looks complicated but it isn't. All you have to remember is, never leave the train. It's all set up for you, in a boxcar. Crude, you'll live like a hobo. But you won't be cold. In a coupla days—" He pointed to an underscored line halfway down the sheet. "—you'll be there. Lorton, Virginia. That's where you get lost."

"Lost?"

"We have an old piece of track lined up for you. Come on. Your train is waiting."

Under gantry lights on a far side of the yard was a train made up of boxcars and mixed flatbeds. Backlund took Cordón to one of the flatbeds. They carried large wooden crates labeled "AGRICULTURAL MACHINERY."

"These are your special babies. Airplanes."

"Planes?"

"Disassembled, yes, airplanes, engines, and spares. As ordered."

"Why are we doing it this way?"

"Assuming we do get the export license, we want to keep these babies off the manifest until the last moment. They know about this too soon, they'll pull out everything to stop us. Have to keep the destination dark. Lorton is only half a day from Charleston. Once they get that far, it gives us a big jump on them."

He led Cordón down the track to the final boxcar and slid aside the door.

□

"This is your parlor car. Abe has fixed it up. You stay with this to Lorton. A guy will contact you there. We have friends all over. Okay?"

Behind Backlund's briskness was a clear affection for Cordón. This bear of a man was soft at the center.

"Yes," said Cordón. "Will I see you again?"

"In Charleston."

In the boxcar there was an oil lamp, a small camping stove, a pallet, some blankets, a saucepan and water, milk, bread, and cans of beans and corned beef. As Backlund had promised, Cordón was going to live like a hobo—but a warm hobo.

■

"There are only two places on this earth I know really well," said Senator Nye. "Wisconsin, where I was raised, and North Dakota. In Wisconsin I was a newspaperman for a while. People there were never much concerned with what happened in other parts. I was twenty-two when the war came. Some of the boys went to France, some never came home. That changed things a little, for a while. People remember that. You know, they don't want to get into any more wars they don't understand."

"I know," said Mary quietly.

"Way I see it is, best way of getting this war from spreading is to get it over fast. If we give the legitimate government of Spain the right to buy the arms she needs, that will achieve that purpose. Seems plain enough to me, after what you've been telling me. Doesn't seem so plain to most of these other gentlemen we've been talking with." He placed both feet on his desk and sank pensively into his leather chair. "You know, they call me a progressive. Way they use the word, you'd think it was a disease."

"It's taking on the tone of a religious argument."

"Yes, it is."

"That Irish lady did a lot of harm to us."

"You know . . ." Nye pulled his feet from the desk and stood up slowly. "You know, I am a religious man. But they make me feel like a heretic."

A succession of senators had come and gone. Their questions to Mary had become predictable: why did the Republicans burn churches; wasn't Franco approved of by the pope; didn't Moscow really run the Republican war. Every time she qualified these generalizations, every time she attempted to explain the factions of the Spanish left, she felt she had left them confirmed in their own prejudices. Nye had coached her into a simpler argument, but this had not made any headway, either. They were now both despondent.

"Hear you had a ride with the First Lady."

"A clever person."

"Not a happy one."

"She listens. She listens better than the senators. If she's not happy it's because she sees the real moral problem better."

"Not exactly my meaning."

She looked at him more sharply.

"The president comes across as a very homey guy. Family man. That's the genius of his radio talks. You know, share my fireside. It's really just another side of that clever and damned devious man. He isn't homey. And there's room for only one morality in the White House."

"But then you're a Republican."

"Nothing to do with it." He grinned and seemed to find reinvigoration. "If I'm a progressive, Franklin Delano Roosevelt is a Bolshevik!"

She left his office depressed. The streets with their Christmas colors provided a sense of illusory well-being.

Someone had been waiting for her at the hotel: Nora Stern.

"I have a request," she said.

"Yes?"

"Do you know of the Theater Committee for the Defense of the Spanish Republic?"

"No."

"Are you feeling okay?"

"I'm tired."

"Well . . ." Stern seemed to consider offering sympathy, but instead picked up from where she had broken off. "There are a lot of these groups now. A lot. The Hollywood Anti-Nazi League, the Motion Picture Artists' Committee. Spain is getting some real star support, big names, James Cagney, Myrna Loy, Joan Crawford; writers like Dos Passos and Hemingway. Well, a lot of these people are joining with us to hold a big rally in New York next week, at Manhattan Town Hall. Very important in getting coverage, newspapers, magazines, radio. I suggested we ask you to speak, and the committee thinks that's a wonderful idea."

"Speak? I've never spoken in public."

"Does that worry you?"

"It terrifies me."

"I think you would be great. Just great. It's so important. It could achieve so much."

Stern was the kind of person who blocked all exits.

"Well, what would I say?"

"That's great. Just great. We have plenty of time to settle your text. You can give us something nobody else can. The real sense of the people's struggle. We need that 'you are there' feeling."

Mary didn't remember accepting, but it was too late. She had misgivings; for all Stern's ardency and quick wits, she lacked spontaneity. Everything she said had a secondhand sound.

Mary missed Cordón. The mystery of his whereabouts was not dispelled by a call from Backlund, who talked like a man being overheard. He was using a pay phone. In the background she heard traffic.

"Your friend is okay. Thought you'd like to know."

"Yes. Thanks."

"How are things going with you?"

"It's a struggle. Nye is a good person, but he seems to be on his own."

"I know. Don't get downhearted, sweetheart. Good guys can win, you know."

"It would be nice. If true."

"Have to go. Take care."

□

The line was dead before she could answer—and before Farrio's man in the hotel had any hope of tracing the call. Backlund and Cordón had slipped away. All they had now was Mary.

■

The train had moved off before dawn, waking Cordón with a jolt. It moved slowly, never, he reckoned, going above twenty miles per hour. After a while the constant crossing of switches with its bone-shaking racket eased off and then finally ended. They had been dawdling for two hours along a single track running over wetlands. Cordón went to sleep again. When he awoke they were not moving. He looked out. The train was in the shadow of a vast granite escarpment, partly wooded. The noon sun was already beyond the escarpment. They were, he worked out, pointing southwest. He heard the regular, asthmatic sighs of the distant locomotive. He was stiff and, in spite of the cold, he jumped out between the train and the trees to pace the length of the boxcar. The air was a tonic. Two gray squirrels scrambled down a pine branch and stopped to watch him. He could have been back in Aragón: resin in the air, wind in the rock, a circling hawk, and snow against the sky. Then, with a shudder that broke the illusion, the train began to roll again.

■

A day more of lobbying left Mary feeling no better. On an impulse, she went to Dann's office, though it was late.

His staff had gone. He opened the door himself. It seemed to her, oddly, that she was expected. He took her coat and led her into his sanctum. The only light burning was on his desk; under an opalescent Tiffany shade it gave him a better color than he really had.

"Sit down. It's been rough on you."

"Joe, I feel scared. I don't know what I'm scared of. It's like—like there's a veiled enemy somewhere out there that I can't see."

He took off his reading glasses and looked at her, blinking. "You feel on your own, right?"

"Like an outsider."

"Nye said you were fine. But I guess it's depressing."

"It's what they don't say. There's something in their faces that doesn't get said. The way they looked at me."

"Yeah." He drew a pencil through a hand. "You feel furtive without knowing why."

"That's right."

"Well, let me assure you, nobody in this is doing anything against the law. Be sure of that. I wouldn't sanction it. What's happening is a necessary subterfuge. Compared with the opposition, we're angels."

"I don't understand who the opposition is."

Dann tapped the pencil on a blotter. It was the only sound in the room. "Don't misunderstand me, Mary. There is no great organized conspiracy. What you have to realize is the scale of business involved in a war like this. This war is potential big business, and there are guys who can smell that kind of business from three thousand miles away."

"Joe. You started to say something last time about First Cape National. Remember?"

"Yeah."

"Why?"

"No mystery. I made a connection. You, your father. You must know better than I do the kind of guy old 'Oiler' Casey is. That crowd—it's your town."

"Yes. But that wasn't why you asked, was it?"

The gnomic face gave nothing away. "Don't jump to any conclusions. It would seem to me—Catholic money, Jack Casey's politics—hell, Mary, do I have to spell it out? It was about you I was thinking. That somebody with your background would do what you're doing."

Somewhere within this explanation—she could not quite fix on the point—Dann had covered an evasion. It was well-meant, but she was certain of it.

He leaned back and put down the pencil. "Large powers and little guys. The men who drew up our Constitution thought that one out pretty well. Of course—" There was an impish flash in his eyes. "Of course, they weren't exactly little guys themselves, the founding fathers. Enlightened disinterest. Ahead of their time. If you're a lawyer in this town, you pretty soon have to decide where you stand on that one. The large powers get larger—in spite of FDR's rhetoric—and the little guys are more vulnerable. It keeps me busy."

"You're a nice person, Joe."

"Yeah. Let's have a drink, shall we?"

■

The coat that Cordón had acquired in the exchange with his decoy was too long in the sleeves and cut like a tent. It was easier to sleep in it than use the blankets. He had slept a lot. The fatigue of months had caught up with him, and the boxcar, dawdling through the remote byways of the railroad labyrinth, was soporific. Behind the closed door, lying on the pallet, he nonetheless gained a sense of a changing landscape from the smells and from variations in the light that seeped through, with the drafts. Once, during the night, he smelled sulfurous air of heavy industry; that gave way to salt water and oil smoke; and then they rolled into mellower land-borne winds. Cordón put aside the coat and eased open the door. Sun flashed into silver woods and picked out, through the trees, occasional mirrors of still water. The land fell suddenly away into creeks. The train ran on high wooden trestles. Below and beyond the reach of the winter light was slate-gray water running under a mill. Dirt tracks rimmed with yellow leaves followed the water to the mill. And then this netherworld, seemingly without occupation, was gone. The train ran between moss-coated granite walls. The trapped sound and sharply colder air forced him to close the door. The country he had always thought of as dynamic and teeming was also a wilderness and, he realized, a wilderness that could reclaim territory from improvident speculators. The dead mill and the unrutted dirt tracks were not sad things to him; he sided with Nature against speculation.

It was an hour before dusk when the train stopped and, after a pause, reversed. He opened the door a few inches. They were on a track coated with rust. Weeds thrived in the railbed. Dark woods rose gently on either side. There was tepid air, and herringbone clouds underlit with mauve and scarlet. There was another pause, a belching of smoke, and the uncoupled locomotive disappeared. Cordón left the door open and sat on the pallet.

He heard no one approach but there was, in a moment, a black face trying to see clearly into the boxcar, and a large hand sliding the door open wider.

"Hello there." The voice was a friendly baritone.

"You comrade Cordón?"

"Yes."

"I'm Solomon and this here is comrade Eddie."

A second face materialized behind the first—white, and emaciated with a stubble beard.

"You had a good ride, comrade?"

"Is this Lorton?"

Solomon grinned. "Let's just say, comrade Cordón, that this is Virginia."

Comrade Eddie said, "There's a problem."

"That's right," said Solomon. "Dave, comrade Backlund, he's having trouble with another consignment. Gonna be late. It's not helping us any, but it's the kind of thing you have to expect in an enterprise of this very nature. You sure look well-rested, there, comrade Cordón." Solomon's great hand moved from the door to shake Cordón's hand. "We're all pleased to make the acquaintance of a comrade from Spain. Dave told us about you. Down here in Virginia we don't get to see so many of our foreign comrades."

Solomon's fraternal clasp went with a laugh that filled the boxcar.

Cordón jumped down.

"The thing is," said Solomon, "Ain't any point in you sitting here in the woods with our babies. You be better employed in other places. So Eddie here is gonna run you into Washington. I'm taking over here."

"What about Charleston and the ship?"

"The ship is there, right enough. It's gonna have to wait for us. Dave wants to load the other stuff first. When it's time he'll send for you. You all set? That your coat?"

Eddie led Cordón down a foot track to a dirt road where an ancient pickup truck was waiting. Eddie reached under the boards of the cab and pulled out something wrapped in old rags.

Unwrapping it he said, "You like this stuff?"

"What is it?"

"Finest moonshine south of the Potomac."

Cordón took a sampling swig.

"Ain't that something special?"

"It's—it's unusual."

"Knew you'd like it. My ole Uncle Motlow makes that."

For the rest of the ride through back hills and down into Alexandria and over the river into Washington they shared the bottle. Comrade Eddie's nursing of the truck was unhampered, but Cordón's mood became uncommonly convivial.

Eddie had suddenly pulled to a stop. "Far as we go, Nick. Daren't go farther. You okay? Know the way?"

"I'll get a taxi."

"Best idea. Good to know you, comrade. Here—you finish the bottle. Got plenty more."

The hotel doorman detected in Cordón's walk a festive spirit, common to the season, and forgave the condition of his coat and the darkness of his beard. He knew the face. It would be good news for Farrio, after a trying time.

□

MADRID

"And now, if you please—"

With the crack of a whip the Jester ordered the curtains to open.

From the wings a small brass band played the first bars of a *pasadobles*.

For a moment the stage remained empty. The music became more insistent and there were impatient shouts from the audience. Then came a flash of scarlet and gold. A figure blurred in motion, leaping in time with the spasms of the *pasadobles*. A yelping archbishop in robe and miter, waving a crucifix.

More shouts.

And out leapt the bull, an uncoordinated bull, front legs shorter than the rear, a bull dragging its hindquarters as if suddenly paralyzed by the sight of the crucifix being flourished like a wand to fend it off. The archbishop confronted the bull, bringing to bear the full mystic force of his office against the black bull with the red ribbon around its neck. The music and the audience demanded more courage from the bull. In reply, the beast exposed its rear to the audience—a large pink human rear with buttocks breaking wind.

The Jester, a Harlequin in tasseled cap, slashed with his whip at the offered flesh.

The bull yelped as the archbishop had done and sprang at the crucifix. With the band playing at full volume, the grotesque pair sped and danced around the stage. The archbishop lost his miter and was revealed, in distress, to be as naked under his silks as the rear end of the bull, his pale white legs skipping with a ballet dancer's agility.

Perot said, "They are real, those robes! Wonderful! From the palace at Toledo."

Rey was enjoying it, too. "Justice!" he cried. "Justice!"

Ferrer was more restrained. She scanned the audience more assiduously than the stage. Almost all of them were in masks: Perot was powdered and rouged like a clown, with a white ruffle around his neck. Rey was Pan in green forest cloak and cap but still, with his glasses, too much the pedant for a lover's meadow. They were among the less bizarre. There were leotards and asses' heads, tutus and transvestite duchesses, several languidly ravishing creatures whose gender Ferrer could not be sure of, and much black leather and chain mail.

Ferrer was herself, in a black *mono.*

The archbishop was about to be impaled. He made one final and fatal leap into a corner and the bull skidded into him, horns ripping into silk. The bull obscenely raised its hindquarters and flashed its genitals. The *pasadobles* and the audience met in a roar of brass and laughter.

The bull relented; the archbishop threw off the scarlet and came to face them, taking a bow in a muslin petticoat.

Perot clapped his hands above his head and flexed his hips, which brushed Ferrer. She pulled away. Rey slipped Pan's arm around her.

The Jester reappeared with both halves of the bull, who were now disporting in G-strings, and they lewdly embraced the archbishop. The four of them blew kisses to the audience.

A drum began a low roll.

The Jester stepped forward. "*To victory! Viva la república! Viva la libertad!*"

The band exploded into the anthem of the republic.

All the bestiary shouted endorsing slogans and then joined in a huge chain dance. Ferrer kept carefully between Perot and Rey as they circled at an increasing tempo under showering confetti—a dust of black and red that collected in her hair. The chain broke. Strangers and lovers embraced.

Perot was almost lost, enveloped by a much taller figure, black leather with a shearling cape and sheep's head. Clown and sheep were mated.

It was a real sheep's head, deboned and padded, but the eyes inside the sockets seemed wolverine and predatory.

Ferrer watched.

Leather bags of wine were taken to the band. Couples disengaged. Perot, released, reached out for Rey.

"Francisco. Francisco—a friend. Meet El Coronel."

The sheep's head bowed and took Rey's felted hand in his leather one.

"And Aneta."

The head dipped once more.

She took the hand. "El Coronel." Predators knew their own kind.

"Comrade."

Perot was still gushing. "What an archbishop Pablo makes!"

Pablo was dancing in the petticoat, with a duchess.

"And what a good anarchist bull!" said Rey.

"The bull was like the government," said El Coronel. "Pulling two ways."

"But victory is coming! And revolution!" said Rey.

The sheep's head was silent. Perot rubbed against the shearling coat and the two of them glided off, unconsciously falling into step with the renewed music.

"They seem happy," said Rey, with tolerant amusement. It was time, he thought, for Pan to play his pipe. He swept Ferrer up and into the dance. She was a mechanical rather than a natural partner, but he was undeterred. He liked the way the *mono* stressed her bust and hips. The music and the assorted lovers were loosening his inhibitions. They seemed to be moving in a steady swell of eroticism. He pulled her close.

"What is *that?*" she said, hissing in his ear.

The hiss sounded ardent to him. "Don't you know?"

She could not loosen from his lock on her waist.

□

Without breaking step she brought her right knee up sharply into his groin.

His eyes bulged and watered and he screeched out, releasing her and doubling in pain, though in the throng it seemed just another contortion of pleasure.

There were whoops of laughter around them. But Rey, struggling for breath, had seen a mask fall from an unmasked face. He could see no trace of pity in her.

NEW YORK

She had washed the debutante curls out of her hair and cropped it again. She kept the black dress but added a red silk choker to be loyal to Cordón's colors. There was lots of red in the Manhattan Town Hall, but it was subsidiary to gigantic stars and stripes draped at the back of the stage. Patriotism had been subtly interwoven into the slogans: "America Fights for Spanish Freedom"; "Communism Is Twentieth Century Americanism"; "Support the Abraham Lincoln Battalion." This last was the only poster Mary was on any terms with—the Lincoln Battalion had arrived with the International Brigade late in the battle for Madrid, and had taken heavy casualties. She looked out at the hall from the wings of the stage. There were still rows of empty seats.

Nina Backlund was with her. "It's too bad," she said.

"It says something."

Stern overheard. "It doesn't matter. The radio people are here, the *Times*, the *News*, everybody except the Hearst papers."

"My legs are Jell-O," said Mary.

"You'll be fine." Stern patted her shoulder. "Norman will break the ice for you."

Cordón was back in his own coat. He said, "I cannot understand, what does it mean? Communism Is Twentieth Century Americanism?"

□

"It means," said Stern impatiently, "that we are, first of all, good Americans."

"And communists?"

"Why not? Where is the problem?"

Mary watched closely. She had never seen Stern so deflected from the rote.

"Where is the problem?"

"What about the revolution?"

Stern was stuck like a vehicle in mud trying to find the right gear. First she sighed. Then she shook her head. Then she laid a hand on Cordón's sleeve, with another more tolerant sigh, and the gears finally meshed. "Our principles and program embody the future development of our country."

Nina said, "That's Popular Front hogwash."

Before Stern went into another paroxysm Mary said, "Isn't it time we went out there?"

Stern gave Nina a quick and venomous glance and then led Mary away.

"She's lucky Dave isn't around," said Nina. "He hates that Moscow stuff. The amazing thing is, I think she really believes it."

"Oh yes," said Cordón. "They all believe it." He watched Mary join the other speakers on the platform. "She is so scared. She is not sure about this."

"She shouldn't worry. We need all the publicity we can get—even with these people running it."

Farrio was sitting four rows back. He saw Cordón and Nina reappear and take reserved seats in front of him. Next to Farrio was a much larger man in a pea coat and blue watchman's cap.

Pea Coat said, "That's the bastard who gave me the slip."

Farrio chewed gum, sucking the flavor out of it.

"Don't see the other guy," said Pea Coat.

"No. No, he's gotten clean away from us."

"This is a fuckin' roll call."

"Yeah."

"These people make me sick."

Latecomers took seats around them. Farrio took the gum from his mouth and pressed it under the frame of the seat in front. They both tried to look like fellow travelers.

Nina had been careful to take seats out of Mary's eyeline—"We don't want her to see us. It would throw her."

But, sitting second in the line of speakers, Mary was looking for them. Cordón saw how tightly her hand clutched the notes.

Behind him two reporters were talking.

"Who's the chick?"

"The redhead?"

"I see only one chick. Nora Stern is a turkey."

"Yeah. Cute. Must be the kid who was in Madrid."

"What's a chick with that kinda class doing with this bunch?"

The lights went down.

Stern introduced the first speaker, a bald man in a loose tweed suit. He had to have the microphone raised from Stern's height to his. Despite his professorial appearance, he was a rabble-rouser. Mary was aware of a long right arm punching the air. As he worked up to his climax, saliva came off him like flying spores. The final burst brought stamping feet and an ovation.

Mary felt paralyzed. Stern was introducing her. She got up but could not see the audience beyond the lights. The power of her voice in the microphone surprised her. Her left hand settled on her hip. The notes in her right hand were not needed. She felt steady.

"Everywhere you look in Europe, democracy is in retreat. England and France are the only democratic powers of any size left, but they seem scared out of their wits. Too scared to stand up to Hitler and Mussolini. Too scared to deal with Franco . . ."

Nina touched Cordón. "That's our girl."

". . . Spanish people are our last hope in Europe. It is the Spanish people, not the German people, not the Italian people, but the Spanish people who have stood and fought against fascism . . ."

For the first time, Cordón heard pencils behind him beginning to scratch over pads.

". . . they started without an army of their own . . ."

Pea Coat said, "This lady has got them."

". . . if the Spanish people are beaten it will not be because they lacked the courage. It will be because they have been denied the means of defending themselves . . ."

"Here it comes," murmured Farrio through mint.

". . . if they are allowed to be sacrificed like this it will be true to say that wars are not won by the people who face the bullets and the bombs. This war will have been decided by the men in Rome, Berlin—and, yes, by the hard men in Washington. By men who have never heard a bullet fired."

There was more, but she had won them. Cordón saw it around him. When she finished, the audience stood to applaud.

Standing at her side on the stage, Stern whispered, "You have a new career."

"Jesus, I hope not." It was corrupting, the pleasure it gave her.

The other speeches were anticlimactic.

Nina and Cordón slipped backstage to wait for her.

Pea Coat said, "Where the fuck is the Swede?"

"He worries me," said Farrio.

"Yeah."

"This is over."

They got up in the middle of a speech and pushed to the aisle, arousing complaint. Pea Coat trod on feet.

Mary thought that she had lost pounds under the heat of the lights, and her mouth felt lined with dust; but with the crush of congratulations backstage it was several minutes before she could get water, and then Cordón fetched it for her.

"It was a very good thing for us," he said.

"Oh, I hope so. Joe Dann wasn't so sure it was a good idea—in this kind of company."

"The reporters took notes."

Behind Cordón and Nina she saw a small man in a gray coat and black beret; he had been there awhile, watching her.

He stepped forward. "Miss Byrnes."

"Yes?"

"My name is Isaac Mandel. I am the editor of a magazine, the *New Nation*. Have you heard of us?"

"A monthly, right? With the cartoon cover?"

"That's right. We're independent, don't have a party line, or any other kind of line. My interest is in journalism, good journalism."

"Yes?"

"Miss Byrnes, I would like you to write for me about Spain. That is, if you're planning on going back."

"You would?" She looked quickly at Cordón. "Yes, I am going back."

"I have to tell you, I don't want the wire service kind of stuff, anything that depends on a deadline for its significance. I want the stuff that somebody could read ten years from now and say, that must have been what it was like. You follow?"

"Yes."

"I want what you feel, Miss Byrnes, as well as what you see. I could tell, listening to you up there, that you *do* feel. You can have as much space as you need. And your pictures. How about it?"

"You mean—you'll actually pay me for writing what I want to write?"

"That's correct. It won't be a lot. But it could make your name."

"It's a deal, Mr. Mandel."

"Ike. My writers call me Ike."

They shook hands, and she introduced Cordón.

Mandel smiled at Mary. "Now I understand the significance of your colors—black and red." He glanced across to where Stern was talking and back again. "You keep dangerous company. You know, I always remember a moment, it was in London, 1924. I was one of the young utopians then, excited about Russia. We gave a dinner for Emma Goldman and we thought we would hear wonderful things about Russia. She told us what the Bolsheviks were really doing. We didn't like it. In fact, to be honest, we behaved very badly, as only a disabused utopian can. She was ahead of her time."

"Some lady," said Mary.

"We learn, we learn," said Mandel.

"You know," said Cordón, "I do not think there will be a revolution in this country."

□

All of them—Mary, Nina, and Mandel—broke into laughter and in that anteroom of the pious it was like voicing heresy.

"Well," said Mandel, as they subsided, "we'll just have to beat the bastards without one."

Nina was distracted. "My, my," she said, "what do you know? We've even pulled in a priest."

The rest of them looked round.

"Tom!" said Mary, "it's *Tom*! And *Liam*!"

Tom and Liam advanced.

"Oh, *Tom*!" Mary surprised her brother with an embrace, holding him fast.

"Congratulations," said Tom, "we have another preacher in the family."

"Oh, Tom. I'm sorry. I must be such a trouble to you."

"Just remember that I love you. You should always remember that. And you should *always* call me when you come home."

"I know. I know, Tom. Tom—" She broke away and realized Cordón's confusion. "Tom, this is Nicolás. Nicolás Cordón."

The two appraised each other from their distant poles.

"Nicolás, this is my brother, Tom. It's okay, he's the good Byrnes."

Mandel watched with fascination.

Liam said, "I've told Tom about Nicolás."

"Yes," said Tom, "and so he did." He put out a hand. "I would be proud to shake your hand, Nicolás."

"I think I might cry," said Mary.

"Don't," said Liam. "It wouldn't be in character."

"I'm *happy*."

"You were very impressive," said Liam. "They loved you."

"Preaching to the converted."

"Oh no." Tom smiled. "Not *entirely*."

They all laughed.

Mandel said, "This seems like family. I'll say good-bye."

"No," said Mary. "Why don't we all go get something to eat? And no more politics."

"I know a great deli," said Mandel.

"Lead us," said Mary.

Pea Coat, watching them all spill out of the stage door together, cursed to himself. He was hunched for warmth over a subway grille. He walked some distance behind them, hoping the party would not last too long.

■

Dann brought them back to earth. He invited Mary and Cordón to meet him at the Yale Club, and sat them in a paneled corner.

"See you lost those lovely curls," he said.

"I am still in the dress, Joe."

"Yeah." He was too pressed to sustain the joke. He pulled out a note and his reading glasses. "I have an early copy of the bill they're drafting for the embargo. It's worse than I thought. The relevant passage is—this is what the embargo will cover—quote, all arms, munitions, implements of war to either side, *and* munitions to neutrals for shipment to Spain unquote. Oh, and this is the sting—all licenses already issued will be invalid from the date of the president's signature."

"To *either* side?" she said.

"You got it. It sounds evenhanded."

"But?"

"But, one, there is no prevention of credit being made available by a bank or banks, and credit is as good as arms to the other side. Two, nothing about oil. Now the trick there is that oil has to be on a strictly cash-and-carry basis. Nobody is shipping to a government port, because they claim it's unsafe for the tankers. So that door is left wide open."

"It's outrageous," she said.

"Yes. It is. And it's going to be law."

"How soon?"

"They're moving fast. They'll get the votes. The House is a walkover. The Senate—well, Nye hasn't got the weight."

"How soon?"

Dann put away the paper and his glasses. "They hope, by Christmas. I don't think so. We can stall it, but only days." He looked at Cordón. "What's the word from Backlund?"

□

"The problem is the spares we need for the aircraft."

"My advice is, don't wait."

"The aircraft would be useless without them."

"You're running out of time."

"I know." Cordón tried to convince himself. "We will do it."

"I hope so." Dann turned to Mary. "I hear you're quite a public speaker."

"We had two paragraphs in the *Post*, one in the *Journal-American*, one in the *Times*. Nothing else. Not exactly an opening-night hit."

"Ike said you were compelling. That was his word. Compelling."

"You know Ike?"

"We go back some."

"You mean—*you* put him on to me?"

"He would have been there anyway."

"*Joe*—"

"Yes?"

"Never mind. You're a very devious and a very nice person. He seems okay, too."

"Yes. Yes, he is. Once . . . well, let me just say, it took Ike a while to find the chosen instrument. There was a time when I thought it might turn out to be a bomb."

"*That* little man?"

"Listen, Mary. Just remember the arrogance of youth when you look at an old man like me."

"Joe, I think I would like to have known you then. I think . . ."

Dann winked at Cordón. "Yes?"

"*Autres temps, autres mœurs*."

"I couldn't put it better myself."

■

Ferrer had had to wait for two days to see Yanin. Now it was nine in the evening and she had been called to a new address—a school. Yanin never seemed to be in the same place twice. There were still coat hangers placed low on the wall for small children, with military coats touching the floor, and school maps on the walls. Everybody there seemed to be Russian, even the women. Yanin was in what must have been the principal's office. There was no heating, and he sat in a fur-collared overcoat with gloves on his hands—the exposed tips of his fingers, as he put away papers, were the only part of him that seemed to contain blood.

He made no effort to mask impatience. "You said it was important."

"I realize that you must be very busy."

"Yes." But as he watched her sit down there was the slightest of concessions to an interest in her. "I am. But I am sure you will not waste my time."

She reported on Francisco Rey, and the story of the masque.

"These people are poison," he said.

"I am sure the man El Coronel is the spy in the army."

"You have done well."

"Thank you."

"Some of this must have been distasteful for you." He folded the gloves into his lap—it seemed that in spite of the coat he was chilled to the bone. "To have won Rey's confidence so completely."

"I didn't—I—"

"No. Of course. But you would—if it was necessary?"

"Yes."

"Will he lead you any further?"

"El Coronel is the top. Perot is incidental."

"I wonder." Yanin's strained breath made even his meditations seem a burden. "I wonder."

The thought of more embraces with Rey sickened her—and she knew that Yanin was reading her mind.

"What do you think I should do?" he said.

Another test, another trap. She smiled sweetly. "I remember a story Dolores, La Pasionaria, used to tell us. The story of the belfry of Huesca."

"Go on."

"There was once a king of Huesca called Ramiro who passed laws which the aristocrats refused to obey. Not knowing what to do about it, the king turned to a certain abbot, his old tutor. The king sent his most loyal servant to see the abbot. The abbot listened to the problem of King Ramiro but said nothing. Instead, he took up a knife and went with the servant into the garden. He began to prune the trees—but only the highest branches. The servant said, 'What am I to tell the king?' The abbot said, 'Tell him what I am doing.' King Ramiro at once understood what the abbot meant. He cut off the heads of all the aristocrats and formed of them what came to be known as the belfry of Huesca. It's an ancient story, but—as Dolores says—one that is always up-to-date. As many belfries of Huesca should be created as are needed to purge us of the traitors."

Again there was just the sound of his breath, until he lifted the gloves and rubbed his fingers together.

"Comrade Ferrer, you are a credit to Dolores. And you are right."

She wished devoutly that she could do something for his weakness; she was wet for him.

MASSACHUSETTS

"There must be a window open somewhere; I *know* there is."

"I will check, Mrs. Casey."

"Is it a window, Andrews—or perhaps the door of the study? There are so many drafts."

"I will check, Mrs. Casey."

"Just *look* at the candles. The flames won't keep still."

Miriam Casey picked up a fish knife and held it to the wandering light of a candelabra, then smelled it.

"Andrews. There is a smell of soap on these knives."

The butler took the knife and sniffed it. "With respect, Mrs. Casey, the bone handles always have that smell."

She snatched back the knife and wiped it with a lace napkin.

The butler waited for her to complete her survey of the table.

"Very well. Do see if you can stop that draft."

The butler withdrew.

In a room above, Heidel looked out through a partly open casement window. A screen of pines bordered the road. The lights of a car flashed intermittently until it turned into the drive and began the steep ascent to the house. More *Schloss* than house, thought Heidel—and built to attract all four winds. He needed the air after a catnap. He closed the window but remained to watch the robed man walk from the car, followed by the young priest. The house echoed every movement below—he even fancied he could tell the age of the feet on stone going to the door. The butler and a footman. He went to his dressing table and finished his brandy; he always needed a warm stomach to face a bishop.

In the drawing room Jack Casey and Patrick Byrnes got up from their chairs, and Casey smiled as he looked at his watch.

"To the second."

Byrnes stubbed out a cigarette and wished he felt warmer.

Andrews announced, "His Excellency, Bishop Spellman."

"Jack," said the bishop.

"Frank."

Casey's handshake had no hint of genuflection.

The bishop looked from Casey to Byrnes.

"Patrick."

"Your Excellency."

"And where is Father Tom?" said Casey.

"I believe he is checking something with the driver."

"Your timekeeper, Frank."

"Yes, yes he is. And a very fine secretary."

Byrnes beamed.

"Well," said the bishop, "You're not going to keep me waiting for a drink on your birthday, Jack."

Heidel came down the stairs and met Liam.

"How do I address him?" he asked.

"For the first time, Your Excellency. Thereafter Bishop would be okay."

Tom came into the hall. Liam introduced him to Heidel and they joined the others.

In her dressing room Miriam took a final look at herself—the dark blue velvet gown was fine, but she changed the diamond brooch for a ruby. It seemed more pious. Flecks of snow began to thicken the frames of the windows.

□

Through the dinner the candles burned more steadily, and she never knew where the draft had originated. Everything progressed, her menu gave pleasure, the bishop was expansive—but the table had no place for her; she was an adornment like the candelabra and the vases. She was drinking more wine than usual. Byrnes, she saw, drank water as though he enjoyed it.

"Yours is a good age, Jack," the bishop was saying, dipping into the sorbet. "A time when a man can take a seat on the hill and look back with satisfaction on the climb. A most distinguished climb."

"That may be," said Casey, "but it started with the blessings of a good home and a fine father."

Miriam coughed and wiped the wine from her lip.

"Did you know, Herr Heidel," said the bishop, "that Jack's grandfather was a pig farmer in Ireland? Can you credit the distance from that?"

"America is the place for ambition, Bishop."

"Yes it is, it is. But your country is making a show, too."

"That is so."

Tom said, "Herr Heidel, may I ask you a political question?"

"Of course."

"What is Hitler's intention toward the Jews? We hear confusing accounts."

Heidel shook his head. "There are a few fanatics who take this too far. For me, frankly, life in Berlin without the Jews would be like a long meal without wine."

Casey grunted. "That so? Well, Otto, I'll tell you this, there are not a lot of Jews living here in Brookline, and that doesn't do anything to spoil my appetite." He offered an encompassing grin.

Nobody responded until, from the end of the table, Miriam said, "I have always noticed that criticism of the Jews comes invariably from philistines."

For a moment it seemed to Heidel that Casey would rise and take the table with him, but the movement was curtailed and he behaved as if deaf. He settled on Heidel as his escape. "Well, we're all of one church here. Isn't that the main thing?"

"Yes," said Heidel helpfully, "one church."

□

"It is a bond," said the bishop. "And one that knows no frontiers."

"Could I ask you," said Liam, "is it a fact that His Holiness is encouraging the support of General Franco in Spain?"

"A tragic country, Liam, a tragic country."

"But do you think—as a church—we should take sides?"

"I would not presume to guide His Holiness on such an issue, Liam."

Tom was across the table from the bishop. He leaned forward with sudden intensity. "Well, Your Excellency, I would have to say for myself, I have been taking a look at the man's record—Franco—and I can find nothing to support the belief that this general knows anything of the spirit of Christian mercy. If anything, I would say it was the reverse. If we as a church back him and the Spanish Jesuits we are backing the most reactionary wing of our church. That doesn't seem either good Catholicism or very American."

Only when he stopped was Tom aware, as though absorbing an echo of himself in the hollowness of the vast room, that he had been so vehement—and that the bishop's eyes implied a violation, even if his mouth did not. His father had paled.

"I do not think that is for us to judge," said the bishop.

"You surprise me, Bishop," said Liam mildly.

The bishop made a greater effort to seem resistant.

"I have been in Spain, Bishop," persisted Liam. "Matter of fact, I don't see the rightness of it in any clear-cut way. But I can testify to the nature of General Franco. I have seen his indiscriminate bombing of Madrid, and I can assure you it sickens me as a Christian and a Catholic. I've seen mothers nursing dead babies. I've seen a dog lapping at a man's brain—"

"Liam! *Really!*" Miriam held a napkin to her mouth.

"Mother. This is not a question of etiquette. I want the truth heard here."

Tom realized how much Liam must have drunk.

Jack Casey had the panic on his face of a man used to keeping control of a situation and finding himself losing it. He looked from Liam to Tom, not knowing which to blame.

"I am sure," intoned the bishop, "that we all want to hear the truth." He paused the way he did in the pulpit and, by force of will, brought them all under his attention like a congregation. "It must be very distressing, seeing these things. However, I would like to know a lot more about the people you so obviously sympathize with, Liam. Anyone who believes that Soviet Russia is concerned with the freedom of the Spanish people is deluding himself . . . and others."

Casey had simmered long enough. He set the silver jangling with a smack on the table. "You're too polite, damn it, Frank." Suddenly he was jabbing a finger at Byrnes. "Got a red in the family, Pat. Don't look so damned witless. There's a red in the family, you can't help it. Mad, bad, and red, that girl of yours." He moved his assault to Liam. "She's so damned smart she's here in this room. Got you like she's some damned ventriloquist, boy."

The bishop held himself aloof.

"Isn't that it?" bellowed Casey. "*Isn't that it?*"

"You'll have to excuse me," said Miriam, still holding the napkin to her face. "Bishop."

She fled.

It was silent around the table until the bishop said, "I would like to get back, Thomas Aquinas, while the weather permits." He rose, and the others rose with him. "You'll be coming to the Christmas Eve mass, Jack? It's a time for renewal of the holy spirit."

■

One of the houses in the street was outlined from ground to roof in colored lights. The lights followed the pitch of the roof and framed the windows; at night it was disembodied by its brilliance, a flashing trinket against the sky of pitch. The Backlunds' children had gazed out at it through frosted panes and conjured their own fanciful explanation: that it was a doll's house come down with the stars attached, from where such things were made.

In Backlund's absence Cordón had played Santa Claus, but his accent had betrayed him. It was a house where exposure of the bogus seemed second nature. But, having exposed him, the children went on with their own secular fantasies, and the garish house sent them happily to sleep.

"I'm all played out," said Mary, stretching on the sofa with a tinsel boa around her neck.

Nina laughed. "The kids had a great time."

Cordón took off a garlanded top hat. "They are wonderful. I love them."

"Yes, they are," said Mary, reaching for her cognac.

"You would make a fine father, Nicolás," said Nina.

Cordón covered his awkwardness with a laugh.

Nina looked from him to Mary, exaggerating her mischievous implication with the question left in her eyes.

"Forget it, Nina."

"One day, perhaps?"

But Mary was as awkward as Cordón—it was impossible, in a house so extensively blessed, to be indifferent—and she, too, laughed. "I guess we'll have to work it out."

"I'm sorry," said Nina. "I shouldn't have. You're both such nice people, though. It sure is a hard world."

"I envy you, Nina," said Mary. "You do so much, and yet you keep your perspective. Here we are, it's easy to forget what brought us here. Sometimes . . ." She trailed off.

"I know," said Nina. "I'll make some coffee."

Cordón lay on the floor next to a sleeping cat and put the top hat over his face.

Mary said, "I wonder what Eleanor is doing tonight? The cat, not the lady. Our cat."

Memories of that spartan room were shared in silence. It was a way of placing themselves together without touching. And a way of knowing what tied them.

It proved to be their last night in the house. Before dawn they were awakened by Backlund's return.

"Everything is moving," he said, as Cordón forced himself awake.

"God, you look frozen," said Mary.

Backlund sat on the bed with the chill still on his breath.

□

"It's been a long haul. Couldn't get everything we wanted in time. Can't risk delaying any longer. Joe says we'll never get anything out if we don't move now."

"What about the train?" said Cordón.

"Joe is applying for an amendment to the export license today. It'll throw them."

"Won't they stop it?" said Mary.

"They can't. Joe is sure. They don't have the legislation to do it. And they can't get that bill through for days yet—thanks to Christmas."

"Smart," said Mary.

"Yeah—that's Joe's strategy. Can you see their faces at State, when they see that manifest? A trainload of airplanes rolling out of nowhere."

"You're sure they can't pull something?"

"Oh, they'd love to. Just love to. The black Ford is outside, by the way. They picked me up on the Fifty-ninth Street Bridge. Gave them a wave. Those guys love me. It's out in the open now. Nothing they can do."

"When do we leave?" said Mary.

Backlund didn't reply at once. He looked untypically evasive.

"What is it, Dave?"

"Okay. You have to know. They want Nicolás on that boat. There's a deal in the works to have the spares put on board in Mexico. He'll have to take care of that. And stay with the boat to Spain."

"Can't I—?"

"Sorry, babe. No. It can't be done. You'll have to let him sail out of your life for a week or two. It will make his arrival all the sweeter, if you're there waiting."

She pouted but was resigned. "I guess I can live with it."

"I hear you were both great with the kids."

"I could not fool them," said Cordón. "They are just like you."

"Listen," said Backlund. "I'm sorry about the boat. It would kind of made an interlude for you both—like a honeymoon trip."

"Not for me," said Mary, with more humor than she felt. "I am one lousy sailor." She put an arm around Cordón. "We've had a great time here. Now the honeymoon is over."

□

■

The *Mar Cantábrico* was the farthermost of three freighters on the wharf. The long delay in loading her had produced a domestication of her deck: three lines of laundry were strung out in the morning sun, and several of the crew were playing chess on the bridge. Idleness has a certain smell in a boat: of inadequately ventilated quarters and of the flotsam locked between the hull and the dock. Mary caught both of these as she followed Cordón and Backlund up the gangway.

The captain was Greek, and for a Greek he was unusually tall and slim, more an Athenian aristocrat than a Salonika mercenary. His cabin was book-lined. He, of all the men they saw on the boat, was the most philosophical about the delay.

"I like it here," he said. "Charleston is a good port. They have a civilized way here. Not like Baltimore, New York. Gentlemen here."

Backlund pressed the point. "The train should be here in two hours. We want to load through the night."

"I have a problem with Customs."

"I know about that. We'll have a revised license by the time the train gets here."

But they didn't. The train was held outside the docks.

Dann called Backlund.

Backlund tried not to dispirit Cordón. "It's temporary. They're stalling on a technicality. Joe says twenty-four hours." He looked at Mary. "The president is giving a press conference tomorrow. It will be on the radio. Joe expects it will involve us."

"I don't like the sound of that."

"I do not understand," said Cordón. "Everything is legal."

"That's right," said Backlund. "They know it."

The captain said "Please. You join me for dinner. The cook is very good, the shrimp is very good. You like creole?"

The train was still outside the gates the next day when it was time for the broadcast of Roosevelt's press conference. Solomon came from the train to listen to it with them, on the captain's radio.

It began with the kind of badinage that suggested that the president was sitting around with familiars; they even talked about his Christmas presents.

□

Solomon said, "Those guys would kiss his ass."

The elegant and slightly effete voice played easily with its more baritone partners. Mary could picture the large head tilted superciliously while waiting to answer, the cigarette holder, the quick eyes behind the light-framed glasses.

"Mr. President," said a reporter, "you'll have seen that there is a boatload of weapons, even some airplanes, going from here to the Republican government in Spain. Isn't that contrary to all the statements you have made on not involving ourselves in that war—and what do you propose to do about it?"

"Well, Stanley, I have to repeat what I said before."

The radio crackled with static as they waited.

"Any attempt by us to discriminate between the parties in this civil war would be dangerous in the extreme. Our people have no desire for it." There was another pause, broken by coughs. "On the specific point you raise, as you know, we have a bill before the Congress now. I support that bill. It will effectively prevent this kind of thing from happening. I would say this, to you and to the people involved. This shipment is perfectly legal at this moment—but it is a *thoroughly* unpatriotic act."

"Mr. President—"

Mary looked at Cordón, who was shaking his head.

"Mr. President, you're saying you can't stop it?"

"I'm saying that while there may not yet be a legal embargo, there most certainly is a *moral* embargo."

The reporters moved on to other things, and the captain turned off the radio.

"What cant," said Backlund.

"I think," said the captain, "you should get that piece of paper pretty quick. Otherwise we will not get out of this port."

Dann called again. Sentence by sentence Backlund relayed what he said.

"The license is on its way.

"The House vote on the bill was four hundred one for and one against. The Senate is rushing its vote.

"Joe says the bill is badly drafted. He might be able to get it delayed a day."

□

"How long will it take to unload the train?"

"Eighteen hours; not less," said the captain.

"It's going to be close."

■

The last of the crates swung over the deck and sank slowly into the hold.

"That's it," said Backlund.

The captain said, "They are still there."

On the dock alongside the gangway were two cars. One contained Farrio and Pea Coat, the other was for the Customs men who had checked every item loaded.

Farrio said, "What are those fucking people doing?"

"Washington," said Pea Coat, making an expletive of it.

"Let me see these guys again."

He walked to the other car.

"Can't you think of something?" he said.

The four men looked at him as one power.

"Fake something, for fuck's sake. It's only a matter of hours. You guys are usually good at fucking people. Why can't you do it when it really matters?"

The one of the four nearest Farrio wound up his window.

Farrio kicked at the car.

Backlund saw this and said to Mary, "I think they know they're beaten."

"Yes. I guess Joe has done it again."

She turned to Cordón. Satisfaction mingled with tension, though neither wanted to display it.

Backlund went to the bridge with the captain.

Mary said, "I'll miss you, my love."

He pulled her head onto his left shoulder and held her there. "This is something to have done," he said. "Together."

"You keep away from those Mexican girls."

"I love you, Mary."

"Oh, my love."

"I will see you in Cartagena."

"Yes. Take care. Please take care."

From the bridge Backlund watched them part.

Without much fellow feeling the captain said, "Nothing is harder to live with than the kind of love that you find in a war."

15

CONNECTICUT

Across the lawn, white cast-iron love seats were set out at intervals, each with one facing chair. Without their cushions they were abstractions on a shallow lake of snow—all white, white on white, with only the silver tree line to divide it from a white sky. The house, too, was white—inside as well as out. Only Dr. Buller was not neutral. Among his smocked nurses he alone was allowed to be positive. His suit was blue serge and his face the beacon that gave hope amid the hopeless. He had composed himself deliberately, and there could be no doubt that he had composed it all, down to the exact placing of the love seats.

He led Mary to the door, opened it, and then withdrew.

Encountering the whiteness was like walking into a spotlight: reflected from the windows, concentrated in the white room. The door closed behind her.

Something licked her ankles.

A few colors became discernible, a gold crucifix on the wall and, as her eyes adjusted, the two people on the white sofa. One was an obese man who wore gray, all gray, and a woman who was in an orange silk gown and had red hair.

"Hello, Mother."

It was a chow at her feet.

"Come here, my baby."

□

She meant the dog. It went to her and clawed up to her lap, where the silk was already worn to a paler shade.

"My last born," said Mary's mother.

The fat man smiled.

"Wise in ways too wise for me. I could not wean her. Not enough of me for her." She peered forward. "How could you understand?"

Mary pulled a chair—a plain pine chair—from a shadow and sat in the light with them. "Mother."

The mother was of the same color and build but for the shrinkage of age and a stronger, broader brow.

"She loved me though. Named for the Holy Mother. And it was Tom who was holy. You see how wise she is?" She put a hand on the much-creased lap beside her. "Conceived for hope. She gave us wisdom instead."

"Mother, you look well."

"You did. How frightened he was of you and your wisdom. Still calls it—" Her voice, until now like a low, warm wind, gained sudden force. "Does he still call it the Devil's work? *Ha!* Then if it was *his* work it is!"

The man rubbed her hand with his, pushing it into his pliant thigh. The dog licked at the silk.

"She loved me. To be sure."

"I have always loved you, Mother."

"Will you *look* at her!"

The fat man did, with a wavering and then fixed smile.

"Still on the run!" She became truculent. "It's true!"

Mary stiffened.

"Yes. You see. It's true. Still on the run! The firstborn was not wise enough to run. Will you *look* at her!"

"You should introduce me, Mother."

"They said her hair was flame but her heart was not."

The two of them looked steadily at each other, eye-to-eye.

In a voice that descended again to the light wind, word by word, her mother said, "On the third day of April I met with Matthew under the hickory. We have been together since the fourth of April nineteen thirty-six." She stopped. "It was the fifth, I think."

Mary looked afresh at Matthew. The smile slipped away from him and he could not find it again. His blue-tinged eyelids fell.

"Oh!" said her mother, pulling her hand free of Matthew. "If only you would!" The hand waved, and a bone amulet fell from the wrist to the forearm. "If you could. If you could stop running, *then* what a talk we could have."

"We could talk now."

"Matthew knows the way." But she edged herself along the sofa apart from him. There she sat, for the first time really alone. She became bright, and felt her hair. The dog moved from her lap to Matthew's. Her feet pressed the white tile in a testing way that darkened veins, and then she stood.

"Kiss me."

Mary stood and held her and kissed the offered mouth.

"There!" Her mother pulled away. "You see! We taste the same, although I did not wean her, could not. There! He knew that! It was that taste that frightened him so much. When he discovered that, he never kissed her again. *There!*"

She sat down again, pressing each palm into the white velvet and, leaning toward Mary in her own shadow, she squinted and said, "You're changed."

There were steps outside; the dog squealed, but Matthew's hand restrained it.

The door opened and a steward wheeled in a trolley. She went around Mary and set the trolley alongside the sofa. There were three bowls, two larger ones covered by a warmer, and two glasses of water. The steward took the warmer and left.

Matthew dipped a spoon into the smaller bowl, containing what looked like a cold, jellied stew with meat cubes of particular redness. He swallowed a spoonful without chewing.

Mary's mother watched him.

He belched—the only sound to come out of him while Mary was there, and he belched in soprano. He nodded and put the bowl on the floor and released the dog, who jumped down and lapped at the meat with a tongue that seemed too weak.

"Mother, I think I had better go."

□

Her mother watched Matthew sample the hot stew in each remaining bowl. She gave Mary a distracted, perfunctory glance and said, *"A fine thing."*

"Good-bye, Mother."

She left the two of them spooning stew—as he chewed, Matthew took on the hue of hot wax.

"She did *want* to see you," said Buller, divining Mary's mood.

"I hated every second of it."

"Did you?" The point interested Buller.

"What do you expect?"

Buller maintained a honeyed voice. "As paranoid schizophrenics go, she is not a difficult case. Here we sustain her anxieties rather than attempt futilely to dispel them. We sustain her anxieties in a setting that gives her the feeling of being able to control them. Even if this means that her universe must be reduced to the scale of one room. It works rather well. I would say that she is as happy now as she is ever likely to be."

"Who is that man?"

"It was quite spontaneous between them." He looked out to the empty love seats. "Quite spontaneous. A felicitous match. They complement each other in every way."

"He's gross."

"Matthew?" Buller was a degree less honeyed. "Physically, you mean? There is in Matthew a great peace of mind." The moment of sharpness passed. He helped her with her coat. "It was good of you to come, Mary. Do you—do you see your father?"

"No."

"You must not blame him."

She showed no reaction.

"You know, Mary, psychiatry and Christianity do not share much, but I would say that a spirit of forgiveness is a clinical as well as a holy remedy."

"*I* am not one of your patients."

"No." He led her to the door. "No. That is so. Thank you for coming, Mary." He looked through the door to the car. "You must not worry about her. She has moments of quite striking perception.

□

Surely you saw that?" His hand gripped hers and lingered. "Good-bye, Mary."

Liam was pacing in the snow. The old Cadillac, with its engine running, breathed white exhaust like a ground mist around him. He came up and opened the door for her.

"Let's get out of here," she said.

Going down the drive, he said, "Bad?"

"For me. Not for her."

He was silent until they turned into the road.

"Come on, Tiger."

At last there was some relief from the white. The road was completely shadowed by a pine wood and stretched straight ahead.

BERLIN

His name was von Klagen, Walther von Klagen. The pilot from Spain. He had traced her in Berlin. Freda waited for him in Heidel's office. There were large windows on three sides. Through the driving blizzard she could dimly see the lights on the far side of the Wilhelmstrasse. The blizzard had trapped Heidel in Hamburg; the trains were not running. She heard the elevator coming up. It was a private elevator and opened directly into the office.

"Terrible," he said, "like Siberia." He offered no embrace, but stood looking around the office; it was his first time there. "Every comfort. I would really like to know, what does Herr Heidel do?"

"No uniform tonight, Oberstleutnant?"

"I am on leave."

"But not in your head."

"You notice too much."

"I am very hungry. When I am very hungry I see things very sharply."

"I would like to know what keeps a man in such comfort—but you can tell me over dinner."

□

"It would be too boring. Far too boring," she said, and took his arm.

Over dinner he seemed brooding.

"To Algeciras," she said, raising a glass of hock.

"I would not care if I never saw Spain again."

"This is a change."

"Is it?"

"You seemed to like it, once."

"It has changed. Did you think me arrogant, in Spain, that first time?"

"Very self-assured, perhaps."

"You are too polite. We were all arrogant then. It was going to be a short war, a useful exercise. Since then I have lost friends. It was a miscalculation."

"Are you going back?"

"We were flying the Heinkel. It was good enough, at the beginning. Then the Russians arrived. The Heinkel they have for breakfast." He finally raised his own glass, with open sarcasm. "To the New Year. Yes, I am going back. But at least this time I go back with a Messerschmitt."

"Please do not let us talk about Spain anymore," she said.

■

Bare though it was, the room was mildewed, with a hint of coffee in the dampness. Mary raised the window and propped open the door. There was no sign of Eleanor, either in the building or in the courtyard. It was a mild and bright day, more invigorating than any she remembered in Madrid. She took the mattress and stood it by the window and began sweeping the floor and stairs. She amused herself by being so homespun. It was a gentle kind of madness in a city that was still being shelled and bombed—though the bombing had eased noticeably. She had been given two reasons for that: Russian fighters, and mud at the airfields used by Franco. Without the need to file a daily story, she was looking more carefully for changes of atmosphere. There was a new stringency; food was scarcer. The power was turned off for hours at a time. There were fewer cars. It was a city adapting to siege—not yet encircled, but a city difficult to keep running when half of it remained the front line.

She had no way of knowing when the *Mar Cantábrico* would leave Mexico: its Mexican port had been kept even from her. The room made Cordón's absence deeply felt. As she sorted the clothes, she found the scarf she had first appropriated from him, and wore it again, like a talisman.

The war had switched to the south of the city. All attempts to cross the Manzanares from the Casa de Campo had been beaten back, leaving the University City in ruins. It was time, she decided, to find the front line again.

Praeger smiled when she told him that.

"It's not like that anymore," he said. She had found him at his usual table in the Gran Vía bar—it had been oddly reassuring to see him as a fixture. The windows were now taped to prevent splintering, and his face was crosshatched in the shadow of the taping.

"What do you mean, not like that anymore?"

"Order has crawled out of chaos. I quite miss the chaos. You look better, by the way. Home and hearth for Christmas?"

"No. What do you mean, order?"

"The old slapdash militias have gone. Even the anarchists are in barracks now. What you'll notice, though, is the way they deal with us. No lone wolves anymore, I'm afraid." He enjoyed the barb. "More like a traveling circus. Koltzov has a hand in it, naturally. Nobody gets to the front without Russian blessing."

She thought Praeger less assured than he wanted to seem; he was unusually ragged at the edges, hair longer and traces of beard, something strained in the face. Aged.

"What exactly is this paper, the *New Nation,* that you've taken up with?"

"It's not a paper. It's a magazine. Monthly."

"Hardly your pace, I would have thought."

"It's exactly my pace."

"Really? The war is not hot copy in America, it seems. They've pulled out several correspondents."

"It's a long way away, Max."

□

"I can imagine. Look, perhaps we could take a circus trip together. Koltzov, I know, will be happy to see you back."

And it seemed to be true. Koltzov was even playful. When they found him at the Telefónica, he said, "We were not sure whether we should allow you to return, Miss Byrnes."

"We?"

"We the people. But nothing escapes us. Not even a paragraph in the *New York Times.*"

"You saw that?"

"Of course. How could we refuse you after making such a speech? Soon I will be able to call you comrade."

It was Koltzov the various; sounding the same but looking different, he said, "You will be concerned about the progress of a certain boat."

Praeger was nonplussed.

She was surprised. "Yes. I am."

Koltzov pushed a rolled copy of *Pravda* at her shoulder. "Nothing to worry about. Between us, I will keep you informed." He slid from the desk he had been sitting on with a sudden energy that made Praeger seem even more wilted. She had had nightmares of the pit in the field, but looking at Koltzov now she couldn't be sure how she felt about him. She had never been given any proof of his hand in the massacre, and she trusted Esposito less than Koltzov. Trust? Who could she trust? Absence had clarified distrust, not trust. She could not even be sure of Praeger, who in his raggedness looked second-rate, whereas you could never say that of the Russian. Oddly there was in Koltzov a quality that reminded her of Joe Dann—what Ike Mandel had called *chutzpah.*

"When can I get to the front?" she said.

"You have not changed," said Koltzov, approvingly. "I can see."

"Well?"

"Franco has to cut the Madrid–Valencia road. It is only a matter of time before he tries that—to come over the Jarama River, south of the city. To complete the circle. He has no imagination, the Generalissimo. He always does the obvious. We will be ready for him."

"Then that's where I want to be."

"Tomorrow," said Koltzov. "Tomorrow I am taking other reporters to a town called Chinchón; that is as near to the front as the bus will go. You can both join us."

"A bus?"

"Miss Byrnes, no private favors."

■

It was an assorted busload, the reporters of four nationalities. Koltzov was like a tour guide, switching from English to French and then to Italian. Three people stood out as not being legitimate under the label of reporters. One was a Frenchman in a suede coat and fedora; one a black American in an old military greatcoat and black beret; one a grave-looking young woman in a fashionable tweed coat and cloche hat. She, Mary discovered, was a Greek novelist who spoke to Koltzov in terse Italian. The Frenchman was a film director, and the American was Langston Hughes, the poet. Koltzov, despite his warning, gave favored treatment to this trio.

As soon as the bus left the city, the war seemed suddenly to have become pastoral. It was unusually hot, the bus kicked up a cloud of dust, the rolling hills looked pacific. They crossed railroad tracks and a small river and then reached Chinchón. The war lay in waiting in the streets—trucks, tanks, and soldiers everywhere. And yet no fear, it seemed, under the clear sky, of raiding bombers. Praeger slept until the bus stopped.

They were led from the bus across a small square to a truck standing apart from the rest, painted with a large sign, COMISARÍA POLÍTICA. Inside this truck, under a portrait of La Pasionaria, were a desk, a typewriter, and a duplicating machine, as well as a microphone and loudspeakers. Koltzov explained that the men in the truck produced a daily newspaper, *Our Fight!* and other "guidance" for the troops.

Someone imprudently murmured, "Propaganda."

Koltzov swung on him. "Propaganda means lies. We make sure that the men get the truth."

"Where from?"

"Reliable sources."

"That's a big business, reliable sources."

Someone else laughed.

Koltzov was calmly lethal. "And what are *your* sources, Mr. Kelsoe?"

The reporter grunted. "Just a joke, Mikhail."

But no one was left in any doubt about Koltzov's humor.

"Another name for the list," whispered Praeger to Mary.

"What list?"

"Of canceled visas."

"He does that?"

"It's what I meant by order replacing chaos."

Koltzov detached his three favorites and took them off, leaving the rest of them in the charge of an officer from the Comisaría Política. While he began a long explanation of his unit's work, Mary slipped away. The Jarama River was to the west of the town. She could see the ridge of hills that lay between them and the front. People were working in the fields—she walked out of the town and could see the vineyards and olive groves in the foothills. Only the sound of a truck coming from the town broke the illusion of peace. She stepped off the road to keep clear of the dust from the truck.

It passed her and then stopped.

It was not a truck, but an ambulance.

"Mary! Mary!" called the driver.

It was Serena Pollard.

Mary went to the cab.

"Nobody told me you were back," said Serena with mock reproach.

"I just got back."

"What on earth are you doing, wandering out here alone?"

"Escaping."

"From whom?"

"Koltzov's tours."

"For heaven's sakes. Jump in, darling."

Mary climbed up beside her. "Where are we going?"

"I'm trying out a new road they've built down to the casualty station. Nothing has happened here for days."

The ambulance ran down to a bridge and began climbing a hill.

□

"Are you glad to be back?" asked Serena. "Where is Nicolás?"

"A long story. And, yes, I am glad to be back."

"Hmm. Well, we're getting properly organized, at last. There's an American doctor here called Pike. The road is one of his ideas. Saves carrying wounded men in the open over rough ground. When it starts."

"When it starts?"

"They'll have to attack before the wet season. That's only a month away. Giles is here. They were pulled out of Madrid and put in reserve for this. This is the big one, Mary. I can smell it."

Serena looked more vigorous than the ambulance, which was backfiring in the low gear.

"I say, won't you be in trouble, Mary, slipping off the leash?"

"Probably. I can't work in a crowd."

The casualty station was a farmhouse. The floors and walls had been scrubbed, and the place smelled powerfully of disinfectant.

"Bill Pike is a real wonder," said Serena, showing Mary around. "Full of that no-nonsense American thing. He's even getting showers and a disinfection truck. Never seen anything *remotely* like it before."

"It seems you're expecting a lot of casualties."

"There were a lot of men dying who shouldn't have. We can save a lot of lives with the proper facilities."

"What's that?"

Serena listened. "Oh, that's becoming so familiar I don't notice it. It's the aeroplanes."

She led Mary outside and pointed up. Twenty or more aircraft were flying very high, little more than silver blobs, coming in from the west. Another group of about twelve were climbing from the east to intercept them.

"It's become a strange ritual," said Serena. "As though nothing really to do with us. The men at the front just lie on their backs and watch. You can't participate. It's like, well—it's like a show. But, of course, it's not. It's very real. They come over to test our defenses. You see, our aeroplanes are just beginning to break up their formation."

Metal flashed in the sun. It did seem remote. There was a sudden flare of orange that turned to black, and fragments of a plane fell; a large one descended very rapidly, leaving smaller pieces fluttering down like shreds of paper. The sound of the explosion reached them several seconds after the plane had disintegrated—it was a jarring echoing blast, the first thing to seem real.

"It must be a lonely way to fight," said Serena.

One other plane had fallen far lower than the others and left an intermittent streak of oily smoke. They heard its coughing engine. It turned tightly several times, still falling, then straightened out and came toward them.

"He seems—I think he's trying to find a place to get down," said Mary.

"Yes. It's one of ours."

The plane's engine revived, it climbed in a steep turn over the farmhouse and then, trailing a heavier smoke that they could smell, it went out of sight behind some trees. They thought it must be down, but there was another roar of the engine and it reappeared, lining up with the new dirt road. It hit the road hard, bounced in a cloud of dirt, hit again, and seemed to be under control.

"Oh God!" said Serena.

The plane could not avoid a single tree that grew by the roadside. It smashed into it with a wing, slew around, and went cartwheeling into a field, shedding most of the wings and ending up with its nose dug deep and the tail in the air.

Men from the casualty station ran up the road.

Serena and Mary followed in the ambulance.

Another plane had dived and was circling the field, banking to get a view.

"Another of ours," said Serena.

By the time they got out of the ambulance on the edge of the road, two men had reached the wreck. They struggled to get the pilot out, and a third joined them.

"It's still burning!" said Mary.

There was a pungent smell of gasoline and oil.

They got a stretcher from the ambulance and ran into the field with it.

The men reached them with the pilot.

□

The circling plane had seen this and climbed away.

"He's bad," said one of the men.

"Let's get out of here," said another. "That plane is going up."

The five of them lifted the stretcher and got it to the road just as the gasoline exploded—they felt the heat on their backs.

The pilot was unconscious. Serena wrapped a blanket around him and they put him in the ambulance.

At the casualty station they took off the blanket and cut away his leather jacket. There was a trickle of blood from his mouth.

"Rib cage has collapsed—there's glass in him from the instrument panel," said a doctor. "Lungs damaged, probably pierced. A leg broken."

"Can't do anything for him, for the lungs, too far gone," said another man, bending over the bed.

"Nothing?" said Mary.

The doctor shook his head.

Serena wiped the blood from his face. Mary sat by the bed.

The pilot's eyes opened.

"Hi, kid," he said, with surprising clarity.

"Are you American?" said Mary.

"Yeah."

"He shouldn't talk," said Serena.

"You talk," said the pilot, more weakly, to Mary.

"I—I think you'll be okay," she said.

"You're a swell kid. Sound like somebody—somebody I know."

She bent more closely to him and put a hand on his brow and smiled. "Please don't talk."

He tried to smile. More blood came from his mouth. He died.

She took her hand from him and began to cry.

Serena put a hand on her shoulder.

"The thing is," said Mary, trying to get control of herself, "I've seen others die, I've seen much worse. But he seemed so—so close. He was very *close.* Do you understand?"

"Yes."

The doctor covered the pilot with a blanket.

They gave Mary the papers from his jacket: Albert Rockwell, age twenty-four, New York City.

□

Outside, the sky was empty. Rockwell's plane had burned down to a buckled frame. Heat from the charred ground was caught in a wind that also carried the impression of spring.

■

For such a slight figure, Yanin had a peculiar taste in footwear: black boots that laced high above the ankles. Perhaps he felt they provided a substance he otherwise lacked; a military impact in his step. On this bright morning he had been to a military funeral. He wore a suit of coarse black wool and a wide-brimmed black trilby. On his left breast hung a red star and ribbon. The suit's trousers were too long; they bunched over the boots. The air had lent him a more lively color. Walking in quick steps through the West Park, he gave the impression even of a certain jauntiness. The funeral dirge, still audible from the procession passing out of the park, was at odds with him.

"Too much is made of these soldiers' deaths," he said.

Ferrer kept pace.

"It is simpler when they are blown to pieces. Then there is no body to be carried through the streets—this all has, for me, too much of the aftertaste of church."

"It does, yes."

"Still, comrade, in this case it was a matter of appearances. Of showing solidarity. Not a distinguished death. He was in retreat at the time."

She would have liked to have linked arms with him. There was always such a natural sympathy of feeling between them—did he realize that? Black suited him in the bright light. He was enhanced.

"So," he said—with perhaps a glimmer of pleasure—"you have found the address."

"El Coronel was not hard to find. He is unusually tall."

"Without the sheep's head?"

They had reached the edge of the park. He stopped and took off the trilby, holding it to his stomach. The unusual brightness in his eyes gave him youth.

□

She presented a dutiful face to him: no nun could have conveyed a more self-abnegating composure.

"There will be no cortege for the colonel." Yanin replaced the hat, at a more formal angle.

■

Heidel had never worked so hard in his life, but he knew he was lucky. He had found a niche within the new order without having to conform to its political or bureaucratic habits. Old family business connections in Rome, Paris, London, and New York had suddenly proved of use to the Third Reich. The subtle network of bankers and industrialists that Heidel knew, and the parochial master of Germany, both needed a middleman. It had quickly been the making of a new fortune. Only the need to make polite conversation with men like Joachim Rohleder reminded him that there might be a moral cost in this—and perhaps he would never have thought in moral terms but for the presence of Freda Eichberg. She had never suggested that anything disturbed her; she was far too reticent for that. But lately, to his surprise, he had found himself reappraising her. Something had altered in those constrained eyes; nothing alarming, but an occasional way of looking at him that was speculative. In return, he had fleetingly thought that under her expensive but drab suits there might be a more interesting body than he had once thought. His wife, away on his Baltic estate, would have been amused to know that he had been fatigued into celibacy.

Certainly, on this morning, Freda did nothing to tempt him. She stood there in a gray flannel suit that made her androgynous, new horn-rimmed glasses leveled at Rohleder in her strictest governess style. Rohleder was reading something she had just given him.

"Good news, Heidel," said Rohleder. "A copy of a cable from the Büro Lenz to Sonderstab W. You will be interested."

Heidel took the paper.

"You see?" said Rohleder.

"So the V-Mann does it again."

□

"I think so. He was at some risk. Each day it becomes more dangerous for him."

"Well," said Heidel, "my American friends will be relieved of an embarrassment. If we can leave the rest to the Spaniards."

"You know, Heidel, I think I will go to Vigo myself. To make sure of it."

Heidel gave the paper back to Freda. "Yes. Why not? I would not like to see such an opportunity lost."

Heidel realized that Freda, unlike Rohleder, got both levels of his meaning, that she would be as glad to see the back of Rohleder as he.

■

Esposito putted a golf ball toward a china cup on the parquet floor, but missed. He was preoccupied by considerations about Mary Byrnes. She would have made a good wife for a diplomat. Her connections were right. She was smart. The problem was that she was crazy—crazy then in an enticing way, crazy now in a way that made trouble. And she was *his* trouble. Her file had tripled in size in a month. *New York Times,* for Chrissakes. He recovered the ball and found his form. The cup shattered.

It was still lying there when Mary was shown in.

"Look pleased," she said.

"Why?"

"I'll sit down."

She took the chair by the desk and pulled an envelope from her bag.

"These are the papers. All he had on him."

Esposito took the envelope.

"Yes," he said, "we are obliged to inform the next of kin."

"*Obliged?* Is that all?"

"That's it."

"What about the body?"

"That's up to the family."

"You mean, you won't help?"

"That's it."

"What's gotten into you? Jesus, this is an *American*—not much more than a kid."

"I know all about his gang. The Russians trained them. They're called the American Patrol."

"Gang?"

"They're mercenaries—cowboys and brawlers."

"They're defending this city!"

Esposito enjoyed the rage in her. "Listen, hotshot reporter. Let me tell you something. Your little hero pilot here." He tapped the envelope. "This is not one of your bleeding heart pinko idealists, fighting for peanuts. These guys were signed up in Mexico City for one and a half grand a month—yes, that's right, one and a half grand. And do you know, they get another grand for every plane they shoot down? Not so damned heroic, is it? Know what kind of pay a pilot in our army gets?"

She glowered but didn't answer.

"You *hear,* me, lady? Paid to kill."

But she failed to explode. Instead, she looked past him and saw a child in the garden.

He tried to gauge her afresh. The strong legs in tight khaki drill, the open-necked shirt showing cleavage and a copper tan, the roughly cut blazing hair, and the dangerously instinctive intelligence.

"Why do you do it?" he said.

"What?"

"Fool around with these people."

She looked at him with a level temper. "It isn't simple."

"They can't win. If Franco doesn't finish them off, their Russian friend will."

"Tell you something." She leaned forward. "You people have it wrong. Sooner or later you'll get to know that. In the meantime, don't you worry your fat ass about me."

"*Worry* about you?" He laughed. "You're lucky, let me tell you, you're lucky to get through the door. You're damned close to becoming persona non grata around here."

"Really?" She got up. "I'd take that as a compliment."

□

■

Perot went lightly and happily up the steps carrying a bottle of brandy. It was cheap brandy, but it was hard to get anything better, and he knew it would be welcome. The long days were tiring and, late at night, the quality of brandy didn't matter so much. Everyone else in the block of flats seemed already asleep. No lights were on, and even the apartment of the old woman who played Wagner on her phonograph was silent—that was a relief, because the walls were thin enough to hear the *Siegfried* Idyll. It had been a better day for Perot: a new job as a waiter in a restaurant with more class than food and a new friend to produce the brandy. Only the joke about cats in the soup had been off-color.

Where was the cat?

It was always on the Persian runner in the hall, but as he closed the door he saw in the light of the one lamp that the cat was not there.

"Cabrito?" he called, still happy.

All the lights in the living room were on, he could see that.

"Cabrito?"

He went in.

The bottle of brandy slipped out of his hand and smashed on the marble.

The room was devastated. The room with such discriminating taste and thought behind it: the silk sofa was slashed and gutted, the Egyptian vases were shards, the French bureau with its filigree veneer had been demolished, the velvet curtains ripped down and thrown on top of the debris. He imagined for a second that a shell or at least the blast from a shell had done it, but then he saw the deliberate and systematic hand: the place had been searched and anything—even the cushions—that might have concealed something had been torn open. The brandy was running from the marble into the fringe of the rug. His instinct was to wipe it up.

The lights in the bedroom were on, too.

He went like a suddenly demented child running and babbling and holding a hand to his mouth into the bedroom.

It was just as devastated, but in the center of it, arranged with design, was the naked body of El Coronel—intact but for the head. The head, inside its sheep's mask, rested passively beside the body on a pillow. A saturated pillow.

"Cabrito!" he screamed, *"Cabrito!"* He fell to his knees before the once so vigorous body.

"Cabrito?" answered an intrigued voice. "I thought he was a sheep, not a goat."

Perot stared around the room and saw what the horror had made him miss: a small man in heavy boots, a man with a large domed head and a calm, soothing face, sitting on the one intact chair in the place.

"Not a he-goat," said the face.

Perot felt himself dominated, but also calmed. He stopped shaking and repressed the urge to vomit.

"I would like to know about your other friends," said Yanin. "Please tell me about them, will you? All your other friends. Cabrito was unwilling to help."

■

The car pulled away from the Plaza Mayor.

"Just drive anywhere, but not too fast," said Esposito to the Marine driver.

Praeger spread himself like a man unused to comfort.

"Even the Russians have American cars," he said. "Koltzov has a Buick."

"That man," said Esposito.

"A finger in everything."

"And two women."

"You sound envious."

Esposito shook his head. "Not of Koltzov. Life expectancy in that regime is not too great."

"He'll survive."

"You seem damned certain of that."

"I know his connections."

"And how about you? Don't you get nervous?"

"Getting nervous is no help." Praeger reeked of cognac. "A country that can make a car like this can do anything."

"You want to come to the States, afterward?"

Praeger stroked the leather seat. "I don't think so. I don't believe that, at my age, I could quite adapt to it."

"You've been a great help."

Praeger seemed to ignore Esposito. His concentration had gone—he stared out at the streets.

"Where will you go?" said Esposito.

"Go? Nowhere. There is no afterward."

Esposito had never seen Praeger in this state of mind, and did not know how to deal with it.

Praeger finally gave him renewed attention, smiling at him with false harmony. "Two women, but not satisfied."

"Koltzov?"

"Mary Byrnes did something that any other reporter would have been expelled for. She got away from his traveling circus, got nearly to the front line. They don't tolerate that. He didn't so much as slap her wrist."

"Interesting. In a way, they deserve each other."

"My goodness. What *has* she done to earn that?"

■

Pollard saw the guitar case where Mary had put it on a suitcase.

"Does Nicolás play that?"

"Sometimes."

"Funny. I wouldn't have thought—I mean, he doesn't look the type."

"What type?" She was bent over a small paraffin burner trying to brew coffee.

"I'm sorry. Jumping to conclusions on absolutely no acquaintance. Do you need a hand with that thing, or are you going to blow us up?"

She laughed. "I think I can handle it. I'm—it's interesting that you should say that." She took two tin mugs and wiped one. "I've never really asked about his family. I get the idea he doesn't want to talk about it. I have discovered that he goes quite crazy if you call him Don Nicolás."

"You're very good together. That's all that matters, really."

"What about you?"

"Women, you mean?"

The coffee was coming to a boil. She lowered the flame.

"I'll let it stew. Yes. Women."

"Never really had any luck. Just casual things."

He sat down on the bed. The makeshift uniform failed to make him plebian; in repose or movement there remained all the subtle deportments of the born aristocrat, even to the way his slightly over-long hair fell about his collar.

"Can I be personal?"

"We are chums."

"What made you come here? *Really?*"

"Oh dear." He crossed his legs Buddha style. "That one."

She decided to pour the coffee.

"Well—" He took the mug. "It started as something very simple. Doesn't it always? It's become a lot more complicated. I think it must have been rather like that on the Crusades. I've thought about that. I mean, there you are, comfortably in your castle, and someone says, there are all these barbarians who want to—I say, this coffee is amazingly good."

"Do be serious. I don't want to know about the barbarians."

He eyed her respectfully through steaming coffee.

"I'm here because I believe fascism is far too easily tolerated."

She nodded—several times. "*That* I will buy."

"Good. Now you can tell me something. Why are *you* here?"

"For all the wrong reasons."

"My turn to say, be serious."

"It's true, Giles. I am. First, personal involvement. Second, I've found I do like to see my name at the top of a column of print. Third, I'm still trying to come to an understanding of what we mean when we talk about the truth. How's that?"

"I think I approve of the first and the third. And the second is only human. Mary, you're . . ." For a second he was intense. "You are so *clear* about yourself. That's what counts."

"I am?"

"How on earth you made coffee this good from that stuff, I'll never know."

"It is good to see you. And as things go here, a passable lunch."

"Yes. Lucky to get the chance. That's your cat, isn't it?"

She looked around. Eleanor was on the pillow, stretching out.

"Oh, *Eleanor!*" She put down the coffee and bent over the cat, rubbing its upturned belly. "Where have you been? Do you know—I haven't seen this cat since I left in December."

"Must be the smell of the coffee."

"You'll bring me luck, won't you, Eleanor? You'll bring Nicolás back, won't you?"

The cat assented.

"Isn't that a funny name for a cat?"

"Not at all. All we Eleanors must stick together."

There was the sound of a truck outside, and a horn.

"I think my carriage awaits," he said. "Have to go."

He still had a slight limp. "I wonder how that cat manages to be so well-fed?"

"Take great care."

They kissed decorously.

"Serena said you were a help with that pilot chap. I think she's probably an Eleanor, too. Serena."

"Give her my love."

He went down the stairs—one of the people she wished she really understood, could go beyond his elaborate defenses, one of the few about whom it was true to say that their goodness was their mystery.

The smell of coffee and of the paraffin stove and the return of the cat conspired to renew the nestlike quality of the room. The warm weather continued, and there were moments like this when it was possible to feel like the postgraduate student making notes in a garret and not the war reporter in a city under siege, worried on the one hand by the absence of a cat and becoming, on the other, blasé about death. It was this unbalancing of values, swinging from the indulgent to the callous, that she noticed in everyone—it was the way people made a new code for themselves and among themselves in order to carry on. Among the Spanish it sat readily with the old ingrained fatalism: the surrender either to acts of God or to the impositions of the class system, ironically the two powers that the war was being fought to eradicate. For her, without such habitual fatalism, the code had to be recognized for what it was: a special kind of madness, the lapse of sanity that made war thinkable in the first place. Giles Pollard had gone one step beyond, from war as thinkable to war as duty. She could not understand that. But to have settled for the lesser madness was one way to keep some hold on herself.

The new people who came to see the war came not as reporters but to draw from it a stimulus that was not available elsewhere—to use it for whatever insights they hoped it would give their art. She had watched them in Koltzov's party. There was a kind of theatrical wardrobe that they introduced to Spain, each appearing in clothes picked with a mind to what would look right, but picked from outside. The filmmaker's fedora had been a gesture of panache; what more often stood out was the cut of fine tailoring in the tweeds and leathers. Koltzov, she suspected, saw through all this as she did, but he knew its value. Koltzov was the ultimate creature of the whole madness; beneath his virtuosity was an undeviating nature pledged to a madness as fully coherent as a religion. Koltzov was playing with her. Too clever to embrace her, he was keeping her for some future purpose.

□

Four hundred men had gone into the valley the day before, roughly four-fifths of the battalion. During the night, two hundred had fallen back. By dawn the small reserve had been brought from Chinchón to the front.

Pollard stood with his platoon listening to the commissar.

"There are two ridges between the fascists and the Valencia road. The farthest ridge is really two positions, a hill with a white house on top of it, to the left, and a conical hill to the right. Our men still hold those positions, but they're exposed. Behind them, this side of them, there's a valley. Then the next and last ridge. That ridge is yours. So you stand between the fascists and the road."

The commissar was an ex-schoolteacher from Glasgow. He still spoke as though dealing with a class from the slums—a blend of the didactic and the suspicious.

"It would help," said Pollard, "to have some maps."

"I've told you all you need to know."

"Out there it would be useful to have a map. It's confusing terrain."

"*I'm* not confused, Pollard."

The commissar was half Pollard's size and compensated with sarcasm.

"Who's on our flanks?" said Pollard.

The commissar sighed. "Spanish cavalry on your left. That's Lister and his tanks. They can't maneuver in your valley. On your right, in the woods, we have the Franco-Belge boys. They're more forward." He betrayed exhausted patience.

"Then we have the only machine guns between the Jarama and the road."

"Now you're with me, Pollard."

Pollard felt that only war, and only this corner of war, could have involved him with a man like Commissar Benson. It asked a lot of camaraderie. "More forward" didn't sound like military precision, but he let it pass.

"Blimey," said Copeman when the commissar had gone. "What a nark."

Pollard nodded. "The narks don't go any farther forward than this." Copeman was the replacement for Palmer, and a man called Archer had taken Taffy's place. All Pollard's Maxim team were new to battle. Their eagerness gave him the caution of a veteran. All his instincts indicated trouble: the fascists had been over the Jarama for two days; their own line—as the commissar had made clear by evasion—was ill-supported and not coordinated. The companies that had fallen back in the night looked demoralized.

Other things were encouraging, though. Here, before the briefing, they had had a hot breakfast and coffee at a farm. The battalion headquarters was a well-protected and sandbagged position on a sunken road. There was a system of field telephones, laid down well in advance. And when they reached their own position on the ridge half an hour later they found that it had been skillfully placed, with the guns behind a deep stone parapet and sandbags around them.

Pollard tried to make a map in his mind by scanning ahead with his glasses. The white house on the left-hand ridge was easy to pick out, and the conical hill to its right. The valley shrank to a narrow pass under the white house. The fascists would have to try to come through there. The weakest link was where the Franco-Belge Battalion was supposed to be, in the woods to the right. He could see no movement there.

As the sun got higher it baked them; each day seemed hotter than the last, and as they had climbed up through clover and thistle it felt more like summer than winter. On the valley's western slopes the vines were already showing buds.

"Fuck my Aunt Mary!" said Copeman. "Get a look at this."

He sat by an open box of ammunition holding up a belt.

"Wrong fucking ammo."

They found that all the belts had been loaded with bullets for the later model Maxim—theirs were world war vintage.

"There's just one box of loose stuff that's the right caliber. We'll have to fucking unload the fucking belts and start reloading ourselves with what we've got. It won't last."

Pollard said, "I'll send a runner down to battalion headquarters."

"That could take all fucking day," said Archer.

"What a cock-up," said Copeman. But he had already accepted the ineptitude and was organizing its repair.

Pollard said, "You don't know how long a day can be until you've been in this war, that's a fact."

He saw something moving on the white house hill. Little remained of the house—there were a few red tiles at one end of the gutted roof and two walls intact. A remnant of a company remained up there, but they had only rifles to hold a position that needed machine guns. Against them the fascists had deployed light and heavy machine guns and artillery. Pollard could hear that the house was under attack again. Men with rifles had to stand up to get a line of fire down the other side of the hill. He could not see the river, but the river would give its name to the battle. How many men had died for a river—from the Tigris to the Somme? And now the Jarama. Not even a map to show where it lay.

Emptying belts and refilling them was slow. There was barely sufficient ammunition to provide one belt for each of the four Maxims.

At last Pollard saw what the men at the white house were firing on: an assault formation of fascists—Moors—appeared between the white house and conical hills, coming in waves with the object of forcing the valley's narrow neck.

"Christ!" said Copeman, following Pollard's glasses and seeing the Moors.

□

"They can't realize we're here," said Pollard. "Surely they wouldn't make the attempt if they did."

"Three belts, that's all," said Copeman.

"Damn. *Damn.* Just look at them. Nobody knows how to use cover like the Moors. The earth just swallows them up."

He knew he would have to open fire. And once their position was given away, the fascist artillery would seek them out. The pitifully few men on the white house and conical hills were under heavy fire now themselves. The Moors were moving fast toward the gap.

"Nice fucking little party," said Copeman.

"Hold until we have a clear field. We must not waste a bullet. Let them get to the exposed ground."

"That'll be late."

"I know."

The three loaded Maxims began tracking to get range and angle. The belt for the fourth was nearly loaded.

Pollard looked at the white house again. Some men survived.

In the valley mouth it was like a set-piece exercise: the turbaned Moors held precise formation on the open ground; their rifles and bayonets were raised, and they had the momentum of men feeling that their objective was in reach.

"Fire!" said Pollard.

For seconds the Moors did not either singly or collectively react. They might have been storming into a rain shower. They had an irresistible velocity, the rearmost waves running into the foremost as they began to fall. The angle of fire from above made it more murderous. Now the lines fell like fairground cutouts, mechanically and all on the same axis.

"*Christ.* It's a fucking massacre," said Copeman.

But Pollard saw no massacre. For him it was balancing a score sheet, and there was still a lot to make up. There was a whole battalion there.

At the fringes the Moors began to break and run for the cover of olive trees on the slopes. It was a waste trying to finish them off.

"Cease fire!"

The heat of the guns and the stench of cordite filled the sudden silence. It had taken barely two minutes to decimate the Moors.

□

Pollard could see the uncertainty on the faces of his raw gunners—the precarious exuberance that went with too easy a victory, and with the comprehension of how many men could die in so short a time. They made nervous and expletive whoops.

Copeman, a fast learner and cockney savant, said, "Our turn next."

Through his glasses Pollard saw someone at the white house waving a rifle at them, but he swiftly disappeared as the fascist artillery opened up. Sound was capricious in these hills: the distant gunfire was sharper than the friendly fire from the conical hill. No sound at all carried from the layered corpses in the valley mouth, but the Moors who lived could be heard shouting from the olives.

■

Serena had gone a night without sleep. The casualty station was filled with French, Belgian, British, and American wounded. Those who could move were driven to Chinchón. The worst cases stayed.

She stood outside, hoping the sun would give her the energy that incessant hot coffee had not. She saw, coming down the road at reckless speed, a Ford station wagon. It drove between two parked ambulances and braked at the door of the casualty entrance—virtually at her feet.

The driver got out with the same manic urgency he had shown at the wheel.

"Give me a hand, will you, and get some others."

He looked at her more closely.

"You speak English?"

"I do."

"Then do as I say."

"Are you Dr. Bethune?"

He opened the tailgate and handed her a metal case. "Here, take this. Yes."

"I've heard of you."

"Look snappy."

The case was heavy. She faltered, put both hands to it, managed to get it inside, and came back with two orderlies.

"Careful—*careful.*" He gave them more cases. "It's all portable except the refrigerator."

Pike appeared—a small, dark man looking worn.

"Bill Pike. You're Norman Bethune?"

"That's right."

"We sure need you."

"I had to figure that out for myself. Those commissars at Chinchón delayed me for three hours. Papers. Papers. I had to explain the principle of the blood bank; they don't seem to grasp the concept of avoidable deaths. Even then, they wouldn't let me move until I produced my party card."

"No," said Pike, "they wouldn't."

The two of them, thought Serena, the American and the Canadian, generated enough enthusiasm for six men. The sight of it brought back her own energy.

She became Bethune's assistant. He called for the worst cases of blood loss and shock and set up three beds with plasma bottles and tubes, instructing her as they went.

Men who arrived in a coma revived.

"Remarkable," said Pike. "Remarkable. They're not even doing this in New York."

"Don't expect miracles," said Bethune. "I don't have the means."

But it looked miraculous to Serena.

■

The ammunition truck could get to within only a quarter of a mile of Pollard's position; even to get that far put it in peril. A chain of men was formed to pass the boxes up the ridge.

"Don't bloody like it," said Copeman. "I don't see no bloody Frogs, nothing."

He was using Pollard's glasses to scan the wood to their right.

If the Franco-Belge Battalion had been where it was supposed to be the men would have been visible. The woods were leafless.

"It's altogether too quiet," said Pollard.

The fascists had not attempted to storm the valley again; their wounded were left with the dead. Occasionally a Moor would be seen trying to crawl to the cover of the olives.

Fascist planes had appeared once, coming from the south and flying along the line of the river. Farther north they had turned east and strafed a bridge.

The men on the white house and conical hills were unable to communicate back; the field telephone lines were cut, and the valley was too dangerous for a runner to cross.

"I don't like it," said Pollard. We can't be sure of either flank. No sign of Lister's tanks on our left. I want you to go back to battalion headquarters and see Captain Wintringham. I want reinforcements for the men on the hills and I have to know about the flanks."

"Right, comrade," said Copeman.

He was the only man Pollard knew who could make *comrade* sound like a term of endearment. His sweat-rivered face conveyed allegiance and yet also the gulf between their two voices, between the aristocrat and the plebian who conspired together against the gulf, and yet knew how ineradicable it was in their blood.

"Be careful, Copeman."

Copeman put on his helmet—a virtually useless French *poilu* of world war vintage—and went slithering through the thistle and gorse. In five minutes he reached the ammunition truck and in another minute could safely walk within the cover of the sunken road leading to the headquarters.

At that moment the fascist artillery opened up. They tried a few ranging shots. One fell midway between the top of the ridge and the sunken road. A second later another exploded within feet of the ammunition truck. Copeman turned and saw the men come running for the shelter of the road. Shrapnel had punctured the truck's fuel tank. It began to burn. As the men came sprinting toward Copeman, the tank exploded. Then, with a cannonading roar, the ammunition went up. The fireball was followed by detonating bullets arcing in all directions.

When it subsided the men picked themselves up and realized that not one of them had been touched.

"A right fucking mess," said Copeman.

□

"Lucky. Very lucky, mate," said one of the men. "Most of the stuff was unloaded."

The barrage resumed. The fascist gunners, bemused by their early luck, were searching out the Maxims' position, moving their fire in a sweep across the ridge.

Copeman began to run down the road, helmet in hand.

■

Mary was lying ingloriously under Koltzov's Buick.

The fascist planes had come without warning, difficult to see in the sun.

"It's the bridge," said Koltzov, on his back beside her.

"Too close," she said.

At her eye level the road threw up a snaking line of small explosions, only twenty yards or so away. The shadow of a plane flashed across, behind the path of its own machine guns.

As the engines of the first wave died away, there was another, more terrifying sound, a high-pitched scream that seemed to descend from directly above, plunging and reaching ear-splitting level.

"Cover your head," cried Koltzov.

The scream changed note and was swallowed in the whine of a bomb.

The bomb fell farther away, about half a mile, but the Buick rocked in the blast.

"Jesus! *Jesus!*" she said. "This is no place to be."

"It sounds worse than it is," said Koltzov. He did seem to have surprising self-possession for the position he took. "That's their idea. The German planes have sirens; they're dive-bombers, called Stukas. Only one bomb on each plane."

"One is plenty."

The bomb had fallen near the bridge. Others followed, but they were not so close.

Koltzov crawled out from under the car. "It is over."

□

"So am I." She rolled out but lay on her back on the edge of the road. "I think my nerve has gone. My ears feel funny."

Koltzov dusted his suit. "The Germans understand terror."

She didn't move.

"They did not get the bridge," he said.

"Mikhail—don't you *get* scared?"

He looked down at her. "Of course."

"Then show it, damn you."

"What would you think of me then?"

She got up slowly. "I might make the error of thinking you were human."

He pulled off his glasses and wiped the dust from them. His naked and myopic eyes searched her out, giving no hint of his humor. "You will understand, I think, if you survive this war. You will understand what, until now, you have had no cause to understand. You will understand me." He returned the glasses to their place carefully. "You have more to learn about war. And about life in war."

She felt strangely chastened—not exactly *threatened,* but deflated in an unaccustomed way.

Koltzov opened the car door for her. "We go to Chinchón."

■

The artillery bombardment lasted precisely an hour and then stopped.

Pollard checked his watch. "They must be Germans."

Archer peered over the parapet. "They haven't touched us."

"I think we would be wise to play dead."

Pollard thought he would like to meet the man who had chosen and built this position. Only a plane could breach it. He could not say the same for the men on the two hills ahead. There was no sign of Copeman. All the Maxims were loaded, with adequate reserves of ammunition. The sun was weaker, but the heat lingered in the sandbags and stone.

"What the—what the fuck—?" said Archer.

Men at all the gun positions were standing and pointing into the valley.

A stream of men in fascist uniform poured in from the right, but instead of bearing rifles they held up their hands in a clenched-fist salute and were singing. Familiar verses floated up the ridge:

Then comrades, come rally
And the last fight let us face;
The Internationale
Unites the human race.

It was sung in Spanish, but the anthem was universal. Some of Pollard's company were already out of the emplacement and going down the hill holding up their own hands in the communist salute. The Spanish youths who supplemented Pollard's own men went following them, calling out Popular Front slogans.

"I'll be—" said Archer.

"Wait." Pollard held him back.

But the two sides were beginning to meet and mingle, coming up to the guns with arms linked.

Copeman, too, heard the singing. He was beginning the climb from the sunken road, past the burned-out ammunition truck. He saw the line of men clambering over the parapet, still roaring out the song. He could see Pollard, with his slight limp, moving with Archer.

"No!" shouted Copeman, uselessly. "No! You stupid fuckers. *No.*"

He could see Pollard's hesitation. It was impossible now to distinguish the men of one side from the other. Pollard was encircled. Copeman began to run up the hill.

The men who a second before had been saluting were now, in unison, pulling their guns.

One of the Maxims was being manhandled to reverse its fire. Copeman stopped. It was trying to aim at him. He turned and went headlong down on the open ground. The Maxim opened up, but it was still too elevated, and the bullets whined overhead. He rolled into the sunken road. The fury of his mind overlapped the firing of the Maxim—and out loud, spinning in the dirt, he shouted, "The bastards! Bastards! Stupid bastards!"

□

■

Bethune's supply of blood was exhausted. He had gone back to Madrid for more. Serena slept for two hours on a pallet in a room with four other exhausted orderlies; then she took a cold shower and changed into fresh linen and her ambulance driver's uniform. All the transportable wounded had gone to Chinchón. No new casualties had been brought in, though it had been an artillery barrage that woke her. She knew that Giles was somewhere on the ridge, but kinship had the trick of receding as a tie when you were confronted by so many men whose lives were marginal. Thanks to Bethune, more had lived than had died on this day. An unusual statistic.

In an hour it would be dark. The nights were cold. She went outside to smoke a cigarette.

The black Buick came slowly down the road and stopped, briefly, where the plane wreck still lay in its blackened earth. Before the car had reached the casualty station she recognized Mary, though Koltzov was unclear until he stepped out. Mary's khakis were streaked with dirt. She ran to embrace her.

Koltzov, standing by, said, "This time she is here with my permission."

"Darling," said Serena, "does being authorized feel better?"

Mary looked at Koltzov. "I think he trusts me."

Koltzov put out a hand, a degree of charm, to Serena. "I am pleased to meet you again."

"We heard about Dr. Bethune in Chinchón," said Mary.

"*That* man," said Serena, "is one of the most *intractable* people I've ever met. He looks like a mad monk. He is also a miracle worker. There are at least fifteen men who owe their lives to him today."

"Interesting—" said Koltzov, "—for a story."

"You might get two words out of him. Go away, for example."

"Comrade Bethune would cooperate, I believe. It is such a tribute to the party."

"I'm sorry?" said Mary.

□

"An example of the party's commitment to progressive medicine."

"Or, maybe," said Mary, "an example of one man beating the system."

"Please!" intervened Serena. "*Do* behave. What matters is what he's done."

"Correct," said Koltzov testily.

"Dr. Pike is sleeping," said Serena, "so I'd better show you some of Bethune's work and explain as best I can."

There were still three men in Bethune's beds.

"These are too serious to be moved," said Serena.

Inverted bottles hung on improvised stands by the beds.

"Blood loss and shock are the two killers. A man who is not actually critically wounded can die very quickly from both. Take these men, for example."

Though heavily bandaged, with limb wounds, the three men had robust color.

"The blood from donors is kept in refrigerated flasks. We have to check that the blood types match. Sterilization is very important; I'm afraid that's an uphill struggle in Spain. Of course, it's one thing doing this in a hospital. Quite another doing it in the field. We simply don't have the equipment or the blood. If you want to be a darling, comrade Koltzov, you might have a word with your chums about providing another dozen—what's the matter?"

Koltzov stepped away from the beds. He gripped a chair and, even in the poor light, they could see that his face was white and moist.

"Nothing," he said. "I think—I think I need air."

Serena looked at Mary.

"You look rocky," said Mary. "Let me give you a hand."

But Koltzov stepped away from her, letting go of the chair, and went with a wound-up, skipping step out of the room.

"Well!" said Serena.

"It's like Count Dracula throwing up at the sight of blood."

"He *is* very odd, you know. Don't much take to him."

"No," said Mary thoughtfully, as they heard Koltzov retching outside, "it would be a mistake to feel sorry for him."

□

■

"Be very careful," said Pollard to Archer, "in everything you do, in what you say, how you behave." He wondered about the man who had planned the trick, and what the man would do with them.

The mound of corpses in the valley had its echo in the faces of the men who now disarmed them. They were lined up on the top of the ridge, openly, so that they would be in full view of the men on the two hills and of their own rear guard. The Spanish youths were separated from the rest and marched down into the valley.

A fascist lieutenant who spoke English came to Pollard.

"You will tell your men please to keep their hands above their heads. You will be treated as prisoners of war . . . you will obey my orders."

This was not the architect of the trick; he was old for his rank, with the yellow skin and eyes of a veteran of the Army of Africa, a place where imagination in a subordinate would have been fatal.

Pollard repeated the instructions to Archer and the men who were brought together in line of march. They were divided into two sections, one to go ahead of their captors and one behind, carrying the dismantled Maxims, giving the fascists a screen against fire from both flanks. As they started down into the valley, they heard a burst of fire. The Spanish youths, spread out in a chain, were machine-gunned from behind.

"The *fucking*—" said Archer, but he was cut off by a movement of Pollard's upraised hands.

As they reached the valley floor a man near Archer, in the rear and next to a flanking fascist, asked in hesitant Spanish if he could smoke a cigarette.

The fascist nodded companionably.

As soon as the man dropped a hand to reach for the cigarettes in his breast pocket there was a burst of fire—the fascist used his automatic rifle at such close range that two men dropped, the second riddled with bullets that had passed through the first. Pollard and Archer had seen nothing until the firing. The column was halted.

The officer went to the bodies and casually turned one over with a boot.

□

At this, another man broke ranks and began screaming and shaking his fist in the Popular Front salute. *"Cowards! Cowards!* Fucking *cowards!"* He spat the words at the officer.

Archer started to move but Pollard hissed, "For God's sake, man, don't you see that's what they want? They'll shoot the lot of us at the first excuse."

Two fascists ran to the screaming man, lifted him, one at each arm, and hurled him against an olive trunk. He was momentarily stunned by the impact, and with his head flopped forward he slipped down the tree to a sitting position.

The officer very deliberately took his revolver from its polished holster. He walked to the tree and pressed the gun's muzzle at the man's left ear. Then he waited.

The man revived. He looked up. He began to raise his right arm and said, *"Salud!"*

The force of the shot jerked his head nearly from his neck.

All belligerence passed from the men, replaced inwardly by a deep revulsion and outwardly by an erect, parade-ground aloofness that they maintained as they were marched through the gap between the white house and conical hills, under the eyes and guns of their comrades.

■

Koltzov had regained color and composure. They all sat, he and Serena and Mary, at a trestle table drinking coffee and talking to the orderlies.

"I am just a reporter," said Koltzov. "This lady—" He motioned his coffee mug toward Mary. "—this lady is a writer. One day she will write a book, five hundred forty-four pages, and it will be about this war. A real book, with an artist's sensibility. And then we shall all for the first time understand what it was that brought us here—we shall be reading a work of literature. You see, literature is not journalism and journalism is not literature. One of them is the truth." He raised the mug. "But which one?"

All eyes followed his to Mary.

□

"That's a Russian question," she said.

"Answer it," said one man. *"Answer it!"* insisted others.

She looked first at Koltzov and then at the rest of them. "Well—I'll give you an American answer. You can't make that kind of distinction. Truth exists in—in a painting, for example. In a piece of music. In a novel. And in a newspaper—" She smiled wryly. "—though imperfectly, in a newspaper. But I'll tell you one thing for sure. You can deny it, you can suppress it, you can—you can *bury* it, but it outlives all of that, always, and people know it in the end. They always get to know it in the end."

Serena clapped lightly but not facetiously. "*Very* well said."

Koltzov sounded soulful. "You see what I mean? She will write a book." Then he grinned ambiguously. "But it won't be published in Moscow."

The laughter did not entirely dispel or satisfy the curiosity that had been aroused around the table, but they were interrupted.

Commissar Benson came in and looked for Serena. "Comrade Pollard, I have some bad news about your brother."

Serena pressed a hand on the table. "What is it?"

"He's in fascist hands. His whole company was captured on the ridge, complete with their guns."

"Captured?"

"Yes. It seems—" Benson began addressing all of them. "—it seems that they fell for a simple trick. The fascists acted like deserters, they even sang the Internationale. Unfortunately they convinced your brother. Surprising."

Koltzov said, "All of them—and their guns?"

"Yes, comrade. May I introduce myself? Commissar Benson. Comrade Koltzov, I believe?"

Koltzov kept his distance from the supplicant. He put a hand on Serena's arm. "I am sorry."

She nodded, seeming steady. "Thank you."

"It could be worse," said Mary.

Benson murmured, "I wouldn't hope for too much. The fascists are not noted humanitarians."

"I know about fascists," said Serena.

Mary took her hand. "Come and get some air."

□

As they left, Koltzov turned to Benson. "Your place is with your unit at the front, commissar. And this is a place for war casualties, not cases of foot in the mouth."

■

It was dark when Pollard and his men marched into the village of San Martín. The men who had carried the Maxims were exhausted, but all of them were lined up in two ranks in the square, facing the steps of the church. The few lights made it difficult to see anything beyond the church. The lieutenant who had led the operation ordered Pollard to the center of the front rank and positioned guards with automatic rifles on the steps and behind them. Then he disappeared.

They were left for several minutes. Trucks drove through the square behind them and then a car appeared alongside the church and parked, but kept its motor running and its lights on so that the beams picked out the front rank. At the same time a truck parked behind them, keeping its lights on. Fascist soldiers from the truck collected three of the four Maxims. The fourth was reassembled, and mounted at the side of the church steps. An officer left the car and walked up the steps, visible only in silhouette with the headlights behind him. He was short and compact, with cavalry boots and a tasseled cap. He stopped directly opposite Pollard, elevated by the steps to six or seven feet above the ranked men.

Both hands, palms inward, settled at his waist.

"Why did you come to Spain?" he said, in a perfect, neutrally accented English. "Who brought you here? Why did you come? What business is it of yours? *Eh?*"

Only the *eh*—bearing a sharp pitch—sounded Spanish, and it was a sound from the Inquisition, not inviting an answer.

"Do you have a god? You see, I stand here before you on the threshold of the house of God. I stand here. You stand there. Because you are godless men, *eh?*"

The Maxim was being loaded with a belt.

□

He remained still until he gave a glance at the Maxim and then began walking slowly down to Pollard, step by step.

Pollard was dazzled by the headlights and could see no features, but he heard the man's quick breath as he stopped on the last step, to remain a head above Pollard.

"You poor creature. So innocent. You believe my men would desert me for a godless hymn?"

Nothing moved in the square now. The only sound was of the two idling engines, the car's and the truck's. The silhouetted figure raised his right arm slowly. Behind and above him in the darkness the church bell began to toll.

□

“I have to carry on, of course.”

Serena sat with Mary in the *hostería* at Chinchón, where she was billeted with other women.

“Yes.”

“I think one of the things that keeps me here is how unwarlike they are.”

“I don’t understand.”

“Sometimes it drives you quite potty, they are so inept. Then you think, well, if this was a society that really knew how to run a war you wouldn’t want anything to do with it. I mean, it’s all a bit *helpless,* you see.”

The humor was brave, but not entirely convincing to Mary. She allowed, “That’s true.”

“Could you do something for me, darling?”

“Of course.”

“Could you contact the British embassy and give them the details, about Giles?”

“I’ll do more than that. I’ll do whatever I can to find out where the prisoners are held.”

“Mary, you’re a real friend.” She took Mary’s hand. “I’ve never had a lot of chums—not close chums. I hope we’ll always be that.”

"Of course."

Mary knew that for all their differences they had found, in each other, a heresy in common which would be called faithless by the gatherers of flocks but was, in truth, the rarest and most binding of faiths. It seemed then that the war was an incident and their bond was for life.

"It's really quite filthy wine, isn't it?"

Serena had drunk half a bottle, and poured more.

"It sort of bubbles away inside like in a caldron. At least, it keeps you warm, and I think it probably kills off all known germs."

"It doesn't feel so great in the morning."

"Oh, to hell with the morning."

Two Spanish women were playing chess on the communal table. They looked pious. A German girl was asleep on a bench with a copy of *Das Kapital* still in her hand. An old Spanish woman sat knitting something shapeless and gray. It felt sane and homely.

A girl came in. She wore a man's coat that came to her ankles and a *poilu*. When she took off the helmet a cascade of dark hair fell over her shoulders.

"María!" said Mary, standing.

It was María of the precipice wedding.

"Americana!" said María, leaving her coat half unbuttoned and coming to embrace Mary.

The coarse coat with the French brass buttons carried the smell of cooking oil.

"María, you look well—"

María knew why the sentence was unfinished. She smiled. "He is good, Álvaro. He is on the Aragón front. And the captain, how is he?"

"Fine. He's fine. He's away, too. Well, look at you!"

"Yes." María had opened the coat. She patted her swollen stomach. "Álvaro is here, too."

"That's wonderful. You must look after yourself."

"I work in the kitchens. They will not give me a gun now. These people. The captain, he must miss Durruti. We all miss Durruti. Not the same now—it goes well, but it is not the same."

Mary introduced her to Serena.

□

"Yes, I have seen you before," said Serena. "Always with the beans!"

"We have more beans than bullets."

They all laughed, María with the cracking laugh of the girl become woman, her already maternal breasts shaking. She dug into one of the pockets of her shirt and produced a photograph, cut out from a larger one. She showed it proudly to Serena.

"My Álvaro."

The portrait was from Mary's wedding group.

Koltzov returned. He had managed to sponge the dirt from his suit and to get a crease into the trousers; his hair looked barbered, too. In the rough little room he appeared too grand, too urbane.

"Time to go, I guess," said Mary.

She held Serena's hand again. "I'll do everything possible. Please take good care." They kissed.

"And María—you have someone else to think of now."

"Give my love to the captain."

In the Buick she could smell cologne.

"You're very sly," she said.

"I do not understand," said Koltzov.

"You've had a bath."

"Yes."

"In Chinchón?"

"Comrade Goriev never takes quarters without a bath. You know, Mary, when we have won this war I will personally institute a policy of public hygiene. Do you know my first target? Toilets. The flushing toilet has never crossed the Pyrenees in any numbers. It is still done the way the Arabs do it."

"What does comrade Goriev tell you about the battle?"

Koltzov made a show of peering ahead at the road before he answered.

"They have crossed the river but they will not cross the road."

"You believe that?"

"We are taking losses. You have seen that. But we want them across the river. It makes their supply lines vulnerable. When there are enough of them, we will give them a taste of what we can do, with planes and tanks."

□

She detected the putative framework of a communiqué, and left him with it. She dropped off to sleep until the lights of Madrid wakened her.

"You know," she said, "I like General Goriev's cologne. A man who smells like that can't be all bad."

■

"I should like you to know my name. I am Major Felipe Alcalá. I should like you to remember. You are interesting me. I know England well. I have good friends there. In the better class of people. I can see you are a man of class. You have the voice and the ways of a man of class. You are not like the others, this scum we have here. I like to talk to you. Cigarette? American."

Pollard shook his head.

"I like American cigarettes, English whisky, French women."

He lit the cigarette and exhaled into Pollard's face.

"There are routine questions. Have you passport. Do you belong to a political party. How long you have been at the front. How many tanks have you seen. These are routine. They can come later. First you are interesting me. Why does a man of your class fight with these people? What concern is it for you? *Eh?*"

The room was small and bare enough for the *eh* to have the snap of pistol fire.

"My name is Giles Pollard. I am a British citizen. I do not have a passport. I am a prisoner of war and I expect my men to be treated in accordance with the international code and for me to be treated in the same way as my men, in all respects."

Alcalá, when not a silhouette in the night, was not imposing. His skin was white and pock-marked. Although he was groomed with care—thinning black hair at the front brushed into thicker at the back to a plaster-hard layer at the neck, no more natural than a wig, and a short mustache well waxed—it was the kind of grooming that did not include frequent bathing. He looked and smelled unwashed. His nails were broken and had rims of dirt.

He blew more smoke at Pollard.

"To be treated as your men? I think you change your mind, soon. You will not like to be treated like your scum. We know well how to treat them, but a man of class should not want to live like scum." He put down the cigarette. "That is, unless he is a communist, a godless man. There is no mercy for godless men."

"I have told you what you need to know."

"Giles Pollard." Alcalá wrote down the name on a pad, slowly and in large block capitals, with only one *l* in Pollard, and then took up the cigarette again. "It is a nice country, England. A man of class can have a good life; there is the hunting, and riding, the famous English sense of sportsmanship. I am a sportsman. I am a gambler. The English like gambling. I will take a gamble with Giles Pollard. I will say, when Giles Pollard has lived as the scum must live, he will want to live like a gentleman again. I will say, a week with the scum and you will want to be a gentleman again."

He banged twice on the table and sat back, relaxing.

Two of his men came in and lifted Pollard, whose legs were bound, lifted him bodily and took him from the room along a corridor to a door that was guarded. The guards unlocked the door and Pollard was hurled through it into the darkness.

■

The Gran Vía had become like a hotel in a town where the trains don't stop anymore. Within weeks it had deteriorated into a listless, faded place. Many reporters had gone. Other guests who had sat out the battle were in no mood for a siege. They had taken the trail of the affluent refugees, to Valencia and then off on boats to some foreign sanctuary. The staff who remained were perfunctory. The elevator moved ever more slowly, and the restaurant had little to serve. Only the bar lived on, drawing the hard core of journalists still in Madrid.

Mary looked for Praeger. He was not at his table by the window. At the desk they thought he might be in his room, but the phone no longer worked.

She walked up and knocked on the door, and knocked again. She was about to turn away when the door opened slightly.

"Max?"

"Oh." He blinked out from semidarkness.

"I'm sorry. Did I wake you?"

"No. No. Do come in."

The only light was at his desk.

"It's nice to see you, dear girl. I'm afraid I've been rather off-color."

He turned on another light.

"You're *green,* Max. Are you ill?"

"The food is so wretched. I think the water is suspect."

He cleared some newspapers from the sofa so that she could sit.

"I suppose you've been in the thick of battle again," he said, picking up a little energy. "With Koltzov."

"I don't like the way you say that. You don't think—?"

"Good heavens. No."

"You're not to think like that, Max."

He was lugubrious and slow. The air in the room was stale.

He seemed to anticipate her. "It's getting difficult here. The heating seems to have packed up. If I open a window I freeze. Would you like a cognac?"

"No. Coffee later, maybe—downstairs."

"What can I do for you?"

She told him about Giles Pollard.

"I called the British consulate. They were useless. Very polite and very useless. Talked about illegal entry, and how they were inundated with appeals for help with prisoners of war. I got the idea that it made it worse that Giles is blue-blooded. They take that as treachery in their own ranks. *Useless.*"

"I see." Praeger sat down. "It would be a mistake to be optimistic."

"What about the Geneva Conventions?"

"Don't be naive."

"Max. I *have* to do something."

"Yes, well . . . you do have one weapon not open to everyone. Publicity. If you got something in print, they might take notice of that."

□

"I couldn't get it into the magazine in time."

"No. I see. Well . . . perhaps I could try flying a kite. You give me the details, you know the kind of thing, PEER'S SON MISSING IN SPAIN—they might go for that, especially the idea of a red viscount."

"You would? That would help a lot, Max."

"Yes. Look. I'll have a shave and we'll try to get something together over coffee."

"Fine."

She picked up one of the papers he had cleared from the sofa.

When he came back he looked fresher, but he shuffled rather than walked.

"Some pretty weird things happen in this town, Max, even in a war."

"For example?"

"Did you see this? Two lovers in a suicide pact, but they happen both to be men. One was decapitated and had a sheep's head on his face. The other sat in a bath and dropped an electric heater into it. Weird."

"Yes. I saw that."

"I guess there's another way of looking at it, Max. Love and life go on."

Praeger tightened the knot of his tie and made an effort to face the world.

"Max, you haven't any shoes on."

"What?" He shook his head. "Love and life go on? Yes."

■

The passage of day into night was a matter of a sliver of light between rafters, as well as of learning the change in the voices of the guards outside the door. It took several days to learn to deal with the deprivation of the senses imposed by sharing a space of this size with sixteen other men. The darkness was relative: eyes grew accustomed to it. The eyes were more adaptable than other senses: it was not certain what the dimensions of the space were, nor what its original purpose had been. It was part of a large farmhouse that Alcalá used for his headquarters, the kind of farm in which animals and people cohabited. In winter this space might have been used for cows. The stone floor had a gutter and a drain. The drain was their only latrine. It would have been worse in high summer, though it was bad enough now. They had no covering and had to huddle together for warmth. They were fed bread and water. There was no water for washing, and Pollard already had a week's growth of beard. One of the men had an arm wound, and under these conditions it would not heal. The communal warmth developed its own stench.

Pollard knew that the farm was at a place called Navalcarnero. When they had arrived in a truck he had been able to see that it was used for resupplying the front line. Alcalá was not a front line commander—just what he was Pollard could only guess, but the coup of the fake desertion was Alcalá's, and he was riding high. His insistence that Pollard should know and remember his name was a deliberately planted false hope, a show of faith in the hereafter, or an egoist's weakness. Nothing that Alcalá did was simple. It would have been simple to have shot them summarily; it would have been simple to have sent them to one of the penal labor camps that Pollard knew the Franquists had started with German guidance—it would have been too humane to have done either. Alcalá's game was more than incidental sadism, it was a puzzle.

There were other prisoners at the farm. Pollard and his men were in one wing of buildings that enclosed a yard. Occasionally a vehicle would back into the yard—they could tell from the labor of a reversing engine—and they could hear the shouts of guards herding men.

All this gave Pollard something to distract him from the squalor. This kind of squalor was incremental: as the personal filth increased, the collective contamination became impossible to hide. At first men had forced jokes out of it, but it was no longer a joke and there was, instead, the kind of lassitude and resignation that foreshadowed the collapse of self-respect. In finding a way of breaking their morale without resort to open violence, Alcalá had shown, again, a form of malevolent genius. Pollard knew the erosion of his own grip on sanity. The count of days, the movements outside, these were becoming irksome in themselves. They drifted into a space that was not constant but tapered, closing in on them like a trick of perspective. Then it began to rain. Water, with the touch of ice, came in a steady drizzle through the gap in the rafters and they could, one at a time, make an effort to wash in it. Alcalá took some hours to discover this act of mercy.

■

A good magazine article, Ike Mandel had said, was like a good conversation. "Forget the habit of news in the first paragraph; in a good piece you get there from any direction. Don't be afraid to be discursive. Just don't lose track." Mary kept thinking of María's photograph of Álvaro, carefully clipped out of the larger wedding photograph—of what it excluded and what it distilled. The act of claiming Álvaro from his surroundings had changed the face looking into the lens. Instead of gregarious, Álvaro appeared private and intense, something that might never have been seen in the whole. And by possessing him like that in the pocket next to her breast, María had done what Mary had never designed, kept that moment for herself, playing a trick with time. It was a way to begin the article, with the whole picture, and a way to end it, with the suddenly discovered fragment that was really the heart of it, a picture edited by chance into something much greater than its parts. Between the beginning and the end would be the other faces she had on film: Bethune's patients, surprised to be alive; Serena, with a cigarette, scowling into the sun to hide her modesty; the face on Rockwell's identity card. There *was* a track to keep to, Ike: a wedding on the precipice, and all the faces on the precipice.

The old German typewriter she had found in a pawnshop was sometimes slower than her mind. She cursed as it jammed. She sat on the bed with the typewriter on a box and Eleanor flicking her tail at every curse. She remembered Koltzov mocking her about the book of five hundred forty-four pages, and realized that it was Koltzov who intended to write that book. Fat chance. She would have to get Bethune's picture, too, even if it meant snatching it in the old door-stepping style she had used in Boston—COAL MAGNATE'S HEIR

STEPS OUT WITH OIL BARON'S WIDOW. It might be helpful to have had a disreputable past. She looked down at the cat. If only Eleanor could talk. The keys jammed again.

■

Barrington-Taylor paced in short, irregular steps as he kept jabbing a finger at Barea.

"It's becoming quite impossible to function as a reliable correspondent—quite impossible. You're playing a very dangerous game, I can tell you. Putting out one version for domestic consumption and another for the foreign press."

Barea allowed this tirade to go unchallenged, since he knew it was impossible to stop it. He looked on with a mildly bored contentment, wondering why Barrington-Taylor wore brown shoes with a blue suit.

"This new business is typical. Look." Barrington-Taylor waved a cable. "You know this is on Reuter and Associated Press from Biarritz. It's quite clearly true." He stopped for a moment and squared up to Barea, reading from the cable. " 'The cruiser *Canarias* of the Spanish Nationalist navy has intercepted a freighter bound for Republican Spain in the Bay of Biscay. The freighter, the *Mar Cantábrico,* was carrying aircraft and arms from the United States and Mexico. Nationalist sources say that the freighter was boarded and its crew executed.' Now, will you or will you not confirm that this is the case?"

"I know nothing of such a ship."

"My dear man, the departure of that ship from the United States was widely reported. It only just escaped the Roosevelt embargo. And now you act as if it does not exist."

"I do not dispute that a ship of that name may have sailed from the United States. Its business and destination are unknown to me. There has never been any confirmation from us that we were shipping weapons from the United States. We have all the weapons we require—from Russia. It is, on the contrary, well known that the fascists receive arms and oil from America via their German and Italian allies. Why do you not report that, Mr. Barrington-Taylor?"

"There is no point in my being in Madrid. I'm not interested in being an accomplice to your lies."

Barea nodded. "You may leave Madrid any time you wish."

Barrington-Taylor turned and walked out. As he went barreling through the outer office, he nearly collided with Mary.

"Ah, the red lady."

"Always the gentleman."

"I'm through with this place, I can tell you. Damned glad to see the end of it. I suppose you'll go on being vivid. They seem to like your kind of stuff."

"You're leaving?"

"Last straw. Take a look at this. Our double-talking organ-grinder's monkey says he doesn't know a thing about it."

She took the cable.

"What is it?" he said. "Look as though you've seen a ghost."

She pretended to read it a second time, but the words would not focus. She fought to stop herself from shaking.

"Is—is this true?" she said. "About the crew being shot?"

"You tell me, dear girl. It's on two reputable agency wires. But you won't get—what is it?"

"Nothing." She handed back the cable.

He left without realizing that she was on the point of collapse.

It was Ilsa Poldi who went to help her. She saw her falter and was at her side, guiding her to a seat.

"What is the matter, Mary?"

Mary looked up at her. She was beginning to cry. "It's this war. This *senseless* war."

■

It was like watching a rabbit eat. Everything on Yanin's plate was green: raw cabbage, lettuce, sliced apple, cucumber. He ate it dry and chewed every mouthful until it was pulp. Koltzov had to endure long, masticating pauses between sentences.

"The change of destination," said Yanin, "from Cartagena to San Sebastián, and the consequent change of course across the Atlantic—this was decided at the last minute, in Mexico?"

"Yes," said Koltzov.

"That, you see, is both the question and the answer."

"Comrade?"

Finally Yanin stopped eating. "Each time I think I have reached the end of the chain it grows another link, like some eternally reproducing organism. Where did the message from Mexico originate? We have only its source from Berlin. There is, comrade, more significance in our own agent's message from Berlin than perhaps they realize."

Koltzov picked up a sheet of paper. "Krivitsky's agent? You get access to Krivitsky's traffic?"

"It was arranged."

Koltzov frowned. "This tells us nothing of the Mexican source."

"It tells us everything about the Madrid source. The so-called V-Mann. He must have been very reckless, not like him. You see—he used a cable. There is only one way of cabling out of Madrid."

"You knew before, I think."

"No," said Yanin, taking back the paper. "No. I suspected. I took a risk. I left him. This settles it. Except, of course, for Mexico. It cannot be helped. I cannot leave him any longer. He has to be eliminated."

"More difficult than the others."

"It will need Goriev."

"Goriev?"

"I feel a lot better, comrade Koltzov. Time for me to visit the front. I would like you to come with me. To organize the details."

"You know, comrade Yanin, I think you should eat something more—more substantial. Something that sticks to the ribs. Before we go to the front."

Yanin was not receptive. He took time to fold the cable, precisely into quarters, and slip it into his jacket pocket.

"I know my needs," he said.

□

■

A young girl—no more than about ten—came down the steps with a rosary still in her hand. More slowly an old woman followed. It wasn't the likenesses between them—something in the lips, a flatness in the nose—that caught Mary's attention so much as their obvious dependency on each other. The girl stopped; she was still learning what was needed of her. When the old woman reached her, they linked arms. The old woman looked at Mary. It was pernicious, this mutual recognition of death, the submission to death, the tolerance of death. Death flourished. It was the space between the girl and the old woman, linked in their arms. Down the steps they went.

Mary remained at the top of the steps, close enough to the great medieval doors to hear the murmuring inside. She had Cordón's scarf in her hand. Her hair had been darkened by the rain. She put the scarf over her head and tied it at her neck. It had been a long time since she had covered her head. Someone was watching her from just inside the door. Come in, my child. Deeply pouched eyes. A brilliancy behind him. The church was untouched, though all around it there were gaps in the roofline.

She turned away and began to walk down the steps. Then faster, almost running.

She went into the Miami Bar at the same speed, five minutes later. She didn't see Praeger. And Praeger, at first, didn't see her. He heard her. Her voice broke into his recollection. Perot—was it recollection or hallucination?—Perot had been on the brink of saying something when, instead, Mary said, "Cognac, please." Perot dissolved. Praeger didn't get up. She would see him.

But before she turned from the bar, she called for coffee to go with the cognac and, waiting for it, drank half the cognac. She looked strange with the scarf over her head. It dulled her. Older—she looked older. He stood up when she saw him, feigning that only then had he seen her. She came over.

"Max."

"I heard. I'm very sorry."

She sat down and untied the scarf. Her compressed hair framed her face like a medieval cap.

□

"I don't know what's happening to me, Max. I found myself standing at the door of a church."

"Perhaps—perhaps you should go home."

"Oh no."

"Of course, I didn't really know him."

"He—" She poured the rest of the cognac into the coffee. "You gave me this habit." She sipped the coffee. "I've just realized that I didn't really know him, either. That makes it worse. Do you understand, Max?"

"I think so."

"Who told you?"

"Koltzov."

"He's been very good."

"I knew about the boat, of course. But I had not made the connection."

"Bastards. The *bastards.* They shot every man—*that's* why I can't go home, won't go home. I want people to know what those bastards are really like. They did not even land the bodies, did you know that? Threw them overboard."

"You didn't go in the church?"

"No. Max, I don't know why, but it always feels better to see you."

What had Perot been trying to tell him? He looked appropriately embarrassed. He hoped she wouldn't touch him, but she did. She put a hand across the table. What did *she* know about loss?

■

On the Jarama it was now a battle of attrition. The trenches were awash, lice burrowed into the seams of clothes and were impossible to remove. Veterans of the world war compared it with the Somme. Others said it was worse. The machines were more deadly, particularly the planes. Mary picked up a rumor of a mutiny. Koltzov denied it—and coupled the denial with the promise of a free run of the front line. And so she returned to Chinchón.

She breakfasted with Koltzov.

"You should not be so hard on yourself," he said.

"Hard? Look at me. I'm drinking hot coffee. Eating eggs. I have a clean bed. No lice in my clothes."

"You know what I mean."

"Mikhail, I don't need consolation. And I don't have a death wish. I despise death."

"Don't forget, I am responsible for you."

"Officially? You mean it would be bureaucratically untidy of me to get killed."

"I am serious."

"I know. I know you are. I saw a very strange looking man around here this morning. In black oilskins. And the most peculiar hat. A leather hat with an enormous brim. Who is he? Another of your celebrities? I thought they had all gone home, when the weather turned bad."

"A visitor. No one important."

"Mmmm."

"You're looking for Bethune?"

"He's avoiding me."

She had learned to distinguish one kind of artillery from another: what she heard now was the precise bombardment of the German 155-mm guns; guns were a reflection of nationality, the real experts could pick out German from Italian, Spanish from Russian.

"I must go," said Koltzov.

The damp got deep into the bones. A part of her had died, she thought. Despite her assurances to Koltzov, she knew she was less caring about herself—about what she risked.

Then she saw the Ford station wagon. It came and went through the square so fast that it left a wake of mud on the walls. Heading for Pike's casualty station.

From the edge of town she heard tanks. The T-26s were leaving their assembly point. She knew the tank commander, Pavlov. Koltzov called him "Pablo" when he introduced them. She found Pavlov standing by the command tank.

They spoke in Spanish. He was dubious, but she said she wanted to go only as far as the casualty station, and he waved her up to his turret.

□

He gave her a padded cap to soften the din. She appealed to his ego with her camera. His face, pushing into the rain, flat lips and Mongolian eyes, was another portrait in the gallery of violent men fulfilled by Spain. The sensation of riding the tank was barbarian. They rolled out of the town and took up formation with Pavlov's tank a nose ahead of the others. They kept to the fields to avoid cutting up Pike's road any more than it already had been by the ambulances. At the casualty station she pulled off the tank cap, gave it back to Pavlov, and jumped into the mud. The tanks went up into a valley.

Bethune was operating. She went into the canteen to wait. Most of them knew her now.

"I saw you arrive," said an orderly. "Every time I see those tanks I feel good. Those people have saved this battle."

Bethune came in. He came straight to her.

"I have been *warned* about you."

"Doctor, I would appreciate it if—"

"Oh, you would? And what good would a photograph of me do?"

"It's my job."

His face, one second set in aggression, was the next rearranged into charm. "And why not?"

Mary saw Serena behind him.

"It won't take a minute, Doctor."

"Listen, Miss Byrnes. I've decided that I need the publicity. I want to make a point. How would you like to have a photograph of me with a patient? That would be better, wouldn't it? You don't just want this sour old face of mine."

"I would do anything if it would help you."

"That's what all the girls say."

He had become an engaging fox; she knew of his reputation as a lady-killer, and she knew that Serena idolized him. The monkish head was nearly bald, but he had rampant eyebrows and a virile, imposing intellect. The antithesis of Pavlov: an innately nonviolent man.

They were good pictures, very good. She was beginning to believe that she really wanted to go on with the war.

Afterward she said to Serena, "You fixed him."

□

"It was nothing, darling. He's not silly. He got the point. It's doing him absolutely no good to knock his head against a brick wall. Publicity could work wonders for him. Isn't he super when he turns on the charm?"

"My word. You *are,* aren't you?"

"Is it obvious, darling?"

"To me."

"We must do everything we can, darling. It seems to have given you a little bit of the old spark, taking the pictures." She squeezed Mary's arm. "I'll give you a ride back to Chinchón in the ambulance, if you can hang on."

"I need some air. I'll wait for you outside, okay?"

The day seemed now to have been a passage of a kind. The rain had stopped. There was even a sense of longer and lighter days, of leaving a mood behind. She heard a car. It was coming down Pike's Highway—lurching and eccentrically driven. An old Citroen. The windshield opaque with mud. Praeger was steering with his head out the window.

His face and glasses were splattered.

"Max!"

"A beautiful day."

There was cognac wafting from him again.

"Max. What are you *doing?*"

"My job. For a change."

"Do you know where you are?"

"Chasing Pavlov and his tanks."

"In *that?*"

"Don't be rude. It's indestructible."

"This isn't your style."

"Well, admittedly, I am a little out of practice. However, I am under instructions to make sense of this battle and comrade Koltzov has been remarkably cooperative. He gave me the car. And sent me in the general direction of Pavlov."

"I think you're drunk."

"I make it a rule never to go to the front when sober."

Serena had appeared.

"I'm sorry," she said. "I have to help Bethune. Can you wait?"

"Just a second." She bent down to Praeger. "Max, do you know where Pavlov *is?*"

"I'm just taking the road as far as it goes."

She looked back to Serena. "I'm going to take a ride with this madman. See you later."

Serena shrugged. "I wouldn't, darling, but it's up to you."

"Get in the other seat," said Mary. "I'm driving."

■

The aspect of Yanin that Koltzov could hardly take seriously was the hat. He looked like a Bolivian bandit. The wind on the hill forced Yanin to pull the brim lower, and it was an effort for him to speak.

Koltzov had powerful field glasses on a tripod. "Yes," he said, "he's nearly there. The visibility has improved."

"He took long enough," said Goriev, standing by them.

"He must have stopped at the casualty station. That's out of sight behind the trees."

"Good," said Yanin.

Goriev took a turn at the glasses. "He won't get much farther. It's impassable."

They stood fifty feet from a field gun. The gun crew had set the range and elevation for a precise target and sat waiting for a signal from Goriev.

"He's slowing down," said Goriev.

"Ah," said Yanin, gripping the hat with one hand and trying to keep his black oilskins in place in the wind.

"Here," said Goriev to Koltzov. "Look now."

■

"This really is crazy," said Mary as the car lost all traction.

"It's war," said Praeger, taking another sip from his flask.

"How did Koltzov think you could follow tanks in *this?*"

"The T-26 is not everything it's cracked up to be."

□

"This is not a time to analyze the T-26."

"True. I see why you are lucky with your stories. You can't keep away, can you?"

"Fuck it, Max. We're stuck."

The spinning wheels sent up a spray of mud.

"And I don't even know where we are."

"Not in any danger. The front is over there." Praeger nodded to no distinguishable point: the road had led to a shallow gradient, and it was the gradient that defeated the car. She could see no sign of tank tracks.

"It's rather peaceful," said Praeger.

"Oh yes. Ideal for a picnic. You sit tight. I'm going to get out and take a look."

■

Goriev raised a gloved hand.

The battery commander waited.

Koltzov strained to see. The car had stopped, exactly where Goriev had predicted.

Yanin was motionless.

Koltzov tried to get better focus. The car door was opening. He held up a hand but Goriev misread the gesture—and dropped his. The gun's blast echoed in the hills, and deafened Yanin.

■

Mary heard the whine of the shell but hardly reacted: she was wading through bubbling mud as it resettled into the car's tracks. She was still like that, pulling at a leg and trying to get to firmer ground, when she realized that the shell was very close. It fell ahead and to the right of the car, only feet from it, near enough for the explosion to lift the front of the car. The windows were sucked out and disintegrated into a hail of jagged fragments. She was picked up by the blast and thrown yards, landing face down in the mud. A hail of glass tore into her.

The car's back was broken. The engine block was blasted through the bulkhead. Praeger, still upright in the seat, was crushed. Wheels, cables, and metal flew off the gutted car. The ruptured fuel tank exploded.

The mud lapping Mary's body began to run crimson with the blood from a peppering of wounds like buckshot. Her hair, pulled to one side by the blast, straggled into the slime. The coldness forced a muscular reflex, and her face pulled out of the mud. She rolled to her side, snatching for air. She felt no pain, only a kind of penetrating wetness followed by a spreading numbness. She could not move. She saw the sky as a gauze with a faint light behind it.

"Oh fuck," she said, and passed out.

■

Koltzov picked out the body in the mud in the glow from the burning car. He turned from the glasses.

"How did *she* get there?"

"I did not understand," said Goriev. "When you raised your arm. It could not be helped."

"What is the problem?" said Yanin.

"How we explain," said Koltzov.

Yanin was still trying to get the ringing from his ears. He took off the hat and shook his head.

"I liked her," said Goriev.

"Yes," said Koltzov.

Yanin fingered his ears. "No matter."

Koltzov looked through the glasses again, traversing the valley. "An ambulance is going out there," he said.

■

Serena had heard the gunfire and the shell pass overhead. It was odd, unusual, to hear a single shot like that, and from that direction: all the government artillery was farther forward. The secondary explosion, when the fuel tank went up, was audible at the casualty station. Bethune had thought her mad, but she took two orderlies and the ambulance because already she knew what had been hit: nothing else had gone up that road.

When she had her first view of the car she did not see Mary's body. So little was left of the Citroen that it seemed hopeless. The mud forced them to pull up a hundred yards short of the incline. Only then, getting down from the cab, did she see Mary.

□

Major Alcalá began a new game. The bread and water had always come at set times; the guards threw in the bread and pushed in a bowl of water. Now they broke the pattern, sometimes leaving the prisoners for much longer without food, at others bringing it more frequently. The roof was sealed to keep out light and the rain. There was now no way of knowing one day from another, and Pollard lost any sense of how long they had been there. He felt mentally enfeebled, without the ability any longer to concentrate. They were declining into a state where none of them disputed. They clung together like sheep.

Alcalá, meanwhile, spent hours at his desk working on a log of the experiment. He referred to a scientific paper on sensory deprivation among chimpanzees kept in darkness, but the chimpanzees had been both male and female, and this invalidated his comparison. He was surprised how resilient these men were. Their social background had no bearing on their ability to survive. That was his most uncomfortable discovery. Pollard, he thought, ought by now to have shown a superior instinct by making a personal appeal. But Pollard was content to sink with the rest of them. This must be the decay of the godless; Alcalá was a devout man and the personal disciple of the founder of the Spanish Foreign Legion, General Millán Astray, who had one eye, one arm, and one leg and issued the cry "Long live death!" when he saw the godless. The experiment with Pollard and his men was not official, it was a hobby. Another week might bring more decisive results.

He lit a cigar and put the log aside, to turn to the larger problem of the battle. The planners had not accounted for a long campaign. Food was short and the front line troops were less zealous. Even the Moors were losing their bloodlust in the Jarama swamp. Alcalá himself longed for the desert, where battles were never bogged down and the air was always dry. This air got to the bones. When the war was won he would go back to the Rif. There was a new kind of snob in the army that he hated, Falangist officers trained by the Germans, men who sneered at *africanistas* like Alcalá. The Germans were everywhere, and they were either Protestants or godless. The cigar burned down as he tried to decide if there was really anything to distinguish a Protestant from an atheist.

But Alcalá in his spiritual darkness and Pollard in his eternal darkness were both suddenly released. Russian bombers, coming low from the north, caught the German antiaircraft battery off-guard. They made only one run, but their bombs dropped several sticks across the farm and the outlying quarters and made a direct hit on the ammunition store.

Part of the wall of Pollard's prison was blown out.

More frightening than the blast was the flood of light. For men in their condition it was like a blinding flash, sustained. They covered their eyes and huddled closer.

Alcalá was saved by the wall behind him, by its medieval solidity. Everything on the other side of the wall was blown apart, including three of his best officers. The roof of his office went with them. He was left, with the stub of the cigar, at a clean desk staring out into open land. The thick plastered tail of his hair was lifted and splayed into a spiky fan. His eyes bulged, and his brows went up and would not come down. In this condition he wandered silently for several minutes through smoke and ash and howling men until he came face to face with Pollard.

The cigar hung out and then fell from his mouth.

"Long live Christ the King!" whispered a man who had never whispered—the sound puzzled him.

□

Smoke swirled about them. Behind Alcalá were flashes of exploding ammunition.

"Long live Christ the King!"

His voice gained strength and he pulled at his revolver.

"Kill without pity!"

Pollard watched him fumbling with the gun but felt rooted: the spectral madman with incandescent light giving him a halo through the smoke seemed mythic and harmless. Pollard was unsure of his own sanity. His eyes burned from the smoke, something chemical, and from the glare.

Alcalá could not loosen the gun from the holster. He gave up and stepped forward, putting a hand on each of Pollard's shoulders and pushing his pop-eyed face so close that Pollard could smell the cigar on his breath. His weight pressed on Pollard. He moved his right hand and touched Pollard's cheek.

"I see the tears of Christ the King. *The tears of the cross!*"

The hand fell from cheek to holster, and this time he got the gun. He pressed it into Pollard's stomach.

"The cross! *The cross!*"

Pollard heard the trigger click, and click again. Alcalá had forgotten the safety catch.

"Redemption, *eh?*"

A tracer exploded and rose in a brilliant arc, surmounting all else, and was followed by a short burst of bullets.

There was a slight shift in Alcalá's expression. From the declamatory his mouth softened and widened, the upper lip riding over gums. His eyes dulled.

"Eh?"—but this time it was a whisper swallowed in a sigh, suggestive of revelation, and with his left hand tightening on Pollard's shoulder he fell to his knees.

Pollard pulled the hand away.

Like a man supplicating, Alcalá knelt with bowed head, rocked on his wide hips, and began to sink lower. The rocking stopped and he slumped to his left. Three punctures in the back of his tunic began to seep blood. The gun was locked in his hand.

Archer came out of the smoke, wiping his eyes.

"Christ!" he said, seeing Alcalá at Pollard's feet.

Pollard shook his head. "Don't use that word."

"We can get out of here."

Pollard came to his senses. "Where are the others?"

"Wandering all over the bloody place."

"Let's get them."

But the smoke got worse. They had to find a way out of it. More ammunition exploded, this time shells, and shrapnel hummed over their heads. They ran into some of the other men, and into one of the guards, whose tunic had been burned off his back. He stared at them and went staggering away.

Pollard found clear air. There were five of them. They were in a beet field that ended with a dry wall. Getting across the field showed how weak they were.

Collapsing on the other side of the wall, Pollard said, "We'd better stop until I can work out where we are."

From the smoke they could still hear men calling out, until the sound of approaching vehicles drowned them. The smoke was driven low along a valley in an easterly wind. Pollard saw from the sun that it was still morning.

■

At first the light came back to her as she had left it, as a distant glow behind a yellow gauze. She remembered the bubbling at her ears and the suction of the mud and how cold it was. The memory was perversely comforting. Everything had been understood and expelled in her one simple curse; thereafter came a feeling of peace. She was reluctant to lose the memory, but the act of reclaiming it also killed it. Gradually it slipped from the mind and, with the growing light, came a smell. It was her body, her hair, and an overlay of warmth and rubber. Rubber?

She opened her mouth and could taste that smell in the air.

"Mary."

She saw a blur against the light.

"Mary. It's Serena. You're not to speak unless you think you can. Move your toes. Try."

She had not repossessed her body. It was close at hand but still impersonal.

"If you can hear me, open your mouth again."

She did so.

"It's Serena."

She felt the hand on hers: contact, but from an uncertain distance.

"You're going to be all right, darling."

■

"There," said Ferrer. "Some hot water, sugar, lemon, and brandy."

Yanin took the mug and sniffed it cautiously.

"Drink it all," she said.

For a second he found the command insubordinate, and raised an eyebrow, then realized he had misjudged her—it was maternal. He drained the mug in two long swigs.

"You should be in bed," she said.

"First, I must finish my report."

He sat wrapped in two blankets although the room was warm, very warm. His face had a fevered tint, and he had trouble steadying his hands. In the bed socks his feet were as delicate as a girl's.

The drink made him cough.

"You should have a doctor."

"I am not sick."

He would yield no more, she saw. The skeletal stoic reinforced her own will every time she was near him.

"My report is important. Koltzov—Koltzov will have his own version, for sure. And Goriev. They conspire."

"It was your work."

"Yes." Yanin felt a little better. A fire had been kindled in his stomach. "Yes—but I do not want to make too much of that."

She wanted to be nearer to him.

"V-Mann one hundred ten," he said, "their top man, under our noses all the while. Koltzov had no suspicion, not until the damage was done."

"One thing I do not understand. How did Praeger have the information, the information about the boat?"

Yanin coughed again. The brandy aggravated his throat. He found his voice again. "You ask a central question. Very few people knew that the boat's destination was changed from Cartagena to San Sebastián. Yet the Nationalist cruiser sailed from El Ferrol with an exact interception course—finding a boat in the Bay of Biscay at this time of the year is a feat in itself. So there is clearly betrayal. No. I do not know where Praeger got that information." He remembered something, and looked at her with more rigor. "Did you know who the government agent on the ship was? The anarchist, Cordón?"

"Yes."

"Shot with the rest."

"Yes," she said, indifferently.

"You know the American woman, Byrnes?"

"She was in the car, with Praeger."

"She lives. Koltzov seems concerned about that—that she was involved. No doubt Koltzov will have an explanation for it in his report. For myself, I see no problem."

"I do not trust her."

Yanin was no longer sublimating himself to her care. He changed his tone. "I want candor from you as from anyone else. Especially on personal questions. There can be no personal weaknesses, none, if you are to take the responsibility I have in mind for you. Nothing must compromise you. *Nothing.*"

The effort drained the color from him. "You do understand? Because, you see, if it compromises you it would also compromise me."

"Of course."

"You were his lover and she was his lover."

"Yes. It means nothing. It is not for that that I do not trust her."

She felt, as she stood up, that every part of her was naked to him—emotions that were as detestable to her as to him.

□

■

After Mary regained consciousness it was a day and most of a night before she spoke. She floated in and out of sleep, never fully asleep and never able to sustain attention. Serena's voice registered, and gradually she came into focus. Mary knew that other people tended her and came and went, and that Serena seemed always to be there. When, with a surge of clarity, she knew where she was, she found that Serena was asleep. She was in a chair, and there was a light behind her, and other lights beyond. Mary lay watching her. Battle dress did nothing to diminish the grace in her—not angelic grace but the grace of the natural giver. Serena gave out, even in sleep, a sense of occupied space from which things could be expected. By recognizing this with the strangely heightened intuition of a mind just resurfacing, Mary could get her own bearings. She thought of Serena's worth. How did she herself measure up to that? She remembered her earlier morbidity and was ashamed of its selfishness. She remembered Praeger saying, "It's rather peaceful" and taking another swig of cognac. She remembered that with sharp clarity, down to the shine on the knees of his trousers as he hunched in the small car and pretended to be nonchalant. And the mud. But not the rest—not what had blown her into the mud. She knew something had happened to her because she was encased in bandages and a rubber tube ran into her somewhere she could not see or feel. A root beer float would be nice. Her mouth tasted sharp and her tongue was dry. She studied the lights that she could see beyond the room. Madrid. The room didn't seem right for a hospital room. But it did smell like one. The drapes. They were odd: heavy velvet tied by sashes. There was a reflection in the window, of the end of her bed. And of Serena who, in order to accommodate her length in the chair, had folded her legs under her and lay lopsided with a skein of hair over her eyes. These reflections floated in the Madrid night. By moving her head she could play a trick with the reflections, placing them on a neighboring rooftop.

The movement woke Serena.

"What happened to me?"

Serena leaned forward and smiled. "Beth saved your life. You were nearly blown to bits."

"What happened?"

"A shell. It blew up the car. Praeger was killed."

"I don't—I don't remember. I just remember—I remember lying there in the mud."

"Here, have some water."

Serena held Mary's head up enough for her to sip.

"Don't talk too much. You're very very weak. You lost a lot of blood. Beth did two transfusions. One at the station, and another here. He wanted to get you here to operate. This is his clinic. It used to be a consulate or something."

"Operate?"

"You had multiple lacerations. Splintered glass. Down your back and legs. Lucky, though. No artery, no organ hit. Arteries and organs are the things we can't manage. You've still got some in you, the glass. Beth couldn't get it all out. Glass isn't like metal, though. Won't give you gangrene."

"I can't—I can't seem to move much."

"Move your toes."

"Did you ask me to do that before?"

"Yes. There. That's important. Very good."

"It must look bad."

"It's your *back,* darling."

Mary smiled. "So he saved me."

"I think he was worried that if he didn't your story would never get written."

"You're . . ."

"You're talking too much, darling. By the way, you kept saying something funny when we had you at the station. You said, 'I'm not running.' Well, darling, how could you, in that mud?"

She let it pass as a joke with a flicker of a smile.

"It's going to be a long time. Beth says you need work they can't do here. You'll have to go home, when you're able."

Home. Where would that be? She didn't want to give up on the war now. She could not do that.

□

"I'll come back."

"Yes." Serena took her hand. "I know. By the way—we found your camera. In the mud. Apparently it still works."

"A voyeur no more."

"No."

"Serena. It's funny. Praeger, Max. He knew he was going to die."

"Don't be silly."

"He did." She couldn't manage emphasis. "I think he'd known for weeks."

"Don't talk anymore. Please. You've got to start taking solids. Get some sleep. I'll be here."

Where did the shell come from? she thought.

■

In the valleys of the Jarama the war never really took complete occupation. Its violence was localized, to a trench, to a road, to a hill, to the arrows that generals drew on maps. Between these pockets the peasants tried to keep the land alive. The land would be there long after the war, and they had to eat. On both sides of the war the older peasants went unmolested. A cart loaded with weeds for animal feed would move implacably along a track while fascist and government artillery lobbed shells overhead. Pollard and his four companions lay in the grass watching an old woman prune vines. Not more than half a mile away a hilltop was being pulverized by shelling—from which side they could not tell. They were, thought Pollard, the real parasites in the valley. They were irrelevant to the battle and useless to the land. Their value in a place of ruthless values was nil.

"Which way?" said Archer.

"South," said Pollard. "Better hope there. No set lines."

To have any chance they would have to cover at least fifteen miles and they were only in condition to cover five. They were lice-ridden and filthy. They had the eyes of desperadoes, but not the stamina to match.

"We need a hole," said Archer. "Some bloody shelter."

Pollard tried to get the layout of the valley clear in his head. There were several water pumps driven by small windmills. He could see the wall of a ravine. That meant a small river. Three houses were visible, low stone houses with crudely tiled roofs. One was well apart from the others, set against the ravine and sheltered by terraces above. He decided to make for it.

It took two hours of crawling, sliding, and climbing in wet grass and clover, mud and rock to find the edge of the ravine and come up behind the house. At close hand it revealed itself to be larger. There was some kind of kiln and they could hear goats. A pipe ran up from the ravine to a pump. The river had fast-running fresh water. The goats seemed to have picked up their scent and made a racket. No one appeared.

Pollard left three men at the kiln and took Archer along a wall and into a yard, a mess of stone and slime. The house had three shuttered windows and a wide wooden door that did not properly shut. Goat droppings were all over.

They slipped through the door.

The goats were in stalls to the right. On the left, through an arch, was a large, whitewashed room with a high, unshuttered skylight. Pollard was surprised to see how clean it was. There was a stone floor divided by a gutter, a pine table scrubbed almost white, a stone basin and standpipe. On the table were stone bowls, two of them filled with goats' cheese. There were olives, and a jug of goats' milk.

"Christ!" said Archer. "A bloody banquet."

Pollard pulled him away, and they went through another arch into a darker room. There was nothing there except a straw pallet against one wall.

"I feel like bloody Goldilocks," said Archer.

Pollard was pensive. "Yes. This would be fine."

"But?"

"We have no choice."

They returned to the others. One of these, the youngest, was a Welshman called Wright. He had been into the kiln. "I've seen these before," he said. "They make charcoal. They call it *picón*. Whoever uses it does good work. Very nicely kept, thank you. Surprising, really."

"In the middle of bloody nowhere," said Archer.

□

"They'll be back, whoever they are," said Pollard. "We'd better decide what we do when they come."

Despite their state, none of them felt easy about mounting an ambush, but that was clearly what they had to do.

■

Koltzov's driver held open the door of the Buick, and Koltzov waited for Ferrer to seat herself. He put a bulky file into his briefcase, but as he got in beside her he kept one document in his hand. Before the car pulled away he detached a small photograph that had been clipped to the paper and held it close to his glasses for inspection.

Ferrer didn't seem very interested.

"Who is she, do you think?" said Koltzov.

"Does it matter?"

"Of all the things we found in Praeger's desk this is, to me, the most tantalizing. I have no idea of its value. It must be significant. He kept it with the codebook."

"Just sentiment."

"I would say, from the style, it was taken about ten years ago. Background could be anywhere. Just a tree. Nothing in focus. She looks much darker than Praeger, might be the light. About twenty. Good hair."

"We will never know."

Koltzov reattached the picture to the paper and put it in the file, snapping the briefcase and yet not feeling that the Praeger matter was closed. He turned his attention to Ferrer.

"You are a very serious young woman."

She mistook it as a compliment. She didn't know Koltzov well. She crossed her legs demurely and nodded. The car was negotiating around shell craters in the Gran Vía.

"Sometimes it is a good thing to relax. Let your hair down."

She began to reappraise him.

"I mean, comrade, that those of us who work so hard must also permit ourselves a little pleasure."

"Pleasure?" She tasted the word dubiously. "What pleasures?"

Koltzov liked the way she filled out the *mono.* "There is still some life left in Madrid. If you know where to find it. Still some champagne."

She glared more resistantly, but was too aware of his rank to be rude. "I do not drink."

"Never?"

"Never, comrade."

Koltzov could not equate this puritanical declaration with the voluptuous figure. Her lips, though unpainted, were too interesting, especially the lower lip, too promising to be so deprived. She was a physical contradiction of her words, and he suspected something unbalanced—something unnatural. He tried another tack.

"It must be disappointing to you, going to Barcelona."

"No. There is important work."

"It's provincial. I hate the place."

"I also."

"Then why—?"

"Comrade Koltzov. You are here. Surely you would prefer Moscow?"

"Not in April." He tried to endorse his own joke with a laugh, but it choked in her gaze.

"Duty has its own pleasure."

Koltzov fell silent. Her fingers, he saw, were never still.

"Comrade Koltzov, can I ask a question?"

"Of course."

"Do you think that we Spaniards could run a revolution: A *real* revolution?"

"Here? Now?"

"Yes."

Koltzov looked out the car window, as though in need of information from the street.

"Well?" she insisted.

He decided not to evade her. "In truth, no. It's not in the character of the people. Not yet. I have been in a revolution."

"Then that must be our duty. To change their character."

He realized with astonishment that she meant it.

"Read Cervantes," he said.

□

"I would burn that book."

Even his physical interest in her died. He was glad the journey was nearly over.

"You can tell comrade Yanin that you looked after his interests very well."

"I cannot equal him."

"A pity he is so—so delicate," said Koltzov with transparent insincerity.

"He is stronger than us all."

"He should be in the hospital."

"He does not trust hospitals."

"I think we are there."

"Thank you, comrade Koltzov."

"My pleasure."

She was so anxious about Yanin that she ran up the stairs to the apartment. She had not seen him for a day. As she let herself into the hall she had a feeling of alarm: mail lay uncollected on the floor.

A smell invested his bedroom as subtly as the light seeping through the slatted blind on the single window. Yanin was in just enough light for her to see that his head was wet with fever. But the smell was of more than fever—it was the breath of a wasting body. She could hear the struggle for each breath—she felt his will rise and fall with it. She cursed the infliction and she cursed her neglect. There must be more that she could do.

She moved to the bed and sat without shading his face. So far he did not seem to know that she was there. Carefully she laid a hand on his one exposed hand. There was no response. She moved her hand to his brow. It was like touching moss on stone.

His eyes were closed but his mouth moved: all else was moist, but his lips were so brittle from the labor of breathing that there was no saliva and no voice.

She whispered, "Please, do not try to speak."

The large bed seemed to mock his body. He was no more than a ridge in the blanket. She took away her hand and sat as still as he lay. The light's imperceptible movement across his pillow was of the same tempo as his fight against the fever. She had to supplement his will. There must be more that she could do.

□

The sun slipped away.

She got up and began to undress.

Naked, she went to the bed, lifted the blanket, and slipped in.

At first she did not touch him. Her strength and his need seemed to meet in a physical field between them. She could feel the saturated sheet, cold on her own skin. He made no movement. He had no reserves of energy left. But she knew that he wanted—that he needed—what he could not ask for.

As carefully as she could, she laid a hand on his waist and then, easing herself into the last inch between them, she slowly complemented his body with hers, lying bone against bone and breast against breast. The effort of his lungs passed into her and was nourished by her warmth. She gave him succor, lying as still as death to give him life. She knew that an open window would have been enough to kill him. This last resort of hers would save him and, at the same time, fulfill her.

□

“Well, there’s no cause for distress,” said Byrnes. “The cable from Madrid is clear; she’s in no danger.”

But he failed to look as calm as he sounded. There were small signals, left palm brushing his jacket, uncertainty of how to stand, most of all the lack of a direct look. Tom knew them all.

“This man Esposito at the embassy can be relied upon, and I’m getting in touch with Dutton at the State Department to make sure they get her out of there as soon as possible.”

“I could go, myself,” said Tom, “but by the time I could be there she would be on the way home.”

“There is no need of that.”

“I think she’s pretty bad.”

“We’ll have the best people look at her.”

“Yes.”

“A good Catholic hospital.”

Tom never felt easy in his father’s place of business, and it was clear why in this conversation. There was a desk without an heir. If there was anything precarious under the marble pillars of the First Cape National Bank it was that the two men who ran it had, from the beginning, put their hopes in nepotism. One of them still did—though without full confidence. The other had been cheated in a way that he would never voice. Tom’s vocation was a disappointment, but hardly an embarrassment. The disappointment was mutually known and silently manifest whenever they were, as now, in the ledger-lined office.

"I don't think," said Tom, "that the denomination counts as much as the specialty."

"Oh? I know of no deficiency—"

"Well, for one thing, I don't think Mary would exactly insist on it, Pat."

His father disdained the humor.

"And for another, it should be left to the doctors. Of medicine, not divinity."

"I see." Byrnes was a man of assumptions that were never quickly dispelled. "I see." He rubbed a finger on his chin. "I suppose you are right."

"There's a lot I don't understand about how this happened."

"Come now, Tom. What do you expect? It's a wretched situation—why on earth she went back, I don't know. It's clear that the whole situation is dominated by reds."

"She had her reasons. You know that."

But Byrnes was not sympathetic. "Let's just make damned sure she stays away from the place in future. You'd better see Liam."

"Ah yes."

"What does that mean?"

"Liam understands her."

"You know, Tom—"

"Yes?"

"Maybe, maybe this will change her."

"It might. It might."

But Byrnes knew he was being reassured without conviction; in a priest that was a sin, in a son it was, perhaps, forgivable.

"Liam's in his office."

"Right," said Tom. "Right."

They never really knew how to end a conversation. Tom went out and down the corridor.

Liam was a dark outline at the window against the sharp April blue. He had a pipe in his hand, but it was not lit. He turned as Tom came in.

"I love her, Tom. What can I do about it?"

"Let's go and get ourselves a drink, shall we?"

The harbor wind disarranged Liam's hair—it was like flicking back ten pages in the photo album; Tom remembered the unruly Liam of their Cape Cod summers. It had taken Harvard to impose grooming on him. Where the hair blew back there used to be a band of freckles. Now there was just white.

Together again in the booth on those shiny mahogany seats—how many wide Irish cheeks had polished them, how many deals been made? Liam the dealer? Tom knew better.

"You know," he said, "she was right. From the beginning."

"That puts us both in trouble," said Liam.

The waiter, without being asked, set down a bottle of Bushmills, three-quarters full, with two double-shot glasses, two pint mugs, and a bottle of seltzer. He managed that all in one hand.

"Thank you, Sean," said Liam. "How are the boys?"

"Wicked."

Sean looked like James Joyce, even to the circular-frame glasses.

"Some steak, Sean," said Tom. "In about a quarter of an hour."

"Right you are, Father."

Liam had slumped. The deviant hair was left as it was.

Tom poured; they touched glasses and drained them in one gulp. The taste took them back some. It wasn't perpetual youth, but it summoned all the things they knew of each other.

"Being that close to her for that long," said Liam, "brought no advantage, granted no privileges." He considered the bottom of the empty glass. "It's a belief I have that if we had met as strangers on a street one day, say about three years ago, we would never have said good-bye."

Tom poured the two seltzers, but Liam refilled his whiskey glass.

"Do I presume too much?" said Liam.

"I don't know. But it strikes me powerfully that there never was a form of purgatory more sustained or elaborate than the way the two of you have so far carried on."

Liam began to straighten, as though the whiskey had revived him, then said, reciting. " 'My love is strengthened though more weak in seeming, I love not less, though less the show appear.' Shakespeare. The sonnets."

"So it is. So it is." Tom had not touched his seltzer. He brooded as he fingered it. "Do you know what it is about my sister that really troubles me? It's that she seems to find the moral truth in any situation. Without help."

"Like Spain?"

Tom nodded. "There is a terrible certainty in her. I saw it on that platform in New York. When that kind of certainty shines through in someone—she did *shine* with it—it's not supposed to be secular. Do you see?"

"Have another whiskey."

"I will."

Neither spoke again for a while. They noticed nothing of the conversations around them except as the soundscape of a tribe making its transactions in the familiar half-light of its varnished cave. They were assumed to be a part of it. The priest and the banker, a Byrnes and a Casey.

At last, Tom looked around. "This town has made a political people of us."

"We always have to defend ourselves."

"Oh, that's true. But we're not just off the boat anymore."

"What are you driving at?"

Tom kept a coating of whiskey in his glass, toying with it. "It was better, I think, when we were just looking after our own. It's gone beyond that. We're after a lot more."

"What do I do, Tom?"

"About her?"

"About it all. I can't stop it now."

"You could not have stopped it anyway."

"But I went along with it."

"Let me tell you something you don't know. There are things *I* can't stop. I have a very political bishop. You know what the Catholic vote is to the Democratic party. No one makes more of that than Joe Kennedy. Roosevelt trusts Joe to deliver. So what is the favor in return? There is a trade-off, you know. The bishop wants Roosevelt to do something no president has done, to give diplomatic recognition to the Vatican. He's using all his Roman connections to that end, and Kennedy has been acting like it's a deal. You do see what that means? You can't recognize the Vatican and support a government that burns churches."

"You have to know what you can't beat."

"Ah yes. We are but fleas on the flank of a mighty beast."

"Let's drink to that. Fleas can bite."

"Particularly the parts that are most private."

They touched glasses and drank and Sean put before them two charred T-bones.

"Is it a celebration, Father?"

They looked at each other.

"In a manner of speaking, Sean, in a manner of speaking. It's the Feast of the Fleas."

"I don't know that one, Father."

"It's not widely known. Have yourself a whiskey, Sean."

"Thank you, Father."

He retreated with a bemused but convivial smile.

"I love her, too, you know," said Tom.

Liam returned Tom to his rectory. The Cadillac smelled so much of whiskey that the nuns detected it. Liam watched him go up the steps. Brother and sister had the same swing of bones under their different forms. A cassock didn't suppress it—it was the set of shoulders and hips while the arms moved loosely, as characteristic as a facial expression. He sat a little longer in the idling car, feeling that too many things were familiar, down to the way the engine's tired valves sounded like distant birdsong. There was a structure of habit all around him. He felt it more when drunk than when sober. There was a point in being drunk if it stopped self-deceptions. He moved the car gently into gear and headed for Cambridge, taking care not to drive like a three-o'clock lush.

It was truly an Ivy League day. Maritime sky and gothic. America's Athens. As near to Europe as you could get without stepping on a boat. Give us your best and we shall make you wise. And the wisdom will make you rich. All over the campus were the bright faces, brightest of the bright, all with that easily carried supremacy. It was a puzzle. Every piece had been found its place. He had fitted himself into it, his colors matched at every edge. It had been easy. She had been there too, but that piece had not snapped so readily into place. Nonetheless the picture—the picture before him now as he sat in the car—was complete with them both in it. She had made the greater effort. "Make the effort, you can do it."

The problem, the puzzle, was that he had gone on being the good fit. He had accepted his part in the fabric of the place. That, in turn, had brought the structure of habit. Looking out over the common he remembered looking out through the same glass—a prism by Cadillac—on the long straight road with pines on each side as he drove her from the clinic. That road had released her but it had led him nowhere.

Once, she had said, "I think you belong here."

At that time it had seemed no more than a mild sarcasm thrown off in the scrutiny of the early morning as she made the French toast and walked around in that coach's sweater that made her more nubile than ever. Perhaps it had been casual in intention, but, like some casually uttered remarks, it contained enough penetration to get stuck in the part of the brain reserved for painful truths, and it came out again now, on a tide of Bushmills and campus air. There and then, with considerable but undisplayed rage, he wanted the puzzle to fall apart. You could put it together again with another guy in that slot. I *don't* belong. If I swear to that, will you believe me?

You could cross the city line and move up to Brookline, but that only made the air better. Exchanging a street for lawns was no escape. The old house was in the new. The habits carried.

"How nice. You're home early."

But she knew. He could tell.

"Would you have Andrews bring us up some tea?"

She watched him go and return with her mind not quite decided on his mood.

"Liam, I think this is delightful, don't you?"

She held up a figurine with her fingers curled in possession.

"See how the glaze changes in the light."

"It's new?"

"It was sent by that charming man, Herr Heidel. It's Dresden. Of course, there's Dresden and Dresden. You have to know. He's clearly a man of discernment."

She set it down and continued to behold it, rubbing her hands like a girl at Christmas.

Andrews brought the tea. Something in the way he put his nose on patrol, with the utmost of English discretion, told Liam that he had picked up the scent of Bushmills. It was a scent he knew well.

"Thank you, Andrews."

Hypocritical creep. His mother was now arranging herself for interdiction.

"Do sit down, dear."

She poured the milk first, and then the tea.

"I have heard the news, Liam. Poor Pat."

"Pat is not the casualty."

"Such a trial. Such a trial."

"I think he'll recover."

"Please don't be so sharp. Pat is such a loyal man."

"Mother—"

"Yes?"

"She is seriously injured."

"Oh yes, so I believe. Quite primitive hospitals, I recall. Do you remember that time I went to the dentist in Pamplona? I think I can still—you do remember? Don't you want some cake?"

The figurine had a power beyond its size. Someone had given vent to a fury in shaping it. Energy wound through it like knotted muscle, and it seemed capable of suddenly exploding. She had handled it as though it had the innocence of a child; he saw only malevolence.

But it was love that wounded him. That intricate organ of the emotions called the heart was settling into a wasting sickness and, in doing so, had put him in renewed touch with his weaknesses of character. If they were self-admissible, he might correct them in time to disappoint his mother. She had always cultivated his weaknesses as though they were signs of refinement. What they brought to her was companionship. As long as the weaknesses were there, she would not lose him.

"Perhaps we should go to Europe, Liam. France first, then Germany. Nice, Salzburg, Berlin. That would be nice. Venice, perhaps."

□

"I think there's going to be a war."

She turned again to the cake, cutting a sliver for herself.

"Not this year, Liam. Not this year."

He could never underestimate her. She was enjoying herself.

Later, much later, after he had slept off the Bushmills, Andrews came to wake him.

"New York on the telephone, Mr. Liam."

Andrews managed to make "New York" sound like a plague.

The voice on the phone was of the place—brisk, direct, assumptive.

"Had some job finding you. Ike Mandel. Remember?"

Liam remembered supper in the deli.

"Spoke with Patrick Byrnes about Mary. Said I should deal with you. What is it with him?" But Mandel didn't give time for an answer. "The proposal is that we get Mary into a hospital here, in New York. How does that sit with you, Liam?"

"Whose proposal?"

"I've conferred with Joe Dann. He took an opinion. There's a man at Mount Sinai, Abraham Sachs. Best man in the line."

"Mount Sinai?"

"Hell, it's only a name. Nothing biblical about Abe Sachs. I'm told he's the father of skin grafting. You know she's going to need a lot of that?"

"Yes."

"The kid is close to you, I know that. She's going to need you. They get very depressed once they figure it out."

"Just a minute. That's all fine. But what about her friend, Cordón?"

For the first time Mandel was silent. Silent for long enough for Liam to begin to realize what was coming.

"You didn't know? That's the hell of it. Cordón was killed, that boat—that shipment they put all the effort into—the Nationalists intercepted the boat and shot everyone on board. That's the hell of it."

"I didn't know."

"How are you placed? Can you come to New York?"

"I'll be there."

"Good. What about her father?"

□

"He'll leave it to me."

"Yeah. Tell you, Liam. She's got guts. And she can write. The first piece she sent me, it was *all* there. We should take care of her."

"Yes, we should."

Putting down the phone, Liam muttered to himself, *"Mount Sinai?"* What would Tom think about that? And about Cordón?

■

Tom, at that moment, was celebrating mass. He tried to give his mind to it, but there was something mechanical in the way he followed the ritual. There were many familiar faces in the congregation, and on the surface it seemed no different from any other mass. The day was dying in a yellow light. At this time of the year the sacraments took on a beauty related to that light. Faces turned up to it. Standing there in the Latinate vestments, communicating the body of Christ, listening to his own incantations, he was flawed, in as small a way as Liam's disarranged hair had jarred with his banker's suit.

Afterward he sat alone for a while and considered praying. No prayer came to mind. It was not his faith that had failed. He could answer to that. He had changed. It was about submission and fealty—and love. These things no longer sat in harmony as a trinity. The Most Reverent Francis J. Spellman had disturbed them. He had interceded between the priest and his Savior—and now seemed as tangible as a shadow thrown between the yellow light and the cross. It would take courage to confront it. A test of himself that could not be helped by prayer.

Did Sister Sarah know? Of the two guardian angels, it was she who had always made him feel transparent. Both nuns knew about the whiskey but were far too worldly (and acquainted with priests) to raise even a brow over it. Sister Sarah had been directing long and solemn stares at him. The innate mercy of her face searched for an opening, but none came until the morning after the mass, when she brought him the *Boston Globe.*

"Have you seen this, Father?"

He had not. She had folded the page to frame a photograph and story. The photograph was of Mary—an old one with an anachronistic hairstyle. BANKER'S DAUGHTER MAIMED IN SPANISH WAR.

"I'm sorry to know about it, Father. You did not need to keep it to yourself."

Sympathy and rebuke were delivered in the same amenable tone.

He avoided the wide green eyes and scanned the paper.

"They're exaggerating, Sister. She's going to recover. 'Maimed' is one of those words newspapers use to get your attention."

"Well, that's good to know." This time she was not going to let him slip away. "You know, Father, Sister Teresa and me, we always liked her. I can remember the two of you at mass together; Mary always stood out as a girl who never stopped asking questions."

"Yes." He smiled. "That is certainly true."

"People with doubts must never suppress them."

He felt obliged to dissimilate. "Quite so."

"She is not lost yet. I am sure you know that, Father."

He broke the eye contact and looked down at the paper.

"If the *Globe* tries to reach me I'm not available."

She remained there with her breath searching for another tack.

"It's a troubling war, Father."

"It is."

"Hard to believe what you read. For example, one side says the other bombed a church while the priest was elevating the Host, and killed all the poor souls at mass. The other side says they bombed a military target and the communists locked up the priests and nuns and set fire to the church. I'm sure I don't know what to think."

"Ah yes." He decided to be the Jesuit. He put aside the newspaper, paused, and said, "I'll tell you what I think, Sister. I think the truth does not always oblige belief."

For several seconds the unassailed virgin considered the point with something approaching beatitude. Then, shedding all suggestion of innocence, she said, "Then it should be the truth we answer to, to be sure."

Damn your certitude, he thought—but at the same time saw the shaft of reason flashing in the early light, unblunted by piety. She had sparred with the Jesuits before.

□

"Father, we would like to write a note of condolence to Mary. Where should we send it?"

"You can give it to me, Sister. You can give it to me. I will be meeting her on the boat. It's a very nice thought."

"A little thing. I'm glad you'll be there, Father. It's love that she will be needing now."

And with that she went, in a stirring of starch and linen.

"Miss Byrnes," said the *Globe,* "attended Radcliffe College and contributed to the *Harvard Crimson.* Contemporaries recall her as a strongly independent-minded student and something of an iconoclast."

"Oh yes," he thought, "that she was." It was in him also. Their divergencies and their commonalities were not neatly separable: branches from the common root they were. Her renunciation of faith was, paradoxically, only the balancing of his declaration. Up to a certain point they had grown with a shared body of beliefs and premises. Her skepticism had been no greater than his. That he had put his skepticism into his faith and she had not did not seem, at the time, to be so great a schism. Patrick Byrnes, it was true, had not been able to understand this. He lacked the imagination. Tom had even argued that hers was the greater courage. His father had seen, instead, not the daughter but the mother, as though confronting a divine torment.

He put the newspaper in a drawer of his desk. Someday it would be behind them.

■

Liam proposed driving to New York instead of taking the train. Tom saw the game: that road would be the old one. Well, why not? The Cadillac was better company than the parlor car. Through New Haven and jokes about the kind of girls you found hanging around Yale. Old whaling towns and a reflection on the oddities of Herman Melville—Liam was good on Melville and the lunacy of Ahab being like that of a cuckold's; the white whale had done something sexual to him. The sex in *Moby Dick* was all of the inadmissible variety—Liam announced that with the sixth glass of Bushmills, in Hartford, and then slept until New Rochelle while Tom drove. Crossing the Queensboro Bridge caused him to evoke passages of Gatsby going in the same direction, and they ended up at the Plaza. A priest pulling up at the steps of the Plaza in a decrepit Cadillac was not enough to rock the doorman.

Standing in the room, looking out over the park, the two of them realized that the approaching boat brought not only Mary but the end of a number of evasions. She had not engineered it that way. But they felt answerable to her for failures she knew nothing of. The boisterous passage of the Cadillac had not altered that.

"Well," said Tom, "I think we had better put ourselves in order. We look a little disreputable."

"Yes," said Liam, sobering fast, "let's be reputable." He lingered at the window, having picked out something in the park. Then he said, "Tom, would it work?"

Half-turning, he said, "*Would* it?"

"I don't know."

"No."

"Give her time."

Liam gave one last glance out the window, where Babylon's towers caught a western sun. "You know, this city used to scare me a little. I don't feel that anymore." And, more briskly, he said, "I'll call Mandel."

"We shouldn't look as though we're headed for a funeral."

"I'll mend, Tom, I'll mend."

While Tom was in the bath, Liam made the call and then sat smoking his pipe, and it seemed, when Tom appeared, that the mood had passed.

Mandel was waiting for them at Pier Thirty-eight. He stood out among the modish crowd as did Tom—there was a clerical darkness in him, too. Liam was the slicker: brown trilby and scarlet tie.

"It's docked to the second. British timekeeping," said Mandel. "Everything is arranged. The ambulance is at the slipway. They handled immigration and customs on board."

The great steel shed was a bedlam of porters, officials, people waiting for passengers. The Cunarder's hull rose sheer like a permanent fixture; there was no impression of water, only a smell to betray the Hudson.

Mandel showed papers and they were allowed on board, led by a steward through the walnut veneers, chrome, and the warm sweet smell of an imperfectly ventilated hedonism—perfumes, cigars, banquets, and steam had discreetly formed a collective memory of six days and nights of passage, of fidelities and infidelities.

"Perhaps we should go to Europe," he heard her say. This was where Miriam could truly be herself.

The smells changed: antiseptic, linoleum instead of carpets. The ship had a miniature hospital, though it was called the sick bay.

"In here, sir," said the steward, leading Mandel.

The light was also clinical. A starched white woman looked at them with some reserve and with one glance dismissed the steward.

"She's only just this minute had a blanket bath. I'm not sure she's ready."

"Oh yes she is," said Mary's voice from a green-hued inner room.

The nurse shrugged and stepped to one side.

Mandel beckoned for Tom and Liam to precede him.

The green failed to dim the red. Her hair was spread wide over the pillows.

"*Tom!* Oh *Tom!* Liam!"

One went to each side of her, and she saw Mandel, who stayed at the end of the bed.

"And Ike!" She saw them trying not to respond to her appearance. "It's okay. I do know what I look like."

"You look great to me, Mary," said Tom.

"It's good to have you home," said Liam, losing gravity with every word.

"I've been very pampered." She looked past Mandel. "Don't go on first appearances. Matron Harcourt is a demon and a really nice person." She looked at Liam. "I feel like an Egyptian mummy. It's best if you don't see under the blanket."

"I've missed you, Tiger."

She brushed her hair more firmly aside and began to cry.

"No, Ike," she said. "Please don't go. I'm sorry."

Tom took her hand. "Have a cry for me."

□

"Laughing and crying is difficult," she said, doing both.

"I have something for you," said Mandel. He came up beside Tom and gave her a magazine. "You're the cover."

She looked at it. THE SPANISH DEATH OF ALBERT ROCKWELL. Hmmm. Looks fine. But wait until you see the next piece."

Mandel put a hand on her arm. "Just get well, kid."

"Funny thing was," she said, "I got blown up but my camera didn't. Second time that happened. When they took out the film it was all there. Only I don't feel so good about using a German camera anymore."

They heard the matron say, "Yes, sir, they are *all* with her."

They looked to the door.

Tom Esposito appeared.

"Liam—and Father Byrnes, I believe." He nodded formally, and looked at Mandel. "I'm Esposito, from the embassy."

Mandel nodded. "Ike Mandel."

"Ah yes. The editor." Esposito saw the magazine. "Well, gentlemen, everything is set. I understand the destination is Mount Sinai."

"Did you—were you on the boat with Mary?" said Liam.

"It kind of worked out dandy. I needed leave—oh, *how* I needed leave—and she needed a bearer."

"You've been good," she said.

"That's my job."

Tom looked across the bed at Liam, then said, "Well, we're grateful, to be sure."

"Your father not here?" said Esposito.

"No. No, he's leaving this part to us."

"I see." Esposito brightened mechanically. "She's looking better every day. Maybe now she'll behave." He was close enough to read the magazine's cover. "Rockwell? I seem to remember that name."

It was an effect he could not quite carry off; spleen was showing.

She put a hand possessively to the magazine. "That's part one."

Esposito tightened his already tight tie. "It seems to me that I can now formally discharge the patient. You won't need me once you're off the boat."

She said, "Tom. Thank you. I *mean* it."

"My pleasure."

"We are grateful," said Tom Byrnes.

Esposito bowed and went out.

"That was a surprise," said Liam.

"Yes," she said, contemplatively. "Yes. He's full of surprises."

"I'll bet," said Mandel.

"You can ride with me in the ambulance, Tom."

It was, for a moment, the appeal of the younger sister.

"Of course."

■

Following the ambulance in a taxi, Mandel said to Liam, "She's scared."

"Yes. She is."

"Don't worry. Abe Sachs will deal with that."

■

In the ambulance Mary could be cranked up from the waist on the stretcher and seemed more comfortable. She held Tom's hand.

"There's a man I owe my life to. A Canadian called Bethune. What can you do for someone who saves your life?"

"Make the most of the rest of it."

"Your hand is cold."

"It's a strange thing, you know. Why does it take something like this to see things straight?"

"I saw it in your face, Tom."

"Ah yes."

He closed the ambulance's curtains against the glare of the streets. There was something unintentionally confessional about the effect.

"Ah yes. I've been recalling something. I think you must have been about ten years old. We came down the steps of the cathedral; it was in the fall, I think. You wore red shoes and white stockings; it was the legs I recalled first. You had your Bible in your hand, but you held it loosely, sort of away from you. You broke away from Mother's hand. The positions of everyone were, I would call them, definitive. For a second or two, like a painting. Father was off to one side. Looking for someone important. You started to wave the Bible as you spoke. I remember what it was you said. You stood there, very bright you were. You said, 'I don't know. Why must it come down? Where is above? I don't like all this looking up. Why shouldn't it be here with us?' Do you remember that?"

"Not in the same way. I know it happened, of course. I remember your face. You stood there, very warily. You said, 'You mustn't be frightened to look up.' "

"I did. That's true. But I've seen what you meant. I've seen the problem. When I look up I've been seeing a bishop, a cardinal, and His Holiness the Pope. Why shouldn't it be here with us? That was a very good question, Mary. He is, of course."

"Oh Tom. I do love you. But I don't think I can help you."

"You already have, you already have."

■

Dr. Abraham Sachs was short and portly, but the thing she noticed most was his sleepy, long-lashed eyes. They elaborated his nature.

"We'll be spending a lot of time together, Mary."

He had dismissed all of them but Tom from the hospital room, and sat spread-thighed on an uncomfortable chair by her bed.

"I've read Dr. Bethune's report. I want to take some X rays. But I can tell you, I'm going to have to get every one of those fragments out of you. It's like grapeshot. It won't be over quickly. But when it's done it will be done. And then I'm going to do some grafts. I can't say how long that will take. You're in better physical shape than I expected. The problem may be in your head. So I'll be frank with you from the start. There will be scars. I don't want you to get a complex about that. You're lucky. They won't show—under the usual circumstances."

"Don't worry about my head, Doctor."

"It's Abe and Mary, okay?"

"Okay."

He looked across the bed to Tom. "It would be a good thought, young man, if you were to write this Dr. Bethune. From what I've seen, and from what I can imagine about the conditions under which he operates, he's a saint."

Tom nodded. "I will certainly do that."

Sachs got up. "Now you can have a few moments with those other two gentlemen. I want you to have a good sleep. Tomorrow we get right on."

There was a large vase of flowers in the room.

"Tom, give me the card."

They were from Dave and Nina Backlund—"See you soon."

"I've a message for you," said Tom. "I nearly forgot, it's a note from my nuns."

She took it, as Liam and Mandel came in.

"The tie is not like you, Liam," she said.

"There's a change."

"There is? Sit down, for heaven's sake. He's a good person."

"Sachs? He was Joe Dann's idea."

"I fancy Ike had a hand in it."

Mandel was inscrutable.

"How about Esposito?" said Liam. "I've been telling Ike about him. What's his game?"

She took a sip of water. "He really was coming on leave. I *think.* We talked a lot. You know, I think I finally see the way his mind works. He's all knowledge and very little intellect. Basically, he's judgmental. Nothing is allowed to run loose. Do you know what I mean? He's *very* interesting. He has made a judgment on everything. Or almost. That enables him to put all ideas into a parcel. He's *very* unhappy about anything he can't find a parcel for."

"He's in the right business," said Mandel.

"I don't trust him," said Liam.

"Well," said Tom, "I don't see what harm he can be doing right now, do you?"

Liam noticed the card in her hand. "Who sent the flowers?"

"Dave and Nina Backlund."

Mandel got up. "I think we should go."

"Oh, I nearly forgot." She pointed to her bag. "Liam, could you?"

□

She searched the bag and found an envelope.

"Liam, this is for you. From Serena Pollard."

He took the letter.

"It's strictly between you and her. She told me it was none of my business. Don't look so hangdog. I love that lady dearly. She did as much to save my life as Beth—Bethune. Giles was taken prisoner."

"I didn't know that."

"She's very tough. She's staying on."

Liam put the letter in a pocket and bent to kiss her.

"Listen, Tiger. I'm very sorry about Nick, Nick Cordón. We—we all liked him, a lot."

She held his arm for a moment, and began to cry again.

"No—it's okay," she said. "I love you all."

■

When he and Tom were alone together in the room at the Plaza, Liam broke the injunction about Serena's letter. "Here," he said, "you'd better read this."

"You think that's a good idea?"

"Here."

Tom unfolded the coarse gray paper and read the large, erratic script:

> Dear Liam,
>
> I've always thought you would one day see the light. You see, the dreadful Drexel King told me what you were up to in Biarritz. That's really your business, not mine, but I did give you a chance. I thought your path to atonement might begin in that hospital in Madrid. I could see it meant something, though I'm not sure what.
>
> Anyway, here's another chance for you.
>
> Mary will tell you about Giles. I want him back. I think some of those people you were chums with in Biarritz could help. Would you try?

□

It would be nice to think that I didn't waste my hopes on you. I don't think so.

Love, Serena.

P.S. Mary is a brick. I love her.

Tom scanned it a second time, and then looked up to where Liam leaned against the mantel.

"It's moral blackmail."

"That's exactly what it is. I think it's going to work."

Tom brooded, while Liam pulled out his pipe and lit it.

"Damnit," snapped Tom, "do you have to smoke that thing at this hour?"

Unruffled, Liam said, "There would seem to be a lot of love in the world, after all, wouldn't there, Tom? It's quite surprising."

He took back the letter, and knocked out the pipe.

■

None of the steps Tom had rehearsed to himself through that night worked out as he wanted. They depended on his choosing the moment, and that was denied him.

"The bishop has been asking after you," said Sister Sarah.

"He knew . . . ?"

"Oh yes. He knows where you've been. He was just asking after you, Father—when you would be back."

All the symmetry went from his head, but then his head was not well.

"I'll go across there now," he said.

She nodded. "That's a good thing, I think, Father."

Even that did not go as planned. He crossed the inner garden, a diversion in order to give himself time, and walked headlong into Bishop Spellman.

"Thomas." The bishop was aglow in the morning air. "Thomas, I want a word or two. Shall we walk in the garden?"

Tom fell into the stately step.

□

"I've been speaking with your father. A good man. Of course, he's very concerned, about your sister. How is she?"

"She's in good hands, Your Excellency."

"Mount Sinai? Yes. Yes—well, New York is a Jewish state, more or less. But I'm sure that's as well. She's a strong will, as I recall."

"She is."

"But a troubled soul."

"She's—she's finding her way, I think."

"Is she? Really? Finding her way. Then what is it that troubles yourself, Thomas?"

There was no evading it. He improvised.

"It's no surprise to you, Your Excellency, I'm sure, to know of my reservations about our position with regard to the Spanish war."

"I recall your view."

"The problem is, we're making a religious war out of it, and I don't think it is. Not a religious struggle. I think the majority of people see it as political, between democracy and fascism. I think it's a mistake to make it religious."

"The majority? You mean, in a secular sense?"

"Yes."

"Well, Thomas. The first thing is, one side is upholding the Holy Father and the other side is not. That sounds religious to me. The second thing is that we have to deal with it as both a religious *and* a political matter. I see you're surprised. Well, you should understand one thing very clearly. A church that *isn't* political cannot survive in this country."

"I'm afraid of that, Your Excellency."

"Afraid, Thomas? Pray why?"

"We are a minority. Twenty percent. We're isolating ourselves on this issue. I'm afraid because I think that for the first time in our country's history there will be a religious schism, between Catholic and Protestant."

"One percent can be right."

It was said with imperial finality. Spellman stopped walking and looked up. "I think there's rain in the air." Then the eyes came down to earth and to Tom.

"You have a pastoral gift. I've no doubt of that. But you are very naive if you think we can stand aside and let an atheist rabble desecrate, mutilate, and massacre the people of our faith. You are not very wise in these things, Thomas. Are you sure of your faith?"

Finally Tom remembered the thought of the night.

"Yes, I am, Your Excellency. I follow Christ. He's what we have. I recall that Christ never needed a sword. He had other ways of defeating his opponents. That is why his word lives. That was his genius, to me."

Spellman was frigid and silent. The glow had passed from him. Until he spoke his vestments seemed like elements of statuary.

"Christ was incarnate. We are mortal. We are like unto soldiers. We must at all times be on duty or on call and obediently subject to the orders of our superiors. You must answer to your conscience. But I fancy you'll not be of service here any longer."

He held a final silent prayer as he looked at Tom, and moved off, like a monarch disposing of a courtier.

Strangely, Tom was not intimidated. He felt unbound.

■

Spellman was right about one thing: rain it did; the spring storm began as a hurricane in the Carolinas, swept up the seaboard, and became a deluge over New Jersey. The radio reported chaos from Cape Hatteras to Cape Cod. The rain turned to snow.

"It feels like Christmas," said Mary.

"I hate snow," said Sachs.

"What about Christmas?"

"Keep still. There. How does that feel?"

She was lying on her stomach and he was adjusting the gauze on her back.

"I feel on fire."

"That's good."

"How are we doing?"

"We are doing just dandy, young lady."

"How long?"

"I'll tell you when."

"Abe."

"What is it?"

"I'm fine in my head."

"I know. Okay. You can turn over. On your own."

He watched her, and pulled the sheet over her.

"Okay." He looked at his watch.

"What is it?"

"Just make yourself comfortable. You have some visitors due."

He was untypically cryptic, she thought. She pulled the mirror from her bag. The hair was a mess, but it would have to wait. And without makeup she looked, she thought, five years younger. Was that the light? The snow was building up on the frames of the window.

She fancied she could smell the snow. It was like sensing a change of air. You began to develop a kind of ultrasensitivity to things like that when you were incarcerated. Sometimes they were delusions. On the boat she had thought Esposito was good looking. And there was the night before, when in the hospital she could smell baking bread. The nurse had disabused her. This time she was sure about the air. It came in advance of someone—before she heard any doors or any footsteps.

Several people. And Abe's great feet clopping in the lead. She put away the mirror.

Sachs half-opened the door, standing in it.

"I do believe in Christmas," he said.

The others were behind him, bearing the breath and air of the street.

"She's decent," said Sachs. He stepped aside.

Cordón came in, followed by Nina and Dave Backlund.

□

They drank from the standpipe but had not touched the food—not because of an order from Pollard but from some instinctive and yet crazy discipline. Archer kept watch by the kiln. The others rested inside.

In a while Archer heard a mule-drawn cart coming up the hill, but couldn't see it.

He told Pollard.

"Probably just one man," said Pollard. "He'll stable the cart. Best to let him do that, and let him come in here." He looked around the room. "Keep out of sight. We'll take him here."

They heard the cart roll into the yard and then into the stalls where the goats were. It seemed an eternity until they heard clogged steps coming toward them. Pollard had one man on each side of the door—Archer, and Wright, the Welshman. The light from above was fading, and all Pollard saw as the men jumped was a dark and bulky form between them.

After their first lunge the men faltered, and pulled clear.

Between them, standing firm and obdurate, was a huge woman. Pollard was struck most by her eyes. Though dark, they had an angry luminance.

Pollard was the only Spanish speaker among them. Feeling foolish, he said, "I am sorry, Señora—" But the eyes stopped him dead.

□

"Who are you?"

Archer and Wright had moved farther away from her, and she took all of them in in one glare.

Pollard tried again. "I am sorry. We are of the Loyalist army. We are lost, and we need shelter."

"Lost? From the other side?"

"We were prisoners."

The woman seemed the most powerful force in the room, emphasizing their own frailty. She was middle-aged and yet as muscular as a younger man, as well as dark-skinned from a life in the fields.

"You escape?"

"Yes, Señora. We need a refuge and we are hungry."

She looked at the untouched table, and considered this paradox. Appreciating their condition increased her puzzlement. She stepped forward to Pollard. "What people are you from?"

"We are English."

"English?" She was nearly Pollard's height, and squaring up to him. "Is that why you do not eat my cheese?"

He could smell the sweat on her, sweet like loam. Beneath the worn and crusted skin there was a surviving and assertive femininity—she had, with ease, gotten the upper hand in a manner that would not have been possible for a man.

"We do not steal," he said.

She rubbed a hand on the upper curve of her hip and shook her head disbelievingly. "You look like animals. But you do not steal food." She moved to the table. "Here. I have some bread. I want you to eat my cheese. You sleep here. For one night."

As they ate she made coffee and heated a pan of milk.

Pollard wondered about the absence of men. There was no sign of anyone else having occupied the house. It was not something he could ask about: her manner and her language had an anachronistic propriety that he knew he could not breach with such a question. And yet she was hardly virginal. She was in every movement conscious of her sexuality. With the weakened men around her she was a ministering vitality—fecund and worldly.

Pollard asked her about the fascist lines. She explained that the river in the valley was a tributary of the Jarama. They were two valleys west of the front line. It would be impossible to cross the Jarama without being seen. The only chance was to try to work south sufficiently to avoid troop concentrations and hope to go east when out of the battle zone. That could take a week.

She seemed indifferent to the war, revealing no sympathy for either cause. He suspected that the war—and they—were intrusions into her work and could be expected to pass. But she was generous. The bowls of goat's cheese must have been intended for the local market. There remained the question, the puzzle, of the kiln, which, as Wright had said, was kept in surprisingly good condition.

He asked about it.

She set down an oil lamp on the table, adjusting the flame as she looked him over.

"The war makes it difficult to get the wood. It is my brother who uses the kiln."

Pollard would have asked about the brother, but she anticipated him.

"My brother is sick. He has not been here for three weeks."

Satisfied that they would be secure for the night, Pollard thanked her and told the men to be ready to leave at first light. The food and their exhaustion knocked them out. Pollard, wanting to make sure of the early departure, asked the woman to wake him at four, her own rising time. She would sleep with the goats and the mule.

However, it was not the woman who woke him, but the cold—the sudden cold that comes just before dawn. It was after five. At first Pollard thought she must have overslept. Then he found that she was gone.

He roused the others. They were all sluggish, and Pollard himself felt slow-witted.

"Where did she go?" said Archer.

"I don't think she slept here," said Pollard.

The implication sank in.

"We've been had," said Wright.

"The question is," said Pollard, "has she had time?"

"And why," said Archer. "*Why* would she do that?"

"That's academic," said Pollard. "*Listen!*"

□

A vehicle was coming up from the valley. It stopped as they listened, and its engine was switched off.

"Don't want to wake us," said Archer. "How considerate."

"Let's get out," said Pollard.

He led them the way they had come the day before, along the back of the kiln and toward the edge of the ravine. Whoever had arrived in the vehicle was, he reckoned, coming up the main track to the yard. It was already light enough to see the hills enclosing the valley. There was a ground mist in the ravine; strands of it hung on a terraced slope where, if they could reach it, the mist would provide good cover.

It was a disorderly scramble, making too much noise. But Pollard knew they had to put as much distance between themselves and the farm as possible before their absence was discovered. He kept in his mind the woman's display of neutrality and generosity and a detail that still seemed incongruous: she had perfect teeth. It was the only thing about her that had any sign of sophistication. Perfect teeth and coarsened, dirty hands. She had never slept with the goats and the mule. He should have seen that as he saw the teeth in the light of the oil lamp.

Before they reached the terraced hill they heard shouting from the farm. The words carried, clear and alien in the still air—commands in German.

Like Pollard, Archer knew the language.

"Bloody Kondor Legion."

"At least they won't know the terrain," said Pollard, "nor how long we've been gone. With any luck they'll fan out for a search, and that will slow them down."

He seemed to be right. They reached the cover of the mist without the voices getting any closer.

■

To the east the British warships were visible in the shadow of Gibraltar's rock; to the south, across the straits, the mountains of Morocco. It was a pearl of days. From the terrace of the villa the world seemed to have been arranged to exclude any stirring of the war. The war was now a thing of the north. Southern Spain was settling back into its own style—its gravity pulling toward that ocher rim of the Africa that had so marked its history, everything pulled south and away from the character of Europe.

Major Rohleder found himself feeling more amenable to the place the more he saw of it. The Büro Lenz offered a useful antidote to the pressures of Berlin. He had also developed a taste for the sherry. He held the glass by its stem in mimicry of the young man who had introduced him to it. The wine's light amber color embraced, for a second, a refracted image of the young man's face.

"Personally," said the young man, "I could drink it all through a meal. Especially if it were fish."

"Really?" said Rohleder. "With fish a Moselle would be better, surely?"

"Possibly."

"You are a good salesman, Mr. Cox."

"We don't do too well in your country, I fear."

"You should perhaps devote more time to us. You see, you have managed to convert me to dry sherry."

"It takes time. In point of fact, now I think of it, there was a German lady who came to the office last year. I gave her a glass of the dry. She was too polite to say that she hated it. It's not a drink for the virgin palate."

"You entertain virgin palates in your office?"

Cox flushed. "Not as a rule. The lady was looking for a *Lloyd's Register,* to check on some ships. I gave her the use of mine—and a glass of sherry."

"Ah. I see." Rohleder considered the sherry's coloring again. "Was that November—when the lady called?"

"I believe so. In point of fact, it was. Do you know the lady?"

"I think so, yes."

"Very pleasant, I thought."

"Oh yes, certainly. I wonder, Mr. Cox, if I might myself come into your office sometime. I would like to have some sherry shipped to Berlin."

□

"Only too delighted."

The warmth of the day extended to the party. Rohleder could see that Heidel was using the time to attempt the conquest of a tall, Moorish woman.

Leissner had noticed the same thing.

"Heidel has his blood up," said Leissner.

"He is not fastidious with women."

"You are mistaken, Rohleder. She is nobility."

"In Spain, perhaps. Tell me, Leissner, what is Heidel's relationship with that secretary of his—Eichberg?"

"Relationship?"

"You know what I mean."

"Strictly professional. Of that you can be sure. Freda Eichberg is not Otto's type. In any case, Otto does not shit on his own doorstep."

Rohleder finished his sherry and looked ready to leave.

"I think we can leave Otto to find his own way," said Leissner.

"Yes."

Leissner was surprised that Rohleder had stayed as long as he had; there might be some human weaknesses in him after all.

In the car, Rohleder said, casually, "Tell me, Leissner, does the Büro Lenz not keep copies of *Lloyd's Register of Shipping?*"

"No. No—why do you ask?"

"A detail. Not important."

But Rohleder seemed preoccupied for the rest of the drive to his hotel. When he got out of the car he spoke to Leissner's driver—in such a way that Leissner could not overhear.

Leissner was not in a mood to tolerate any more of Rohleder's conspiracies, although he knew his own driver was Gestapo. As soon as they drove away he opened the partition window of the Mercedes.

"What did Major Rohleder ask you?"

The driver was arrogantly compliant. "The major wishes to buy some sherry. I am to take him to the shipper in the morning."

"I see."

Leissner closed the partition. He knew he had been lied to.

□

■

Knee-deep in heather with the mist condensing on their pallid faces, Pollard and his men looked ghostly.

"This mist will burn off," said Pollard. "The thing to do is to find cover for the day. We can move at night."

He remembered a small olive grove from the day before. It ended against a sheer rock face, and between the rock and the trees were thick oleander bushes.

The mist held until they went higher. To reach the olive grove they had to work their way up a shallow hill without paths. They were nearly over this, with the sun on their backs, when a plane appeared.

They heard and saw it at the same instant. It came down the center of the valley following the line of the river and descended below the level of the surrounding hills.

"A Heinkel," said Wright.

It was a biplane. They could see its white fin with the black fascist cross.

"It's going for the farm," said Pollard.

The plane banked and began circling until it saw something and went lower.

"We'd better damned well get cover," said Pollard.

But the only cover—and that was sparse—was the olive grove, still a quarter of a mile away. They began running, but the wet heather made it difficult. While they were still on the hill the plane stopped circling and began climbing and banking in their direction. Their instinctive but futile reaction was to duck as they ran. Pollard knew how visible they must be. He heard the engine note change. The Heinkel was diving right for them.

"Spread out!" he shouted.

As they broke the Heinkel came down behind them and pulled up over the hill. Its slipstream left a wake in the grass, it had been so low. It turned sharply and came again.

They stopped running and threw themselves to the ground.

Pollard saw the flashes from its guns. It laid down a line of fire between them and the olive grove. Exposed as they were they could have been wiped out in that one pass. The pilot seemed to be trying not to kill them but to pin them down.

"Stay where you are," said Pollard.

The Heinkel turned for another run. This time it laid down a line of fire behind them. It climbed away and began circling overhead.

Archer crawled to Pollard. "We're bloody trapped," he said.

"Yes. He could have cut us to pieces. As it is, we'd better not tempt him. He's marking us out for someone else."

They could see the pilot in the open cockpit looking down as he banked over them.

"We're lucky it's the Germans," said Pollard.

"I feel so bloody helpless."

"We are helpless."

"That fucking woman."

"The *bitch.*"

It took only ten minutes for their pursuers to find them. There were three Germans—in unmarked uniforms without rank—and six Spaniards.

Pollard stood with his hands over his head, and the others followed. The plane did a final low pass and flew off.

The German in charge was about Pollard's age, thickset, dark-haired, and tanned. He spoke flawless Spanish but less well in English. He was gravely formal.

"Who is leader here?"

"I am," said Pollard.

"I am Oberstleutnant Dietrich. I take you into custody as prisoners of war. You understand?" His formality covered a certain nervousness.

"Does that mean with the rights of prisoners of war?"

"Of course."

Pollard decided to press the point, looking at the Spaniards beyond Dietrich. "Why should we believe that? We were treated appallingly when first captured. Like animals."

"In my custody you will be treated according to code. I cannot for the future speak."

The men had closed around Pollard, and the Spaniards herded them with bayoneted rifles.

□

Dietrich surveyed them, taking in their condition for the first time.

"You will be taken to camp with other prisoners."

He was trying to reassure them, but the spirit had drained from Pollard's men. All around them, as they were marched off, the valley picked up the rhythms of its own natural order, which they had briefly violated. As they reached the road where a truck waited, Pollard saw at the wall of the farm the woman, watching them—like a raven on a nest with half-furled wings.

■

"All agents are obvious—once they are caught," said Goriev.

"At the end he lost his nerve," said Koltzov. "He made only one mistake. Until then I had no suspicion. No—no suspicion."

"He was too good for them to risk him on one thing like that, the boat. But the boat must have mattered to someone very high up. It's always the same—the field men are sacrificed for whim."

"The boat was a serious loss to us."

"True. But we have learned from it. We will not advertise anymore."

They were sitting at Koltzov's dining table, going through the Praeger file, and drinking vodka.

"Look at this." Koltzov gave Goriev a newspaper clipping, yellow and as crisp as parchment.

Goriev studied it. "What do you make of it?"

"I don't know. It's like the photograph. Perhaps of the same vintage."

"A German newspaper. His own report on the Ukrainian uprising."

Koltzov looked over the other oddments from Praeger's desk: an old French newspaper, an accounts book that concealed his codes, letters, notes—and the photograph of the girl. Everything from the desk still bore the smell of Praeger's tobacco.

"It comes down to this," he said mournfully. "No more than ashes. What would they say of me, Goriev, from my papers?"

Goriev laughed. "Here lies poor Koltzov, still looking for the truth."

But Koltzov was not humored. "Praeger and I had one thing in common," he said, picking up the photograph again.

"What's that?"

"He was a Jew. And an apostate."

"You think that girl was a Jew?"

"I don't know." He put down the picture. "I don't know. Tell me, comrade General, do you think it's better to go like Praeger—without ever having to make the final reckoning?"

"You mean—if we have the choice?"

"I'm serious."

"Better a shell than a Moscow trial."

"Yes. Yes—I think so." Koltzov poured himself more vodka. "We must hope that comrade Yanin never gets charge of a trial. That man is going to give Genghis Khan a bad name."

"Yanin has a disciple."

"What a bitch!"

"Do you think Yanin—?"

"That's Yanin's problem. I don't think he can."

"You don't really believe it's as simple as that?" Goriev took the vodka. "Something tells me that when we look at comrade Yanin—alive or half alive—we look at the future. He is what we have created. The progeny. A system managed by men and yet having none of the human scale—we all meant that something better should come of it, did we not? I thought so. You cannot argue with that. Our youth was not spent in the fire to give birth to the likes of Yanin. I have no idea who his mother could have been. Not Mother Russia. Insemination by persons unknown. That Spanish witch has it too. It will spread. Before it is too late I think, comrade Koltzov, we should pick out all these bastard children and bury them. Just as you did with the fascists in the Model."

Koltzov's melancholy hardened into a sudden belligerence.

"I will take care of comrade Yanin."

Goriev realized how incautious the vodka had made him. He began pulling together the scattered papers from the Praeger file.

"Spain is a curse," he said.

□

■

The pocket battleship *Deutschland,* its aft deck shaded by an awning, seemed as accommodating as a cruise liner as it lay at anchor off Algeciras. Heidel and Leissner were both in white suits and panama hats and drinking their second cocktail before lunch at the captain's table. They watched Rohleder pacing the upper deck with a man they didn't know.

"He's been asking me about Fräulein Eichberg," said Leissner.

"Oh?"

"Whether there was a personal connection between you."

"Those damned people . . ."

"You do not need to worry, Otto."

"Scavengers."

"Rohleder is an ambitious man."

"Yes." Heidel regained control of himself. "I'm sorry—that such a day should be host to the likes of Rohleder; it is the pernicious poison in the system."

"He asked a strange question—if we keep a *Lloyd's Register.* You remember, you asked Fräulein Eichberg to check those Russian freighters that took the gold?"

"What has that to do with Rohleder?"

"He's clutching at straws. Never the right straws. He knows very well that there's a gang of old Weimar communists working for the Russians, run out of the Hague by a Russian called Krivitsky. We watch them, but that's too simple for Rohleder."

Rohleder had parted from the other man and was coming down to join them, looking more agreeable. His chin had a way of tautening under the force of a smile, as though fighting it.

"Gentlemen," he said, "such a beautiful day." He put his back against the rail and looked across the deck and the water to Gibraltar. "Our enemy or our ally, which will they be?"

"The British?" said Heidel.

"Our kin by race, yet different."

Leissner nodded. "They are agreeable."

"But will they come to Moscow with us?" said Rohleder.

□

"*Moscow?*" said Heidel, unable to conceal his disbelief.

"Of course. Sooner or later."

Heidel could not, even then, adjust to the solemnly delivered lunacy.

And Rohleder knew it. He knew Heidel was one of those without the vision. But keeping up his manner of sociability, he said, "Heidel, I have been wanting to ask, have you heard of a woman called von Poellnitz—Gisela von Poellnitz?"

Heidel felt wary and yet compelled to answer. "Von Poellnitz? It's a familiar name, of course, a good family. Gisela? Yes, I think so. We may have met, socially."

"Can you recall the circumstances?"

"I don't think so—one meets so many people in the season; it would have been in Berlin, I imagine." In truth he recalled her very well. "Why do you ask?"

"The signal to Madrid that led them to our agent went from the Soviet Trade Mission in Berlin. We broke their code some time ago. The woman von Poellnitz has been mailing letters to the Trade Mission, which we have intercepted, unknown to her."

"Have you picked her up?" said Leissner.

"Oh no. No." Rohleder moved away from the rail. "She will take us to others."

He said no more of it, but to Heidel it was like a brief play of a cool wind from the water in the otherwise embracing day. It was demeaning that a hand once touched in all innocence should now inflict fear in this subtlest of ways.

■

Yanin was sitting up and taking nourishment. Ferrer had been able at last to open the window. The sour air of fever was dispelled; the scents of spring came on a wind from the south.

She wore Yanin's own silk gown, and watched over him as he spooned the light broth. Her breasts hung loose over him as the token of everything that she could give him and had already given him. He now knew the wholesomeness of her body, and she the ways of his. Nothing had been altered—he was the master and she the apprentice, but in saving him she had entered more deeply his trust. He watched her without any trace of emotion. He had surrendered nothing. And yet, though their relationship was physically unconsummated, they were politically knitted by every sinew. It might, he thought, become one of those liaisons, not unknown in the courts of the ancients, where a bed was irrelevant to the bond.

"I will get up," he said.

"Are you sure?"

"I cannot waste time."

She took the bowl from him.

He drew up his knees and she pulled the blanket clear. His knees were like veined granite; as the shaft of light fell on his body, it picked out all the bones. For a moment, before he moved again, he was almost as a child with a precocious head. He felt the warmth of the sun, and his breath was steady, without the sound of strain. He swung one leg and then the other and sat on the edge of the bed testing his feet. His feet were bluish, the only part of him showing color.

"Are you sure?" she said again.

"Yes."

"I will run the bath."

Through the open window they heard artillery—she paused to count the shells. They always came in threes.

"The end of siesta," he said.

The last explosion was greater than the others.

"A building," she said.

An aftershock rattled the window frame and the bed—as Yanin sat there the tremor passed visibly from the bed to him through his blighted shanks. He looked like a marionette as the strings were taken up.

"I wish you could come to Barcelona," she said.

"Do you not believe you can do it on your own?"

"Of course I can." She had been mistaken to show sentiment and covered it as quickly as she was able.

"That is why I chose you."

□

She pulled the silk more modestly about her and went to prepare his bath.

He did seem renewed. From the bath he went to his clothes. All that he could not manage was his boots. She eased his feet into them and then threaded the laces to above the ankles with head bowed before him. She was still on her knees when he stood up. The boots were his final cement. He was finished with her now.

□

"He just came back from the dead," said Liam ambiguously. "He just *walked in.*"

"Well, God be praised for that," said Tom.

"I guess I should show more charity."

"You should. You should." Tom sat next to Liam in the parked Cadillac, staring out to the harbor. "As a pastor I would expect it, as a friend I know how much more complicated it is. That's the measure of it."

"She's transformed by it. I guess I have to accept it."

"I can't tell you how you should feel. But you can't do anything else."

"I like him. That sort of makes it worse."

"He has a rare strength in him. I can see that. Not worn openly. That makes it a finer thing."

"I know, *damnit.*"

"There's a detail that impresses me, Liam, the more I think about it. He knew that she thought he had been killed with all those other souls on the boat. He could have gotten a message to her from Mexico, but he did not. At first I thought that was callous. Then I saw how *selfless* it was, truly. By making any contact with her he would have put at risk not just himself, but all the work he was there to do. He had to live with that—as she did—but I think that it was harder for him."

"You're very generous."

"Well, I think you'll agree, Mary saw that, understood it at once."

"She would believe it if he walked on water."

"Come, *come.*"

"You're right, damnit. Tiger is happy."

"She is."

"And you. Father Byrnes."

"What of it?"

"Spellman would excommunicate you if he could."

"Ah. But he cannot."

"Father Byrnes, spokesman of the heretics. Catholics for Democratic Spain. Look at you."

They sank into silence, watching the gulls lift in the wind beyond the breakwater. Tom lowered his window a little and turned his face to the salted air.

"The thing is," he said, "I would like to believe that I cared as much about something temporal as I care about my faith, do you see?"

"You mean, because you can make a more tangible impression?"

"That's precisely what I mean." Tom turned from the wind and rested a hand on Liam's shoulder. "It's not that I'm any less of a Christian for wanting that, is it?"

"No."

"You see," said Tom, with sudden determination, "I want to feel strongly enough to do something as fine as Cordón did, to be as *sure* as that."

"You'll not be popular."

"Oh, not with the bishops or the cardinals and not with His Holiness the Pope, but I will be more at peace."

"Tom. You're a finer man than I."

"Not at all." Tom pressed the hand on Liam's shoulder again. "Not at all. You're just beginning to find yourself. And so am I."

"Maybe." Liam pulled himself from his slump. "Time to go."

"Suddenly I wish I could come with you."

□

"This is a one-man mission, buddy. Find the Limey."

"I'll pray for the both of you."

"Just pray for him. He needs it more."

The Cadillac hiccuped a few times as he started it and then settled into birdsong.

"Jesus *Christ,* Tom. I must be mad."

He laughed as he had once laughed when both of them were freshmen, in deliberate mimicry of a spirit outgrown but never renounced. As he swung the wheel and the car kicked up gravel, it seemed that it was trying to hurl that past self at the future, instead of what he had become—as though it offered more resources.

Tom, too, was looking for courage, but not in that way.

They went to the railroad station. Tom was to have the use of the Cadillac while Liam was in Europe. Liam pulled out his bags.

"Tell Mary I'll be in New York as soon as I can," said Tom.

"I will. And look after yourself."

"You're right to do this."

"Am I now?" Liam grinned, to find a way out of being more emotional. "I'm glad you think so."

Tom put out a hand and they clenched. What might once have been a fraternal gesture seemed to assume a political image, from the distant world of mass allegiances, where raised arms and clenched fists were on the march. In the railroad concourse only Farrio's man noted it.

In the parlor car there were several men Liam knew. He felt oddly weightless talking to them about the stock market and Joe Kennedy. They were not very clever men, but they did one thing well; they carried their tight little knowledge with them like a portmanteau and were impervious to ideas beyond it. New York, because of its internationalism, was a dubious place to them, a place where—as they complained—you had to watch out for the Jews. They were men who always went back to Boston. Liam wasn't sure he ever would. He told them only that he was going to Europe, and to them that was enough to generate half an hour on Europe's unreliability as a place for business.

By the time he reached the hospital he had forgotten them as easily as the drinks he had had.

□

The last of Mary's operations was done. She was well enough to be on her feet. She met him at the elevator, displaying her recovery.

"See," she said. "What do you think?"

He thought that in the long pleated skirt, blouse, and cashmere cardigan she could have passed for a Radcliffe girl again. It was not easy for him to take.

"Where is the string of pearls?" he said.

"Liam! What about *me?*" She took his arm aggressively. "Don't you think I'm—"

"Ravishing. You're ravishing, Tiger."

As she took him down the corridor, there was no one else in view and they felt more than either was ready to put into words. She tightened her grip on his arm. Just before they reached the room she stopped and released him, flicking a wave of hair clear of her brow.

"Liam. You're very dear to me. You do know that?"

He wanted to keep her there like that, with that intensity showing against the clinical neutrality of the corridor, and he consciously tried to imprint the image like a negative. He waited for a second or two and then lightly kissed her without holding her.

Cordón was waiting in her room.

Liam knew immediately that they were lovers again. Beside them he felt desiccated.

Cordón shook his hand. "It is a good thing that you are doing, Mr. Casey. Giles Pollard saved my life."

"Liam—please call me Liam, Nick."

Cordón was a confusion of manners: his accent had developed a slur of American, his hair had kept the Spanish gloss, but his jacket was striped seersucker over an oxford button-down. This invitation to drop formality was not yet customary. He tried it for sound.

"Okay, Liam."

Mary sat on the bed, betraying a trace of pain.

"Liam, how has your father handled this?"

"Jack? Jack has me guessing, as usual." He pulled up a chair. "Do you figure it? He couldn't have been a nicer guy. He called the Germans himself. Himself. There's a man called Heidel who has some leverage with Franco. The wheels are in motion."

"No. I don't figure it."

"Well, I do have a suspicion. I guess he hopes that once I see the other side in action I won't waste any more time with the reds—like you."

"Some chance." She looked at him quizzically. "You do *look* their type. I guess you have to play along with it."

"I'm not sure I want to look their type, Tiger."

"Just kidding." She turned to Cordón. "Nicolás, what do you think of the chances?"

"Of finding Giles?" Cordón hesitated. "It is difficult for me to know. He is English. If he was Spanish he would be dead. With the English they are sometimes more careful."

"How much say do the Krauts have?" said Liam.

"The Germans? It will depend on where he is. The Germans and the Italians are usually, from what I am told, they are usually running the war."

"How much longer before you get out of here?" Liam asked Mary.

"Abe is saying a week. I'm healing okay—he's done wonders for me, but it's not a pretty sight."

Cordón looked at her with transparent attachment.

"But then," she said, "what you don't see you don't grieve over. I'm going to be selective in the use of mirrors."

"Will you go back?"

She looked up at Cordón. "Yes. Yes. We are going back. It isn't over. I think we can win."

"Not without the Russians," said Cordón.

"How do you feel about that?" said Liam.

"I do not like it. What choice do we have?"

"*Jesus,*" said Liam, "I get so mad at FDR. What the hell side *is* he on?"

"Ah," said Mary, "maybe he doesn't know."

"He knows."

"He should listen to his wife."

"Not this year. He's already thinking about the midterm elections."

□

This swift interchange was too arcane for Cordón. It also showed a remnant of their old private language. Mary stopped and drew back from it.

"I wish I could come to the pier, but I can't," she said.

"Just see me to the elevator."

By shaking hands with Cordón again he won the consent to have her to himself as he left. Until they reached the elevator they were silent, and did not touch.

Then she said, "Liam, you seem careless. Please don't be careless. *Promise* me."

He was finding it very hard again. With the elevator beginning to answer his call he kissed her on the brow.

"Don't worry about me."

"Until."

"Until."

Nothing ahead of him, he thought, could be as painful as this. He left wondering whether she had seen through his defenses. He could not tell. But she was right about one thing. He did feel careless with himself. Reckless, even.

■

Oberstleutnant Dietrich was true to his word. He remained with his captives until they were delivered to a prison camp thirty miles behind the lines. It was very unlike Alcalá's camp: the main building was an old barracks. The place was overcrowded, the sanitary arrangements primitive, the food mostly beans. But there was a yard to exercise in, and a joint command, a Spanish major and an Italian captain. The Italian was the restraining hand. He kept the regime on military lines, which included scrubbing and cleaning the quarters for the first time since they had been converted to a prison. And during the day prisoners were driven out on road work details where, if they were lucky, they could find bread and wine. Only International Brigade prisoners were held there.

The barracks was on the fringe of a village. When Pollard left on his first detail he found hardly any evidence of the war. They were in a backwater.

The Italian, Captain Malvetti, was anxious to learn English. He picked out Pollard as a tutor when it was discovered that Pollard spoke Italian. Three evenings a week Pollard would be escorted to a house in the village where Malvetti and five other Italians lived. For two hours, sharing the captain's wine and, occasionally, his food, Pollard was able to forget that he was among fascists.

Of the six Italians, Malvetti seemed the most intelligent—as well as the most regal in pretensions. There was, however, a mean streak in Malvetti. Some of the prisoners were Italian communists. They were put in a separate block and given the most squalid duties.

One night Pollard raised this. They had never discussed politics before.

For a moment Malvetti became hostile.

"Why not? Why should you care about them?"

"All prisoners should have equality."

"How can you be a communist and a lord? Tell me."

"I gave up being a lord."

"Then they gave up being Italians when they became communists."

This sophistry inflated Malvetti with truculent assurance, and his five compatriots nodded in agreement.

"They should be treated equally."

Malvetti examined Pollard with ferocious eyes. "You may think you are not an aristocrat anymore, but I know better. That is why I have you in this house. You talk of equality, but you come here and you drink my wine."

"You are right, Captain. I should not come."

And that was the end of it. Pollard never went there again, and Malvetti searched in vain for another instructor.

A week later, when Pollard was summoned to the Spanish commandant, he expected a reprisal. But Malvetti was not there.

Dietrich was.

The Spaniard, Major Blas, kept Pollard standing between his escorting guards while he consulted a file.

"You were first a prisoner at Navalcarnero?" he asked.

"I was."

□

"You are charged that in the course of escape you murdered Major Felipe Alcalá. You shot him in the back. Three times."

Pollard stared at Blas as though paralyzed.

"You understand what I say?"

"It is not true. The camp was—"

"Be silent. I have a report. Major Alcalá was shot three times in the back. I have a photograph of the body. There is no doubt. You were the last person seen with him."

Pollard looked from Blas to Dietrich. "It isn't true. He was killed by—"

"Be silent," screamed Blas. "Put him in irons."

As he was led out he passed Malvetti's open door. Malvetti did not give him a glance.

■

When the SS *Washington* docked at Hamburg a car was waiting to take Liam to a plane, and the plane took him to Berlin. Freda Eichberg met him at the airport.

"Mr. Casey, welcome. How nice to see you again."

"Miss Eichberg. Things really seem to work in this country." Liam looked at his watch. "Just two hours ago I was on the boat."

"Things work for people with your connections. Did you have a pleasant crossing?"

"Just fine. But I'm not sure about those connections you think I have."

"You see those two men?" She nodded toward the porter who was taking Liam's bags. Behind him were two men, conspicuous for their identical raincoats.

"Yes?"

"There will be men like that wherever you go."

"Now you mention it, there were guys like that when I checked through immigration."

"Just so. You are being well looked after."

"They don't look friendly."

"Don't stare at them."

"I don't need it."

"Mr. Casey. Someone has decided that you should think well of us. Don't make it difficult."

"I'm sorry." He saw that she was nervous. "I guess I should appreciate it. If it's really going to help."

"Yes. Herr Heidel wants to help you. Please. I have a car."

She drove the Mercedes herself.

"Is Berlin what you expected?" She said, as they went into the city.

"Listen, Miss Eichberg. Can we speak openly?"

She seemed to concentrate on the driving for a few seconds.

"This is perhaps the one place," she said.

"Yeah, well—I don't intend to make it difficult for you, Miss Eichberg. But I have to say that if the price of all this cooperation is for me to declare my everlasting adoration of Adolf Hitler somebody is going to be feeling shortchanged."

She was silent again for a while.

"Mr. Casey, nobody is going to threaten your moral virginity. You are free to think what you like about the Führer—free, because you are merely in transit. I would appreciate it, nevertheless, if while you are here you observe all the courtesies." She looked at him. "I'm sorry, but I have to say it."

Liam pulled out his pipe and pouch and began pushing the tobacco tightly into the bowl, checking his temper. "I guess I deserved that," he said.

"Yes. You did."

He lit the pipe and said nothing more, looking out at the clean streets and the well-ordered people. He had a recollection of her looking across the table at him in Biarritz. She wanted him to take her as a governess; okay, he would go along with that. But she was the only woman he saw on the whole trip driving an official Mercedes, and he had to wonder why she was able to do that.

She took him to the Adlon, where his suite was baronial. The two watchers were nowhere to be seen.

"I will return at eight," she said. "You are to dine here, with us."

"I thought Herr Heidel was in Spain."

"He is. He is in Burgos. You will find that everything possible is being done."

"You make it sound simple."

"Then I'm sorry. It is not at all simple. No, not at all. Until eight, then."

She left a scent of lavender in the room—a mismatch, he thought, for so avid a figure. Nothing so far had been left to his initiative; he disliked that.

Precisely at eight she appeared at the suite, with someone behind her.

"Mr. Casey, may I introduce Oberstleutnant von Klagen."

Von Klagen bowed formally.

"Come in, please," said Liam too enthusiastically, giving von Klagen more of a pull than a handshake, already out of patience with their formality. "I'm having champagne. Would you join me?"

Freda kept her mask, but von Klagen was more impulsive.

"I think so," he said.

"Not for me, champagne," she said, giving von Klagen a cautionary glare.

"Something else?" Liam waved to a table bearing a variety of drinks. "Vermouth? Gin? Whiskey? On the house."

"Just water, thank you."

When they were seated she said, "The oberstleutnant—"

"Walther, please," cut in von Klagen as he took his champagne.

She began again, irritated. "Walther will be flying you to Spain."

"Yes," said von Klagen. "We leave in the morning, if that is convenient."

Liam laughed. "Convenient? I'm not a tourist."

"Very good. Mr. Casey, may I ask a question?"

"Sure can."

"What is so important about this Englishman?"

"Tell you the truth, I didn't want it to be such a big deal. All this high-powered treatment, I guess that's my old man's work. Maybe it's getting out of hand."

"But," said Freda Eichberg, "what is his importance?"

"Hell, he's a friend. I'm doing it for his—for his family."

"Not many communists have such friends," she said, unable to conceal her sarcasm effectively.

"Oh, you know he's a communist?"

She was fleetingly disconcerted. "That is what I understand."

"I have an idea," said Liam, "that no one would be more surprised than Giles Pollard to know that we're moving mountains to save his skin."

"He is fortunate," she said.

"We have not found him yet," said von Klagen.

Feeling slow-witted, Liam was suddenly and pertinently sober enough to divine that all was not what it was supposed to seem in the relationship of von Klagen and Freda. He was quite sure that they were lovers. The more she played the puritan the more obvious it became. Lavender had been replaced by something much more animal, and it was on von Klagen too. Liam began to smile mysteriously and to act even more gregarious. He should have seen through her before. She was so skillful at dressing to mask her body that he only now realized how good it was. Of von Klagen's part he felt less certain. Von Klagen's mobile eyes took in much more than they gave out, and von Klagen's capacity for champagne did not loosen his tongue; while Liam grew happily drunk over dinner he was alone. The other two seemed never to relax.

The next morning she drove him not to the Berlin airport where he had arrived but farther from the city, to a military airfield, and once through the gate directly to a plane apart from the others.

Von Klagen was supervising the fueling.

She stopped the car thirty feet away and they waited.

"That's some ship," said Liam.

Freda had said very little on the journey. Now she merely nodded.

Liam got out and walked over to von Klagen.

"A good morning for us, Mr. Casey."

"Yes. What kind of a ship is this?"

"A Heinkel, a Heinkel one-eleven."

"A bomber?"

"For the moment, no." Von Klagen was distracted by one of his ground crew. When he returned he said, "We have an extra fuel tank in the bomb bay. We will make the flight nonstop to Burgos."

□

The plane had no markings.

"It is not politic to land in France," said von Klagen. "We will go west and then south over the sea. We will fly over Republican Spain for very little of the time. We will be there in six hours." He looked at the sky. "Perhaps, with this wind, five and a half." He went to the plane and pulled out a bag. "Here, Mr. Casey, you will need this. Flying jacket, and parachute." There was a hint of humor. "You will need the jacket but not, I hope, the parachute."

As he climbed through the hatch, Liam could smell new paint, new metal—and the aviation fuel.

"You have a choice," said von Klagen. "You can go forward and lie in the nose, or take the copilot's position, above you, up the steps."

"I'll take the seat."

Freda stood with von Klagen as they watched Liam clamber upward.

"Sometimes, he is like a schoolboy," she said.

"Yes."

"Good luck."

"It will be some time, I think."

"I know."

"Well—"

There were too many eyes on them for more.

■

For two days—days of increasing heat—Pollard had been driven northwest with a score of other prisoners in a covered truck. They were chained together. The truck stopped frequently, but rarely were they allowed out of it. The sight of so many men urinating together caused merriment among their guards and anyone else who came upon them. The guards walked along the line looking at them and insisted that they always urinate into the wind so that it blew back into their already soiled clothes. Perversely, on the first evening, they were relatively well fed, with stew instead of beans. Only later was it apparent that the stew had been made from bad meat and all of them, through the night, suffered the consequences on a stone-floored barrack room.

Pollard was the only prisoner from the International Brigade. The rest were from fascist units who had been arrested for desertion. His singularity won no friends. Even to deserters he was still the enemy—*el rojo,* the red, and in their minds a cause of their plight.

The stops were caused by the truck overheating—they had climbed the pass through the Sierra de Guadarrama, and the load was too much. By the end of the second day they had covered much of the treeless tableland behind the sierra, and Pollard realized where they must be going: to Salamanca, the old Spain that had been with Franco from the beginning and was now his headquarters. Salamanca's fortress heart was reached by a bridge crossing the river Tormes. It was dusk as they passed into the city. They were taken to a massive sandstone bastion and then led from the truck down to medieval dungeons.

■

Von Klagen slipped the Heinkel down to follow the line of a river and out toward the inland plateau, over a highland lake and foothills dotted with villages and woven with rivers. There was another, lower, escarpment and then, in its lee, was the city of Burgos. They were turning to land.

"Five hours forty-one minutes," said Liam.

"Yes."

"Some ship."

The airfield was full of planes of several kinds, armed and all marked with a black cross on a white disk. They were not bunched, but dispersed. Von Klagen's plane was met by a small open car, which he followed to a parking point.

When Liam and von Klagen dropped from the hatch, the driver of the car was waiting.

"Rudolf," said von Klagen.

He shook hands with a sharp-featured officer of his own height—

they might have been twins. He turned to Liam, who was pulling off his helmet.

"May I introduce Rudolf von Moreau—Rudolf is our, what you would call in the United States I think, our ace. He is in charge of the experimental squadron. Rudolf, Mr. Liam Casey."

"Not an ace, just a pilot," said von Moreau, shaking hands and then turning to von Klagen. "Another Heinkel. They come too slowly. I think they want us to beg for them." To Liam he said, "Mr. Casey, your friend Herr Heidel is waiting for you at the hotel."

This, then, was the other side. Liam measured it against Madrid, and the comparison was disturbing. There was an air of determination and discipline—something in him responded positively to it. It was Jack Casey's voice murmuring about order versus chaos, the appeal of northern ways, the reverence for men who could make the trains run on time. Insidious though it was, he could not shake it off. Von Moreau and von Klagen, professionals who could have been products of West Point. Even the city of Burgos, unscarred, was part of the feeling. And then Heidel, too.

"Welcome, my dear Mr. Casey." Heidel read Liam's mind. "It must seem odd to you; very few people get to see both sides of any war."

"It—it is different, yes."

"I hope so."

The three Germans laughed.

Once von Klagen and von Moreau had gone, Heidel became amicable.

"It is good that you are here. I trust you were taken good care of in Berlin?"

"Sure thing. Tell the truth, I didn't expect things to move so fast."

"But you are an important man, Mr. Casey. I have made everyone here aware of the help your bank is giving. I do know where this man is."

"Pollard? *Where?*"

"It is difficult." Heidel was trying to maintain enthusiasm while being aware that he had reached a critical point. "I did not understand the true situation until yesterday. I thought he was merely a prisoner of war."

"So what's the problem?"

"Giles Pollard is charged with murdering a Spanish officer while trying to escape."

"What?"

"Naturally, the death sentence is automatic."

Liam sat down. "*Jesus!* I just don't believe it."

"He has been taken to Salamanca. I am trying to get more information. And I have asked for a stay of execution in order that you can see him. Frankly, I cannot do more."

"What about a trial?"

"A *trial?*" Heidel looked at Liam as though he came from another world, and then realized that he did. "A trial? In Spain? In war? All cases are settled personally by the Caudillo—by Franco himself."

"Then by heavens we'd better find out how much it costs."

"Costs, Mr. Casey?" Heidel's bromidic mood had evaporated. "I'm afraid it cannot be done like that; I am afraid you do not understand the Caudillo."

For the first time Heidel was beginning to see the father in the son. Liam was looking at him as though he, too, had a cash value. "No, it is not that simple."

"So what do we do?"

"There is another possibility. I believe your best course would be to see the archbishop of Salamanca. The archbishop knows of your family's standing with the Vatican, through Bishop Spellman. If you can persuade the archbishop, then perhaps the archbishop can persuade the Caudillo."

"You mean the appeal should be to God?"

"I think you are beginning to understand Spain."

"This part of it."

It became clear to Liam that an effort was under way to keep his mind distracted from the fate of Giles Pollard. That night the Germans organized a dinner for him, and the host bore a familiar name: Lieutenant Colonel Wolfram, Freiherr von Richthofen, cousin of the Red Baron. Von Moreau, von Klagen, and four other young officers were assembled.

Heidel introduced Liam.

Von Richthofen was something of a puzzle: he had the bearing of an aristocrat, but Liam noticed that his hands were coarse and as darkly grained as a mechanic's. His officers were in awe of him. When he was formal, so were they; when he was political they deferred; only when he was ribald were they relaxed. All three moods came in swift succession.

Liam introduced politics. "One thing greatly interests me," he said, looking across the table at von Richthofen. "I hadn't realized the extent of your commitment here. Why is that?"

"What would you say, Mr. Casey, was the greatest danger to the world at this moment?"

"Getting into a big war."

This annoyed von Richthofen, but he kept control. "The danger I am talking about is colored red. Maybe we can stop communism with a little war. Maybe not."

Heidel smoothly intervened. "We draw a line," he said. "Here, in Spain. We stop them here."

"Washington is a lot farther away from Moscow than Berlin, Mr. Casey," said von Richthofen. "That is the difference."

"Yes, well—" But Liam had no stomach for more, and the conversation drifted to the ribald as they drank on into the night.

"Mr. Casey," said von Richthofen harmlessly, "what are your recreations?"

Liam raised his glass. "Wine, women, and song."

"Ah well, you have the wine. I play the flute. And we have special arrangements here for the women. An excellent brothel for my pilots. We ensure that the girls are clean. Is that not so, Rudolf?"

Von Moreau seemed slightly embarrassed, but assented with a nod.

"So, Mr. Casey, you are our guest."

"You know something?" said Liam, fixing his eyes on von Richthofen in a way that drew the attention of the rest of them. "Never had a whore. And never will." He smiled benignly. "A whore is a whore, clean or not."

Von Richthofen looked like a man who had detected a fart. His face puckered and then flushed.

Heidel again saved the moment. "Mr. Casey has to meet an archbishop tomorrow."

□

When Heidel left Liam at his room he said, "You know, Mr. Casey, the American sense of humor is not a good traveler."

"It wasn't a joke, Otto."

Heidel hesitated.

"Otto, the man was offering me a whore."

This was not the son of the father. Heidel had to be careful. "I think we all had too much to drink, perhaps. I will see you in the morning."

They flew to Salamanca in a Junkers trimotor. It was a different kind of town, Liam soon discovered. The Gran Hotel had the mark of journalistic occupation, a well-stocked and populated bar, but what stood out was a raciness, almost a chic, that Liam hadn't seen in Madrid. There were glamorous and well-dressed women with eyes predatory for newcomers.

There was hardly time to take this in. A Spanish major was waiting for them, and they were driven into the fortress. The stone itself seemed repressive; it was a place that many men had entered and never left.

Heidel remained with the prison commandant. The major led Liam downward. Each level admitted less light and at the same time intensified sound. Incarceration, degradation, extinction—those were the layers of it. In the dead air of its core Liam's city shoes rang like jailer's boots. They reached a vaulted passage. The major was met by a corporal who led them to a cell and opened the door with a key the size of a pistol.

At first the light was too poor for Liam to see anything in the cell. The corporal unhooked an oil lamp from the passage and set it inside, on the floor.

Pollard sat on a stone slab against the rear wall. His feet were in chains. He blinked into the light.

"Giles. *Jesus Christ.* Giles."

"Who—who is that?"

"Liam—Liam Casey."

"Casey?" Pollard bent forward and then, pushing himself slowly from the stone with one hand, stretched the other toward Liam.

"Casey? Here?"

The chains dragged.

□

Liam took his hand and embraced him, feeling the offense of his own worsted against the tainted rags and the fetid moistness of Pollard's skin. He was surprised by the strength of Pollard's grip, holding, holding.

"Casey. So it is. So it is," whispered Pollard.

They were eye-to-eye in near darkness.

"I'm not broken, you know." He challenged Liam. "D'you see that, old man? I'm not broken." But there was something antique in his voice. He pulled at a lapel. "You're real, Mr. Liam Casey. Real. What are you doing here?"

Behind Liam the major and the corporal, neither of whom spoke English, remained at the open door.

"How did the bastards let you in?"

"Serena asked me to find you."

"Is she all right? I think of her always. You know . . . she's the finest of the Pollards. She is."

"She's okay."

"That's good."

"I have to ask you some questions. I don't think we have much time."

Breaking the embrace, Pollard pulled at a sleeve of his shirt and, with an effort, straightened himself.

"Questions?"

"They say you shot an officer."

"Rubbish. Rubbish. They've never—you know—they've—" He broke off, glaring past Liam at the two men in the doorway, seeing them for the first time.

"Giles. What happened?"

"Funny thing is, he did have three bullets in his back, but he was about to shoot me. Not a very good case, is it, old man?"

"How?"

"The place was bombed. That's how we got out. Ammunition went up like a bloody fireworks display. That's where the bullets came from. He saved me. Funny that."

"Did anyone else see that?"

"Somebody saw me with him. That was on their report. No chance to argue with it. They don't allow that."

□

"I'm going to get you out of here."

Pollard began to sag. He sat down again as though drawn down by the chains, and his head dipped.

"I'm going to get you out."

Pollard shook his head. "Good of you—good of you to try."

"I'm going to get you out. This is hell."

At this mildly expressed rage Pollard was able to raise his head again. "Hell? Oh, no. This isn't hell. It's degrading but it's not hell. Hell is to be in a place like this and to think you're wrong."

For a moment Liam felt the weaker of the two of them.

"I know I'm right," said Pollard. "They've made sure of that."

Pollard was no Lutheran fanatic seeing vindication in his chains. He was the epitome of what was supposed to be holy grace, but in his case it came from within himself, his last reserves, without mystical assistance. Liam knew he had no belief to match this; that was his weakness.

The major stepped through the door.

"Hold on," said Liam. "I'm going to get you out."

By the time he rejoined Heidel, he had tempered his anger into a metallic determination.

"He didn't do it. I want him out of there."

Heidel misjudged him. "I understand how you feel."

"I don't think so. I don't think you do. You didn't *see* him. The man is in chains. *Chains. Goddamned chains.* They've never given him a chance to explain. What kind of —what *kind* of a damned system is this?"

"Please—"

"These people are still in the Middle Ages."

Heidel looked nervously through the door to where the commandant was drinking coffee with an aide. "It will not get us anywhere to insult them."

"They are beneath insult." Liam grabbed Heidel by a lapel. "We have to get him out. He didn't shoot the officer. They were in a bombing raid, the guy was killed by exploding ammunition, *they have to know that.*"

"You are sure?"

□

"It took me two minutes longer to be sure of his innocence than it took them to be sure of his guilt."

"You must not talk like this to the archbishop. You must calm down."

Liam freed Heidel. "Yes, I guess you're right. Let's go see the archbishop."

But they were kept waiting until late afternoon. Then, arriving at the episcopal palace, they found that Franco had taken over most of it for his own headquarters. The gilded roof had been strung with telegraph wires. The courtyard and garden were patrolled by Franco's personal guard. If the ancient powers, the church and the state, were in alliance again, there was no mistaking who was on top.

Inside, the colors were by Velázquez—or, more exactly, it was a place where, as in Velázquez, the colors failed to come to color, they were suggestions: of ocher, of scarlet, of purple, of woods and silks and a face that was skull clad in parchment. The archbishop sat on velvet and they on oak.

Heidel had to interpret. The interval between pronouncement and translation heightened the ex cathedra tone.

"Yours is a family of distinction in our church," said the archbishop.

Liam looked suitably humble.

"Then tell me this. You come on a merciful mission, and I see mercy in your heart. But this man is a communist. Why have you such love for him?"

As Heidel waited, Liam had to reach for unaccustomed pieties.

"He is from a noble family, he is a personal friend, and I believe that he is innocent."

The archbishop inclined his head slightly to his left to hear Heidel out. He let the words rest in the air for his absorption before replying.

"He is a communist. Anyone proposing that the basis of Christian belief is a fallacy is out to destroy the whole mechanism of our life and society as God ordained them. For that reason alone the atheists must expect the church to muster all its powers to defeat them." He paused for Heidel to repeat this, and then continued, "We have an army that will prove that Christian fire is as remorseless as any. That must be."

"But Christianity must also show justice," said Liam sharply.

The archbishop seemed to find this an exotic thought. He gazed upward for a few seconds, took a long-drawn breath, and settled his eyes more acutely on Liam.

"Only believers can expect . . . justice."

It was a trap, and Liam saw it—"justice" had suggested to the archbishop something too mundane and progressive.

"If we show forgiveness to an unbeliever we may yet win his faith."

Heidel admired Liam's agility, and translated this solemnly.

The archbishop looked at his ruby ring, dull but still intense in the gloom.

"What is the evidence of this man's innocence?"

Liam told him.

"The Caudillo has already decided that he should die. If I am to intervene, I must be convinced that this is a soul that can pass into God's care. I am not convinced."

He waited again for Heidel, and then added, "It is only because of your own merciful nature and because of the piety of your family that I can persuade myself to consider this case at all. But I will raise it with the Caudillo."

Having translated, Heidel stood and bowed. Liam followed.

The archbishop nodded in a curtailed way, then, suddenly rising from the velvet, held out his hand for Liam to kiss the ring.

As Liam was about to withdraw, the archbishop spoke again—in English, but an English with an archaic Latinate pitch that rang like an incantation in the stone and veneers.

"We are not God. But we are Spain."

"Blessed be the Lord," said Liam.

The archbishop was motionless as they left.

"I congratulate you, Liam. May I ask—are you a believer?" said Heidel when they went down the steps.

"I've learned one thing. Cant has to be met with cant."

"But—"

"I am a Catholic, Otto."

□

"He is a different kind of Catholic, I think. The archbishop."

"Will he do it?"

"I cannot be sure. I think perhaps, yes." Heidel stopped. A black Mercedes came into the courtyard and the guards became rigid. In the shadows between the car and the door two men appeared, one towering over the other.

"Liam! That is the Caudillo. The small man."

Liam fleetingly saw a wide-hipped short-legged man in khaki, but no face.

"Who is the giant?"

"General Hugo Sperrle. The Kondor commander. A *peasant*."

"You sound like a snob, Otto."

"I have standards."

"I need a drink. Several drinks."

"I also."

The shared stress had brought them slightly closer. In the bar of the Gran Hotel they took a table and shared a bottle of champagne.

"Otto—do you like doing what you do?" said Liam.

"Why do you ask?"

"I don't like what I do."

Heidel began to sound paternal. "You do not, I think, realize how lucky you are. *One,* you are young. *Two,* you are rich. *Three,* you are American."

"And *four,* I am not a banker." Liam pulled out his pipe. "You didn't answer me, Otto."

"I do what I can do."

"I don't think that's an answer. You don't mind the pipe?"

"No. No, I do not mind the pipe, and no, it was not an answer."

"You know, Otto, you're like a man out of your time. Nothing is going to be how you want it anymore. Take that general, what was his name?"

"Sperrle."

"Guys like that are running your show. By your reckoning Hitler must be a peasant."

Heidel was uncomfortable. He took his time to reply. "It is a phase. We are going through a strange phase. The times produce the men, you know. Hitler. Mussolini. Franco. It cannot be chance."

"Too glib, Otto. The question is: why *do* people want leaders like that?"

"The old guard is dead. As you said, I am out of my time. I cannot explain it."

"That's—" Liam broke off. He saw a familiar figure walk through the lobby to the street, head held like a viceroy. "*I don't believe it!*"

Heidel followed his gaze. "You know him?"

"Sure thing. Had a swing at him in Madrid. A real jackass. What's he doing here?"

"Barrington-Taylor. Yes, I know him. He was expelled from Madrid."

They watched Barrington-Taylor ushered into a black Mercedes.

"Sperrle's car," said Liam.

"Yes."

"Well—I'll be dipped in shit."

□

22

CALIFORNIA

"And what the hell is that supposed to be?" asked Casey, not forcefully but in pained wonderment.

"It's a woman," said May Lindt. She straightened the frame of the picture and stood back from it while Casey regarded it from his bar stool. "I think it's just perfect in that spot. The California light is like Spanish light."

"If you say so."

"You don't like it?"

"I buy paintings as an investment. If I'm told the guy is undervalued—then it has a certain worth."

She turned away from the bright veranda and squinted into the shade where he sat. The slight puckering around the eyes and over the upper lip flawed her like a breeze lifting a veil.

He disliked being made to feel crass by her modish talk. "Looks like crazy stuff to me," he said.

"It's a Picasso."

"Yeah. Here, come have a mimosa."

When the two of them were in the villa in the Hollywood Hills, Casey drank more than usual. She didn't mind. The slightly ponderous "Come have a mimosa" was as near to being amorous as he ever managed. She took the drink and sat on a stool with one foot tiptoed on the floor and the other on the crossbar so the knee was up to her waist; the seersucker pool skirt rode high enough for him to see her pubic bush, as well-tended as the Japanese garden.

But he was jaded. California forced him into unnatural plumage. The flamingo villa, the orientalism of the garden, the scents and the servants, the sluggish air that was like an enveloping narcotic, and the passing parade—these things were paid for and suffered. So there was no stirring of his rogue limb when he was offered a sight of that golden pocket of pleasure.

"What is it, Jack? It's not just the painting."

"*Hell,* May."

"The place? You know, Jack, you don't get like this in Palm Beach. I don't see the difference."

"*You don't?* I'll tell you the difference. This is a place for people from nowhere. Palm Beach is a place for people from somewhere."

"It's important for me to be here, Jack."

"I know."

He was indulging her with less patience.

"Jack."

"What?"

"I have to get seen. You know, seen with the right people."

"Hell, don't we have enough of them here? Short of buying the studio I could hardly do more."

She put the knee down and sat with a pouting chastity. "You've been very good, Jack. But we don't get all the top people—people like Robinson, Crawford, Cagney."

"We get that effeminate dago who likes your fucking tits."

"He's a very old friend. I like to see him."

"What are you driving at?"

"You can get along with those people if you're smart. Speak their language."

"What language is that?"

"You know—they're—well—" She made an effort to play a part that she had practiced, assuming an ill-fitting solemnity. "—they have strong opinions on things, they're not just movie stars. They have *concerns,* take Chaplin—"

She got no further because at this name Casey erupted.

"*Chaplin?* Chaplin is a goddamned pinko pervert. You want to be seen with Chaplin? What *is* this? You—you damned bubble-head."

She tautened so much that for a moment she seemed paralyzed. But her arm lifted from the bar in a sharp swing and emptied the mimosa over his head. Then she stood and stamped a delicate foot with surprising force on the marble.

"*I am still loved!*" she screamed.

He grinned, dripping though he was. "You think you're Garbo?" In a deadly mimicry of her he said, "I am still loved. I want to be not alone." One line flowed into the other.

But stripped of her adoptive voices she at last found her own—and a lethal dignity. "This is Hollywood. In Hollywood *I* know the roles. In Hollywood you're just another dirty old man trying to buy a better class of cunt."

She walked out.

She kept a small notebook bound in pink leather with a gold-leafed inscription: "May Lindt, Her People." She had never let pass a name that might at some time prove useful. In eleven years they had been gathered in the book, using a version of her normally erratic script that was so condensed it resembled an ancient cuneiform. She leafed through the pages and found Father Thomas Aquinas Byrnes.

Sister Sarah, when the call came through, had heard of May Lindt—not only heard, but knew her every role. Thus disarmed, Sister Sarah explained that Father Byrnes was no longer resident. She gave a number in New York City—with a hint of wistful devotion and hoped-for salvation.

Tom Byrnes, when the California operator finally connected with him, was happy to be diverted from the vigilance of Nora Stern, whose office he was sharing.

"You remember me, Father?" purred Lindt.

He realized that she meant personally rather than professionally.

"Of course, Miss Lindt."

"I saw your advertisement, Tom."

"Not mine, Miss Lindt. I am just one of the organizers. But I'm glad that it's been noticed."

"Well, Tom, I feel the way you people do about the fascists." (She said "fayshists.")

□

"So do a lot of other people."

"I just want you to know, Tom, I would be happy to give my support to what you are doing. I feel *really* strongly about it."

"That's good to know. Can we expect you at our rally in Los Angeles?"

There was a theatrical hesitation, and then, "Well, yes, Tom, you can. You can include me."

Tom admired the subtlety of *include.* He could not suppress a smile before he replied. "That's fine, just fine, Miss Lindt. You'll appreciate, I'm sure, how important to us it is to have distinguished names like your own. Your name will help us to reach all your fans."

"Anything I can do, Tom."

"We're looking for this rally to raise a lot of money, Miss Lindt. A lot. We need dollars. So anything you can do to bring donations would be a fine thing." He cast a quick and firm eye at Stern. "You can say that this is strictly nonpolitical as a rally; all parties are welcome. What matters is the issue of freedom in Spain and how our government responds to it."

"I understand. Yes. Nonpolitical. Is—is Mr. Chaplin going to be there?"

"We certainly hope so. But—and I know you'll appreciate this, Miss Lindt—we're not asking our more famous supporters to speak or to sit on the platform. We think they should just come as ordinary citizens and sit where they wish."

There was another hesitation, and then she said, "Oh sure, Tom. Sure. I guess we can't dodge the cameras, though."

"No, Miss Lindt—but I'm sure you've gotten used to that." Without betraying his amusement he added, "I wonder, would it be possible for us to use your name with the others in our advertisements?"

"Oh, of course," she said—too quickly.

"Well, I'm very obliged to you, Miss Lindt. I look forward greatly to seeing you again, in Los Angeles."

After he put down the phone Tom sat back and shook his head. "I wonder—I wonder. We do have to be charitable and believe in the highest of motives, I'm sure. But the last time I saw that lady she was surrounded by some of the most reactionary people who walk this good earth. *May Lindt.* May Lindt against the forces of darkness. I don't know."

Stern was curt. "A whore."

"That's true." He shook his head again. "The fact of the matter is that even a practicing harlot can do a little good just by showing her face. It's not to me a question of Christian charity—" He broke off to flash a mischievous eye at Stern. "—as much as the natural broad-mindedness of the mendicant."

"You're a funny kind of priest."

"Ah yes. It must look like that to you."

"You've never considered giving it up?"

He was surprised to detect the unwelcome personal interest. "No—no, I never have. I never have. It's a vocation, you see."

She stiffened to her usual consistency. "No. I don't see. What I see is a first-class mind working inside an archaic postulate."

"Oh, that's what you see, is it?" He got up and brushed his coat. "Well, to be sure, it's one of the curiosities of the Spanish civil war that it is able to unite such a combination of forces as ourselves—the holy and the unholy, against the diabolical. I think that's more to do with the eternal verities than our respective personalities, Nora."

"You're a silver-tongued anomaly."

"And you're a very faithful servant of a false god."

"I'm hungry."

"How can anyone eat so much and stay so thin?"

"I'm paying. It's my treat."

■

Mary had never seen Abe Sachs in natural light. Walking with her and Cordón in Central Park, Sachs presented a leonine and different aspect. All the reservation of the surgeon was gone; he strode out like a man to whom everything was worth noticing, from the age of the granite outcrops to the types of birds nesting by Sheep Meadow.

"Without the park," he was saying, "I would not tolerate Manhattan. It was a work of vision, to put it here before the barons could buy the land."

Cordón looked over to where someone was horse-riding. "I would like to do that—to ride a horse through New York."

Sachs laughed. "Not up Fifth Avenue." He, too, watched the rider. "Time was when I could do that."

"Why can't you do it now, Abe?" said Mary.

"No time. Someday, a farm in the Berkshires. When I'm too senile to get on a horse."

"*Oh, Abe!*" She took his arm. It was a day too easily exclusive of care. The three of them seemed like everyone else. No far bugle could be heard. But Cordón never dropped his restless, reined-in look. The horse had suggested where his heart was.

"Not tired?" said Sachs.

"No," she said, though she was.

He slowed down without challenging the lie. "You'll do," he said.

"Abe, I don't know how to—"

He put up the intercepting hand she had grown used to.

"Now let me tell you something," he said. "It's been an education to be with you people. I live in a cocoon up there. Most of my patients remain only bodies to me. Listening to you, and watching you, I've opened up my mind again. Got a little air. Now, when I read the *Times* on Spain it doesn't seem a far-off irrelevance to me. Tell you, I think we are all being too damned casual about the drift of things over there in Europe. If you're a Jew you have to worry a little more than anyone else."

"Tell Roosevelt," she said.

"*Roosevelt?*" Sachs grunted. "What does *he* know?"

"You a Republican, Abe?" she said impishly.

He stopped. "*Me?* This is *New York,* lady."

Standing there with his imperfectly anchored tie, his gut pushing at his shirt, and his trousers stopping short of his ankles, he was spilling enough energy for a man half his age.

She kissed him on a cheek. "Sorry," she said.

"You know," he said, "you're the first real redhead I ever knew. Won't forget you." Then, winking at Cordón, added, "Free for dinner?"

□

"Am I officially released?"

"I'll write the release. Tomorrow. Tell you, don't go crazy. You'll tire easily."

"But I can go to California?"

"The slow way. On the train."

"I am free for dinner."

"Let's take a walk over to the Plaza. And bring your friend."

■

Miriam closed the partition between herself and the chauffeur as the Rolls-Royce pulled up outside First Cape National. Byrnes stood there like a windblown sparrow. Too lacking in poise to wait until the chauffeur came around to open the door, he slipped clumsily into the car.

"Windiest corner in Boston," he said. "Always was."

"Yes." She looked over gold-framed lenses. "You're working too hard, Pat."

"Me? No." He patted the ruffled hair. "No, Miriam. I don't truly believe I am."

"You should leave Jack something to do."

The car moved into the lunch-hour traffic, with others giving way to it.

"Jack does the work only Jack can do."

"Yes." She pulled a glove more tightly up to her elbow. "Yes. That's always been the problem."

Byrnes did not enjoy this kind of wit. He had no talent to respond.

"You must relax a little, Pat. That's the point of this little lunch. *I* want to see the *old* Pat Byrnes."

"Hmmm."

"The bishop thinks Tom will get over this nonsense. I think he—the bishop—is being most considerate."

"He is."

"So can we please forget all that plagues us?"

Suddenly and surprisingly he smiled. "Why not?"

She patted his knee. "I'm going to Venice. You should come."

□

He piously regarded the hand that had come to rest on his knee.

"Couldn't do that."

"I've arranged for you to see my doctor. I think it would be easier than you think."

"Doctor?"

But the subject was closed. She withdrew the hand and sat back.

"I did want Liam to come. No hope of that now, of course. But once he's home I'm sure you can hand everything over to him."

"Liam?"

"Do stop asking questions like that and do try to look just a bit interested."

■

The train had revealed other Americas to Cordón: prairie, desert, Rockies, and now a strange, half-familiar place giving views of the sierras, lower hills, and a palm-dotted littoral. And all the time he was moving farther from where he should have been, another three thousand miles farther.

"It's worth it, my love," said Mary, touching his hand and reading his mind.

The train's shadow absorbed colors and became blue-green.

"Yes. I know."

"We will be going back soon. You're a very good fund-raiser."

"Other people can do this. Other people—"

"No one else can speak from your experience."

He closed his hand on hers. "Together we are very good."

"Yes, we are."

Together they had become known in their group by his colors—the Black and the Red. Cordón always wore black now.

The conductor called out the imminence of Los Angeles.

She still had trouble standing. He held her by an arm.

The station gave the first dreamy breath of what was to become a balmy, subtropical caress during day and night. Like the air, the light had a lack of sharpness. Edges were never quite defined. Sun fell into the station as into a cathedral, in beams of intercepted and softened brilliance. And Mary had a sense of herself being diffused: it was all too lacking in contrasts, the kind of disharmonies that made New York so vibrant.

There was a car waiting, a convertible so long that it could have been a boat, drawn up in the concourse with a liveried driver on hand. An army of redcaps scooped up every piece of luggage. Even her camera. Cordón fell mute and grasped her arm as though in fear that they would take her also. The owner of the car had the manner and girth of a plantation baron; he wore a white vested suit and wide-brimmed straw hat. Mary almost expected him to spit tobacco.

He advanced, white buck shoes an andante on the marble.

"Miss Byrnes? Señor Cordón? Don Chambers."

His hand was pink and warm.

"Welcome to California."

"Thank you."

Cordón, still dumb, nodded as the hand came to him.

"My friend Mr. Dann told me to take great care of you." He concentrated on Mary as though searching for physical damage. "I have to see that you have every comfort. I have instructions that you are not to tire yourself." He seemed less and less convinced that she was in any way impaired. "And I am reliably informed that such an ease of habit is not your normal disposition." Finally he grinned—a great and embracing grin forewarning of inescapable hospitalities.

Whitewalls and curling chrome exhausts, buttoned hide and ivory steering wheel, walnut dash and fitted blue pile carpet that deadened the road, and the smell of the hide as they drove in the sun; they floated to the house on the edge of Pacific Palisades. Borne rather than driven. And Chambers on the jump seat, facing them, pointed out all the landmarks of the lotus-eaters.

Finally Cordón said, "What is the work here?"

"The *work,*" repeated Chambers, confronting the question slowly. ". . . well, the work is plain hard to see from here." The car was climbing the Pacific Palisades with a view of the bungalows on the beach. "Out in the valley there is agriculture." He acknowledged the asperity in Mary's eye. "It falls short of paradise. Then there is oil. Construction. This part of the state is late in blooming. That leaves Hollywood. Hollywood is work, I guess."

□

"I see no poor people," said Cordón.

"Oh, they are here," said Chambers. He pulled his vest more securely over his belly, and allowed gravity to take over his face. "My position may, I appreciate, seem something of an anomaly to you people. I'll put it as plain as I can. Miss Byrnes, I don't know that you are aware that you write for my magazine."

"*Your* magazine? *New Nation?*"

"I'm a kind of sleeping partner. There is not a snowball's chance in hell of that magazine ever being solvent, on account of its basic opinions. I happen to hold those opinions myself, and I can afford their propagation. Hearst, I do believe, has an easier time with his contaminated opinions."

She could not mask her unease.

"Ike Mandel," said Chambers, leaning forward against the angle of the climbing car, "is not a bought man, Miss Byrnes. I never touch a word in the magazine."

"No—I didn't think Ike was a bought man."

"But you can't square the magazine with me." It was a declaration rather than a question and he had her right. "That's not so offensive to me and it's to be expected of you. I hope that in the course of the next few weeks here as my guests you'll come to understand the lack of apology in my wealth and the sincerity of my opinions. Miss Byrnes, I read your article on the life and death of the pilot, and I sincerely hope that you will practice your honorable profession and your considerable gifts for many years to come. You will not be short of the opportunities. And now, if you please, we are at my home and you are to allow yourselves something I believe neither of you people have had anything like enough of—a few of the creature comforts."

■

Farrio's room was airless and thin-walled: intimacies carried even through the plumbing. Pea Coat's room was worse. The two of them sat in the light of Farrio's one window.

Farrio moved air with a folded newspaper. "Hypocrites," he said.

Pea Coat (now in rucked cotton) said, "I don't get it. I just don't get why a man like that plays around with pinkos."

"You see the advertisement? They're gonna have half of Hollywood along. I tell you, everybody is on the bandwagon now."

"No point in taking names."

"Dutton doesn't like it. He thinks they could begin to turn things around."

"This is a shit hole."

"The tab on this job is getting noticed. *Jesus,* what a fuckin' dance."

"Not a lot to show for it."

Farrio gave up with the newspaper and lit a cigarette. "I don't agree. It doesn't look productive right now. Have to remember this is foundation work. Later, it's all gonna be very useful background."

"Later? Later we'll be too old."

"No. Don't think so. This work has a future." Farrio convinced himself and moved on. "What we have to do here is to give them a scare. Stop it looking like the kinda show you can take your kids to."

"How do we do that?"

Farrio stood up and pulled the wet shirt free of his spine.

"Plenty of bums in this town looking for work."

Liam could not shake off the memory of Pollard in irons, not even in sleep. In the dream, the vision of Pollard overlapped with the archbishop, the archbishop's inquisition, the archbishop's effeminate eyes searching him for weaknesses that could be attacked, making him feel accountable for unnamed transgressions—touching that seam of guilt that was always there, guilt without reason. There was a chain clamped cold to his own legs.

Someone knocked urgently at his door.

It was bright morning. He pulled himself out of bed.

Heidel's face was as bright as the day.

"Good news," he said. "Pollard has been reprieved."

"He's free?"

"No. Not free. They want to exchange him for one of their officers held by the Republicans."

"Can they do that?"

"It has been done before. The exchange will be made at Gibraltar, with the British taking Pollard."

"How long is it going to take?"

"I am not sure. You should be pleased."

"Yeah. I guess so. Feel like hell. The archbishop delivered."

"To your credit, Mr. Casey. I think they see that it is good for them, too."

"Yeah, they'll make it look that way. That's the price."

"You can see him once more, before they take him south. They have moved him from that place and taken off the irons."

Later that day Liam was driven to a barrack block at the edge of Salamanca—it turned out to be an officers' barracks.

Pollard was in a dormitory—to himself, with one guard on the door. He was lying on a bed, head propped up, reading a book. Already he seemed to have gained color, though he was still gaunt.

"I don't know what you did or how you did it, old chap, but you saved my life. Funny thing about it is, I can't believe it. It was all—all too fast."

Liam motioned for him to remain on the bed, and sat beside him. "It surprised me."

Pollard looked him over sagely. "I hadn't realized quite what influence you had."

"It's Uncle Sam."

"Is it? Is it? And which side is Uncle Sam on?"

"He's neutral."

"Ah." Pollard closed the book and laid it down. "They gave me this. An extraordinary work. *Mein Kampf.* The faith and policy of Adolf Hitler. Difficult to remain neutral about ideas like those."

"They say I can't come with you. I wanted to."

"That's all right, old man. You've done enough."

"What will you do—when you get to Gibraltar?"

Pollard looked beyond Liam to the door, which though closed conveyed the presence of the guard. "Let's cross that bridge when we come to it, shall we?"

"I'll make sure Serena knows."

"Do you believe in God, Liam?"

"Why do you ask me that?"

"Something in your face. You have the look of a believer."

"I guess you should know. I saw the archbishop. It was the archbishop who intervened with Franco."

Pollard's haggard features seemed all the more interrogatory. "Was it? *Was* it, indeed? You *do* have influence."

A lot more should have been said, but not there, not at that time. They both had to concede that.

□

"Well," said Liam, standing up, "I hope I see you again."

"I have a feeling you will." Pollard pushed himself up from the pillow. "I'm sorry. I owe you a great deal. I haven't been very good at showing it."

"You owe me nothing." Liam took his hand. "What I've seen here has been an education. An education that came late."

As Liam left Pollard, he realized that he had for the first time seen the common thread in the brother and the sister, perhaps more acutely than they knew it themselves. And he heard Serena's words, in her letter to him, "I thought your path to atonement might begin in that hospital in Madrid" and wondered how much she had told Giles.

"Well, Liam?" said Heidel smugly, waiting at the Gran Hotel.

"He's okay. He's okay."

"So. We can relax a little." Heidel took his arm. "It would be a good idea, perhaps, while you are here, to see the war from this side."

Liam looked at him sharply. "That sounds like my father's idea."

"No. It is a courtesy. I am sure you can appreciate that there is an anxiety that you have a balanced view."

"Just what do you have in mind?"

"I have to leave for Berlin. In the meantime arrangements will be made to get you to Lisbon, it is quicker to New York from there."

"And what do I do, in the meantime?"

"We return to Burgos. Von Klagen and his colleagues would like to entertain you."

■

When the Pacific sun began to spill into a double image on the water, the terrace of Chambers's house caught the fire in its banked flowers, and for three or four minutes suffused it.

Mary lay on a sun bed that Chambers had found especially for her: it cranked up to three different angles and took the weight off the spine. She tried to count the colors as they changed, and thought:

how do you define a color like vermilion? Blue-red? It sounded like it looked. Anything seemed to grow here. There were more colors than she could name. Blacks and reds. The Black and the Red.

Cordón brought her a cocktail with as many shades as the flower bank.

"What is it?"

"Don calls it a sundowner."

"It—" She tasted it. "It's *delicious.*" She looked up and reached for him. "Don't you feel good? What are you drinking?"

"Cognac."

"You're not happy."

"I am happy to see you happy. But I cannot change—even with all this."

"No." She gripped his hand. "I don't want you *ever* to change. I was thinking how lucky we are to have so many good people—Don, Ike, Abe, Joe Dann, who make up for all the others who don't give a damn."

He took a chair beside her. "You want to come back to Spain with me?"

She put aside the drink. "Have you any doubt?"

"I have to fight."

"I know that." She sat up. "I know that. I know it will be different this time."

"There is nothing for me in Madrid. I will go where I am needed."

"Nicolás. I know. I *know.* And I, too, am going where the war is." She stopped. They could hear a car pulling into the drive. "You must not try to protect me, Nicolás. We both know what can happen. We don't deceive ourselves."

He leaned over to kiss her shoulder. "I will not ask that question again."

■

Von Klagen pulled his chin to his neck, puffed his cheeks, and opened his eyes to a mad, popping stare. "Physical fitness is the basis of every successful officer's career. *Push one-two! Up one-two!*" His neck turned bluish-scarlet. "You see, you fools? Duty, willpower, decisiveness, dedication. All begins with a fit body."

It was in perfect mimicry of von Richthofen—the voice sprang from the contorted face in a strident bark.

"It is essential that every effort be made to eradicate weakness."

Von Moreau raised his glass. "Duty. Willpower. And always check your undercarriage."

They collapsed in mockery.

"What do *you* think of our leader, Liam?" said von Klagen.

"It's a good impression."

"Ah," said von Moreau, "our guest is too tactful."

"The man who does not go with whores," said von Klagen, returning to his own face. "You will be remembered for that."

Von Moreau laughed. "You must understand, Mr. Casey. Syphilis and gonorrhea are as dangerous to pilots as antiaircraft fire."

"So," said von Klagen, "you see that fifteen minutes with a clean girl for one hundred pesetas keeps a pilot flying."

"Very practical," said Liam. "Let me ask you, your own question. What do *you* think of your leader?"

Von Moreau watched von Klagen alertly.

"I think, Mr. Casey," said von Klagen, "our leader is bombing his way to a place on the General Staff. He knows that Spain is shit, but the man who looks good in Spain will get a real war to prove himself."

"A real war?"

The three of them sobered at the same instant.

From the next room in the hotel they heard lusty song through a paper wall.

A thousand miles from Hamburg
A lonely flying lad
Lies dreaming of the
Reeperbahn
And all the girls he's had . . .

Von Moreau looked at his watch. "Time for bed, I think."

Bawdiness and nerves on edge; orderlies carrying polished boots;

□

strong coffee and the smell of farts; waiting cars and the night dying into a day of brilliant clarity—Liam slept little that night and realized that something very big was under way. Heidel had left the day before. At the airfield Liam had been kept at a distance from the military area, and transparent diversions had been offered to him—an inspection of a captured communist tank, a tour of the cathedral, and, finally, the dinner with von Moreau and von Klagen. Bad weather, they had said, had kept them on the ground for a week. But now it was a bomber's sky. You could fly to Berlin over cloud but you could not bomb through cloud with any precision. Von Richthofen was a man who liked precision.

He went back to sleep. It was afternoon when he woke—was wakened by planes. The sky seemed full of them, pulling up over the town.

And then it was empty. It was warm enough to sit in the small courtyard of the hotel. He ordered coffee and lit his pipe. Burgos seemed a backwater again, the kind of place where his mother, making one of her grand tours, would take one look at the cathedral and leave. Nothing to collect. Hate had peculiar dynamics in his mother. She wanted to build around Jack Casey a museum to commemorate her own refinement; all her tours were made with their ultimate shipments of art in mind. Jack at bay, ringed by porcelain and jade. Liam had never settled his loyalty on her, and she still hoped. There was certainly nothing in Burgos worth buying for her.

Suddenly his thoughts were curtailed: Barrington-Taylor was standing there.

"Pipe of peace, old chap? Powwow?"

Barrington-Taylor was either tired or mildly drunk or both.

Liam waved his pipe at the vacant chair at his table.

Barrington-Taylor settled in folds.

"Bit under the weather. Gippy tummy. Dreadful food. Heard you were here. What do you think?"

"About—?"

"These Luftwaffe chappies. Isn't that why you're here, to take a look at their show?"

"If it is, they're not showing a lot."

"No." Barrington-Taylor summoned fellow feeling. "No. Very

cagey with me, too. Bring me here, but feed me scraps. I say, I would like some more coffee. How about you?"

Liam nodded.

Barrington-Taylor treated the waiter as he would have done a dog.

"I rather gather you have some high-level connections," he said, pulling out his own pipe.

"Nothing political. Just business contacts."

"Mmm. No bad thing, the way things are going. This is the right side for that. The Germans really know how to run a war." He sucked needily at the pipe. "They chucked me out of Madrid, did you hear?"

"Yes."

"Yes. Thing I can't stand is the man with untested opinions. In my racket you have to know the difference between likes and dislikes and opinions. An opinion should be formed by experience. Do you see? I mean, you might not much like the look of some of the chaps around Herr Hitler, they're all a bit *arriviste* for my taste, I can tell you, but one needs to keep an open mind. A weak Germany would be no damned good for Europe. A case of *realpolitik,* old chap. I'm quite sure we can moderate the coarser tendencies in Herr Hitler. Need to have a powwow or two, that's all. The essential thing is that we have an enemy in common. Comrade Stalin. Moscow purges. Now there's a bloodbath for you."

"There's barbarism here, too."

"Oh yes. Don't hold any brief for that." Barrington-Taylor nodded with happy vigor. "Just dragging themselves into the twentieth century, of course. Look here, a pity about that little bout of fisticuffs in Madrid. Got us off on the wrong foot."

Liam was depressed enough to concede. Barrington-Taylor's meandering platitudes had a soothing quality, and eventually the two men turned to cognac until the sun moved off the courtyard. Then both of them went back to bed.

The pilots returned in one riotous surge.

Von Klagen found Liam in his room.

"You were sleeping?"

"Too much brandy."

"I will take a bath. We will go together for dinner. A good day. Then, maybe, some women."

□

Liam got von Klagen more clearly into focus. There was something too effusive in him. An adolescent had replaced the contained and sagacious adult. The hotel began to sound like one vast locker room with the winning team in the baths.

"Sure. Why not?" he said.

■

Freda should have opened a window, but an instinct deterred her—as a child in a room very much like this she had felt more secure when street sounds were dulled by the overlapped chintz drapes. She remembered her mother coming in from the street, her face still like a lamp burning too brightly, and making her open the window. Even in spring her mother always wore the red scarf wound tightly like a choker around her high neck. The tail of the scarf was flung over her left shoulder, and the wind would lift it like a streaming pennant. She could always pick out her mother, no matter how dense the crowd as it came up the wide street past their house, and afterward, when it surged into the gothic square, she could see that pennant like a separate animated thing bearing the color of the people more brightly than the banners. First it had excited her. Then, gaining wisdom too quickly, she had grown fearful of those days when her mother went to march. The drapes had not totally screened her from the gradual change in the voices. As in a symphony advancing from tentative theme to a climax, projecting dissonance and consonance to resolution, it was possible to fit the first notes to the last. One day, not long before the end, her mother had looked up as she surged past the house and seen drawn drapes. When she returned she tore them apart and opened the window and only then looked at her and said, with intense love, "Freda, you must not be afraid." Weeks later the red pennant had fallen, probably picked out by a sniper grateful for such a good target.

Freda Wandel; Freda Eichberg—child without trace, woman without a past.

The drapes had the same smell of cigarette smoke gathered through the winter. The room should be aired. She opened the window from the bottom, pushing hard to break the fit of swollen wood. It moved suddenly and then stuck a quarter of the way up, where she left it. The street sounded hardly at all. Small leaves moved in the wind.

"I don't think so," she said, looking each way but holding herself back. "I think it's all in the imagination."

"I thought I saw them yesterday, the same car."

"It doesn't mean anything. Just looking for a house, probably."

The "probably" was an effort.

Gisela von Poellnitz sat at a small lace-covered table. She was reluctant to accept the reassurance, but said no more.

"Where will it all end?" said Freda, returning to the table. "Sometimes I feel my nerve going. I try not to take chances, but the temptation is always there." She sat down. "It cannot always be like this."

"So you want a predictable future?"

Freda smiled wanly. "No. No—I want to know that it is worthwhile, that is enough."

"You have had a success. You have made a difference."

"The thousand-year Reich."

"I have not seen you like this before."

Freda felt the weariness in herself. "Three lives to lead."

"You chose the third."

"Yes. It is madness. He is not coming back for a while."

"We need some madness, all of us."

At first Freda had thought of von Klagen as a dalliance, then as a useful part of her cover. Now he was more. And that was the cause of her dispirited mood.

■

As soon as Heidel came back from Spain Freda knew that he had scented something. He was untypically surreptitious. Several times she knew he had been looking at her when he thought he was unnoticed. It felt like someone had been through her desk. He was not very good at this and, with mounting impatience, she had waited for him to come to the point.

He had done so like a crab.

"Your friend von Klagen is very impressive, well thought of by his superiors."

"Yes?"

"It is a good idea to be careful choosing friends."

"Herr Heidel, are you talking to me like a father?"

He was annoyed, but made an effort to remain civil. "You know how much trust I put in you. You have always been dependable. Exemplary." He faltered, curiously unsure of where to step next. "As it is, there is an atmosphere around us, you know what I mean, an atmosphere where we do need to be careful."

"Careful? About Oberstleutnant von Klagen?"

"No." He saw through her obtuseness. "No. Of course not. I recall several times meeting you with Gisela von Poellnitz."

She went cold to the bone, but kept the same expression and—precariously—the same casual voice.

"Yes. You did."

"A good family, I know."

"Yes."

"Have you ever had cause to discuss politics with her?"

"Who can say they never discuss politics, Herr Heidel?"

He gave up the crabwise approach. "I think it would be wise for you not to be seen with her."

It was a sickening feeling now. "Why?"

"Take my advice. Please."

He was more personally insistent than he ever had been with her.

"It is good of you," she said.

He relaxed a little. "I am sorry to be the one to say it. God knows, we are all of us vulnerable. We are going through a strange phase."

He remembered using the same euphemism with Liam Casey, and the repetition of it underlined its moral bankruptcy. Freda, he unexpectedly recognized, was not merely vulnerable but, in her admirable poise, a very consolable young woman.

Deferring this fancy, he became businesslike. "Is the Du Pont file ready?"

She realized that her hand had left an imprint of sweat on the manila where she had gripped it. "I have a final check to make." She kept the hand in place. She felt simultaneously hot and cold.

"Yes—well, I want to study it tonight. What of the sailings for America?"

"There is the *Bremen,* sailing on Sunday, or the *Washington* from Hamburg on Tuesday."

"The *Bremen* is always full of *lumpen.* I will take the *Washington.*"

The following minutes seemed like hours to her, until Heidel went to his bank. Even then, she felt observed. It was absurd, because no one could be in the offices without her knowledge. The oppression did not need physical form. A net lay before her, awaiting one false step to trip it. She had to find a way to warn Gisela. Gisela had been right. Who was the weakest of them—and who the pursuer? Her own last refuge, once the others were warned, was Heidel. She had seen and read that single and swiftly suppressed flare of interest in his eye. Poor Heidel—a stranger still to the lawless night that had long since crept into every street. She changed the binder on the Du Pont file. Her handprint was as ineradicable as a stigma.

Heidel returned, took the file, and leafed through it as he stood over her desk. His fingers on each page expressed a manner of breeding: he had a head for figures but absorbed them dispassionately, the fingers never looked acquisitive. He nodded assent as he progressed; given that he stood to make a small fortune if these figures were correct, she marvelled at his detachment. He would avoid *lumpen* on the Atlantic and, in a way, that was why he could be so unperceptive about the regime he served. Heidel's failing was the dereliction of a whole class, deluded into mistaking brute force for will. Not "poor" Heidel. Stupid.

"Good," he said.

"I will book a stateroom on the *Washington,* then?"

"Yes." He hovered on a thought but left it. "Telegraph Mr. Casey. He will want to know my day of arrival. And Mr. Lammot Du Pont."

It was hard that evening to recover the sense of threat that Heidel had unwittingly conveyed. Berlin was warm and people were walking home instead of taking streetcars. The streetcar she took was unnervingly empty—only three other passengers. At the Tiergarten she walked for twenty minutes until sure she was not followed, and then took another streetcar back into the city.

The church stood in a corner of a small square, one of the medieval pockets left in Berlin, and only its spire was visible from where she left the streetcar. The church was reached through an alley, and walking down it was like going to a sanctuary. She went up the steps. The doors were open. Ahead of her the altar was lit from behind by a deep window of stained glass. Only the yellow and blue glass had any splendor. Otherwise the church was unadorned.

She avoided the center aisle and went to the left, through into the vestry. An old man in a black suit came from a passage with movements like those of a disturbed mole. He had thick white hair parted in the center so that it fell like a divided mat over his ears.

"Freda," he said, with bestirring interest. "Little Freda. We have not seen little Freda for many months, have we?"

"Dear Erasmus."

"Many months. You are taller now."

"Yes. Is Pastor Gregory here?"

He was muddled by associations. The interval between her childhood and her womanhood had been mislaid. He stretched himself so that his trousers rode up and revealed white socks. Then he reached out to take her right hand.

"Painted nails." Her palm lay flat against his. "Pastor Gregory will not like painted nails, child." His hand moved and closed on her wrist. It smelled of embrocation. "Erasmus will take you." He released her and led her along the passage he had come from and then up a spiral stone staircase. There was a short gallery at the top and a door at the end of it. Erasmus left her at the door.

"Go in," he said.

She knocked and went in. It was a library with one high wall; a gabled roof curved down to another wall half as high. Both walls were lined to the ceiling with books.

Pastor Gregory rose from a desk at the far end of the room.

"Freda."

"I'm sorry. I had to come without notice."

The pastor was, like his library, built on a bias. His left shoulder was lower than the right, his mouth and his hairline tilted in the same direction—he was like a man trying to keep balance on a listing ship. The left arm was withered and tucked into a jacket pocket. Yet despite this he was not frail. He came quickly from the desk and lay his good hand on her shoulder.

"What is it?"

"I made sure I was not followed. I want you to get a message to Gisela. They are watching her. I think they must have traced her letters. She should leave."

"Please, sit down."

His touching her had been slowly effective, a counterpoint to her tremulous torrent of words. He was a man of pacific force, able to absorb and neutralize her distress within those few seconds.

When she had taken the chair by his desk, he went back to his own place.

"How do you know this?"

"Heidel. Heidel warned me; he knows her only as a friend of mine, he suspects nothing more."

"What else?"

"Gisela had a feeling she was watched. I thought it was a false alarm. I can't go to her now."

"No. I hope you are safe."

"I think so."

He considered this in silence for a minute. Then he said, "You could go to Wollweber in Copenhagen. We could arrange that."

"No. There is no need."

"It is getting harder for us. We must not take risks." It was said not as a stricture but inclusively, all in the same ameliorating voice, a voice like an amplified whisper. "You are certainly your mother's daughter. Not my brother's."

"I do not remember him."

"An elephant, poor soul. Your mother took pity on him. Pity and certitude were her passions. As strong as a hurricane. She could not pity me. That was what made us incompatible."

"But she loved you."

"Of course. And I her." He smiled. "I was the rock against which her passions were useless. We were such a thing to hear. There was a day . . . a day when she had just heard Rosa Luxemburg, and I had convinced myself that I was the heir to Martin Luther." He tightened at the shoulders and rolled forward. "Such gods. Such a day." He ran beyond his words in memory before he spoke again. "You have all of that, but more—more animus. That is dangerous. They might see that in you."

"I will be careful."

"Yes," he said with a trace of doubt. "We will warn Gisela."

She had often wanted to prolong her time with him. The paradox was that although he knew this and knew his power to steady her, it was Gregory who always terminated the meetings. For the first time she suspected the cause: there was no real intimacy in this gift of his; he wished it to remain so, to remain above any charge of preference or partiality. She represented a reincarnation of something he could not trust himself with for too long. He could no more make a favorite of her than the withered arm could grow again.

She could only imagine, when the door closed on him, how much of this havoc he conceded to himself.

■

"No whore for Mr. Casey."

Von Klagen held a glass of champagne unsteadily. His shirt was open to the waist.

"No whore for me."

Liam could not recall how they had reached this room. He had preserved full dress; not even his tie was loosened. All his drunkenness was turned inward and gave the illusion of solemnity. They had eaten and drunk prodigiously. "No whore for me" was a declaration made to a curtain that was drawn across an alcove used for washing. He sat with von Klagen on one side of a huge baroque bed.

Von Klagen rose, and fell over one of his discarded shoes, spilling champagne.

"No whore for the American," he said, and pulled open the curtain. The brass rings grated on a rusted rail.

A woman, naked, was revealed. A fleck of rust fell on her shoulder.

She seemed sullen and stood with arms loose, like a wrestler before a clinch. She was oddly proportioned: short in the calf but long in the thigh, narrow-hipped, heavily busted, but with a swanlike neck and a full-lipped Moorish face.

"Special reserve," said von Klagen. "Finest vintage. Officers only and officially approved. Not public property. Not a whore. A lady of rare qualities. She will demonstrate."

He stepped aside with the flourish of a master of ceremonies.

Before Liam had fully concentrated on her, the woman sprang at him, into a double somersault, smacking hands into the thin carpet and ending up at his feet in a handstand with legs slowly spreading wider for balance.

Von Klagen's face was framed in the apex.

"You see," he said, "rare qualities. A fine acrobat."

The legs snapped together like a trap. She remained on her hands for a few seconds, then did a backward somersault ending with legs facing Liam and hands behind her on the floor so that she was positioned like a table. Her black hair fell in a wide span to brush the floor. Her stomach contracted and her hips flexed, making her breasts settle to each side. Her thighs, Liam noticed with a selective and fixed focus, had been developed to the tone of a man's. All her movements began with the thighs.

Von Klagen took the bottle of champagne from a sideboard and slowly poured it between her breasts. It ran in a bubble-fringed rivulet across her stomach, gathered momentarily as a pool in the navel, then flowed again into her pubic hair.

"Please," he said, "champagne and Black Forest gâteau. A fine dish. Taste."

The champagne had filtered through the bush and began to fall in a drizzle between her legs.

"Please," urged von Klagen as the bottle ran dry.

The woman's thigh muscles rippled with the strain of holding her position. Liam was suddenly aware of her strong, gamey smell, lifted in the effervescence of the champagne. He appeared to try to rise and move toward her, and von Klagen waved him on. But once his weight was on his feet he pitched forward from the bed and slumped to the carpet—comatose, and still wearing a look of bemusement.

□

■

Freda was closing doors behind herself. There would be people she could not see again. Not only Gisela von Poellnitz. It had all been prepared for: abandon the outer ring, and wait. Change as little routine as possible.

By the time she saw Heidel again she had done everything she could, and she felt surer of herself.

It was Heidel who was edgy.

"Have you reserved the stateroom on the *Washington?*" he said.

"Yes. It's done."

He pressed his hands under his chin as though in prayer. "What do you think—about the zeppelins. Are they reliable?"

"The zeppelins? I do not know, Herr Heidel. I have never been on a zeppelin."

"Last night I met a friend who works for the Graf Zeppelin Company. I happened to mention my trip to the United States. He told me they have not been able to fill all the berths on the *Hindenburg.* It is making its first flight of the season. He has been calling the press offering them berths."

"I have seen the *Hindenburg.* So big."

"Last year the *Hindenburg* made ten flights to New York without any problems. It would be an interesting change from water. To be aloft over the Atlantic. The accommodations are luxurious. No *lumpen.*"

"You should try it."

"Yes. I think so. You think it reliable?"

"I think so."

"It is insured by Lloyd's of London for half a million pounds at five percent. If Lloyd's have confidence in the *Hindenburg* I should also."

He seemed still unresolved about something and turned away from her to shuffle some papers. Then, and with rehearsed casualness, he said, "They have offered me one of the finest staterooms on the *Hindenburg.* Rather an extravagance for one person."

She did not choose to make it easy for him. "Perhaps Mr. Casey, Junior, would go, if he comes back from Spain in time."

"He is leaving from Lisbon," said Heidel with a trace of testiness, and then his annoyance fathered resolve. "What I am saying, Miss Eichberg, is would you like to join me on the *Hindenburg?*"

She played her primmest face, with no hint of salacity in her voice. "I have never been to the United States. I have often dreamed of it. And, of course, I am familiar with the Du Pont transaction. I am sure I could be of assistance to you, Herr Heidel. It is very generous of you to propose it."

"Well—will you?"

"Of course."

"Then cancel the *Washington.*"

She felt for a moment far from assenting to the idea of sleeping with him—she was being taken as a servant. He was brusque for the rest of the day as though, by being so, he preserved the facade of rectitude. She did not mind. He could have anything he wanted. To get out of Berlin at this moment and to get so far away was merciful. Laughter and champagne would do no harm.

□

24

Obscene verses in German echoed harshly in Liam's head. He pressed his head to the pillow but the chorus rang on. His mouth felt lined with soot. He reached out for water and, having gulped it, realized that the hotel was silent. There were no singing pilots. It was not yet dawn. And he was fully clothed. Reality soaked into him like a new pain. How many times had it been like this? The dark and cheap room in Burgos was like other rooms in the wake of drink. In the wake. The wake. Something was over. Strange how the mind logged impressions not heeded at the time. Now he had a very clear picture of von Klagen with the acrobat's legs framing him and saw what was really there. Helplessness. Von Klagen could not help himself. What was over was a prelude, something like the *Siegfried* Idyll. Wagner. Liam had argued with Mary about Wagner. Necromantic slush, she said. The idyll had a sound like wind in a slope of pines. He liked that slush. Von Klagen had been there. But now not. The interlude had given way to the full orchestra and chorus. Distant hills caught in lightning. Von Richthofen on the hill. Mary had said, "Hell is reached through Wagner's graveyards. Valhalla." There was pain of an irreducible voltage in hearing Mary. Laughing at him as she said it. Her mind against his emotions. What a rat hole this was. Finish it quickly, said von Richthofen, with his bucolic finger held aloft at the table. Not a good face. Pumped up from the neck at full pressure.

Thighs like the acrobat's. Champagne dripped like semen. Take off shoes.

Where were the fucking shoes?

He sat up. A man could be made ridiculous without shoes.

He went to open the window. The shutter swung suddenly and hit the wall, waking several dogs. Good air. Across the street one light was on behind a half-open window. A boot moved up and down at the wrong height for a leg. An arm in the boot and a cloth on the toe. An orderly preparing for the march of the gods. Valhalla.

His shoes were gone. Not in the room.

Later it amused Barrington-Taylor.

"I missed the party," he said, looking down, then up, Liam as he came into the lobby. "Rather glad I did, old chap, from the look of you."

"Have to find some shoes."

"Let's get some coffee, shall we?"

All the aircrew had already left the hotel. They had the dining room to themselves.

"Everybody was very much the worse for wear this morning," said Barrington-Taylor.

"Where were you?"

Barrington-Taylor was suddenly shifty. "Oh—trying to get some stuff to London. The phones are appalling. Of course, all the main international lines go out through Madrid—or did, so it's a question of getting through to Lisbon and then having stuff relayed from there." He paused to pour Liam's coffee. "Think this show will be over soon. Yesterday's little exercise should hasten the end. I say, your hand is shaking."

"It didn't seem little."

"Figure of speech. You going to hang on here?"

"Why?"

"I think we might be given a tour of the zone. Had a chat last night with one of the staff officers, quite cocky they are now."

"What do you mean? Go to the front line?"

"Question of catching it while it lasts. You would need shoes."

"I should be getting out."

□

Barrington-Taylor smiled. "They're working very hard on you, old chap. Are they wise?"

"I don't get you."

"I get the idea you're not impressed."

Liam was careful. "I didn't say that."

"No. You didn't."

The trouble with having taken Barrington-Taylor as a fool from the start was gauging the cost of the mistake. The English were always good at not seeming dangerous. There were layers of falseness born with them. Or bred into them? Liam felt at a disadvantage.

He went in search of shoes. The old concierge, a fat woman with kiss-curls plastered permanently to her brow like tribal marks, came out from behind her kiosk and examined his feet. She found them big—this she made clear with a hand movement and much shaking of the head.

As this left her nonplussed, a man came into the lobby and heard Liam trying to ask about shoe stores.

"Excuse me," said the man in a voice that reminded Liam of Pollard—it had the same English honey in it—"are you Mr. Casey, Liam Casey, please?"

Liam noticed particularly that the man had very fine shoes, black brogues, and a superbly cut dark gray suit.

"That's right."

"Allow me to introduce myself. My name is Julian Molero. Captain Luis Bolín sends you his compliments and has deputed me to escort you to the forward positions of the army."

"As you can see, I have no shoes."

Molero did not laugh. "I can solve this problem, Mr. Casey."

Shoes were found. Molero drove a Hispano-Suiza more suitable for the grand tour than for a theater of war. There was a large wicker hamper in the trunk with enough food and drink for a party. Molero displayed it while Liam loaded his bags.

"I do not like the northern diet," said Molero. "Beans, beans, beans. I never travel without proper provisions."

"I can see that."

"It will be good for you to get away from German tastes." Molero strapped down the trunk and nodded across the street to a line of Kondor Legion trucks. "They think they can ask for anything, those people. The iron ore, the iron ore—all the time that is what they ask. It is like asking a friend to your house for dinner and finding that he takes the cutlery."

"Doesn't look like a dinner party."

Molero didn't reply as he got behind the wheel. It was some minutes later, as they drove north out of Burgos toward the mountains, that he said, "The Germans can rehearse their war here if they wish. I have no complaint. But they cannot take Spain with them. General Franco is a great man and not a fool."

"Who is Captain Bolín? You said a Captain Bolín sent you."

"Captain Bolín takes care of our relations with the press and all our foreign friends. He was with us from the beginning. When we were just a few." Molero drove with his chin always thrust forward, as though conscious of profile. "He has met your father, I think."

Always that damned shadow. Molero had a knowingness of Liam's discomforts. Liam decided what Molero resembled: an under manager of a good hotel who pimped for the richest clients and knew the price of discretion. About twenty-eight, Liam thought, and likely to start going to fat in a year or two: that was why the chin was kept so proud. "When we were just a few." An opportunist who was lucky. He would know Juan March, so why had he not said so? Holding for future use. In spite of Molero's speed, Liam fell asleep thankfully.

He woke to find that they were parked in a town square. Molero was talking to two Spanish officers while the car was being refueled. Liam's neck was stiff where he had slumped against the seat, and he was overdressed for the heat. He got out and threw his jacket into the rear seat. The town was full of troops.

Molero returned. "The war is moving fast. We are going to Durango, but I am told that our forces are to the west of there now, pushing to Bilbao. Everywhere the enemy is in retreat. The line is changing all the time."

"Where are we?"

"Vitoria. To get to Durango we have to go through the mountains. We can be there by nightfall if we eat on the road."

□

Some time later, having been silent since they left Vitoria, Molero took one hand from the wheel, pulled out a map, and passed it to Liam.

"Can you read maps?"

"Sure."

"There was no sign at the last junction. Can you check the route from Vitoria to Durango?"

Liam realized that Molero did not read maps. He traced their route to the junction.

"Durango was the right fork. We took the left."

Molero was annoyed, and slowed down. The road had narrowed to go through a valley. There was a wooded slope to the left and a river gorge to the right. Molero found a cart track in the trees and began nosing up it to reverse. "This is an attractive spot for lunch."

The pines gave good shade from the heat.

Molero spread out a blanket and began selecting food from the hamper. Napkins were unfolded. Foie gras was sliced, olives divided equally between black and green, onions and lemons quartered. Wine selected.

"At one time," said Molero, "one could live quite well in Madrid. Not as well as in Paris, of course. I always hoped Madrid would become the equal of Paris."

With the foie gras in his mouth and the wine in his hand Molero tried to manifest his worldliness, but Liam gurgled the wine and wolfed the food, playing Falstaff.

Neither of them heard a step until five men surrounded them.

Molero was caught with a suspended wafer.

The men all wore berets and gun belts and battle dress. They leveled five rifles.

■

Freda wrote out the address: Max Winkler, Berlin W8, Post Schliessfach 81. Von Klagen had given it to her with the warning that as the clearinghouse for all mail to and from the Kondor Legion it was also a censorship filter. She had written in an unnaturally inhibited tone.

It might have been a note from a chaste cousin. It was no medium for lovers, and no medium for guilt. The guilt was unreasonable but there: the clumsy guilt of a novice lover, anticipating the embrace of Heidel. She talked of wanting to see America and of the novelty of going there by zeppelin. She tried to imagine von Klagen's reaction: his manner with her had slowly changed; in him tenderness was as illicit as treachery in her. She went cold at this thought of what was required to be German in 1937.

She sent new telegrams to America and received one from Boston confirming that Heidel would be met at the zeppelin field at Lakehurst in New Jersey, by Patrick Byrnes.

Heidel was an old woman about his wardrobe. He always took several trunks on a ship, but luggage on the *Hindenburg* was restricted for the sake of weight. He fussed about his suits. Was it cold on the airship—would she inquire? New York might be humid or it might be cool. Boston was always windy. He needed several suits for each eventuality. Evening dress could be comfortably worn on the *Hindenburg,* she reported. The staterooms were heated.

She bought herself two evening dresses which she considered modest enough for the role of traveling "secretary." It would alarm Heidel to show a bare back. Discretion was more important than fashion. She gathered her hair in a spinsterish bun at the nape of the neck.

But when they arrived at the airfield in Hamburg and went to a reception for the passengers, she spotted at least two other women who looked brazenly vampish on the arms of men more than twice their age. The airship's captain looked at her as though pitying Heidel for having such a plain companion.

The airship overshadowed all. "More than eight hundred feet long and nearly one hundred and fifty feet high," explained the captain.

A light wind sang in the mooring ropes. The *Hindenburg*'s engines were a dull throb from above. An official photographer asked the passengers to make a group before they went up the tower to board. They stood with the silver-edged shadow across them.

Heidel had already met a Swedish industrialist whom he knew

and scented more business in the making. It was going to be that kind of company: money, politics, and roving eyes. She smiled for the camera and felt the odd one out among them.

■

Major Rohleder was reading the next day's paper in bed when he saw the photograph. He had forgotten that the new season of zeppelin trips was starting—that was negligent. And when he saw Freda Eichberg's gray self-effacement in the group, he was already thinking of someone to blame for the oversight. He reached for the phone and was bellowing into it for some time.

■

Liam understood nothing the five men said, but their accent was strikingly at variance with Molero's.

Molero seemed more outraged than alarmed. He began shouting and waving his arms.

One of the men leaned down, picked up a corner of the blanket, and pulled it, so that food and drink spilled over Molero's lap.

Liam sat where he was. Molero leapt up.

One of the men fired. The bullet shattered the wine bottle. The single shot was deafening, and echoed several times through the pines, sending birds squawking.

Molero stopped shouting.

The leader of the five emerged. He was short and bulky with wire-rimmed glasses. He looked from Molero to Liam and then asked Molero something.

Molero answered with cowed obedience.

The man spoke again.

Molero looked at Liam. "He says we will not be harmed if we go with them."

"Who are they?"

"Basques. Basque national army."

The youngest of their captors, who looked no more than sixteen, said, "You are English?"

"American."

The youth spoke to his leader. He turned again to Liam. "We must see your papers."

Molero said, "Bandits."

The youth followed Liam to the car, where he found his passport.

All five of them looked at the passport in turn; it was passed along like a rare and mysterious object.

The leader spoke to the youth.

"He says, why are you here?" said the youth.

"I am here to observe the war."

The youth pointed to a page of the passport. "You have been in the Republic."

"I was in Madrid."

The youth was puzzled. "Why you come here?"

"I am an American. I want to see both sides."

The youth considered this slowly and then spoke to his leader. The leader looked from Liam to Molero as though assessing the relationship. He spoke to the youth.

"You are in no danger with us," said the youth. "I keep your passport." He nodded to Molero. "This man can tell you, the Basque people do not shoot their prisoners. That is the truth. We do not murder. And—" He spat at Molero. "—we are not bandits." He kicked at the empty foie gras can.

They all clambered into the Hispano-Suiza. The youth drove. The leader and Liam shared the other front seat; Molero was between two men in the back, and the fifth sat on the open trunk, toting his gun. The leader had a high smell and kept pulling at Liam's clothes—the jacket and then the shirt—and muttering *"americano,"* beaming congenially. Liam began to feel in better company than before. The youth had trouble changing gears on the frequent bends and gradients. After each misplaced gear Molero could be heard groaning.

The car seemed alone in the mountains, its noise thrown back from below. Sometimes the road was so enclosed by trees it was like a tunnel; at others, when they edged a ridge, the sun was intensified by reflection from sheer rock. Still they climbed. Before the summit the youth turned into a dirt track without lessening speed. It was like driving into a crevice, a progressively narrowing one. Then one wall of the crevice gave way, and they drove into a small plateau. Three vehicles were parked under the trees: an ancient truck, a car, and a wood-framed bus.

Before they stopped, men came out of a cave. One of them did not wear a beret. He had a great mane of hair so white that in the shade it remained brilliant. He wore no ammunition, carried no weapon. The others fell back as he reached the car.

The leader of Liam's captors got out and spoke to him.

Molero was taken from the backseat, but it was Liam who was the curiosity. No one pointed a gun at him anymore. He got out of the car.

The youth said, "This is El Roque."

The commander was not misnamed. He was clearly by far the oldest of them but had great physical presence. His face and neck were lined finely like a milled stone. The white hair fell long over his collar.

El Roque spoke to the youth.

The youth said to Liam, "El Roque says we have no argument with the *americanos*." He looked beyond Liam to where Molero stood trying to reassemble his dignity. "The other he says is shit in the milk."

Liam wished he could talk directly to El Roque. He knew that the Basques were a law unto themselves. In this mountain redoubt they had the look of an implacable force.

Their capture, the youth explained, had been pure chance. The front line was uncertain, and the five men had come down from their base looking for evidence of the Nationalist advance. They had heard artillery and seen planes, but made no contact. Then they had heard Molero's Hispano-Suiza, and thought it was a fascist scout car. When they saw the picnic, they thought it was, said the youth, "crazy like a dream." From Molero's papers they realized his importance. "We would like to throw him back to them, but he has seen this place. So we have to send him to Bilbao. You can go to Bilbao. Get a boat to France."

□

It was said politely, but Liam knew that he was an encumbrance. He wanted to stay. For the first time he felt among people who had no design in mind for him—here, he had no connections.

"I am Juan," said the youth.

"You speak English fine."

"My father has a small hotel, in San Sebastián. I learn English by talking to the people."

"Juan, I don't feel right in these clothes."

"Horacio likes your suit." Juan nodded to the leader of the five. He was about Liam's build. "I get you something. Maybe Horacio can have your suit."

Liam laughed. "He can have the shirt, too. He liked that."

They found some trousers as thick as woodman's pants, a sweater, and an old leather jacket. Liam gave Horacio the Brooks Brothers suit and the shirt.

El Roque summoned Juan and Liam.

"He says," said Juan, "it will take two days to reach Bilbao. We leave early in the morning. You eat with us, tonight."

They slept in a cave. It was cold, and the cold woke Liam just before dawn. They let him walk from the cave, and he went to the edge of the plateau with a blanket wrapped around him like a heavy cape. He was looking east. In a while the first light—swiftly sharp at this height—outlined a tapering range of peaks as far east as the Pyrenees.

"I think of my woman at this time, always."

Juan was at his side.

"Where is she?"

"She is in Bilbao."

Liam moved along the rock to make room for him.

"She waits for me. War is no good for love."

"No."

"Where is your woman?"

Liam pulled the blanket more tightly around his shoulders. He seemed to get colder with the light, especially in the feet.

"I have no woman."

Juan surveyed him for a few seconds and said, "You have a woman."

□

Liam cursed Juan's intuition. The youth made him old. Faced with a dawn of unsurpassed beauty, he was not prepared to satisfy Juan's impertinent sympathy.

"No woman," he said, too sharply.

Juan settled back on the stone, silent but unchastened.

Mist began to detach itself from the valley basin and slide up the ridge in long strands.

It was time to move. El Roque deputed Juan and Horacio to take Liam and Molero to Bilbao in the Hispano-Suiza. Horacio wore Liam's jacket over shapeless corduroys. His hips were too wide for the jacket to fall properly, but the ensemble gave him a new swagger. His broken teeth clicked as he ordered Molero into the car. Molero had slumped into a broody passivity, no longer even looking at Liam.

"It is fifty kilometers by the best road," said Juan, "but we cannot go that way. We must keep to the bad roads."

They were hardly roads at all. The Hispano-Suiza remained mostly in low gear as Juan looped mountains and followed tracks only shepherds normally used. For most of the time they were in the cover of trees, until after three hours or so Juan reached a river and followed it into a valley. He picked up speed. Horacio urged him to go faster.

At first Liam thought it was a change of note in the engine. There was a deeper roar increasing as they increased speed. Then a shadow flashed over them and the deeper noise took on a separate life. The plane was flying little higher than the telegraph lines that marked out the road.

Juan braked and the car slewed in a cloud of dirt.

They watched the plane begin a climbing turn to the left of the road. The sun caught metal and the white disks with a black cross.

"German," cried Juan.

They were about half a mile short of trees on a stretch of road otherwise without the prospect of cover. He straightened the car and began racing for the trees. None of them could see the plane anymore. It was behind them. The car was misfiring and losing grip. Liam saw the plane, this time to their left, coming lower across marshland and heading for them. Before he could warn Juan he saw orange flashes on its wings. The road in front of the car erupted in a twin line of explosions.

Juan braked again.

Before the car stopped Horacio was jumping from the back, pulling Molero with him. All four of them leapt from the road blindly and landed in mud and marsh grass.

The plane climbed again. Liam could see that they had no cover. Yet the instinct was to press down prone into the grass. The plane took its time, almost lazily banking to take another look at them.

Horacio was hurling oaths at it. Juan said simply, *"Messerschmitt,"* Liam thought of von Klagen.

Before they realized what was happening, Molero was springing out of the mud. He lost footing, pushed again, and made it to the road. His suit was smeared green. He ran to the car. Its engine was still running. He was in it and driving away before the rest of them had moved.

■

The large windows were canted inward from the top, giving the *Hindenburg*'s passengers on the promenade deck an unobstructed view below. The western coast of Ireland had slipped away half an hour earlier. Now there was nothing but the Atlantic, clear enough for Freda Eichberg to see wavecaps broken into spray by the wind. It was a sea without any transparency, even under bright sunlight. There seemed a skin to it.

"The wind is against us," said Heidel. His hand was lightly on the base of her back—it was still enough to join the other indiscretions carefully noted after the first night by the more vigilant stewards.

She felt only the slightest sense of motion. If you had not looked at the water, the great ship would have seemed almost inert. This suited the wishes of most of the passengers, who had quickly become lighter than air themselves.

"Yes," he persisted, against her distracted downward gaze, "at this time of the year the prevailing winds are from west to east. However,

Captain Lehmann assures me that this is taken into calculation. Captain Lehmann likes to be punctual."

"It is important to be punctual," she said.

Was she goading him? He had not been able to be sure of her humor from the moment they had gone to bed together. Thereafter, the prim Fräulein Eichberg had been put aside and replaced by a woman both intimate and aloof, sometimes simultaneously, body yielding but eyes not.

"Please, I would like to smoke," she said.

"Of course."

They had been out of bed for an hour, and she always wanted to smoke after sex. He worried that this routine might become too obvious. There was only one place on the *Hindenburg* where an open flame could be allowed, a smoking room reached through a system of double doors. The inner doors opened automatically only after the outer ones were closed. The air in the smoking room was kept at a slightly higher pressure, ensuring a tight air seal.

It had never occurred to Heidel that she might be socially vulnerable. Now, lighting the cigarette for her as she hunched toward him on the wicker seat, he saw what he took to be the desperation of someone feeling unequal to her surroundings. There were a number of very large cigars and all the habits of dress and manners that went with them. He wanted suddenly to reassure her. She belonged. She was as entitled to be there as any of them. She sat too stiffly as she deeply inhaled the cigarette.

"These are good times, I think," he said.

The idea did not seem to take root. She did not alter her position or even look him in the eye.

"Things go well for me," he said, cutting the end from his own cigar. "When things go well for me it can be good for you, also."

This time he had her attention.

"It is a pleasure to be with you, Freda."

She settled more comfortably in the chair. Only the avidity of her smoking remained to suggest stress.

"Well, I am enjoying it. Yes. It takes a little time to leave Berlin behind." She looked at him as she had done several times in bed. "Yes. Success is good for you. Really." She looked quickly around them. "There are no failures in this room." Then she laughed in a crackling way that sounded less amiable.

"No," he said, made nervous by the attention drawn by her laugh, "no failures." Was it a mistake to have brought her? He hoped not.

■

Horacio began to try to get out of the mud and grass, but Juan restrained him.

The Hispano-Suiza was still misfiring and slewed from one side of the road to the other. Molero pumped the throttle.

The Messerschmitt had gone higher and this time ahead of the car. It completed its turn and began to descend again, going head-on for the car.

Lying where they were, the three of them saw only the plane's sharp black outline. It was even lower, and firing again.

Everything was a blur. The Messerschmitt's shadow passed them before it did, its engine overrode all other sounds, they felt the slipstream. Along the road there was a twin fountain of smoke and dirt. Curiously they had missed the explosions. The smoke drifted away. The car had not reached the trees. It was almost at right angles to the road. For seconds it seemed unscathed. The smoke had gone; the plane was an echo in the hills. Nothing moved. Nothing in the car. Its engine was still running.

Horacio stood up.

At that moment the car exploded. As it left the ground—it was the gas tank that had gone up—it was whole. Before the flame engulfed it the wheels spun high above, and then other parts, and Molero's body—spinning like the wheels.

"Jesus!" said Liam.

Juan turned away and looked for the plane. It was climbing in a spiral high above the mountains.

Horacio had been immobilized by shock, his hair blown back from his brow and his glasses hanging from one ear. He started to laugh, first with a whistling pitch and then, as his arms came to life, with a deeper rasping.

□

Juan and Liam clambered back to the road. The Messerschmitt was only a fading sound. Oil and rubber burned with a heat strong enough to feel on the face. None of them cared to look for Molero. They walked past fragments of the car and reached the trees. In a while they found why the Messerschmitt had been in the valley. Their road joined a main pass through the mountains. It was thick with refugees and retreating troops. Wrecked trucks lay in a burning line outside a village. Juan was told that a pack of Messerschmitts and Heinkels had strafed the road. Casualties were being treated in the village. Civilians and soldiers seemed equally demoralized.

Juan talked to an old officer who was waiting for a doctor to attend to a gash in his arm. The man seemed quickly irritated.

Juan shook his head as he returned to Liam. "All they talk about is the Iron Ring of Bilbao. They think if they reach there they will be safe. The fascists are only kilometers away."

As if to confirm him, shells began falling on the road short of the village. There was a stampede of people.

Juan stood calmly listening to the fall of the shells. "German eighty-eights."

Since the end of the Hispano-Suiza, Horacio had ceded leadership to Juan. Horacio was walking as though in a trance, occasionally and inaptly laughing. He stopped several people to discuss the quality of his jacket, announcing *"americano."*

Juan led them north out of the village with the retreat.

Several trucks came weaving through the people, more purposefully than the rest of the apathetic troops. They were full of men.

Juan saw them and shouted, *"Cristóbal! Cristóbal!"* and held up a clenched fist at the trucks. The last one stopped. Juan leapt to the running board of the cab and spoke to the driver.

"Come!" he said, jumping down and running to the rear of the truck. He pushed Horacio over the tailgate, helped Liam climb up, and followed them into the truck. There were about twenty men in there who—despite Liam's memory of Molero's earlier slander—looked more like bandits than soldiers. There was no common uniform, but they were heavy with gun belts and had a mixture of huge revolvers in holsters and automatic rifles. In the gloom and dust of the truck, suspicious eyes settled on the newcomers.

□

"Where are we going?" said Liam.

"These are Cristóbal's men," said Juan. "They do not retreat. They are going to hold the line."

"Who is Cristóbal?"

"Cristóbal leads the Rosa Luxemburg Battalion. Communists. The best fighters in Spain."

"Where is the line? Where are we going?"

"Guernica."

■

Von Klagen feared few things more than riding in von Richthofen's Mercedes.

"I believe in knowing the breaking point of everything," said von Richthofen as they hurtled toward Vitoria. "The Mercedes is a good car, but on German roads you cannot give it this kind of test."

"No," said von Klagen.

"They send me the spare parts. That is not enough. I write to them suggesting changes. After all, we do it with the Heinkels, we should be listened to when it comes to a car. Yes?"

"Yes."

"Speak up."

"I said, yes—it is a good idea. After all, we must have a car capable of conquering the world."

"You joke?"

"No."

Von Richthofen returned his attention to the road without being sure of von Klagen. They were nearing Vitoria, and it was prudent to slow down. There were always stupid Spanish dogs.

"It is annoying," he said, "that the American has disappeared. I have no time to be concerned with such things. That is a diplomatic problem. It is not a good idea to have such people wandering the front."

"Berlin is very anxious."

"Berlin. Berlin. Berlin. *Who* is Berlin?"

□

"I am responsible for Mr. Casey."

"Yes." Von Richthofen had no sympathy.

Waiting for von Klagen were the three people who had last seen Molero and Liam. Two of them were the Spanish officers who had talked to Molero when the car was being refueled. The third had seen the car leave the town. Thereafter, there seemed no trace. Von Klagen discussed the map with the two Spaniards. If Molero had gone astray, it was impossible to know where to look in the maze of the mountains. Bridges were being blown up as the Republicans retreated. With that kind of confusion it could be days before a clue would turn up.

Von Klagen was supposed to be flying, not looking for strays. He was aware that von Richthofen was suspicious of his Berlin connections. It pleased von Richthofen to have von Klagen in a political mess.

Von Klagen was ordering a consoling cognac when Barrington-Taylor came into the hotel.

"Am I the first?" said Barrington-Taylor.

"The first?"

"There are no other reporters here yet?"

"I have not seen any."

"Good. I'll join you if I may." Barrington-Taylor ordered a whisky, but there was only brandy. "Been tipped off that you will be in Bilbao in a week. Understand it's a rout."

"A week? The main attack has not started."

"Even the Spaniards are looking very cocky, very cocky." Barrington-Taylor pulled out a sheet of paper. "Perhaps you can explain this, old chap."

Von Klagen took the paper.

"Just issued by Franco from Salamanca."

Von Klagen read aloud as he translated from the Spanish: "We wish to tell the world about the burning of Guernica. Guernica was destroyed by fire and gasoline. The red hordes burnt it to ruins. They have uttered the infamous lie of attributing this atrocity to our noble and heroic air force . . ."

Von Klagen stopped reading and handed back the paper.

☐

"Well, old man?"

"That is official."

"Look. I know. You know. The place was bombed. I dare say the reds want to make political capital out of it. Probably they did set fire to the place to make it look worse. An old trick of theirs. Irún, after all, was dynamited as they pulled out—know that for a fact. Case of turning defeat into a moral victory. Thing is, it would help if I could get there myself. London says the atrocity story is running in all the usually gullible quarters. London would like another view."

"Guernica has not fallen, yet."

"First come, first served."

"I am sure you will have preference."

"Good. Good. That's good. I say, you look a bit down."

It took von Klagen another half an hour to shake off Barrington-Taylor. Then he went in search of von Richthofen.

The commander was supervising an inspection of the underside of his Mercedes.

"You see, von Klagen—the axle, again." He bellowed over the sound of the hydraulic lift. "Always the axle. So simple to make it stronger. Look, you see the casting."

Von Klagen bided his time, peering under the car.

"Well—*what is it?*" said von Richthofen, stepping back, and rubbing his oiled hands.

"There is a statement from Salamanca. It denies that we bombed Guernica."

Von Richthofen did not alter expression, but he took von Klagen gently by the arm and steered him to a corner of the workshop.

"My dear von Klagen, it is your friends in Berlin. *Officially,* Guernica did not happen. You understand?" He waited but no answer came. "Unofficially I have been congratulated on the success of my experiment. *Politics,* von Klagen. *Politics.* The glib and oily art."

There was, to be sure, oil on von Richthofen's hands. Not blood. Von Klagen was expected to look slow-witted. He could not give von Richthofen that satisfaction. His unveiled contempt was as near to a court-martial offense as anything unspoken could be. He turned and walked out.

□

■

A light drizzle lifted the fragrance of blossom from the orchards. Only when they were closer to the town was it overlapped by another, heavier smell that the rain had trapped in the streets. Liam had known that smell before, of incineration. But not on this scale. He was looking at the incineration of a whole town. Things not usually combustible had burned. Steel window frames and beams had melted and left scorched brick shells. The men in the truck fell silent as they slowed to crawl around the debris. A tree had been turned to a crisp stump, and yet within yards of it geraniums on a balcony were unscathed. What had consumed the town had moved as capriciously as a god, annihilating and ignoring. The smell became rank and reeked inimitably of death, drifting on smoke rising from within the ruins of Guernica.

Horacio had not spoken since they had been in the truck. His hair was still like a displaced cap, and his eyes had not lost their glaze. He crossed himself.

Sharply, Juan said, "This is the work of those who claim to follow God."

All Liam could say was, "Why? *Why? Why* would they do this?"

"To show us," said Juan quietly.

Liam recalled von Klagen's ambiguous elation when he came back to the hotel.

"We have no defense against this," said Juan.

The men around them suffered the same collapse of spirit.

The trucks stopped in what must once have been a spacious plaza. It was now the center of a military operation. The men were ordered from the trucks by brisk commissars.

Juan led Liam and Horacio through the crowd.

"This, this was the station—the line to Bilbao," he said.

The remains of a hotel were spilled across the plaza. The station building survived in part, precariously. It had been occupied by soldiers. Juan found a seat and directed Horacio to it. The man who not so long ago had been the epitome of a bandit leader was a vacant bystander. He meekly followed Juan's instructions.

□

"He will recover," said Juan, seeing Liam's concern. "You—you are not too good?"

Juan's transplanted hotel slang was inadequate. Liam looked at Horacio in the Brooks Brothers jacket, and then around them, from the waiting room open to the rain, through the entrance where one twisted door hung where it had been blown, and out into the devastation. He had seen carnage in Madrid, but Madrid still lived. This town, which von Richthofen's finger must have punched on a map, was no longer an entity. He could not vent his feelings—they were half directed at himself and half at an unassailable evil, not particularized in the form of von Richthofen but in the phenomenon those men represented—their *science.* Unassailable, because it had no personality. He was still new to lunacy of this nature.

"No—not too good," he answered.

Juan could not assess where Liam was damaged. Liam had a rude health in his face, and the rough clothes filled out his figure. He didn't stand out here as an interloper unless you noticed his shoes. Although smeared with the slime of the marsh, they were too fine. Juan thought they were like a gold watch stolen from a corpse and worn by a robber. He had seen watches taken like that.

"We must go to Bilbao," he said.

"No," said Liam. "*No.* Not yet. I have to know what happened here."

Juan scowled. "What happened?"

"I know it was bombers. I want evidence."

"*This* is evidence," said Juan sourly, raising his arms.

"I have to talk to—to people."

On the bench beside Horacio a cleric had been slumped, apparently asleep. His cassock was streaked with mud, and his face was so dark with grime that it was impossible to tell his age. The bulk stirred and straightened and spoke.

"I will tell you what happened," he said, in an English that trilled like a chorister's.

Liam gaped.

The cleric rose. "I am Father Alberto de Onaindía. I am a canon of Valladolid Cathedral. As the Lord would have it, I was passing through here when the bombers came."

□

"Father, I want to know. What you saw."

"You are American?"

"That's right. Casey—Liam Casey."

"There have been reporters here. I spoke to one of them."

"I have to know for myself."

Father Onaindía gave a placid smile. "Yes. You are a Christian, I assume?"

"A Catholic."

"I thought so."

There were those who always knew; Father Onaindía would probably have divined how tenuous Liam's faith was. Something about the priest was quietly indomitable and, to Liam, instantly and desperately necessary.

But Juan was suspicious. He stepped back a pace and looked at Liam more than the priest, as though Liam was revealed in new colors.

The priest saw this. "You are together?"

"This is Juan," said Liam.

Juan resisted the priest's benediction. "I am not a Catholic. The church is an oppressor."

"Do I look like an oppressor?" said Father Onaindía.

"In this war you can never trust a priest."

"Then trust God."

Juan's exasperation turned to Liam, "*Listen to him!* How many planes does God have? What can God do in Guernica? Look at this. *Look* at this!" He punched air.

Only Horacio remained undiverted by this outburst.

"You come with us; I will show you what God can do."

Liam took Juan's arm. "Come with us."

For a few seconds it seemed that he would not, but as Liam persisted Juan relented. Each of them went at a different pace into the plaza: the priest first, sure and erect; Liam, the tallest but stooped to the priest's height; and Juan, putting Liam between himself and the priest and hanging back.

"Many of the survivors have gone to Bilbao," said Father Onaindía. "Those who remain still look for the many who are missing. It is impossible to know how many have died. We have counted hundreds of bodies. Many will never be found. Of course, the people are confused about what happened. I have talked to perhaps thirty or forty. I am making a report, you see. But it is not possible that everyone agrees. In this—in this terrible thing there can be no memory that is easy to talk about. Of one thing I know. There was no mercy shown. It was very deliberate; the planes came and came again and again for nearly three hours. The fires burned through the night and into the day. The night was long. No, there was no mercy shown."

"You are making a report?" said Liam. "Who will see it?"

"I will send it to the Holy Father."

"The pope? The pope supports Franco."

"Do you think the Holy Father would support this?" They had reached the center of the plaza. Father Onaindía lifted his arms as he asked the question. "Well? Do you?"

"The Holy Father is not here. He will never see this."

"No. You are right. He will never see it. That is why I must make this report. I must hope that it will be seen to be the truth."

Juan watched them. He said, "One priest against the Vatican. Not too good."

"They will not bury Guernica," said Father Onaindía.

"I will pray for that, Father," said Liam.

Father Onaindía took his hand. "Then I bless you. You are right to believe in that."

Juan walked beside them thereafter, though without any trace of piety.

"There was only one plane in the beginning," said the priest. "Its bombs came here on the plaza. I think perhaps it was three or four hundred people here. Many died."

Their first call was on a captain who was organizing the search for the missing from a small bar. He had helped Father Onaindía gather evidence, and the two of them recapitulated it for Liam, with Father Onaindía translating for the captain.

"It was methodical," said the captain. "It has not been like that before, with the bombers. They came at intervals, about twenty minutes. After the first bomber we thought it was over. But the first, I think now, was marking the town. The next ones came lower. They realized we had no defenses. The bombs were mixed. High explosive and incendiaries."

□

"And then machine guns," said Father Onaindía.

"Yes," said the captain, "that was also methodical. The smaller planes flew low, up and down the streets, machine-gunning the people."

"Many people were shot in the back while running—women, children."

"Even at the end they were doing it as we were trying to fight the fires."

"What I don't understand," said Liam, "is how this could be called a military target."

"There is one thing in Guernica," said Father Onaindía, "one thing you might call a military target. The bridge. It is the main route behind our lines to Bilbao. The bridge was not touched. I know that, because I took shelter under it."

The captain added something.

"Also," said Father Onaindía, "there is an arms factory, and it was not touched."

"Calle Santa María," said the captain.

Father Onaindía nodded. "Come," he said.

They left the captain trying to pacify people calling out the names of their missing kin.

The drizzle stopped. In the still air it was easy to hear artillery exchanges in the east.

"Nearer," said Father Onaindía, listening. He led them into a broad street where few buildings survived intact. The road had been ruptured, and water still poured from shattered pipes.

"It was market day," said Father Onaindía. "There were cattle and sheep, refugees from the front, as well as the people of the town. There were shelters, places that were thought to be safe. Here—you see this—here was one of the largest shelters."

Nothing identifiable remained. Water gurgled through a gulley where rubble had been clawed away to find bodies. They saw blackened brick and an enormous crater.

"One hundred thirty, perhaps one hundred fifty people died here."

Father Onaindía stepped back from the crater so that Liam and Juan could look down. Half of a blackened horse, head and forelegs, hung out of a collapsed wall. The horse looked arrested in motion, its mouth agape.

Liam stepped back. Juan remained. He began to ease himself down into the pit. He pulled at a stunted wooden beam. Rubble fell away. Something silver lay wedged between the beam and more rubble. He pulled it free, revealing a metal canister. He called to Liam to take it.

Liam leaned down. It was heavy.

When Juan had climbed back, Liam had already seen the German script on the canister.

Father Onaindía said, "Others were found that did not explode. A firebomb. They contain a mixture of aluminum and iron oxide. They are designed to burn at five thousand degrees Fahrenheit."

"This is evidence," said Liam.

"Yes. I will keep it," said Father Onaindía.

"I would like a photograph."

"I will arrange that." Father Onaindía looked at Juan. "Thank you."

"Give it to the pope," said Juan.

Father Onaindía looked at him tolerantly. "These bombs have no religion. This is not a holy war." He picked his way back to firmer ground and turned to Liam. "There are evils beyond our experience being foretold here." He seemed absorbed in a massive bewilderment.

Liam found himself confronted as he had never been before by a tangible evil, but also by a man its equal in holiness.

■

Von Klagen found Captain Klaus Gautlitz cursing the quality of aerial photographs.

"Bilbao," said Gautlitz, showing von Klagen a print.

Von Klagen looked at the picture, but not with much concentration. "Gautlitz, do you remember the debriefing details for the last twenty-four hours?"

"Not all. I do sleep."

"Have there been any reports of bombing the roads?"

"That is all we are bombing."

"Do you recall any report of a car—a large car, a Hispano-Suiza?"

"You see this photograph? How can I tell a car from a pig?"

"Yes. I see."

Von Klagen gave up. He wanted to sleep. "It is better, not to see too much," he said. "We should not see what we cannot admit."

The sarcasm surprised Gautlitz. He looked from the wet print to von Klagen, noticing for the first time how wild he seemed. "I heard you are going home," he said.

Von Klagen nodded. "*Home?* I don't know. Back to Berlin. A new assignment. Good night, Gautlitz."

But at one-thirty in the morning he was awakened by an orderly and called to the phone, and it was Gaulitz.

"I have something for you, Walther. I can tell some cars from a pig. You know Mueller?"

"Mad Mueller."

"Mueller the Messerschmitt man, yes. He is still hunting alone. In spite of von Richthofen. Yesterday he was supposed to be with the others, strafing the roads to Bilbao. He made two or three passes and then, as usual, said his guns were jammed. He went climbing to unjam them, then he shot up a car on a back road. From the description it could have been your Hispano-Suiza. He was low enough to read the number."

"It was destroyed?"

"Of course."

"Did he see people?"

"Mueller does not bother with details."

25

Byrnes slowed the car to look at the road signs; a car behind him honked and honked again.

"Damn people, damn place," said Byrnes.

"Pat, I think your eyes need attention." Miriam leaned forward. "Next right," she said. "Lakehurst, three miles."

The car behind them swung out and passed with a final burst of the horn.

"Godforsaken damn place," said Byrnes, leaving the main road.

Miriam put a soothing hand on his thigh.

"Nothing wrong with my eyes," he said. "It's the light."

"Of course."

The light *was* difficult: heavily overcast, and yet a brightness was reflected from the road, bouncing off the signs. The signs had a starkness about them, and were canted to the same angle as the few trees to the prevailing winds that came over the New Jersey scrub-land. Blown sand snaked across the road.

"Of course," she said again, withdrawing the hand to the silk scarf at her neck. "I had no idea it would be such a dreadful place. No idea."

"Not like taking the boat to Europe."

"Why can't this airship leave from somewhere civilized; I mean, shouldn't they call in at Boston?"

"I think they have to have maneuvering space, Miriam—it's a hellofa size." He peered upward as though expecting to see the *Hindenburg*. "I always thought the Germans were punctual. Already seven hours late."

"Perhaps I should have taken the boat after all."

"Well—" Byrnes became more affable. "—it's daring of you, Miriam."

"Yes. It is." She seemed happy at the thought. "It is. We should be daring more often. Last night was very nice, Pat."

Byrnes seemed nervous about being overheard, though they were alone.

"You do promise to see my doctor?" she said. "He will understand."

"Yes, Miriam. That must be the place, coming up. The hangar. It's colossal."

"And when you see the doctor, you should suggest the vacation."

"Colossal. Look at it."

"Oh dear, it's beginning to rain."

"Looks like we may have a storm."

"What will the airship do?"

"Don't know. I guess it has to come in anyways."

"There are movie people and things here."

Before they reached the main gate of Lakehurst Field they saw the cars parked near the hangar with movie cameras on their roofs. Men were draping them to protect them from the drizzle. There were already many other cars there, including the Casey Rolls-Royce, sent ahead with the luggage.

At the gate, Byrnes asked a policeman about the *Hindenburg*.

"She's over New York City right now, sir. Should be here in a few minutes." He waved them through.

■

"I feel I could reach down and touch it," said Freda.

The faint sun caught the southwest corner of the Empire State Building and glinted from the binoculars of several people peering up from the observation platform. Other people waved at the *Hindenburg;* the colors of their clothes were visible.

Heidel and Freda were among a score of passengers looking down from the promenade deck. Manhattan did seem touchable.

"It's the most magical place I've ever seen," she said, waving down.

"I have never seen it like this—yes, magical," he said, and pointed out Fifth Avenue, striped by the shadows of buildings.

A steward came along the promenade deck announcing that luggage was to be collected in preparation for arrival. The *Hindenburg* turned west over the Hudson and began very slowly to descend.

■

"I see it," said Byrnes. "*My God,* what a size!" He handed the binoculars to Miriam.

The glasses were too much of a technicality for her. She fumbled with them for a moment and then gave them back to him.

"I see it," she said. "I don't need these things." The *Hindenburg* was coming directly toward them—it became more substantial against the cloud. "I'm sure I don't understand how such a thing is possible. It seems so—so pagan a thing."

"Pagan?"

"Unnatural."

The *Hindenburg* was now less gray, more silver and lower.

"They don't seem able to tell us what the hell is going on," said Byrnes, listening to an announcement from the crackling loudspeakers on the roof of the passenger building. "Something about landing conditions uncertain."

"Where does one sit?" she said.

"It's only gas in there, Miriam. Hydrogen. The passengers are in the things underneath. Gondolas. You can see them now."

"Oh."

"I don't think he's coming in."

Men stood around the mooring mast, staring up, but the *Hindenburg* turned at the end of the field and began rising again. A parachute carrying a small cylinder dropped and floated down, and was collected. The airship moved away to the south.

"What is happening, Pat?"

The speakers crackled again.

"A message from the captain. Waiting for the wind to drop. Landing at six. Another two hours. Damn business."

"Oh *dear.*" She gripped his arm. "Where does one *go* in a place like this?"

■

"Time for another drink," said Heidel. "There is not much of interest to be seen now."

"Yes. A drink."

They left the window of the lounge and went down the companionway to the double doors of the smoking room. Other passengers, irritated by the delay, were already drinking, and the general nervousness was expressed in even louder voices than usual. A man played Strauss on the aluminum piano. Heidel found a table as far away from the others as possible, knowing now Freda's distaste for the cigar smokers.

"Are you worried?" he said.

"You mean—about the storm? No. I think it is not a problem."

"Good. Good. You did seem nervous."

"No. I cannot see anything to be nervous about. I was worried sometimes when we were over the Atlantic. Then you feel, we are so far away, if anything goes wrong there is only the water. Here, well, there is America below."

"There is no cause to worry."

She suspected though, as he took the drinks from the waiter, that he might be on edge himself. The whisky seemed slowly to relax him. During the course of the journey he had seemed lighter in mood and younger, as though finding an age he had never had. He had become uncaring about the curiosity they aroused. They had stayed longer in bed, and the more they had made love the more he had seemed to want. She was happy with him, but expected him to revert to his old self when they touched earth again. She realized that now he might be on the brink of saying something, needing perhaps one more whisky to do it.

A steward came to him.

"Excuse me, Herr Heidel. Captain Lehmann would like to see you."

Heidel was puzzled. "Now?"

"In his cabin."

Heidel looked at her with apologetic frustration, and then left with the steward.

"Delaware," said the steward, trying to be amicable.

"What?"

"The mouth of the Delaware, below."

Heidel was too irritated to look down. "We are too long delayed."

"Captain Lehmann will take no risks."

"Risks?"

"These are difficult conditions. The wind is a problem for mooring. It is better to wait. We will be on the ground before nightfall."

On the catwalk the webbed metal groaned and the whole craft seemed animate. Lehmann's cabin was aft, near the control car, and as they reached it Heidel could hear the engines pulsing with the assurance of a heartbeat.

Lehmann stood looking out at the control car. He was a model of calm and command. Beside him was a man Heidel had seen from time to time during the trip, a man who was always on his own and always in sharply pressed gray suits.

Lehmann waited for the steward to leave.

"Herr Heidel," he said, "this is Captain Strelow of the Abwehr."

"Abwehr Three," said Strelow in a manner as precise as the crease in his pants. "I believe you know Major Rohleder."

"Yes."

Lehmann produced a sheet of paper. "This has just been received by radio from our embassy in Washington. Captain Strelow decoded it. From Rohleder."

□

Heidel was hoping the whisky was not too noticeable on his breath. He made an effort to hold the paper steady as he read it.

"You see," said Strelow, "how serious this is, and how lucky we are to have this signal before we landed."

Heidel had sobered very rapidly, and read it a second time.

"You had no suspicion?" said Strelow.

"I do not believe it," said Heidel.

"You think Rohleder would make a mistake?"

"Rohleder is . . ." Heidel put down the paper. "It is hard to believe. Hard to believe."

"She must be very clever," said Strelow.

Lehmann nodded and, with a sharp eye on Heidel, said, "Perhaps, Herr Heidel, you were too close to her to see it."

Heidel surprised both of them by laughing—though not engagingly. "*Too close?* I suppose it looked like that to you. The truth is that I did not know Freda—that is, in the biblical sense—until I boarded the *Hindenburg.* It had never been one of those relationships. She is—she was—very professional in her work and not that kind of woman."

"And what kind of woman do you think she is now?" said Strelow caustically.

"I don't know. She did not seem—she did not seem to be political."

"She cannot leave the ship," said Strelow. "She must be detained."

"You mean, taken directly back to Berlin?"

"She should be able to be very helpful to us."

"You think she would do that?"

"What do *you* think, Herr Heidel?" Strelow picked up the paper and folded it. "Better the Abwehr than the Gestapo. She could save her own neck."

"For *what?*" said Heidel stridently. "Prison for life?"

"A camp, yes."

"You make a camp sound like a place of pleasure, Captain."

"You will come with me now to her?"

Heidel glared at them both. "She has great courage."

"Red filth," said Lehmann.

Heidel turned and went out, leading Strelow.

□

■

"Do come over here, Pat, and do stop worrying. I've met this marvelous man who knows all about porcelain."

Byrnes had been checking Miriam's luggage as it was readied to be taken to the *Hindenburg.* He was sure, from the slightness of a glance from her chauffeur, that the man had detected their assignation in New York the night before. That would be only the beginning of the wretched thing, thought Byrnes, and he had no way to stop it. Now she wanted to talk porcelain.

"This is Herr Bueller from Dresden."

Bueller was a small, fragile, and very bald man whom she had plucked from the crowded benches and now presented to Byrnes like a collected piece: his shining skull was as unblemished as a china bowl, and he moved with an old world-grace.

"Patrick Byrnes. Pleased to know you, sir."

"Friedrich Bueller. A very great honor, Mr. Byrnes."

"Herr Bueller," said Miriam, "has a factory in Dresden."

"More a workshop," said Bueller.

"He has written a book on porcelain."

"More a monograph."

"So we will have an interest in common to discuss on our voyage."

"Flight," said Bueller.

"Damned late," said Byrnes.

"So much concern with time in America," said Bueller. "We must be the masters of time, or it will be the end of perfection."

Byrnes stared down at him intemperately, but checked himself.

"Quite," said Miriam. "Pat, don't stoop so. I'm getting an altogether better feeling about this voyage since I met Herr Bueller. A very nice class of passenger seems to be attracted to the zeppelin."

"The storm is clearing," said Byrnes.

"Oh good," she said, "then we should be on board in time for dinner. I have quite an appetite."

"I also," said Bueller, who seemed to Byrnes to have dined off birdseed.

■

With the few steps it took Heidel and Strelow to reach her from the air lock of the smoking room, Freda knew what had happened. She had noticed Strelow before.

Heidel was awkward and stricken. "This gentleman is from the Abwehr," he said, putting himself between her and the closest group of people, in the hope of discretion.

"Yes," she said.

"Captain Strelow."

She turned from Heidel to Strelow. "I think you would like to talk to me, Captain?"

"If you please."

She remained seated and took another sip of her drink, dead in the eyes.

"Why?" said Heidel. "*Why* a woman like you?"

"What kind of a woman am I?" she said quietly. "Do you think? Look around you. Do you think I am a part of this?"

Heidel was too agitated to be provoked. "They will not let you leave the ship."

"No." She looked at Strelow, finished the drink, and rose.

"I will do what I can," said Heidel, still on the same spot.

"No. You must not. It is not worth the risk. You are not involved." She picked up her purse, straightened her skirt, nodded, and smiled at Strelow as though leaving for a promenade.

Heidel went to the window and looked down at the patches of brightness where the sun was beginning to filter through the cloud, but he saw nothing.

■

Byrnes had left Miriam with the expert on porcelain and walked to the restraining fence alongside the huge hangar. His hat was damp from the drizzle and the brim sagged about his ears, completing the impression of a man gone too far from his familiar comforts. He watched the newsreel cameramen climb to the top of their cars and take the shrouds from their equipment—the rain had stopped. The cameramen joked about the girls in the restaurant bar, where they had spent most of the afternoon. Everybody was staring in the same direction, south. One of the cameramen, using his lens like field glasses, called out that visibility was about five miles.

"Nothing there," he said.

In the circle of wet sand around the mooring mast the ground crew came out like a baseball team to a diamond. There were crackles of static from the loudspeakers—the storm, not too far distant, still had life in it. The announcer cleared his throat—sounding as jaded as Byrnes felt.

"The ship is expected in a few minutes," he said.

Byrnes checked his watch. It was 7:16 P.M.

■

Strelow had been very agreeable, she thought. He had asked a few questions, cited Rohleder, and said that there could be no formal interrogation until she was in Berlin. As far as she could tell, Strelow was the only agent of any kind on the *Hindenburg.* His cabin was half the size of Heidel's stateroom, and austere. He said she would have the berth next to his but—since neither of them would leave the *Hindenburg*—she would be free to move around. He even helped her move her clothes. He showed no curiosity about her motives, assumed that she was, like him, a professional with an alternative chain of masters. This disinterest annoyed her—it was like being in the care of a zookeeper. Did he have any moral sensibility at all? There was plenty of time ahead of her to find out.

Used bed linen was piled at the end of the corridor. Most of the passengers had reassembled in the main lounge for the customs inspection. A bust of President Hindenburg was on a pedestal at the head of the stairway near her berth.

For the first time, as he carried her last bag, Strelow showed humor. He patted the bust and said, "He sees as clearly now as he always did."

□

She could not give him the satisfaction of a response.

They were getting lower and—from a change in the fall of light in the corridor—she realized they were slowly turning. The linen slid from one wall to another.

Strelow looked out. "Not long now."

So close and yet never to be touched: the urge to look again at the land below had gone. She took the bag from him and went into her cell, closing the door. His face, as she sealed herself from it, was bemused rather than offended. Perhaps he was as reasonable as he seemed, though she would not trust the thought. Only then was she able to take stock of herself. She would have to find a way, long before they got back to Berlin, of ending it. Strelow did not expect that of her. Everything in the berth flexed as she looked at it: the ship was tilting downward. She sat on the bunk.

■

"There she is," called one of the cameramen.

It was still some seconds before Byrnes saw the *Hindenburg*. By then all the cameras were swiveling to pick up the first shots, and the reporters came spilling out of their cars.

Byrnes watched for half a minute. The *Hindenburg* was about two miles off, not coming directly toward them but crabbing, as though finding the right line of approach. The wind was fitful, imprecise in direction.

The ground crew filed out again.

Byrnes walked back to the passenger building. At first he could not see Miriam. All the other passengers gathered at the windows. Behind them, on their bench, Miriam and Bueller were still talking. Bueller was laughing. Byrnes felt quite surprisingly malicious toward Bueller. He hoped that the German would discover in the course of the journey how all-devouring Miriam Casey could be. Then Bueller might sweat. Byrnes thought Bueller's dome had never been blemished by a bead of sweat.

"It's here, Miriam."

She shifted her attention reluctantly. "Oh good." She noticed the crowd at the windows. "No need to act like cattle. Could you let me know when you think we should go?"

Bueller looked complicit.

"Very well, Miriam." Byrnes left them and went back outside.

The *Hindenburg*'s engines were audible. The red setting of the swastika on the fin was clear. It was low and turning toward the mooring mast—turning quickly, Byrnes noticed, more nimble than he expected for so huge a machine. The cameras had to incline sharply to follow it. Something flashy in this maneuver, thought Byrnes, something not quite correctly German, in the way he thought of their character. It would be good to see Heidel again. And good to see Miriam go.

The first mooring rope snaked down as the *Hindenburg* pitched gently to a stop.

The ground crew moved to secure it while another dropped to the sand.

Byrnes was surprised by the stability of the ship: it had settled very close to the mast and began inching closer for the final mooring while the ropes were secured. One of the wonders of the world, truly. A business to get into, the future. Anybody with investments in the steamship companies had better consider it. To see ahead, that was the thing. He liked that in Heidel: Heidel was conservative and yet progressively minded.

Even the hard-boiled newsmen were gaping.

And the sun came out for it. Very brightly. Was that the sun? Byrnes squinted into the glare. Somewhere above the ship. Brighter still. A plume of blinding brilliance and a shower of meteors, or so it seemed, all above, lighting the upturned faces. Men running. The ground crew, kicking up the wet sand as they ran, were caught in that growing light from above. She's on fire. My God. She is. Running along the ship's upper spine toward the swastika at the back. Engulfing her. The nose reared up.

Men crying out now.

One, two, three hundred feet of fire. Unthinkable speed. You could feel the heat.

□

■

Freda felt the ship steady itself and saw the flexing stop. Several people went down the stairway—she heard the steps on metal. She opened the door. Strelow's door was open. She thought he was one of those she had heard on the stairway, but then she heard him moving inside. She went into the corridor and looked out the window.

Strelow came out.

The sudden brightness was reflected from the sand below. She saw two ground crew men at a rope stop working and look up.

There was a shout from beyond the stairway.

Strelow said, "Something has happened." He went to the stairs. At that moment the ship reared up. Strelow gripped a rail but went tumbling down.

She held the handle of a door. It swung open, and she slid to the opposite wall. The bust of Hindenburg and its pedestal keeled over and went down the stairway. The brightness from above changed from its initial reflected yellow to a burst of enveloping incandescence. She lost her grip and went skidding, feet first, over the edge of the stairway and down—it was now so steeply tilted that she hardly touched a step. She ended up in a mess of the linen and the shattered bust, and saw that Strelow was pulling himself from under the linen. There were screams from nearby, but she had no time to get any coherent grasp of where she was. The aluminum superstructure was coming apart. One second Strelow was there, free, and stretching an arm toward her, the next he had disappeared through a funnel ringed by fire. That was fearful, a fiery mouth opening to take her, all else poured into it. She let go and gave herself to it.

■

Byrnes lost his hat in a surge of air that seemed to spring from the ground—it lifted his trousers. Suction—the fireball had grown in one blast and now gulped air. Amid the screams and shouts someone yelled "Get an ambulance," and it was the only distinct voice Byrnes heard. Getting an ambulance would not help a lot. How long? Twenty seconds. The whole thing, end to end, consumed. Swastikas burning, the tail end nearly gone and falling fast. Look out for people. The nose right up there, maybe five hundred feet, and the fire was into the clouds. Men running from under. Byrnes couldn't move. The heat. Stupefying. The smell. Chemical. Sand blowing through his hair. Newsreel camera still turning. Heidel in there. It made a difference if you knew somebody. Otherwise . . . Byrnes crossed himself; his eyes were smarting.

In the passenger building people were screaming, but they didn't leave the windows, even when the explosion came. From behind, as they were frozen there, they looked against the inferno like figures from a wall at Pompeii—that's what Miriam thought. She recalled the outlines burned into a wall there, and it was volcanic here, too. How strange. She gripped Bueller's arm to the bone. Bueller was all bone. He felt brittle. His hot breath on her neck—something like vapor from a kettle just under the boil. A cry that never found voice.

■

Strelow crawled across the sand toward her. They seemed inside a dome made of a phosphorescent web—she lay, unable to move, something heavy across her legs. Strelow reached out for her and she gripped his hand. The fire was like liquid: it showered in droplets and turned instantly to steam in the sand. She saw a drop fall on Strelow's jacket and burn out in a crisp bubble. He was pulling. She could not move. Beyond—what was beyond? Air on fire. Figures moving in it but not moving in any earthly way. Strelow pulled again. He was saying something, but the roar was too great. Then they were engulfed. A torrent. She was saturated—soaked with water. Whatever had trapped her was gone. She crawled and fell into Strelow. Water still poured over them. He pulled her to her feet, and then, still holding her hand, began to run into the cascade of fire.

■

People came out of it. People ran toward it but were driven back. Some of them met—those coming out and those bent on reaching them. The ship's nose was the last to settle and collapse into the rest. It seemed to Byrnes that the whole field was on fire. The clouds glowed. How many people were in that thing? He had no idea—but it was astonishing to see anyone come out. There was more coherence now: fire trucks appeared, though the hoses were useless. Survivors were carried on litters. How would he find Heidel?

He realized that not all the people in the passenger building had been waiting to go. Some were relatives of those on board—a few Germans, mostly Americans, including children. He was looking for Miriam and Bueller. It was more distressing in here than outside. He couldn't see them. Then he saw her chauffeur who, it turned out, was looking for him. They—Miriam and Bueller—were in the Rolls.

She had a rug around her and sat in the backseat like a monarch with mute consort. Bueller was still correct in every detail.

There was ash on the roof of the Rolls, and some blew into Byrnes's hair as he bent to the half-lowered window.

"I wish to go," she said.

"To *go?*"

"Of course."

"What about Heidel?"

"Your business."

He put a hand on the window as though it might detain the car.

She patted the rug to her thigh. "The traffic will be awful."

Bueller's face, in the glow from the fire, showed the first sign of sweat.

Byrnes dropped his hand from the window, gave her one final and contemptuous study, and turned away.

The Rolls began to move.

Byrnes wandered for a while, but it was not the wandering of a confused mind. His mind was unusually clear. Purged of delusions by the catastrophe. A religious clarity: he had the renewed devotion of the spared. Only one sin to be confessed, and that would be put to rest early. The survivors were accounted for, and there were a merciful number: perhaps sixty of the ninety-seven passengers and crew on board. He tried to find Heidel, but no one at first bothered with names. The first casualty center was the airfield dispensary, but it could not cope. Byrnes followed the ambulances to the nearest hospital, ten miles away.

It was an hour or so before he was able to see a list of names. Heidel was not on it, but he found Freda Eichberg. They said she was burned, but not badly, and that he could see her. No one else had asked for her.

Most of her hair was gone.

"Mr. Byrnes."

"Miss Eichberg. Glad to find you. Very glad. Terrible thing."

"I am not too bad, you see."

There were dark blue rings around her eyes and a rawness in her voice.

"Remarkable, just remarkable that anyone could walk out of that."

"I was saved by a man. What has happened to him I do not know. His name is Strelow."

"Strelow? I believe I saw that name on the list of survivors."

"The strangest thing, Mr. Byrnes. In the middle of it, that fire, we were soaked in water. Water. But for that we would have died. Really. Somebody said it was the water tank. I do not remember —"

He saw that she was shaking. "You take it easy. Miss Eichberg, I'm looking for Herr Heidel. You see him?"

"Herr Heidel?" She spoke as though just recalling him. "No. No. I was not with him when it happened. I do not remember—"

"Okay," intervened a voice, "let the lady rest, please. Please, sir."

A young nurse went to the bed.

"Of course. Miss Eichberg." He looked at her. "I'll take care of everything. Don't you worry."

He set about doing that directly. The Paul Kimball Hospital was handling the emergency well, but it was no place to leave Freda Eichberg. He found the immigration officer who was going through a passenger list with a zeppelin official and arranged to take responsibility for her. There was still no trace of Heidel—ten or so people were unaccounted for. The *Hindenburg*'s crew had fared worse than the passengers; by the latest count more than twenty had died.

"This man Strelow," said Byrnes, confirming the name on the list of survivors, "where is he?"

"Why do you ask?" said the zeppelin man.

"He saved Miss Eichberg's life."

"Really so?" The German looked too whimsical for the circumstances. "Herr Strelow is not here."

"But I thought—"

"Not here."

"You heard the man," said the immigration officer, who was besieged.

Byrnes swiftly forgot Strelow. He was called to the phone.

It was Casey, from California. "Miriam called me. Where is Heidel?"

"He's missing."

"You mean, dead?"

"Not confirmed. It's chaotic here."

"Awful. Awful. The radio is putting out an eyewitness account. The goddamned reporter broke down and cried. You okay, Pat?"

"I'm taking care of Heidel's assistant, Miss Eichberg. She's in pretty good shape. Going to get her into a New York hospital."

"Yeah. Take care of it. Say, what do we do if Heidel is dead? Who do we deal with?"

"I will talk with March about that."

"Yeah. Yeah—maybe we don't need the middleman anymore, Pat. What the hell is going on there?"

"People are trying to find people."

"Awful. You going back to the Plaza?"

"Guess so."

"I'll reach you there. Say, Miriam seems to have taken it pretty well."

"In her way."

Byrnes's tone surprised himself and Casey.

"What was that?"

"Yes. She's okay."

□

"Better get her on a boat, Pat."

As Byrnes hung up, he realized that the zeppelin man had been waiting outside the phone booth.

"Mr. Byrnes."

"Yes?"

"About Miss Eichberg."

"Yes?"

"It's good of you to be concerned, but you really do not need to go to such trouble. We will take care of her."

"We?"

"The Zeppelin company."

Byrnes felt unfamiliar with himself: after the sharpness with Casey he was now vigorously disliking the German—following his instincts.

"It's no trouble. Miss Eichberg is a business associate. I have an obligation."

"It would be better if we took care of her, I think."

"*Better?* For whom? *Listen,* Miss Eichberg is going to have the best people in New York take care of her."

The German hesitated, trying to contain his habit of command.

"Very well, Mr. Byrnes."

Was he frightened of something? Byrnes was puzzled.

Hesitating again, the German looked around Byrnes to the phone, and then, stepping halfway into the booth, said, "You know, Mr. Byrnes, this disaster could have been avoided. It was the fault of you Americans."

"Pardon?"

"We wanted to use helium gas for the *Hindenburg.* We asked to buy the helium from your government. They refused. We had no alternative but to use hydrogen. Helium does not burn."

"You sure have a strange sense of responsibility, sir. In this country the guy who runs the show takes the rap."

Byrnes walked out through the bedlam feeling at the beginning of something, rather than the end.

□

"I would just love to own a piece of that newsreel, Jack. Just about every movie house in the country is running it."

May Lindt held up the morning paper for Casey to see the sequence of photographs, stills from the newsreel, of the *Hindenburg*'s last moments. The rim of the paper had already curled crisp in the sun.

"Yes," he said, glancing over the top of his half-frame reading glasses and then returning to his own paper. "Zeppelin stock sure isn't worth a bean today. It's the end of those things." He checked his watch. "Ten o'clock in the east. By now I should have a piece of Pan American."

"Jack, you're still quick on your feet."

"With you I need to be."

"You say the sweetest things, honey."

"Please don't call me honey."

"It was a joke."

Without looking up he said, "This other damned joke of yours. The pinko parade. I don't like that, either."

"It's good for me. I'm getting interviews again."

"Forget it."

"What do you mean, *forget* it?"

He looked up. "You're a memory."

She stood up as she had under the direction of her favorite Austrian, himself a pupil of Eisenstein. Now, as then, she was too brittle for a queen. The swan spoke with a crow's voice.

"You have never understood. What do *you* know about the public? *What?* What kind of a public have *you* ever had? How many people love you?"

He leaned back into the sun, putting his glasses on top of the paper. The liver spots and freckles on his brow had combined into a kind of hide: he looked, with the creases of ill-humor, like a disturbed iguana.

"Public?" he said. "I despise the public."

She took a few moments to stop listening to herself and to take in what, with open spontaneity, he had said. The truth of it came as the taste of something unexpectedly sharp, puckering her mouth into more than a pout, less than a gasp.

Satisfied, he returned to Wall Street, while she went inside, still absorbing the enormity of his attitude. It was not morally offensive; it didn't hit her on that side of the mind. It was more an insult to loved ones. Combined with his insult to her personally, it revealed him as unfitted to be there at all, in *Hollywood*—she recalled one of her Babylonian epics where all the pleasures of the palm gardens had been foreclosed by a gothic tyrant who had shown the same contempt for popular sentiment. As this parable flowered in her mind, the telephone by her pillow trilled into the satin. On the patio he wouldn't hear it, and the Japanese manservant was in the kitchen. She picked it up.

"Yes?" she said, weakly.

"Mr. Casey there?"

"Who is this?"

"Farrio. Vincent Farrio."

"Hello, Mr. Farrio."

"Miss Lindt?"

"Yes. Mr. Casey is busy. Can I give him a message?"

Farrio paused, but his breath conveyed to her that he was one of her public. "Would you do that, Miss Lindt? Just tell him that everything is set. Oh, Miss Lindt."

□

"Yes?"

"I saw your name on the list of supporters for the rally."

"That's right."

"Can I give you some advice, Miss Lindt?"

"That's very sweet of you, Mr. Farrio."

"Stay away from that rally. There could be some trouble."

"What kind of trouble?"

"You know how it is, Miss Lindt. These things get out of hand. There are a lot of crazy people around; this sort of thing attracts crazy people."

"I see."

"It's been a pleasure speaking with you, Miss Lindt."

"It's very kind of you to give me your advice, Mr. Farrio."

"Yes. Well—you've always been one of my idols, Miss Lindt."

"Thank you, Mr. Farrio. I most certainly will give your message to Mr. Casey."

It was a day when her mind seemed to get clearer by the minute—successively shocked into perception. She lay looking at the pink telephone and then formed a resolve. It seemed to offer a dramatic opening for her—a role altogether modern, from the more European-minded studios.

■

"Well, it was a deliverance, to be sure," said Tom. He tried to show in his voice how agreeable it felt to have his father call from New York.

"Yes, it was, Tom, just as I feel about it. Of course, poor Miriam is too distressed to see it that way."

"Ah yes. She would be."

"Tom."

"Pat?"

"I understand that you must follow your conscience. Of course, it's not my point of view. But I think a man, and especially a man of the cloth, must follow his conscience. You'll not have a lot of friends in the church—but I imagine heresy brings its own companionships."

"I don't see it as heresy, Pat," said Tom, wondering how far the novelty of wit had dawned with his father.

"No. No, I don't suppose you do, Tom. Well then. The thing is, you keep yourself well away from those Bolsheviks."

"I'm not one of them, Pat." Tom looked across the desk to where Stern was composing a speech, and permitted himself a smile. "Pat, have you called Mary?"

"No. No, I have not."

"She would like that."

"You can give her my love, Tom."

"I will."

"Yes. Have you heard from Liam, Tom?"

"No. Mary thinks there's no cause to worry, that loss of contact is not unusual there in that situation."

"I'll see what I can find out."

"It was good to hear from you, Pat."

"Yes. I'll call you from Boston, Tom."

When Tom put down the phone Stern put aside her fake concentration.

"Your *father* called you?"

"He did. He did. It's a strange thing. He seemed changed. He was at Lakehurst when the *Hindenburg* crashed."

"On business, I'm sure."

"The man he went to meet was killed."

"Sounds like an act of God."

"That's blasphemous, coming from you."

"I thought you couldn't talk to your father."

"There is always hope of redemption, with anyone, Nora."

"You said, 'I'm not one of them.' You know something? You never will be. Sad to say."

"How is the speech?"

"I'm sorry. I couldn't help overhearing."

"Eyes and ears."

"What does *that* mean?" She squared up to him in her rabid way.

He held up a peaceable hand. "Please. It was a joke."

□

As ideology struggled with affection she was momentarily maladroit, dropping notes on the floor.

Neither of them saw May Lindt at the door.

■

"I went to my room to finish packing, we had been in the smoking room. I never saw him again." Freda spoke quietly. "Chance. They could not fill all the berths. He was offered it at the last moment."

"Well," said Byrnes, "there are things to be thankful for. It seems remarkable to me, only thirteen passengers died. Doesn't seem possible, so few . . . I can't forget, the sight of it . . . terrible."

"I remember little."

Byrnes seemed not to hear her; only part of him was present, she thought; the rest had been mislaid. He looked out the window as though thinking the rest might be coming across the lawn. Distraction with a touch of charm in it. Her mind was clearer than his.

"He had been happy," she said.

"Heidel?"

"Things were going well for him."

"A man needs only so much money . . . after a certain point . . ."

"Mr. Byrnes, you've been very kind."

"Least I could do. Beautiful place, this. Before it was a hospice it was in the same family two hundred years. Tom Paine stayed here. Sanctuary." At last he moved his attention fully to her. "You're looking much better."

"I hope my hair grows back."

"The superior says you can be out of here in a few days."

"Mr. Byrnes—"

"Pat. Please call me Pat."

"Pat—I—"

"What is it?"

"Do you know what happened to Herr Strelow?"

"No. No—tell you the truth, it escaped my mind. I guess you'd like to thank him."

"It's all I remember, him pulling me out."

□

"You'll miss the cortege. They're expecting a lot of people. I guess Strelow will be there, when they take the caskets to the *Hamburg.* Full military honors."

A nun came into the room with a new flask of water.

"Well, Miss Eichberg, I have to go." Byrnes was collected now, and bright with some undeclared resolve. "You come stay with us in Boston when the sisters have done with you, would you?"

"You're very kind."

"Good. Fine. Fine. She's mending well, Sister."

"She is, sir," said the nun.

Freda recalled the desiccated Byrnes at the table in Biarritz and wondered whether it was simply the glow of the hospice that had infected him, or whether she had misjudged him, that in an alien setting he just hadn't been himself. Whatever. She liked America. It made it easy to forget. Pastor Gregory and the Lutherans would scorn these nuns with their bucolic retreat—full bellies and virgin faith ringing from the chapel each dawn over the lawns and the pond. It was too easy to forget.

■

Liam saw Mary and Cordón standing at the gate. The DC-3 swung to a stop with a last rasp from one engine, and the slipstream caught Mary's hair, lifting it sharply away from her brow as the wind used to when they walked the beach at the Cape—hair alive like fanned flame. A few seconds to assess them without their seeing him. She looked more senior; the glimpse had the feel of portent, of her filling out into a role, distinctive and public, that would be set for the rest of her life. A public woman.

Cordón held himself back in her shadow. He must know it too. California hadn't been able to soften him. Liam knew Cordón better now for having known his enemies. He could not fight Cordón, not even for her. Especially not for her.

Then he was stepping down aluminum into the sun.

"You look one hundred percent, Tiger."

"I am."

"Nick."

"Liam."

"You didn't waste any time," she said.

"There's a lot to explain." He didn't quite know how to touch her.

She kissed his cheek and took his arm, to walk. "We're going to do that—take the plane, when we go back east."

Liam turned to Cordón. "How much has come out on Guernica?"

"Very little in the newspapers."

"It's not been clear," she said. "Contradictions."

"I was there. Two days afterward."

"You *were?*" They were inside the terminal. She stopped. "I want to know everything. *Everything.*"

"That's why I'm here."

"Yes." She looked at him more carefully. "I can see it in you, Liam."

A porter brought his bags.

"Jesus, Tiger. Whose car is this?"

She laughed. "It belongs to a man called Don Chambers."

"California."

Cordón opened a door for him. "I cannot take California seriously," he said. "But there are good people here. Some good people."

Liam and Mary sat together, with Cordón facing them on a jump seat.

"So you're really feeling as good as you look, Tiger?"

But Cordón answered. "She will not rest."

"I am fine."

"It is no good arguing with her," said Cordón, too passively for Liam's taste. "But you must know that." Then something drew his attention to the road behind the car as they came into a straight, climbing stretch. "The same car, every time."

"What is it?" said Liam.

"Our shadows," said Mary.

"Who?"

"FBI. Still with us."

"They do nothing," said Cordón.

"Well—I don't like it," said Liam.

□

She put a hand on his arm. "Don't let it bother you. What can they do?"

"Makes me feel like a hood."

"Makes me feel we're necessary."

Liam settled only reluctantly. "Who is this Don Chambers?"

■

Rohleder was in uniform, Strelow did not. They stood side by side with heads briefly bowed. The final bars of "Deutschland über Alles" echoed against the hull of the SS *Hamburg,* not quite loud enough to exclude the sound of traffic beyond Pier 86. The ceremony had caused congestion and provoked horns.

"What does that man think he's doing?" whispered Rohleder.

A photographer disregarded the anthem and stepped to the line of caskets. He knelt to get a low angle on the row of Nazi storm troopers with hands raised in salute.

"America," said Strelow. "Nothing is sacred."

"Yes. America. So big. So weak."

There were twenty-eight caskets, each draped with the Nazi flag. Thousands of people had come, many more than the police had been prepared for. The only disciplined calm was here, where the storm troopers formed the final avenue for the assignment of the *Hindenburg*'s victims to the boat.

"Lehmann is remarkable," said Rohleder.

Captain Lehmann stood with the other survivors of his crew. A singed raven.

At that moment a reporter, as heedless of the protocol as the photographer, broke ranks and went up to Lehmann.

"Captain Lehmann, is this the end of the airships? What do you say, sir, to the people who say that?"

Lehmann appeared not to hear the question.

"Captain Lehmann—" insisted the reporter, and two others joined him. Lehmann stared past them.

Two storm troopers came from behind him and began to pull the reporters away.

"Hey, buddy," said one, standing his ground. "This is the United States. Not Germany."

Another storm trooper appeared and the reporters were bundled away.

"Good," said Rohleder.

Lehmann remained at the head of the caskets like a gatherer of the dead. Strelow could have answered the pertinent question: no Graf Zeppelin would cross the Atlantic again. He, like others, had always thought the airships a grand folly.

"Good," said Rohleder again, switching his attention to Strelow. "Just one other matter left for us."

"You can leave it to me, Major."

"Yes." Rohleder was not warm. "Yes."

■

"Appalling," said Chambers, "really *appalling.*" It understated his emotions; though flamboyant in dress and furnishings, he was old-world when it came to voicing feelings. Although intent on everything Liam had told them, he had gradually moved his eyes away, to a private focus in the direction of the ocean—without seeing it. "The problem is, people won't want to believe it, you see. I don't think I would have believed it, without getting it from someone who saw it for themselves. People just don't want to believe these things. You see."

"Liam," said Mary decisively, "*Liam,* you have to tell it to the people just like you told it to us."

"You mean—on the platform?"

"Why not?" said Chambers.

Mary nodded, and so did Cordón and Tom.

"That's right," said Tom. "*You* tell the story of Guernica. Then people will listen."

"I'm no good at public speaking. Never was. It terrifies me."

"It's not public speaking," said Tom. "Not rhetoric. You tell them what you've just told us, in the same way. In the same words."

"You carry a unique conviction," said Chambers.

"I'll introduce you," said Mary.

□

"I don't have any choice, do I?"

"No," she said. "What was done at Guernica makes it unnecessary for us to make any more speeches which are just slogans. We do not have to explain the character of our enemies. They have done it for themselves."

"Yes, they have," said Chambers. "Beyond any argument."

"And you can quote a priest as witness," said Mary.

"I'm going to need all the help you can give me, Tiger," said Liam, coming to her as Chambers led them out to the terrace for lunch.

"You'll be fine. Looking at you, as you told that story—I saw something in you I've never seen before, Liam." She hesitated, wanting more privacy than was possible, and therefore wondering why she was not able to say what she wanted to say. Instead, she said, "You were wonderful, what you did for Giles. He's in Gibraltar now?"

"Yes." Liam had not missed her evasion, but was in some way satisfied by it. "Yes—I confirmed that before I left France. He'll need a while to recover." He made a show of being casual, giving her a plate from the buffet, but spoke more as he felt. "He'll go back. In his eyes he had the same absence from his surroundings that you have."

"Liam." She touched him on the sleeve. "You have the look of a man who's no longer sure what kind of clothes to wear."

"That's the climate."

"No. Don't be so light."

"That's not easy. Since we're both trying to look so light."

She stopped talking and jabbed a fork into the food in an aggravated way.

"You *are* going back," he said.

"Of course."

■

This America was more English than she had thought it was going to be: Freda watched two women riding horses, dressed as for an English hunt. She sat at the window of her room. The riders were some way off, black against the emerald, spiky with bearing. She hadn't heard the sister open the door.

"Miss Eichberg, there's a friend to see you."

Normally she heard every step on the parquet. Puzzled, she looked beyond the sister.

It was Strelow.

Earthbound, he was somehow smaller and not to be feared. He smiled. He, too, it seemed was dressed for England, in a tweed jacket and flannels, very barbered. No. She was not frightened.

"How are you?" he said.

"I'm well." She stood up and patted the bandana that covered her scalp. "Probably I look worse than I am. And you. You look unharmed, really."

The sister left them.

"Yes, I was fortunate."

"Best not to remember too much. Please. Sit down."

He was sanguine in every movement, like a man with the natural habit of reassuring others. She had to remember who he was and what he did.

"So," he said, taking a chair at the other side of the window. "This is pleasant. I understand you will be leaving soon."

"At the end of the week."

They examined each other in the benign light, aware of their connection being a profanity in such a place.

"You saved my life," she said.

He didn't respond.

"Why?"

"It was possible."

She thought that to be an answer worth judging him by, and sat there in silence for a whole minute.

"I am worth more to you alive," she said.

His blandness was only so deep, but he held to it.

"It is true, I see," she said.

With a kindling of anger he said, "I could not have left you there to die."

"Why not? What is the difference, really?"

But he recovered his composure, looking warily once to the still open door, and then not answering.

"You know, Captain Strelow, you have a weakness, I think."

He looked at her sharply.

"Yes," she said, "you are human. They need people like you. They could not exist without people like you."

She had won the temporary advantage—but little comfort from it. On different ground he would deal with her more belligerently.

"At least you didn't bring me flowers," she said.

■

"The lady didn't take your advice," said Pea Coat.

"I guess she needs the publicity," said Farrio.

"Still looks like a million dollars."

"It's where they stop the car," said Farrio. "That marks the pros. See. She had the car pull up in the middle of the goddamn street. Then she has to walk twice the distance."

"Some walk."

May Lindt's progress between the police barriers was a measured work of art. Her dress was at least ten years out of fashion. The skirt went to her ankles, weighted with a brocade hem and split up the calf. Her derriere (she called it that) was clad and yet as good as naked. It was a silver mirage—never settled, never definite in contours, unattainable and irresistible. Most effectively it was her own signature, something remembered fondly and undiminished. She walked as its originator and sole possessor. And she was loved for it: vocally and avidly. She had destroyed fashion in twenty seconds.

"Hope she knows what she's doing," said Pea Coat.

"She knows." Farrio had to remember what else was on his mind; he looked at the people beyond the lights. "A full house."

"They don't know Spain from shit."

"They pay. This is money."

Inside the theater Stern watched the stalls from high above, from a window of the cubicle where the lights were controlled. Tom stood with her.

"You're sure it's going to work?" he said.

"Sure I'm sure. Most of them were obvious."

"Most of them," he repeated.

"The rest, wherever they are, we can get to. It's all worked out."

"Nora, you have unsuspected resources."

She turned from the window. "Unsuspected? I thought everything was revealed. To people like you."

"You're a series of revelations, not all of them expected."

She pushed a hand into his stomach. "Then learn."

Below them, backstage, Cordón sat with Liam. They both wore black suits and red ties. Liam was sipping a Bushmills.

"You know, Nick," he said, "I never was taught anything I needed to know."

The voices and laughter coming through the curtains left Liam and Cordón as isolated as if they were in a hotel room above a traffic-filled boulevard. And in being isolated they knew how close they had become, though neither was able to say so in words. With so little in common they stood together.

Farrio and Pea Coat found seats near the back. Farrio said, "Count 'em. Some show."

Stern took one last, lingering bird's-eye view. "Robinson, Cagney, Loy—it gets better by the minute. And May Lindt—of course."

Tom had watched May Lindt go down the center aisle. "She tries too hard."

"I like her."

"A pity about the company she keeps."

"Let's go down, Tom. I have to be there when they make their move."

"They'll wait. Farrio is the one to watch. I wonder how Liam's feeling. It would intimidate me." He led her to the iron steps.

Mary heard them coming. She had suppressed her dislike of Stern, but it was an insecure truce, made easier by the way her brother had made his own adjustment. Tom absorbed all Stern's aggression like a pillow smothering a pistol.

"How many of them are there?" she asked.

"About twenty," said Stern. "Not difficult to pick out. They have a smell."

"Bastards."

□

"Don't worry. They're all marked."

"I saw Farrio," said Mary. "Last time I saw him in a clear light was on the dock at Charleston."

"How is Liam?" said Tom.

"Liam is very odd. He's gotten modest."

"Ah yes. I know what you mean. Like something inside of him has departed."

"Stage fright," said Stern briskly.

"No." Tom shook his head. "*No.* Not at all."

"That's me," said Mary. "The stage fright. I've never seen an audience like this. It's knowing so many faces."

"You'll be just fine," said Tom with—he heard it himself—a shade too much of the benediction. Both women were impervious to benedictions.

"Chaplin isn't here," said Mary.

"No," said Nora.

"You know," said Mary, "they're showing *Modern Times* in Madrid. I thought we could expect him. That is a very political film."

"Time to get up there," said Tom.

Farrio looked around the theater. "They know what to look for? All of them? You sure?"

"When you take off your hat."

"Right. This should be beautiful to see."

The curtain went up. Liam, Cordón, and Nora Stern sat at the rear of the stage in front of a blank screen. Mary stood center stage at the microphone under a stagewide banner, AMERICANS FOR A DEMOCRATIC SPAIN. Her black dress was full-length and hung in folds gathered togalike at one shoulder. She was such a strikingly austere figure and so still that the audience fell instantly silent.

"Thank you, ladies and gentlemen, for coming, and for your generosity." The steadiness of her voice surprised her. "We are a very long way from Spain, here tonight. Not only in distance. We are a long way from Spain in the condition of our lives. We are free. We are Americans. So—why should we care about Spain?"

Pea Coat murmured, "I don't give a shit, lady."

From the wings Chambers thought—as Mary let the question hang in the air—that her control of the audience was already absolute.

"We should care. We should care because we believe in nations like our own, ruled by consent and not by arms. From the beginning this war in Spain was an insurrection, an armed insurrection planned by people who do not uphold anything remotely like the kind of freedoms we enjoy. We should care because our own good fortune is also our own responsibility. A standard we have to carry. And, ladies and gentlemen, anyone anywhere who looks to us for help in carrying that standard must not be turned away. They must not . . ."

Farrio's hat remained in place. It gave him a feeling of capricious power. Yet he found himself having to concede her guts, Mary's guts. He knew about her injuries. A copy of the hospital report was in his file.

". . . and now I would like to introduce someone who has just returned from Spain. Someone who has seen both sides of the war. An eyewitness without any political affiliation—"

"This is the one I'm waiting for," said Farrio.

Liam came to the microphone.

The theater lights went down, leaving a single beam on the screen at the back of the stage.

"I want to show you a town," said Liam. "It is called Guernica."

A still flashed up on the screen.

"This is what Guernica once looked like."

The still faded and was replaced by another, of a street hardly recognizable as a street.

"This is what Guernica looks like now."

There were gasps from the audience.

The picture faded and the lights went up.

"I want to describe to you what I saw in Guernica. I want to take you on a walk through that town . . ."

Farrio removed his hat slowly, wiping his brow.

"Lies! All faked! All lies!" came a shout from somewhere near the front. *"Red propaganda! Damned red propaganda!"*

Liam paused and looked down, unflustered. He saw two men standing in the second row—one shouting and raising a fist. Then others, dispersed through the audience, rose and took up the chant, *"Lies! Lies! Lies!"*

□

Tom, standing with Chambers in the wings, said, "Handpicked for their size."

"And voices."

"Very nice," said Pea Coat.

But Farrio was watching the man who had risen next to the first provocateur in the second row. He was not one of them. All over the theater, while the audience began to protest, other men rose alongside or near Farrio's men—and they were just as big.

Laim said, "Ladies and gentlemen, please remain in your seats. We have been expecting this."

Lindt looked up at Liam and then she stood, finding a voice that she hoped would be heard and remembered by the famous German director she had seen in the front row. Lifting an arm that had been seen on the Babylonian ramparts she cried, "Away with them! Agitators! *Fascists!*"

Farrio stood. "What the fuck . . . ?"

Stern was placid at the rear of the stage. She turned to Mary. "Aren't they beautiful? My longshoremen?"

Pea Coat was bewildered.

Within a minute all the provocateurs were being bundled up the aisles. Some tried to fight, but were instantly overpowered.

Suddenly the entire theater was applauding.

Liam held up a hand and waited for it to subside.

"Well," he said, "*they* talked of lies." He nodded into the silence. "And *I* want to talk of lies. You'll find that, according to some newspapers, Guernica was blown up by its own people. As Ernest Hemingway says, and Hemingway has been there and knows, fascism is a lie told by bullies. A writer who will not lie cannot live or work under fascism. So let me continue the walk through Guernica . . ."

Farrio and Pea Coat were still in their seats. Farrio had to restrain Pea Coat. "We can't—we can't do any more." And they had to sit and wait until the audience rose in sustained applause for Liam.

Mary came to Liam's side at the microphone.

"You were wonderful."

Bathed in light and seen by so many they were alone, aware of the old intimacies of skin, hair, and smell.

□

Then she held up a hand. "Finally, a man who wants your money. A Spaniard . . ."

Outside, Farrio heard the new burst of applause for Cordón. Pea Coat was opening the door of their Ford. Out of the darkness behind them four or five large men came running.

Farrio leapt into the driving seat and shouted, "Let's get the fuck outta here." Pea Coat had to sprint to get in the car. Without lights Farrio swung around and headed straight at the pursuers. A baton hit the trunk and another the roof.

"They were *ours,*" said Pea Coat with confused rage.

"Fucking bums," spat Farrio, turning into Hollywood Boulevard and, still without lights, attracting the notice of a patrol car that began, unseen, to move after him.

■

Freda could not be sure; the picture in the *Daily News* was packed with faces. She picked out Captain Lehmann with certainty. Behind Lehmann, overshadowed by saluting storm troopers, she thought it might be Rohleder, but Rohleder had a face that readily evaded. She was still looking at the paper when Byrnes came in with the superior.

"Well now," he said, "I'm told you want to go."

"She is not a very patient patient." The superior smiled.

Freda put aside the paper. "I am grateful to you; you have all been very good to me. But I think it is no good to me to be spoiled. Really."

"I'll leave you with Mr. Byrnes, then," said the superior.

"Thank you for coming," said Freda, beckoning Byrnes to the chair by the window. She waited until the door was closed. "Mr. Byrnes, I have to tell you something, something that I think you will find hard to believe. I have to put my life in your hands."

He frowned. "Your life . . . ? But you are in no danger now, Miss Eichberg."

"You see. It's hard to believe it. Lying here, everything so good, these kind people, such a beautiful place. All so far from Germany. Mr. Byrnes, Captain Strelow came to see me."

"The man who saved you."

She shocked him with a brassy laugh. "Yes. Yes. Captain Strelow saved me. He saved me so that he could take me back to Berlin. You see, dear Mr. Byrnes, before the *Hindenburg* crashed Captain Strelow had arrested me. He is—he is a kind of policeman. We have so many kinds of policemen in Germany."

To her surprise Byrnes assumed a kind of imperturbable sagacity that reminded her of Pastor Gregory. He looked at her as though more familiar with her than he had been a minute earlier.

"A strange thing, Miss Eichberg, a strange thing. Back in Biarritz I had a feeling. It hardly registered. Fact is, I really didn't know until now that it had registered. Let me tell you, strange things are happening to me like—like a premonition in reverse, an ignored memory. Know the kind of thing? Like something surfacing from a dream. But it wasn't a dream. I thought you were—you were what? Not what you seemed. Do you follow? Freda? Do you believe that such things happen?"

"Yes."

"If they arrested you, you must be working against them. That takes a lot of courage."

"For me, there never was any question."

He considered this with a slowly confirming eye. "Yes. Yes. My father felt that way—about the British in Ireland. I remember that. Conviction. It's in my children, you know. It passed to them. I—somehow I was frightened of it. I met Jack Casey. Two smart kids on the make. I'm sorry. Not the time. I've been blind to a number of things." With sudden resolution swallowing his introversion, he got up and said, "Well, Freda, this is America. This man Strelow can't just . . ."

"They will if they can, Mr. Byrnes."

"I guess they might. I guess that's the kind of people they are."

"I have to get to Canada. There are people there who will be able to get me to Russia."

"Russia?" The idea settled into him more with curiosity than shock.

And he repeated it without the question, "Russia. There's a lot I don't know about you, Freda."

"Can you help me?"

"Of course. We should not waste any time."

He seemed stimulated, rejuvenated, she thought, having never seen such purpose in him.

■

"My press agent," said May Lindt, "says this is something we can build on."

Casey didn't reply.

That morning's papers—the Chandler paper and the Hearst paper—had been clipped before he came out to breakfast, and he sat trying to read a page that had been eviscerated—May Lindt's style with scissors was cavalier; she cut in grand gestures, enlarging a one-line reference to herself with its surroundings as if it were a footprint on the highway of history. She had severed the last third of a stock market report, and Casey had to switch papers. The Hearst report of the rally had made more of the interruption than of the speeches.

"You hear me?" she said.

He looked but did not speak.

"I was *noticed,*" she said. "Cagney kissed my hand afterward." Irresistibly drawn to his ill-temper like a flame advancing erratically along a fuse to a bomb, she tightened the belt of her robe, took a bite of toast, and picked up the discarded paper. "Liam was just wonderful. I cried."

He grinned without mercy. "You sure it was your hand that Cagney kissed?"

But she remained placid. "Jack," she said, after another bite, "you really shouldn't be here. I see that now. It makes you too sensitive."

"What?"

"Jack, you're insecure." Fearlessly—angelically—she went to him and patted his scalp. "A man like you. Imagine. *Insecure.* You're a man's man, Jack. It's the place. Things aren't like that here."

The fuse had burned out just before reaching the charge—he intercepted her intention.

The Japanese gardener moved through the shrubs pumping a shroud of insecticide in which the sun was diffused into chemical shades.

"My God," he said, "you do believe your own fucking publicity." He pulled loose the belt of her robe. "Okay. Let the dago take another look at these. That's *all* he does, I'll bet." He took one breast in his grip and squeezed hard. "I'll leave you to it. I'm heading back east."

Through the tears she smiled without hurt or malice. A strand of marmalade glistened on her lip.

■

"You know, Freda, you're a very handsome woman. As well as a brave one."

Byrnes helped her out of the car.

"I look terrible, Mr. Byrnes. I have no hair under this hat."

"Not at all." He surprised himself with his display of emotion. "I'm really sorry you have to leave." He pulled his own hat lower on his brow. "You must write me, from Russia."

"You have been very kind to me." She leaned forward and pecked his cheek, with a discreet touch of the tongue.

The chauffeur came around and gave her one bag to a porter. Another man came toward them across the concourse of the railroad station. He was dressed in bright tweeds, wore wire-rimmed glasses, and carried a cane. He nodded to Byrnes and took off his fedora for Freda.

"Miss Eichberg," said Byrnes, "this is Sean Doyle."

"Pleased to meet you, Miss Eichberg," said Doyle, speaking as brightly as he was dressed.

"Mr. Doyle will be riding the train with you as far as the border at Niagara. You'll be in good hands."

"Yes," said Doyle, "I understand you are being met at the border."

"Yes."

"Well," said Byrnes, "I have to say good-bye. I've never done this kind of thing before. Makes me on edge, I can tell you." He looked to Doyle. "It seems hard to believe, Sean, that Miss Eichberg is in any kind of danger. I hope our little plan works."

"Don't worry, Mr. Byrnes," said Doyle. "I'll not let anything happen to her."

Without warning she kissed Byrnes again, her cloche hat brushing the rim of his trilby and knocking it slightly askew.

"I'll always remember you, Mr. Byrnes." She settled on her heels again and admired the rakish tilt to his hat—such a small thing made him look younger. "And I would be very grateful if you would say good-bye to Mr. Liam Casey for me. I am sorry I could not wait for him to return. That was such a fine speech he made."

"I will tell Liam," said Byrnes, resetting the line of his hat.

"We should get the train, Miss Eichberg," said Doyle.

As he watched them go, Byrnes felt caught on an unfamiliar tide, pulling clear of what once had seemed permanent anchorage. The way that Freda Eichberg walked was assured, and suggested what he felt was possible within himself—that anchorages could be broken without sorrow.

■

It was dark in the canyon, at least as dark as it ever got. That was another bitch of his about California. It never really was dark. He always liked a good dark night with some earthy smell to it, a night that clamped down hard. Trees and bog darkness with wood smoke. Not clear skies and oriental scents on a clammy wind, wind like a perfumed woman in heat. That damned painting had eyes like the Japanese gardener's. Looking every place except at you. In the semi-darkness the Picasso was full of deceits of line and intention. Then, caught momentarily in the beams of a car, it burned with color. It took the slammed car door to snap Casey out of it.

"Mr. Liam, sir," said the houseboy, backing away before Liam stepped from carpet to terra-cotta. Without being asked, the houseboy switched on the lights. Casey was surprised to see how dark

Liam was, not a California tan, much less cosmetic, leather-grained at the neck, peeling to roughness on the forehead. He was strengthened. No longer dressed by Miriam. Sweater under a linen jacket. Looking *ballsy.* Not a word he would have used for Liam before. Hostile with it, too. Not on his own. Somebody else talking to the houseboy.

"Jack."

"The prodigal returns."

"I wanted to—"

"You wanted to what?" cut in Casey with more edge than volume, barely above a whisper. "To explain?"

"I owe you that."

"You're too late. I read the papers."

"It was your idea—your idea that I should see both sides."

"It was." Casey nodded. "It was." He no longer looked like the aggressor. He stood for a few seconds, still flushed but assessing Liam with detachment. Then he went behind the bar.

"I'm having a drink. What about you?"

"A Bushmills," said Liam, transparently wary.

"A Bushmills," repeated Casey, reaching for the bottle. "You and me must be the only people in California who drink this stuff." He poured two straight glasses and gave one across the bar to Liam. "You look like you could use it."

They eyed each other as they drank.

"Yeah," said Casey, "I read the papers. I never knew you had it in you. A real rabble-rouser."

"It wasn't a rabble."

"They've got you, those people."

Liam put his glass on the bar. "Look, Jack. I've joined no party. I know what I'm against more clearly than I know what I'm for."

"That so?"

"I wasn't uninvolved. I know that. I was implicated. Giving March that line of credit was as lethal as dropping the bombs. It's the beginning of the chain."

"What did you suppose it was for—Hershey bars?"

"It took the evidence of my own eyes to understand."

They both finished their whiskeys.

□

"Jack, I'm not expecting any more of you. I'm expecting more of myself."

His father's eyes mocked before his voice did. "Until iniquity is pardoned?"

"You're not at all troubled by what's happening out there?"

Casey shook his head. "Let me tell you the difference between you and me. I recognize the guy who's out to steal my lunch."

"I won't be coming back to the bank."

"That's right. That's right. You won't." Casey refilled the two glasses without spilling a drop. Then he raised his own glass and nodded toward the Picasso. "You make as much sense as that guy."

Liam had not noticed the painting until then. He downed the Bushmills.

"What's the trouble, Liam? You disappointed we haven't had a fight? That what you wanted?"

"It might have been better."

"It's not that easy, Son."

More steps left the carpet for terra-cotta.

"Your moral support has arrived," said Casey.

Mary came to Liam's side.

"Good evening, Mr. Casey."

"If you were not Pat Byrnes's daughter you wouldn't be in this house."

"No, I wouldn't."

"You wouldn't expect me to be hypocrite enough to be polite."

"No. I wouldn't."

"Red Mary." Casey looked from her to Liam. "But not Red Liam. A lot of guilt. But no cause. Sanctimonious and stricken." He looked back at Mary. "You look more and more like your mother."

She tautened.

Casey raised his glass. "You both represent the best argument against nepotism that I ever saw. Now get out."

Outside, they were about to get into their car when they were caught in the beams of another car coming up the driveway between the palms. The driver pumped the horn, and it echoed through the canyon. It was a foreign convertible, lustrous pink. Lindt swerved to a halt beside them and leapt out in a breeze of silk and perfume.

"Liam, *darling!*" She put hands to each cheek and kissed him fully on the mouth.

"And *Mary!*" She caressed Mary. "You were both *so* wonderful. I tried to come backstage afterward but—my darlings—I had to oblige the photographers. You know how it is . . . Mary, I thought that you and your Spanish beau made such a striking couple, just like Loretta Young and Tyrone Power. Did you see them in *Love Is News?* You could *feel* the electricity." She suddenly paused and gazed at the house. "You've seen Jack?"

"We did," said Mary.

"Well, I'm truly sorry I missed that."

"Did you choose the Picasso?" said Mary.

"I did. I did. Don't you love it?"

"That was clever of you."

"Jack *hates* it."

"I know," said Liam, "I know." And he laughed. "Miss Lindt, you have a lot of guts."

"Yes, I do, Liam. However, your father has at last decided that he isn't happy in California. It's too—too wild for him."

"I can believe it," said Liam. "Well, we have to go. Mary and Nick are going back to Spain."

"My heart will always be with you," cooed Lindt as she embraced Mary again. "Take care now."

Driving away, it took Liam some minutes to lose the humor that Lindt had infected them with.

"She's the only person who has ever taken Jack," he said, "and I'm really glad."

"She *is* beautiful."

"Yes."

She watched Liam go, by this train of thought, to his encounter with his father—there was more speculation in his face than melancholy.

"What is it?" she said.

"I don't know. It seems crazy. But—"

"But what?"

"Well. He looked at me in a way that he never has before. It wasn't—it wasn't hostile."

□

"It sure felt hostile."

"No. No—we weren't talking. Just taking a slug of whiskey. I felt it. *I had become what he wanted me to be.* That make any sense? And the crazy thing is, the more I become what he wants me to be, the more we are pulled apart."

She put a hand on the back of his neck and felt the fall of his longer hair. "That makes sense. Fathers are hell."

■

The mother superior looked up warily as the two men were shown into her office. They were altogether too propelled. Barely a nod of reverence between them, and decidedly pagan in manner. Overdressed for the heat.

"Gentlemen," she said, hoping that the word would materialize in them.

Strelow got the hint and pitched his voice more respectfully than usual. "There seems to have been a misunderstanding, Reverend Mother, with regard to Fräulein Eichberg."

"Oh?"

Rohleder was less disposed to respect. He snapped, "Fräulein Eichberg was our responsibility. She has been released without our authority."

"Authority? And what authority is that?"

Strelow persisted in being more diplomatic. "I had arranged that we would take Fräulein Eichberg home."

"That was before Mr. Byrnes kindly offered."

"Byrnes?" said Rohleder.

"I am sorry, we have not been introduced."

Strelow said, "My apologies. This is Herr Schmidt, from our consulate."

Rohleder snapped heels as he bowed.

"Well, Captain Strelow and Herr Schmidt, Miss Eichberg seemed very happy to be in Mr. Byrnes's care."

"Mr. Patrick Byrnes?" said Strelow.

"Yes."

"I see." Strelow looked at Rohleder and managed to restrain him, then back at the superior. "We did not know that Mr. Byrnes had done so. I wonder, could you tell us where Mr. Byrnes took Fräulein Eichberg?"

"Herr Schmidt used the phrase, 'released without our authority.' You did not explain to which authority you referred."

"A figure of speech. Naturally, the consulate feels itself responsible for any German national who is unfortunate enough to be in an accident."

"Well, Captain Strelow. You will be happy to know that Fräulein Eichberg is making an excellent recovery. We were a little concerned for a time, not about her physical condition but about her spirit, which seemed to have succumbed. Understandable, after such a terrible experience. Happily, when she left with Mr. Byrnes she had quite recovered her spirit. The spirit is the great healer—wouldn't you agree, Captain Strelow?"

"Most surely. I am sorry—we are, of course, most pleased to know that Fräulein Eichberg is so well. No doubt Mr. Byrnes is taking good care of her."

When they were outside, fanning themselves with their hats, Rohleder vented his fury. "You should have taken her when you came before. Abwehr—this is Gestapo business, not Abwehr. You can be sure that this will go to the highest level."

Strelow was not cowed. He carefully replaced his panama and said, "I am sure that Mr. Byrnes will cooperate with us—once the situation is explained to him. We have to remember where we are, Rohleder."

"Oh," snarled Rohleder, "I know where we are, Strelow."

■

"I did not like this country, when I first came here. It takes time to understand it. Time to like it." Cordón stood at the porthole of their cabin, looking at the west side of Manhattan.

"I remember the snow," said Mary, "and Dave Backlund's face when he came into our room. Remember?"

"So many good people."

"We should go. They're waiting for us in the saloon. French boats smell French. Don't they?"

"It is like a honeymoon, a cabin like this."

She laughed. "That's unusually romantic of you."

"We should be romantic. While we can."

"My darling. Please. I know."

"I am not leaving what you are leaving. For me it is much easier. I am not leaving what I love."

"I am not leaving you." She held him and then broke away, saying, "We must go. Do I look okay?" She wiped her eyes.

Tom Byrnes had gathered everyone in a corner of the saloon on the promenade deck, and he stood apart from the rest, waiting. When Mary and Cordón came through the doors, he stepped forward.

"Nothing formal. You understand."

Behind him were Dave and Nina Backlund, Joe Dann, Ike Mandel, Abe Sachs—and Liam.

"Oh God, I'm going to cry," said Mary, taking Tom's hand.

"Go ahead," he said.

"I'm okay."

She looked at Sachs. "You see, Abe. Totally new." And then she cried.

"Pull yourself together, Tiger. We can't take it."

"Oh Liam!"

He seemed boyish again.

Cordón took her arm. "We owe much to all of you," he said.

Backlund said, "We'll miss you both. You have made a big difference."

"Hell," said Dann, "isn't anyone going to have a drink?"

Two stewards were waiting with champagne.

"This is on me," said Dann. "Drink."

As she took her glass, Mary pulled Tom to her. "Where is your lady?"

"You'll be meaning Nora."

"Where is she?"

"Nora went to Chicago. Nora has an unerring instinct for trouble."

"You were a team."

"Such an alliance cannot be made in heaven."

"What a pity." She teased him. "Tom, I have an idea that it's celibacy that makes you so sane."

"That's quite possible. Quite possible. However that may be, you are not going to believe what it is that I am beholding. I cannot credit my own eyes . . ."

She slowly lifted her head from his shoulder and followed his gaze.

Patrick Byrnes was coming toward them.

"Father!" she said.

"Father," said Tom more moderately.

"Tom. Mary."

He stood there very calmly, conscious that the others had now stopped talking.

"It was Sister Sarah who told me," he said. "Otherwise I fear I would have missed you."

"Father," said Mary, "I didn't think . . ."

"No. I doubt that you did, Mary. That was my fault. There is not a lot that can be said now. Being here is a beginning."

Tom took his father's arm. "Pat, I must introduce you."

Mary looked at Liam, who was as stunned as she, and it was Liam, when Byrnes had been introduced to the others, who introduced Cordón. By then Mary was with Cordón, and more coherent.

"Señor Cordón," said Byrnes, "I have made the mistake of allowing my daughter to become a stranger to me. You are wiser and also more fortunate. It is an honor to know you, sir."

Cordón took his hand. "An honor for me to know you, Mr. Byrnes."

Everyone began talking at once, but Tom held up a hand.

"One moment, please. I have a duty to perform." He pulled an envelope from his pocket—an envelope that had been slightly crumpled by several embraces—and drew something from it, holding it up. "This is a check representing the proceeds of the Los Angeles rally, after the deduction of costs. Nicolás, may I present you, compliments of the people of California, with a check for twenty-one thousand two hundred dollars and seventy cents."

They put down their glasses and clapped.

Cordón took the check. "I accept this on behalf of the people of

Spain—all the people of Spain, those who are free and those who are not. Thank you."

They clapped again.

Byrnes turned to Tom. "He is a good man. Sister Sarah keeps all the clips on you people. She told me about him."

"Yes. He is a good man, to be sure. And I'm very happy for Mary. Father, it's a fine thing that you've done in coming here."

Byrnes's hand overlay his son's and closed tight on it.

□

27

CASTILIAN PLAIN, WEST OF MADRID

The heat lay in the ground at night. There was no wind; the warm air retained the smells of the day's battle, dominantly the smell of tanks—overheated engines, oil, cordite, and hot steel. By the time the sun went down the tank crews were so baked they could barely speak. Water had become the first famine of the battlefield. The Guadarrama River was dry.

Six tanks were pulled off the dirt road while their crews slept in the open. A quarter mile away on the same road, after having tried to sleep in her ambulance, Serena Polland sat on a sandy mound. She could hear birds, earthbound and clacking as they picked over bodies down in the river valley. She hated this place. It was worse than the Jarama. Nothing gave cover. The topsoil was too shallow for trenches. Bodies turned black in a day. The battle had a heartlessness that was new, a fanatic quality in its direction. The waste of lives couldn't be concealed from the field hospitals. Stretcher-bearers only brought in men they thought they had any chance of saving.

She felt perversely energized. All her faculties were at a peak. She identified the nationality of a voice half a mile away. And she knew it was Koltzov's Buick before she saw it turn off the Las Rosas road. The night was so clear that he hardly needed his lights to come up the dirt road. She looked at her watch: three-thirty, near enough. Light in less than an hour.

□

Koltzov was driving himself. He stopped alongside the ambulance and got out.

"Comrade Pollard."

"Back again?"

"Like you. I do not sleep. Why are you here, alone?"

"Not very. Alone, I mean. Not a place for solitude."

Caught with one side of his face in the lights, Koltzov was half of the day and half of the night.

"You like solitude?" he said, as though raising a point of etiquette.

"There are times when a little bit of it would be nice. One needs a private place."

"A private place?" His glasses moved in and out of the light as he laughed. "I'm sorry—but it sounds so unlike you, comrade."

"Does it? Does it? I suppose so." She, in turn, laughed. "Anyway, it's not very likely, is it? In the middle of a battle."

"No." He changed tone. "I have just come from the American Hospital. A woman photographer, a German, died there an hour ago. After all this time, we had not lost any journalists until now. She did not take my advice. She insisted on being at the front line."

"What happened?"

"One of our tanks collided with her car. She fell under it."

"How awful."

"She was fearless. That is always a mistake."

They both thought of the same thing at the same moment.

"Like Mary," said Serena.

"She is coming back."

"Mary?"

"Yes."

She was silent for a moment, and hunched. "Well," she said finally, "I thought she might. And yet I hoped she wouldn't. What is it?"

Koltzov was staring upward. "Bombers."

"At night?"

"Only the Germans fly at night."

He went to the car and turned off the engine and lights.

"Not going to Madrid," he said.

The planes were high. They watched them with the fatalistic calm of veterans—infinity and proximity were equally felt.

□

The bombs fell several miles to the south. A town's roofs were suddenly sharply clear against the flashes. The blasts could be felt in the ground.

"Brunete," said Koltzov.

She felt the air stir. They watched the fires take hold.

She said, suddenly insistent, "Are we winning?"

"To believe otherwise, comrade, would be treason."

He turned to his car; he had a way of intimidating that needed neither force in his voice nor physical expression. It was a dismissiveness that came as quickly as a knife, and she felt its sting long after the Buick had disappeared toward the flames. Her father could do the same.

BARCELONA

"You work yourself too hard, comrade."

Aneta Ferrer didn't respond.

"You have lost weight since you came to Barcelona."

The car turned from a plaza toward the cathedral. He was right about the weight, but she didn't want any sympathy from Francisco Antón. He might be La Pasionaria's paramour, he might be on the Central Committee, but he was weak and vain, and he held handshakes too long.

"It's the heat," she said.

"Dolores thinks you should take more care of yourself."

Ferrer laughed. "Look at her! She never stops!"

"She has an iron constitution."

"Comrade Antón. I have only just begun." She leaned forward and spoke to the driver. "Next right, then the eastern corner of the Plaza del Rey."

"You do have a sense of humor, after all," said Antón.

"What do you mean?"

"Choosing the gothic barrio for your operation."

"It is ideal."

"It would not appeal to me."

"In the cellars it is as cool as December. You see. This is it."

"A convent?"

"Why not?"

The car stopped at an archway sealed by huge doors of bleached oak. In one door was a small sliding panel, no deeper than a visor. Someone was there, looking at the car.

"Forteen seventy-six," read Antón, looking at the top of the arch. "Five hundred years of chastity."

"Will you come in?" she said.

Her lack of enthusiasm was explicit. He shook his head. "This is where your world and mine divide, comrade."

Not until she was out of the car did a door open for her.

Antón watched her go—barely more than a girl; her conceit was of a kind becoming more common: that of the possessors of the future. The women were the worst, the most remorseless. A year of war had given Ferrer an indifference to her body that chilled him. The black *mono* was caught in the brightness of the courtyard before the door closed.

There were palms and magnolias in the courtyard. And yet its peace seemed to be joyless, to have been planned that way, with the flower beds too precisely placed. No one had sat in the shade of the trees, and no one had taken a bloom with the impulse of love. The door made a bleak fugue as it closed.

Ferrer went through cloisters and into what had been the chapel. The altar, with the cross and the other holy furnishings, had been removed. It had been replaced, on its stone plinth, by a bench with six chairs behind it. The result was a raised presidium that faced the original plain pews and the center aisle. Over the stained glass that had lit the altar was draped a large red banner with the portraits of Marx, Lenin, and Stalin. Their faces had been woven into the linen in yellow thread. In the morning, when the sun fell on the stained glass, a radiance suffused the new trinity—rendering them more benign than the design had intended. Lenin's yellow skull gave off the semblance of a halo.

□

She walked up the aisle to the bench. The work had been finished while she was away. She stepped up to the chairs and looked back to the pews. Then she saw Ernö Sletin at the door, watching.

"You like it?" His voice was as soft as his footfall.

"Excellent."

"They are good carpenters. But a little superstitious, I think."

"Superstitious?"

"Nervous when they took down the cross."

"Ignorant."

Sletin wore rope-soled sandals and liked light, loose clothes that she thought bordered on the effeminate—a white embroidered shirt hung outside black cotton trousers. He was an exotic and, in one thing, an expert.

"There is something else for you to see."

Before she joined him she turned and looked at the presidium again. "I would like a picture of Dolores under the banner."

"Of course."

"She was magnificent. She dominates the Central Committee. Now—show me."

He led her back into the cloisters. She could smell the garlic on his breath. Sletin chewed whole cloves. A draft of it came with each sentence.

"It is better, much better, than the house," he said.

They turned under an arched doorway and went down steps. There was brick dust and the sound of hammering below.

"The cellars are older than the convent," he said. "I think they were built by the Moors. You can tell that from the style of vaulting. African."

The light that came from the few grilles was supplemented by electric bulbs on a cable stapled to the roof. They followed the line of lights to a man breaking bricks with a mallet.

Sletin's thick black hair had picked up some of the brick dust. "This is what you want to see," he said.

There was more new electrical wiring. A main cable ran to a junction box on a wall. Some flagstones on the floor had been removed and replaced by cement, over newly laid pipes. Other men worked in a passage that ran off to the left. He led her along it.

□

"My three chambers. Ready by the end of the week."

In the first chamber a man was working on the floor.

"Stage one. Reception. The floor will be made up entirely of these broken bricks, with their rough faces upward. The chamber can take from one to thirty people, and whether one or thirty there is nowhere to lie down."

He moved to the next door and switched on a light.

"This is finished."

There was a metal chair, a wooden table, and a single large, shaded light over the chair.

"The chair, you see, is bolted down. It is connected directly to the electric cable. When the interrogator pulls a switch under the table, the whole chair is live. We can control the amount and area of the current."

"Have you done this before?" she said.

"It is a proven system." He turned off the light. "The electric chair does not prove to be enough on its own. This next chamber is my own design." He unhooked a lamp. "There is no light in here at all. When the door is closed it is as black as the blackest night."

The floor of the chamber had been dug out into a concrete-lined pit sloping steeply from the door to a depth of about six feet at the far side. He held the lamp so that she could see the ceiling. Four perforated pipes ran across it.

"The pit is flooded from above. There is no grip on the concrete. The subject is forced by the water to the deepest level. It fills in three minutes. Cold water. And all in darkness, total darkness."

"Good. Excellent."

"Sink or swim. We control the depth. And the time. Experience suggests that an hour is more than enough, in most cases. There are exceptions, but not many. It is extraordinary what the human imagination can do to the most stubborn subject under such conditions. There is often no physical damage, it is entirely psychological. Darkness and water. It goes to the core of our ancestry, to the transition from fish to man. Under different circumstances it would make useful scientific study, comrade." He stepped back from the door and held the lamp so that he could see her reaction more clearly.

"Comrade Sletin, you sound wistful."

□

"Wistful?"

"Like a scientist who has been frustrated."

"Not at all. This is a science, in its early stages. This is not the Inquisition. There have been too many wasted deaths."

"Wasted?"

"A bullet in the head is nonproductive. Every subject is an asset. My object is to use these assets, not waste them. Every subject has a story to tell. The science is to extract the story without needless violence." He put the lamp back in the bracket. "The minimum of violence. That is my idea—nothing in these chambers is intended to kill. What happens afterward is a political decision. This is a place of interrogation, not execution."

He was serious; the choreography of his walk and manners was all of a piece. His disciplines were those of a temperament and culture unfamiliar to her, at variance with Spain and the Spanish. The idea of "wasted deaths" would take time to get a hold. Where had Yanin found him, in what academy?

■

Drunks spilled out of the train clutching their goatskin wine flasks. Cordón and Mary let them go, as they gathered their own luggage. Then Mary saw a bearded man, in a flapping black leather trench coat and a cap, pushing through the drunks toward them.

"Captain!"

The bearded man broke from the mob.

"Captain!"

"Álvaro," said Cordón, and the two embraced.

"Welcome home, Captain."

He could have crushed Cordón. Mary was astonished. The adolescent Álvaro of the wedding picture had aged and enlarged.

He released Cordón and beamed at her. "Miss Byrnes. We are pleased to see you here again."

"I'm Mary to you, Álvaro. Always." She kissed him.

"And María? How is María?"

"She is here. With our son."

□

"A son! I am so pleased."

Cordón, with purpose, said, "Who are you with, Álvaro?"

Álvaro's effusiveness was curtailed. "I am on Mera's staff. Officially. With Fourteen Division."

"I thought Fourteen Division was based in Madrid."

Álvaro was hesitant. "Yes, Captain. Mera is in Madrid. Officially."

"What is this *officially*?"

"I will explain. In the car." He picked up Mary's bag and led them from the platform.

■

Italian bombers from Majorca bombed Barcelona with impunity, and at random. The streetcars no longer bothered to stop during the raids. Francisco Rey was unaware that another raid was in progress until he saw people scattering in the street. The streetcar continued to a regular stop. A bomb fell about three hundred feet away, knocking out the front of a three-story building. Rey got off the streetcar, but it clanked on its way. A few people gathered at the bombed building. Other bombs fell, but at some distance. Rey joined the onlookers.

An old man said, "The place was empty. Lucky. A doctor lived here. The doctors have gone." He laughed mysteriously to himself and suddenly noticed Rey. "Are you a doctor?"

Rey shook his head.

"Too young," said the old man through a squint.

A small fire had started somewhere under the remains of the building. The bomb had not hit squarely. Blast had scooped out everything to the basement on one side, but the ground floor on the other side was intact. The fire gained a hold there, in paneling. There was no furniture.

Someone pointed at the revealed basement. The dust was settling. The man who pointed kept back from the edge. Others joined him.

A fire truck arrived.

Rey looked down into the basement.

More than half of it was in shadow. It was hard to pick out what they were looking at. Before he did, Rey noticed stains on the tiled basement floor—blood, long dried, in streaks and several large pools. In the shadow were five bodies. All men in suits. Even with the lingering smell of the explosion and of the fire there was a new, detectable stench. The bodies were lined up neatly against a wall, bent as though in prayer. The suits made them look more whole than they were.

Someone said, "What was this place?"

No answer. Instead, they began to slip away.

The head of the fire crew, a fat, youngish man in unmarked overalls, looked into the basement and then at Rey, the only one left.

"What are you looking at, comrade? They were fascists."

Rey stepped back and went down into the street. Debris had caused a minor diversion, otherwise traffic had returned to normal. He made a mental note of where the house had been. Even the fire trucks were in the hands of the party: classic Stalinist doctrine—from the taproots up. Taproots. And basements.

■

"They sat there," said General Goriev. "For *two days* they sat there."

Goriev and Koltzov stood on the bare plateau with the dust blowing at their backs. Meandering all around them were men and vehicles, trucks, tanks, and artillery. Koltzov's Buick had a tidemark of the brown dust to its waist. Although the sun was low in the west, the heat made the dust scalding to the skin.

Shouting over a passing tank, Goriev said, "They use tanks as though they are artillery. They *sat* there. The moment was lost."

A whole division was pulling back, a sight eloquent in its abjection—and inadmissible.

"Brunete is lost," said Goriev, still shouting although the tank had gone. "Thanks to this man Lister. Tanks should not sit on their arse." One foot kept heeling into the dirt as though into the flank of a horse.

"Lister was trained in Moscow."

"Not by me."

"Comrade General. What should we call this? Consolidation?"

"Call it what you like."

"Consolidation. Our heroic armies have consolidated twenty square miles of their advance. Brunete. Brunete was of no significance."

"Eighty percent of our armor, thirty percent of our aircraft. Thrown away. *No significance?*"

"Comrade General, you see the dust on my glasses."

Goriev was sick of Koltzov's joke about his glasses. He turned and slowly lifted the glasses from Koltzov's nose and clear of his face. Koltzov did not move. Goriev had never seen Koltzov without them. Koltzov's eyes, without focus, were unblinking and larger than they seemed when refracted. It was a face that suddenly belonged to a tribe. The oldest of tribes. The one that none had been able to extinguish.

■

Mary lay in the bath for an hour, occasionally adding hot water. That there was hot water, that there was a bathroom, was anomalous. The small hotel was more like a rooming house. There had been no sign outside. No name. No lobby. A concierge of great age remained behind a grille. Álvaro had kept the car waiting while Cordón saw Mary to the room, and the two of them had then gone off into the night. She had barely any sense of being in Barcelona. In these early morning hours the street had seen no traffic since their car left. Were there others in the hotel? She heard nothing. She had a copy of *Life* magazine in the bath. It covered the war's first year. Who was this photographer, Robert Capa? She should be in *Life.*

She got out of the bath and put on a robe. No hope of sleep. The robe smelled of Paris. She put her camera case on the bed and checked the equipment. Two Leicas now, and new lenses. The stuff kept rolling into the sagging center of the bed. Film bought in Paris—fast film, almost impossible to find in Spain. She had loaded one of the Leicas and was checking the viewfinder when Cordón came in.

"Couldn't sleep," she said. "God. What's the matter?"

When he sat on the bed the lenses rolled back to her.

"What *is* it, Nicolás?"

"I am not going to Madrid." He reached out for her hand. "We should fight Franco. Instead, we make war on ourselves.The Stalinists are wiping out the Trotskyists. Here, in Barcelona. A purge. And everywhere."

"You're not a Trotskyist."

"We will be next."

"They can't turn on the anarchists, not here. You are too strong."

"Not anymore. All our best men are at the front."

"Nicolás—what kind of danger are you in?"

"This city has changed."

"What is this—*this* place, Nicolás?"

"We are safe here."

"I don't *believe* this. *Who* is the enemy?"

"You should go to Madrid."

"And—and where are *you* going?"

"I am going out of the city. It is better if I do not say where. For the moment, it is better for us not to be together."

"Oh God." She gripped his hand. "I had a feeling at the station. I ought to be able to rise above the selfish, I know. When I was lying in the bath I already felt left out—excluded. I just didn't—I just didn't expect it to happen like this. Before we've even seen daylight."

"You will be in no danger in Madrid. You must go."

"I'm going to fuck you first."

"There is no time. Álvaro is waiting for me."

"There is time."

She slipped out of the robe and stepped behind him, pulling his head between her breasts, covering his eyes with her hands.

"Like the first time."

"No."

"Like the first time."

"It is not the first time."

She took away her left hand and forced it over bone inside the neck of his tunic to the knot of hair.

"Do you remember the first time? You put your head into my

breasts. I got the smell of you then. I couldn't stop. Not then. Later, we talked about the effect of death on life."

"I remember." His right hand gripped and took her right hand from his eyes and held it on his thigh.

"And I found your scar," she said. "Your secret scar. Right here. Right by your balls. We are both scarred now. Kiss my scars, Nicolás."

She freed her hand and lay across the bed, pushing away the lenses. She heard him stand and, arms outstretched, she gripped the frayed satin, pulling the sheets up into it. But he came to her gently at first, fingering the band where the scar tissue was a shade lighter than the surrounding skin, following its line to the base of her spine. Then his finger ran into the first crease of her buttocks and pressed harder, opening out where she was already wet. He kissed and licked the scars.

"Animal," she said. She heard his boots catch in and scrape the bare boards of the floor. His finger ran into her and her knees dug deep into the satin.

"Now. Now. *Now.*"

The silence of the hotel and the street gave an illusion of privacy. She heard his breath like a voice unformed, coming close to her. She felt a button on his tunic as definite in outline as if she were looking at it, pressed into her haunch. The buckle of his belt, around his feet, began to punch out his rhythm on the boards. She bit into the satin. He filled her. *Which of them would die first?* The question burned into her as he did, a fear without voice or answer.

"No," she said.

He was standing as she sat up.

"Not before I kiss your scar."

She held him by his tunic and found the ridged skin of the scar with her tongue. Both their tastes were there. A thin line of hair grew along the scar and was brittle on the tongue.

He ran his hands through her hair. There was still the impression of her body in the bed. Everything in the room seemed of the same tiredness and color. He saw himself from the waist up in a mirror. Her hair was the only assertion of color there—strands of it ran like liquid through his hands in the reflection. *Which of them would die first?*

□

"What are you thinking?" she said, easing away from him.

"That we touch the edges of life."

"Is it you that makes Barcelona so dangerous for me?"

He buckled his belt.

She put on her robe. "Maybe one day there will be no secrets," she said. "My love, take care. Take care." She embraced him. The embrace was painful. Her scars were on fire. She gave no sign of it.

So much left with him—abruptly gone. She had not been prepared for that.

In the street, Álvaro stood by the car.

"I am sorry," said Cordón.

"It does not matter, Captain."

Before he switched on the engine, Álvaro smiled. "She is good, Mary. I like her."

Cordón nodded perfunctorily.

"Captain—why do you not marry her?"

Cordón glared at him.

"Marriage is good, Captain. I could marry you, like you married me and María. I would like that."

He started the car without risking another look at Cordón. In the disappearing night Álvaro had acquired a responsiblity for Cordón and he felt good.

Mary watched them go. With the first light came the realization that the skyline ended at the sea. A ship lay out there—a warship. She got into bed, but the pain kept her awake. Someone walked across the floor of the room above. Gradually it began to sound like a hotel. But nobody laughed.

■

"I know the style." Ferrer nodded. "There is a voice. I know the voice. I know it." She looked up from the newspaper, at Sletin. "It is unmistakable."

"That newspaper was closed down more than a month ago. Somewhere they are still printing it."

"I can hear him dictating it." She read out, ". . . the house of death in the Calle Fernando, opened to our eyes by Italian bombs, is only one of the dark places where the gangsters of Stalin do their work. Where was our brave leader Andrés Nin taken? Where did they torture him? Nin was beaten to a pulp before he died, but he did not break. The Stalinists cannot break us. No matter how many houses of death there are, the POUM will not be liquidated. This is not Russia. We will show these tools of Stalin that the Spanish people will make their own revolution . . ."

When she stopped reading she drew back into herself. The intensity of her concentration seemed to shrink her. There was, thought Sletin, an aspect of beauty that was without emotional appeal. It appealed to the intellect in a way that he remembered feeling at Bukhara when looking at the ice-blue tiles of a mosque. Ferrer was a thing of undeniable beauty—beauty shorn of veneer and decoration.

"I know the Jew," she said, in a voice barely audible to Sletin.

■

"Nothing, Captain."

Álvaro slowed down at the end of the street.

"No car," he said.

"No." Cordón waved for him to pull into the corner curb. "I have a feeling. I don't like it." He tilted the rearview mirror. There was enough light to see the length of the street in the Ramblas. Not a thing moved.

Álvaro was slightly impatient. He kept his hand on the gear lever.

"The next street," said Cordón. "I can go through the school to the apartments. Stop short of the school, and wait."

The school was closed for the summer. Cordón knew the way through the yard. A line of washing hung at back of the apartments. There seemed to be a score of women's stockings. He went up the stone stairs and rang the bell. The door opened almost at once.

"Come in." The woman stepped aside for him.

Berneri was at the door of the big room, wearing a black silk robe.

"Nicolás."

Cordón was surprised by the robe.

"You are not ready, Camillo?"

"Come. Sit down. We will have coffee."

"We must leave."

Berneri waved him into the room. The drapes were drawn and every lamp still burned. A large porcelain ashtray was full of cigar butts. Beside it on the marble table was a leather-bound book, open where fresh notes had been made.

Cordón went in, but did not sit down.

"I am not going, Nicolás."

"We—"

"I know. At first I did agree." He glanced at the woman who crossed the lobby to the kitchen. "Not for myself. But we have talked." He took in the room with a low movement of a hand. Collected it. "This is my life. I cannot leave."

"We have a safe place. Others are coming."

"Safe? And after that, where? I cannot run anymore. Please. Sit down. Nicolás—I am sorry."

Cordón sat, and looked at the book on the table.

"Perhaps the others should go," said Berneri, sitting opposite. "They may be in danger. I do not feel in danger. They are after others now, what they call, in their elegant way, the 'vacillating elements.' An old theorist without a university and without a publisher is extinct to them. Barbieri feels the same.Trotsky is their Antichrist. It was Nin's misfortune to have been Trotsky's secretary."

"We will be next."

"There is no car outside now."

"They are more discreet. They are there. Probably in one of the houses across the street. You do know how they are organized? The Servicio de Investigación Militar? The tribunals of espionage and high treason?"

"Oh yes. SIM. We call it the Russian syphilis. Except for their new techniques, a Marxist version of a Bourbon tyranny. Atavism—nothing changes. Stalinism is Czarism. Nazism is the Holy Roman Empire. They all exist—they all depend on—phobias. Jews. Trotsky."

"Camillo. You are in great danger."

□

The woman silently brought and poured the coffee. Berneri looked up, took her hand very briefly, and when she had gone looked at Cordón with melancholic composure.

"Much of what I am I could not take," he said. "I could not live like that." He put a hand on the open book. "There is one thing that you could take. My diary. The thoughts of the night. Not a polished work, I am afraid. No. A lack of symmetry." The joke froze in his voice. "But the essence of it is there. To hold that three things are inviolable. Truth . . . freedom . . . beauty." He closed the book. "Art cannot offer any resistance to political terror. I accept that."

They sat in silence for a minute, during which the room imposed itself as something extramortal.

"You should not cry, Nicolás."

Cordón took the book and stood up.

"I am glad you still carry the gun, Nicolás. I remember I said to you before, so many of the best are already dead." He hugged Cordón and kissed him on each cheek. "You must not join them."

"What I owe you cannot be measured."

Berneri broke away and led him to the door.

Nothing more was said between them. They knew they would never speak again.

■

"When it comes to Stalin, Dolores has a brown tongue."

The old printer flicked cigarette ash over a copy of the paper *Frente Rojo*—over the colum he was reading. His laugh crackled deep in him. "She licks him every day. No priest is more a supplicant. And she has no love of language." He tilted the paper so that the ash went on the floor. "She violates the words. Pulls out their guts until they are empty. And she incites. How she incites. She kills more people with words than Franco does with shells."

There was a bare bulb above him. He was myopic and had lost Rey somewhere in the darkness.

"Listen to this—'No measures will ever prove excessive that are taken to purge the proletarian camp of the poisonous growth of

Trotskyism . . . ' And so on and so on, words to kill, make no mistake; she fills graveyards." He coughed convulsively.

"Then why do they love her, Luis?"

The printer loosened his collar. "I can't hear you, Francisco."

Rey came out of the darkness. "Why do they love her?"

"She is a *sabia.*"

"You believe that?"

"Yes. I am old enough. She has that power—there was a *sabia* in my village. Her mother said she cried out from the womb. With her it was a holy force. I saw it. She could drive away the demons. Dolores can summon the demons."

Rey picked up the paper. *" 'To be a disciple of Stalin is an honor for every proletarian.' "* He stopped reading. "I don't believe in the supernatural. This is—"

"Well?"

"—I don't know, Luis. I knew a woman in Madrid. She was a disciple, of Dolores, and of Stalin. I thought she had some kind of power. Sexual, in a way. But she was dangerous. Not *sabia. Calio,* perhaps."

"Some women have that. I have seen it."

"No. I cannot really believe in it."

"What did she do? This woman?"

"She—she had people killed. She tried to kill me."

The old man could see Rey quite well now; the bulb brought out the sweat on his brow and under his nose.

"I have seen a woman with *calio* break glass with one look. They exist. And I think that you have seen it."

"It's—it's a part of Spain that I do not really know. It's not rational to accept it."

"Rational!" Luis laughed explosively again. "What is rational about what is happening here? *Rational!* You would know it if you had seen the *calio* in her. You would feel it, *here.*" He put a hand, discolored by ink and nicotine, on his groin and closed it like a claw.

Rey backed away from the light. He did remember. The printer pulled cigarettes from his overalls. He did not need to peer out at Rey again.

Rey thought, there is no fear in the old man. He had the sanguinity of someone who had spent half his life in clandestine work. His first love was words. Words had so often been driven underground that for Luis they were like a sustained illicit love. He corrected all the proofs himself: when he dropped the lines of lead into a galley he caressed them. Reading *Frente Rojo* made him crazy. Its corruption of language drove him into the arms of those he felt he could trust with words. He carped at Rey's rhetoric, but had seen in the fugitive newspaper a kind of honor. Mocking Rey for blind faith in the rational, allowing his own superstitions, he was wise in ways that were beyond Rey's reach, and Rey knew it.

A handful of men stood bowed at the grave. They were stripped to the waist, still sweating from the effort of digging into sand and stone. One of them had just finished painting the inscription on the improvised cross.

Serena had seen them digging as she brought the ambulance down to the riverbed. A hygiene truck and water wagon were already there, parked in willow bushes. She walked over to the grave. The inscription read, "He died so that Spanish democracy may live." She spoke to one of the men, a Negro.

"You've taken a lot of trouble. That's unusual these days."

The Negro nodded. "We were together from the beginning. Came through the Jarama. Came through Brunete. Thought we would make it. A sniper got George."

George Graham was the name on the cross. "All from America?"

"All from New York. Left the same day." He turned from the grave and put out a hand. "Name's Oliver Law. You English, ma'am?"

"Yes I am."

"I saw you come down this morning."

"You had a bad time on Mosquito Hill."

They walked toward the hygiene truck, where men were lining up for a shower.

"Sure did."

□

"All Americans up there?"

"No. Canadians too."

"They've merged the Lincoln and Washington battalions."

"That's right."

She sensed he didn't want to talk more. Like the other men, he was raw-eyed and filthy. They had had no shower or change of clothes for two weeks. And very little water.

She looked up to the low ridge that sheltered them: a line of telegraph poles marked the skyline, the road to Villanueva de la Cañada, main line of the retreat from Brunete.

"Still quiet," she said. "Perhaps you'll get the rest you need."

He nodded without conviction and joined the line for a shower.

Two weeks earlier, when the battle began, the men—even under fire—had been full of boyish humor and conviction. Now the silent line at the shower, and those sitting with canteens around the water wagon, had no spirit. Geiser, the commissar, sat alone under a willow. A mule was tied to the same tree. The mule was the only survivor of six they had used to carry down the wounded. Mosquito Hill had won its name from the sound of the bullets.

She returned to the ambulance and lay in the back, in the shade of one closed door. Even under the willows the ambulance was torpid, and she dropped off to sleep almost instantly.

A magpie fell on a scrap of bread and flew with it into a tree.

Law saw the bird as he came out of the shower. One bird. No more. It seemed to exchange the perception with him as it swallowed the bread. Only a crazy bird—or a starving one—would be in such a place. Law put his tunic under the tree and lay there waiting for the magpie to spot another scrap and swoop on it. But the bird fidgeted. It edged sideways along a branch, tilted its head, opened and closed its tail feathers. Law understood birds. Its agitation passed to him.

■

Heat and vibration had begun to prize the coachwork free of the Buick's frame. Leather curled away from metal like skin from a carcass. Wood warped loose from screws. Carpet wandered underfoot. Madrid was like the car—it worked as it shed the inessentials.

The domino players were back in the cafés, necks left proud by loose jackets. Many people looked as though their clothes were a size too large.

The car rode badly, down low on its rear shocks. The blistered leather on the dash smelled vaguely vegetable. Mary had the window down as far as it would go, but something was shot in the works and it stuck. The smell of Koltzov's cigar didn't help. Koltzov had not been touched by the general decline. Nor did he worry about the Buick's dilapidation. His foot pressed hard on the accelerator, and they climbed the road west out of the city fast enough to pass a convoy of trucks. He had only his right hand on the wheel. With the left he flicked cigar ash out the window; then he kept that arm in the wind.

"You see," he said, "three weeks ago this road was under Franco's guns."

What she saw was a truck heading straight at them as he swung out to pass a water wagon.

Koltzov held to his course. The horns of the oncoming truck and the water wagon blared. At the last moment the truck pulled over. Mary looked back. In the billowing dust she saw it come to rest against a low wall.

"I'll take Franco's guns," she said.

He threw the remant of his cigar out the window and pulled out another.

"Here," she said, and took it. She bit off the end, spat it out to the road, put the cigar in his mouth, and lit it for him.

"Where did you get that lighter?" he said.

"Paris."

"Hmmm."

"What does *hmmm* mean?"

There was no more visible traffic on the road ahead; he leaned back and drew on the cigar. "I am pleased you came back."

"Mikhail—"

He waited.

"Mikhail. I still find it hard to believe that Max Praeger was an agent."

"Why—why is that so hard to believe?"

"He was a Jew."

Koltzov flicked ash and lay the cigar, unfinished, on the dash. "I am a Jew."

"You're not working for Hitler."

"In Spain, after the Inquisition, some Jews remained. They were called the secret Jews. One of them was Columbus's navigator. It is something, to feel indispensable." He picked up the cigar again. "To have a worth, and to know it, that is something."

The taste of the cigar was addictive in her mouth. She reached out and took the last one from his shirt.

"Max hated himself," she said, before she bit it.

Koltzov put his foot down to the floor. The Buick reached a state of balance halfway between traction and flight.

■

Serena heard nothing until a blast lifted and dropped the ambulance. The closed door that had shaded her swung open and slammed shut again; the other door hung on one hinge. In the few seconds that it took her to focus there were more explosions. Then screams. A piece of hot shrapnel the size of a plate hit one of the stretchers hanging from the side of the ambulance and set it ablaze. She bent double and pushed her head into her knees, covering her ears with her hands. All the screams merged into one—they could not be shut out. The earth shuddered. A short, sharp wind showered her with sand and grit. When she heard the machine guns, she realized it was planes—planes so low that the noise made her ears feel like bursting. And all the time, waiting for the next explosions. The ambulance filled with smoke. It kept shaking and began to sink on one side. No more explosions. She knew all the smells and she had heard many screams, but this time she was inundated from every side. Something that had fallen on top of the ambulance slid from it. Her head rang as though invested by snapping wires. She began coughing.

Law pulled her out.

The first thing she saw was a man lying at the side of the ambulance with a bird, the magpie, crushed into a gaping wound in his chest.

"Blown into the tree," said Law, a little wildly. "Blown right into the tree with the bird. I never saw a thing like that."

The body had falled onto the ambulance roof and then to the ground.

She held him.

"You're all right, ma'am," he said. "You're okay."

She still held him. His voice was lower and steadier.

He said, "We should get out of here."

She looked beyond him.

"I have to do something."

Little survived of the hygiene truck. Water from its ruptured tank steamed on the hot sand and filtered away. Blood ran with it. Two men who had been in the shower were lying one over the other. Another body lay under the truck.

Commissar Geiser stood under the willow where previously he had sat. The tree was shorn of foliage and bark. He was blackened and stared across at Law and Serena. Between them, in the dry riverbed, were some men who had been machine-gunned after the bombing as they ran. Some were still alive.

"Oh God," she said, almost under her breath, as Law supported her.

Her ambulance was canted because on one side the tires had been ripped open by shrapnel. The only intact vehicle was the water wagon.

"I must help those men," she said.

One first aid orderly was unhurt.

There was little the three of them could do—Law, Serena, and the orderly salvaged some dressing from the ambulance. Of the injured there were only two with any chance of surviving to reach a hospital. Geiser walked around in a trance.

"We must get out," said Law. "The airplanes could come back any time, and now they've marked us the Moors could come."

Law drove the water wagon, with the two wounded in the cab beside him. Serena and the orderly stood on the running boards. Before they left they tried to get Geiser to join them.

"Report. I must report," he said.

□

"Get up here," shouted the orderly, putting out a hand as Law revved the engine.

"Report to General Gal," said Geiser, turning away to walk down again to the riverbed. When they reached the main road and took a last look back, Geiser was a small figure advancing up the other side of the valley with an erect stride.

■

"I'm sorry," said Mary, "I feel sick."

Koltzov glanced at her without slowing down.

"I think it was the cigar," she said. "How much farther?"

"A few miles only. Do you want to stop?"

"You'd better."

No sooner had the Buick pulled over than she was out. He heard her retching.

It wasn't the cigar, she knew, and it wasn't the speed, or the heat. For several days she had been vomiting like this.

Koltzov switched the car off. He could not see her, but the retching had stopped. The only sound was a light wind in the telegraph wires. They might have been in a place that had never seen war. She seemed insensitive to his mood. But that was too kind. He could have laughed at himself for that. *Insensitive?* People like Mary Byrnes had no background to understand. She could not even imagine it. Praeger had found that. Praeger had been safe with someone of her innocence. Her face appeared in the mirror. She was standing against the car, pulling hair clear of her face. Scared about something. She composed herself before walking up beside him.

"I'm sorry, Mikhail."

"There are moments when it seems like a bad dream that has passed."

She followed his eyes over the landscape.

"I hope you remember it like this," he said. "For your book."

"Oh. That book. Five hundred forty-four pages."

"I see it all the time. People who write one thing for their newspapers and—" He tapped his forehead. "—and another up here. They store it away. It's just material to them."

"I—I try to put it all down. I don't keep a store."

He laughed. "Then I will have to be careful about how much you are allowed to see."

The sun's glare dissolved into his glasses—they became pools of mercury. His laugh had the same opacity. But it wasn't Koltzov that scared her so much as realizing how much they had in common. He was really a loner, a lot farther down the road than she.

■

A disused railroad tunnel served as a dressing station. It was narrow, with room for only one line of beds. A pinhead of bright light suggested that at the other end lay a safe and brilliant valley. But this end was like a fragment of hell. The low, sooted brick acted as a megaphone for every voice, every moan. A few oil lamps supplemented the exterior light. At least the place was cool.

The two wounded men had survived the ride in the water wagon.

Serena took off the dressings to clean their wounds.

"We must get them to a hospital," she said.

Law nodded. He had been a wordless helper since they arrived.

There were no ambulances. Many of the wounded had been waiting all day to be taken to Madrid.

When an ambulance did appear it came from the front, loaded with new casualties. Serena helped select those who could be dressed there, in the tunnel.

One of these men recognized Law.

"Hey—lootenant, you okay?"

Law nodded.

"We lost you."

"That's right."

"I feel this is all happening to someone else."

"That's the morphine," said Serena. She was puzzled by Law's reserve with a compatriot.

□

"I need—Jeese—I need someone to talk with. Someone beautiful."

She found metal in the wound.

"Don't worry, you'll mend."

He tried to lift his head to see Law more clearly, but she gently restrained him.

"Lady."

"It would be better if you didn't try to talk."

"How are the other guys doin'?"

"Please. Don't worry."

"What will you do with us?"

"Get you cleaned up, then back to Madrid."

He lay back and seemed to drift off. Law moved away to other men.

She was completing the bandage when his eyes opened again.

"My own people shot me," he said.

"Don't be silly." Delirium had to be dealt with sharply.

"We were running away. We had enough."

"Keep still."

"They turned a machine gun on us. There was a mutiny."

"It would be better—"

"Listen, Lady. I have to talk. What kind of hospital will they send us to?"

"You're not badly hurt. You won't be in hospital long."

"You know what they do with guys like us? They put us in mental hospitals. The nuthouse. We ain't never seen again. I know."

"That's nonsense."

"Listen. I know." He tried to raise his head, looking around for Law, but sank back. "You gotta stop them sending me there. Do I look crazy? I'll tell you who is the crazy man . . ."

Law had returned.

The wounded man was coherent enough to stop talking.

"He looks okay," said Law.

She stood up and picked the metal fragment from the antiseptic bowl.

"What kind of bullet is that?" she said, holding out the palm of her hand for Law to look.

□

"All look the same to me, lady. Why?"

"It seemed . . . I've not seen one like it before." She closed her hand around it and slipped it into a pocket. Law, she realized, had been collecting papers from the men's tunics.

■

The sign said, VILL NUEVA E LA AÑ in white on blue tiles, and each missing tile indicated that very little of Villanueva de la Cañada remained intact. Plaster on the wall bearing the sign had gone the way of the tiles. Wooden beams in the roof of the house were exposed. Very few people were left in the street. The town appeared to be in an advanced state of demolition. There was so much rubble that Koltzov had to stop the car. A few Russian tanks had pushed themselves into partly collapsed buildings for concealment. Their crews lay on them, asleep.

"We can go no farther," said Koltzov. "You have seen as much of the front line as possible."

"This place is a mess."

"When we left Brunete it was no more than bricks in a field."

"I want some more pictures."

She got out of the car. And when Koltzov blinked his way into the street she got a picture of him.

"The censor will not pass that," he said. "I am a secret weapon."

"I realized I didn't have one shot of you."

"I would like one of you."

She gave him the Leica.

"Against the tank, please," he said.

The tank had its gun dipped into the street. While Koltzov focused the tank crew stirred and greeted her. She climbed up among them and they arranged themselves around her. He framed and took the picture.

"Good," he said. "Very good." He helped her down, gave her the camera, but held her hand fast.

"The weight of this sad time we must obey," he said. "Speak what we feel; not what we ought to say."

She allowed him to keep his hold, and said, "The oldest hath borne most: we that are young shall never see so much, nor live so long."

"You surprise me."

"Why?"

"King Lear. To recall it so quickly."

"Ah. Speak what we feel? *You* surprise *me."*

He released her hand. "There was something in your face."

"There was?"

"The lens found it for me."

She took his arm, waved one last time to the tank crew, and walked to the car. "It doesn't feel right here. Why am I getting this treatment? What are you keeping from me?"

He cooled in annoyance. *"You*—you are like a gourmand complaining to the kitchen about disappointed expectations. You came late. *Too late."* He flicked a hand at the dust. "The other diners have long since left."

One of the men on the tank had a guitar. He had begun playing, and the others sang with him. Koltzov's outburst, not disclosed to them by any gesture, was underscored by a contrary voice, his Russian basilisk against Spanish fiesta in the decimated street. It carried the prospect of madness.

Koltzov's teeth sealed his attack, bared like those of an old tiger snarling to reaffirm his potency.

"I'm sorry," she said, but without concession. "I'm doing my job. Or trying to."

The soldiers sang more lustily, kicking heels into the hull of the tank.

Koltzov absorbed her answer without any hint of softening; he bore not the slightest resemblance to the man she had photographed only a minute before.

■

Two more ambulances came to the dressing station from the front. Serena knew the drivers, and sat smoking with one of them on the cab's running board. Several times she saw Law come to the mouth of the tunnel, watching her.

□

She finished a cigarette and looked up. "Too high for us."

The other driver saw the planes. "I think they're ours. Russian."

"I have to stretch," she said. "Stiff as a post."

She walked behind the ambulance to the edge of a wheat field that had been crossed by tanks. Two women squatted in one of the swathes cut by the tanks; they were picking out crushed husks and putting them in a basket. It reminded her of a painting, something evoking the lost medieval simplicities. Pieces of life broke away from their surroundings like that, to become familiar touchstones. As crisp as it was, the wheat gave off a scent of the late summer hay wagons. She failed to hear Law come up behind her.

"I'm sorry, ma'am," he said, "if I surprised you."

She was swallowed in his shadow.

"Sorry to disturb you, ma'am. Could you tell me, are those ambulances going back to Madrid?"

"Why do you ask?" she said, recovering her attention but not, altogether, her nerve.

"Those men of mine in there. I want to be sure to get them into the right hospital."

"The right hospital? What do you mean?"

"I want to get them into the American hospital at El Escorial. They are Americans."

Slowly she put a hand to his elbow. "I think you'd better join me for a walk. Come on."

■

"You should be the last person to forget . . . " said Koltzov, ". . . to forget that it was Praeger's signal that betrayed the *Mar Cantábrico.*"

They were crossing the Manzanares into Madrid, pulling clear of the checkpoint.

"I've thought a lot about it." Mary was slumped in her seat. "A lot. It bothers me. It bothers me that he knew. How did he know?"

"Idiot!" Koltzov swung the car violently. "These people are crazy. Crazy. Driving in the blackout is killing more people than the bombs."

"How did he know?"

□

"He was a professional."

"Don't you have any idea?"

"Not my responsibility."

In the dark, driving with shaded lights, she realized that Koltzov was virtually blind. Comprehensively blind and dumb at this moment.

"You can drop me here," she said.

He slowed down and tried to see the curb.

"You should move to the Florida, with the other writers."

"I don't like hotels."

One wheel slammed the curb and the car scraped to a stop.

"Good night, Mikhail. Thank you."

Leaning over to retrieve her equipment from the backseat, she sensed he had been on the point of saying something, but had changed his mind. When she closed the door, he was watching her and she felt, as she walked away, his eyes on her in the same way that, when under fire, she always felt that she would be hit in the exact base of her spine. The Buick didn't grind free of the curb until she turned into the side street.

"Mary!"

She was going through the archway to the courtyard when the voice came from above.

Serena was sitting on the staircase, her face momentarily bright in the glare of a cigarette.

"Serena!"

"Darling! It's been *ages."*

They met and embraced on the stairs.

"My God, darling. How many cameras have you? You're *festooned."*

"It's so good to see you. I can't tell you—" Mary kissed her and held her face in her hands. "I'm just glad to see you're alive. Come up."

She unlocked the door and switched on the light.

"Eleanor has gone. I miss her. Sorry about the mess."

"You are *amazing,* darling. No sign of the war casualty."

"They took eleven ounces of steel out of me in New York. Oh, Serena!" She lay down the equipment. "You—you look fine, too."

"Oh?" Serena sighed. "I find myself worrying about things I haven't given a thought to for ages. The right color lipstick, is my hair too thin, should I use a diaphragm. I'm getting careless in that department. I don't know what I feel anymore. I don't know myself. I've been here so long and I'm not at all sure I know what it is that we've achieved for so much suffering. And yet I know I must go on. Do you—do you think my hair is too thin? It's the diet. I suppose I should dye it. What do you think? You have such gorgeous hair, darling."

"I think you are a very fine person." She brushed her hips. "Where is Giles?"

"I'm sorry. It's a defense mechanism I suppose, to turn it on oneself. Giles isn't too well; they found a spot on his lung. Went from Gibraltar to hospital in London. He's in Switzerland now. I think that's good for him. I miss him. Of course, it was Liam who saved his life."

"Coffee?"

"Please."

"Come downstairs while I brew some."

They stood together, with the gas burner as the only illumination, catching the one's darkness and the other's sheen.

"I've been with Koltzov all day," said Mary, filling the pot. "He's so damned volatile. It seems he remembers who he is meant to be only after showing you what he would like to be. You know? He can't square the two roles, nor can he settle for either one. You have to learn to deal with both. That tends to make you as crazy as he is. I can't deal with it."

"Darling, it's been a disaster, this battle. Appalling casualties."

"We have to talk about that. Here, can you take the mugs?"

When they were seated on the bed Mary said, "Serena, how—how do you keep going?"

"Oh, I just do. No tenets damaged. But I'm no longer sufficiently enraptured with Spain. It smashed up poor Beth. He took to the bottle. Everything he wanted to do, all the lives he was saving, they obstructed him at every turn, poor thing. So he went. We've had three doctors killed in the last week." She had turned brighter in the steam from the coffee. "How is Liam?"

"A changed man."

"You're very fond of him."

□

"Yes, I am."

"But Nicolás—I haven't asked about him."

"Nicolás is in Barcelona."

"Nasty things happen there."

"Yes."

Serena kicked off a shoe. "Dear Liam. In other times . . . but *what* other times will we ever see?"

"I've missed a period. I throw up a lot."

Serena put a hand on her knee. "Darling! That's—that's wonderful." Her first rush of enthusiasm abated. "Or is it?"

"I don't know. I'm frightened."

"Of course you are."

Mary smiled wanly. "I'm not so reckless, that's for sure. Some war correspondent."

"How certain are you?"

"Well—it's only a period."

"Nicolás doesn't know?"

"No."

"No. Well, don't worry, darling." She kept the hand on Mary's knee and changed tone. "Mary. Something happened today. I can't do anything about it, but I think you could. Can I tell you about it?"

■

Rey heard the beat of the ancient flatbed press as he went down the stairs. The newspaper was reduced to one sheet, but Rey lived by Napoleon's belief that hostile newspapers were more dangerous than bayonets.

Luis slept at the bench. It often happened. The rhythm of the press did it. Head sunk into chest, hands in lap, yellow skull under the bulb. A smell of garlic, stronger than the ink and lead. A proof page on the floor by Luis's feet. It was as though all the obsessive felicity had fallen, like the proof, from him, that the hulk had relapsed into the blubber of an infant. Rey was annoyed: he wanted to get the paper on the streets, to wage war.

More clearly seen, there was an oddity about the hands in the lap.

They gripped lewdly or—Rey was suddenly alarmed—in a thrombotic seizure of the whole body. The body was without breath. Only the machine had life. Beat and swish, beat and swish.

Rey faltered. A natural death was something he had never seen. The idea was too liturgical for his taste. There was no hereafter, and Luis had the face of a monk who, in his final spasm, had resentfully realized this. Closer. The shadow of the layered chin concealed another oddity. There was a discoloring around the neck like a distended vein. From this angle the body had the look of recoil.

Beat and swish, beat and swish.

Rey didn't want to touch Luis.

"The final edition," said Sletin.

He stepped from behind the press as lightly as a dancer and looked as though he might take a bow like one. The embroidered shirt moved losely over the hips. He smiled virginally; the voice reminded Rey of Perot.

BUENAVENTURA DURRUTI
14 JULY 1896–20 NOVEMBER 1936

The inscription was newly cut. Durruti now lay in a mausoleum. Too much of an edifice, Cordón thought. Durruti would have despised it. Built by a guilty conscience, tribute safely made.

"The day we brought the body here," he said, "we could not get near the grave. There were so many wreaths that the paths were impassable. Thousands of wreaths. More flowers than I have ever seen in my life. Then it started to rain. You know, Barcelona rain. The water came pouring down and it looked like the wreaths had been thrown into the sea. All those flowers were floating away, a great tide of flowers, and people, soaked to the skin. We left the casket in the mortuary. He was buried the next day. That night—" He broke off. "The night we brought him here—" He broke off again.

"What?" said Álvaro.

"That night I went to see Berneri."

There was no shade by the mausoleum. The sun had turned crisp the one wreath resting by the inscription.

"Berneri said it was a death that should not be solved."

They stood for a further minute, Álvaro one step behind Cordón, looking several times around the cemetery. Some distance away a spade bit into gravel. Another grave. Apart from the two gravediggers no one could be seen. Álvaro wondered why a grave was being dug during the siesta. He tugged the strap over his shirt, the strap of an automatic carbine.

"Yes," said Cordón, turning. "I know. We should go."

In turning his back on the mausoleum, Cordón felt the remoteness of the days with Durruti. An age had been buried with him. Once they reached the shade of an avenue of plane trees he stopped.

"Mera was right," he said. "We cannot survive by being a band of brigands."

"I—I would have liked to have been one of you," said Álvaro.

Cordón punched his shoulder. "You are a married man."

From a distance they looked of the same age and as lawless as two gunmen come down in high spirits from the hills. Hunters.

Aneta Ferrer waited for them to reach her, and then stepped out from the trees.

Cordón might have seen her before but for the distraction of the gravediggers nearby. As it was, he was completely taken by surprise. Álvaro, too, was gaping.

"Nicolás."

Cordón pushed Álvaro's carbine back into its sling. "It's all right." He was within a few paces of her. She wore a black dress, unadorned, and she was unarmed.

"I have been looking for you," she said. "And I thought, if he is in Barcelona, he would come here—to pay his respects."

"Why?"

She was luminous in the shadows. The black dress set off the force of her face; the face had aged but become more compelling. Her power had always been part intellect and part animal attraction. She was compelling.

"This is Álvaro, yes?"

Álvaro hardened.

"Nicolás. Walk with me."

Cordón turned to Álvaro. "Stay here. Wait."

Álvaro reluctantly conceded, fingering the carbine.

She stepped to Cordón's side but did not touch him. "You are very elusive."

Her body scent brought a flash of other places and other days. They walked together.

"Why are you elusive?"

"This way you talk. Am I supposed to believe this is a meeting of old lovers?"

Her walk stiffened and her voice pitched more sharply. "No. I wanted to warn you."

"You came here on your own?"

Silent for a few seconds, she looked up at him with eyes that were straying from her voice.

"Does it mean anything to you? That I came?"

"Once, once I used to think that it would never matter, never, that we followed different ideas. It should not matter. The catastrophe is that it does."

"Get out of Barcelona. This is not your problem."

"When Durruti died, everybody was an anarchist. For a day."

"Do you understand what I am saying?"

"Are you the law here?"

Her laugh was as metallic as the spades. "Do you think I do not know what you are doing here?"

"Russian syphilis."

"Trotskyism must be exterminated."

"I've heard that song. Dolores sings it. Purging the rear—always, she talks of purging, exterminating, liquidating. This blood feud of yours is the real enemy in the rear." He stopped walking and confronted her. "Why are you warning me?"

"You don't know?"

"To show me your power."

She sighed. Her left hand gripped and pulled at her dress where it was slack just above the hipbone, an old mannerism, more that of a child than of a woman. And, like a child, she was petulant with sucked-in lips. She would have pulled the wings from a butterfly.

"Oh," he said, *"oh* for what we were."

He felt pathos in the momentary peace of the graveyard, in the light brushing of the wind in the planes, in the dying light of a beautiful woman. Better both to have died than to have become like this. A hundred feet or so behind her, Álvaro stepped clear of the trees with the carbine across his chest.

"We were nothing," she said. *"Nothing."*

He allowed her to believe he was deceived, he had to allow her that. So he walked back to Álvaro without another glance at her. Starlings broke from a tree in a small, wild pack and scattered among the headstones like hail.

■

"Keep moving—and don't slow down," said Law.

Serena missed a gear in trying to heed him and, at the same time, to look out the side window. The noise of the ambulance bounced back from a high, white plastered wall.

"That's the place," said Law. "I know, for sure."

"How do you know?" said Mary, sitting between him and Serena, crammed into the cab. She craned to get a look at the building behind the wall.

"Because I was there."

They were nearly at the end of the white wall. Then the road took a right curve between trees. Mary saw only a tower—a watchtower like a penitentiary's. And then they were in the shade of the trees.

"You were there?"

Law nodded. "That's right. You see, I drove a truck there with my commissar, Commissar Geiser. We took a carton there—all documents, papers. Papers and passports. They belonged to some of our men who had been sent there. Geiser said—don't slow down, keep moving—Geiser said the men were being treated for shell shock. I knew they didn't have shell shock."

"They deserted?" said Serena.

"General Gal is a madman. It was deliberate. He sent us over the hill knowing we would be mown down."

"So—" Mary settled back into the seat. "—so what happens in there?"

"There are Russian doctors. I don't know what kind of doctors. But nobody ever gets out of there."

"You saw Russians in there?"

"Heard them, too, Geiser was laughing with them. Laughing. Well, Geiser got his."

Serena recalled the lone figure striding out toward the Moors.

"You're taking a risk, telling me this," said Mary. "You know that?"

Law nodded. "Yes, ma'am. I do know that. You know, I came here back in December. We came over the Pyrenees. About sixty of us. In the snow. All volunteers. That's how we saw it, ma'am. We were volunteers. Somehow it always gives you the sense, if you begin like that—well, it makes you feel you can quit any time. You're a free man, right? If things don't turn out so good, if you—well, if the heart goes out of it. You have your passport. You can leave. It isn't like that. They took all the passports. You have no freedom. Not even the sense of being in a real army. They watch you all the time."

As if to underline that point, he tried to get a glimpse in the mirror.

"All the time."

■

Arturo Barea and Ilsa Poldi were no longer running the censorship from the Telefónica. Mary found them in the Foreign Ministry in the Plaza de Santa Cruz—or, more exactly, she found Ilsa there, waiting for her at the foot of the monumental staircase that divided two large inner courts.

Ilsa, usually able to convey calm under any pressure, was openly anxious.

"Mary."

They kissed.

"This is a palace," said Mary.

"The Telefónica became too dangerous. The shelling. Come, let's walk."

She led Mary across a court, between a circle of marble statues.

"It's strange, Mary. Arturo says, if you want to run away from death you run straight into her arms." She managed a tenuous crease of the lips. "I thought that was his Spanish morbidity. No more. You remember, at the Telefónica I was always at my desk at five sharp."

"I remember."

"The day after we left the Telefónica a shell came through our office window and made a direct hit on my desk."

She held Mary by the arm. "Arturo is falling to pieces before my eyes. It's not the shells. It's not the work. Things are different, politically. They look at us almost as if we are fifth columnists. All they want is an excuse . . ."

The encircling statues seemed attentive. Military boots rang on the flagstones. Somewhere above a shrill telephone went unanswered.

"Who—who are *they?"* said Mary.

"New men. A new order."

"You want to go."

"Arturo doesn't see that."

"Ilsa." She broke off, partly in a surge of despair and partly to think. "These statues are *awful."*

"They're official. State-subsidized." Ilsa, too, seemed suddenly struck by this vision of absurdity. "Let's get a drink."

■

Spain was but a darker band of haze slipping to meet the horizon. So much had dissolved within the haze—an episode was over and liquidated. The smell of the boat, hot steel and coal dust, reestablished a sense of the real world, where the engines made the future.

One of the crew came to the stern.

"Too bad, comrade. All those señoritas left behind."

Yanin's face, which the sailor had never seen until now, turned on him slowly.

"They are a hopeless people."

□

■

Serena heard the cat from the bottom of the staircase. It saw her and arched its back and cried out again. Serena ran up to the door. It was locked. She pulled at the handle and then pounded.

"Mary! *Mary!* Are you there?"

She heard the voice faintly.

Eleanor pushed her head into the door.

Serena had to throw herself at the door several times before the catch broke away from the jamb.

"Oh—you poor darling," she said as she saw Mary on the bed.

Eleanor sprang ahead of her and leapt up to the pillows, sniffing at the blood.

■

Sletin's mouth was a small purple-ringed hole between his spongelike cheeks, cheeks like buttocks, nose vestigial, mouth like an arsehole. Rey saw it like that—and told Sletin so in vivid, staccato defiance. Sletin was bending over him. The light was very bright and caught a bald patch under Sletin's brushed-back hair.

"Yes," said Sletin, unprovoked. "You will eat your own shit, spoonful by spoonful, before I have finished with you." He held his head there a little longer, looking into Rey's dilated eyes. Then he stepped back and out of the light, where Rey could not see him.

"More," said Sletin.

The man at the desk moved a lever and held it down.

The black straps holding Rey to the chair pulled tight as he jerked under the repeated shocks. There was a smell of urine and of burning cloth—Rey's trousers gave off smoke. He screamed on a high and drawn-out note that, in the stone room, was choral.

Ferrer stood behind the man at the desk.

"You see—no balls," said Sletin. "Castrato."

"I want the names," said Ferrer.

The pool of urine under Rey broke its bounds and began to move over the floor in a yellow rivulet, oddly straight, headed for the man at the desk. Ferrer moved away to Sletin's side.

"The names."

Sletin contemplated Rey in the wake of the higher voltage. He didn't like to be pressed. This woman was always pressing, even when silent.

"Let us see how well he swims," he said.

■

It was, by some chance of allocation, Durruti's old car. The one in which Cordón had heard Durruti's dying curses. They had been given it in Barcelona by a man unaware of its associations—just another car the worse for wear. And that was the way things were going.

Álvaro wanted to drive. He put his carbine on the backseat, not mentioning the stain that was still there, making the leather richer.

Now, after a day driven in the heat, the Packard was missing on one cylinder and hard to drive slowly. They reached Madrid an hour after sundown. Only then, at a roadblock, was the car recognized. A man remembered the license number.

"That was Durruti's car," he said.

Álvaro nodded while the man looked at their papers.

"Did you know him, Durruti?" he said, still holding the papers.

"Everybody knew Durruti," said Cordón.

"You're from Barcelona," said the man. "In Madrid he was never one of us." He looked at Cordón's papers then at Cordón. "Durruti had balls—but a big mouth." He gave them back the papers and waved them through.

"Madrileños," snarled Álvaro.

Somewhere, thought Cordón, Durruti was laughing.

Ten minutes later they pulled onto the paving by the courtyard. Cordón went in. The light was on in the room above. Serena sat in a chair at the top of the stairs, flicking at mosquitoes with a magazine. She stood up and waited for him.

"I'm glad you're here, Nicolás."

□

She stepped aside to let him pass, but put up a finger to her lips.

Mary was asleep in the bed.

He was shocked by her appearance.

"What happened?" he said, hardly able to restrain his voice. "She's as white as chalk."

"She's had a bad time but she will be all right. She lost a lot of blood. She'll be anemic for a while."

Cordón stood looking down at the bed.

Álvaro came up the steps too noisily, and Serena waved silence into him.

"It was very hard to locate you," she said. "I tried for days. I'm glad you could get here, Nicolás. She's—she's pushed herself too hard. Too soon. She wasn't as tough as she thought. She ought to get away from Madrid. Get out of this place."

Eleanor uncurled from the counterpane and stretched and then came nonchalantly to Cordón's feet.

"You will take her, won't you? Whatever she says?"

He nodded. The cat was purring loud enough to wake her. "Who told you where we were?"

"Koltzov. The Russian. He's been an absolute darling. Much to my surprise."

■

Already half stunned, Rey could keep no sense of balance as he was thrown onto the sloping concrete. The door closed. In the darkness he slid slowly down the damp concrete and touched something cold—a metal grille at the end of the slope. There he lay with his head back on a wall and his legs folded under him. He could dimly make out the limits of the space around him. The metallic shock, the only cold thing he had touched in hours, reassured him of his functioning senses, and slowly he could feel himself breathing and know that, apart from the dull burning in his groin, he was still intact. There was even anger in him. He moved sideways and banged a fist on the grille. For a few seconds the air moved in a quirkish draft. Then there was a gurgling above, followed by a surging roar.

The water came like a tide down the slope. Within a few seconds it was up to his waist. Trying to pull himself up, he was knocked down again by a backlash of water from the wall. He floundered, trying to keep his head above water. But once the water took the weight of his body, he realized it required little effort to float—the water was cool rather than cold and cleared his head. He became amused. Amused like a child, kicking into the water, arms spread out, head thrown back, ready to laugh above the roar of the pipes. Pipes. Where were they? He pushed from a wall and kicked across to another. The water came from above. He looked up. The ceiling was there—he could see ripples of seams in gray concrete, could even have touched it with a raised arm. The water continued to rise. There could be only a foot or so of air above him.

■

The hills were so bright with blooming lavender that the color seemed to lift in the heat and tint the air. The air was sweet. All the windows in the Packard were down. The warm air played through Mary's hair, spreading strands of it over the pillow and the leather. From the driving seat Cordón had watched in the mirror as she slept.

This slight shift of his head to see her was what she first registered when she awoke. She saw his eyes in the mirror.

"Where are we? I can smell lavender."

He half-turned to smile. "You slept for a hundred miles. We are halfway to Valencia."

She moved her head to get a view over Álvaro's broad shoulders. "It's beautiful . . . doesn't seem like the same country."

"Going south," said Álvaro, with more cynicism than affection.

She kept her head in that position on the pillow, feeling that her weakness was something she should disguise with curiosity and alertness in her voice. Then she caught Cordón looking at her again. He couldn't be fooled. She offered a smile conceding the truth, happy that they could be so close. Within minutes she was asleep again.

■

Ferrer and Sletin were drinking coffee. She also smoked a cigarette, consuming it very quickly and periodically jabbing it across the table at Sletin in emphasis.

"At first he made me feel angry. He seemed to doubt my conviction. It was like—" She crushed the cigarette on the table and pulled out another. "It was like not being trusted."

Sletin lit the cigarette for her.

"Then I realized he was testing me. Finally, I understood. My political education was just beginning."

Sletin blew out the match. She didn't seem to want any response from him. She had the intensity of the self-obsessed. Her eyelids hardly rose, and when they did there was a great distance in her eyes—the inner distance of subjection. He watched her hand, her left hand. Her fingernails were long and carefully kept and they bit into the table, into the grain. To him her hands were her one attraction.

"He gave me my purpose," she said and—at last—looked for a reaction.

Sletin pocketed the matches, patting them into his shirt.

"I knew so little. He is my teacher."

"He has gone."

For a moment she kept the same expression and then it crumbled away.

"What?"

"Yanin has gone."

"Gone? He—"

"Recalled to Moscow." Sletin nodded and drank in the pleasure of having completely ended the eulogy. Her face was gray, and now the eyes were fixed open. "No need for alarm,"he said soothingly.

"But—but he could have told me."

"It was very sudden. It usually is."

She slumped at the table, shaking her head and draining cold coffee.

"Such men cannot be personal," said Sletin.

Her hands gripped the coffee mug as he hoped they might grip him. But there was a disconcerting narrowness in her when she looked again across the table—momentarily he had a sense that she had changed substance and was about to take wing around the room. His irony—all irony—was lost on her. With alarm he saw that she had swallowed literally what he had said—like a flame, wanting it to burn.

"No. Of course," she said.

She was solid again. She was thinking of high, laced-up boots in association with the sound of a guard pacing the courtyard outside. Through an open door she could see the passage with Sletin's three chambers. Rey had been silent for some time. Rey—Rey had been like a blue-winged fly that made a lot of noise and that you never quite caught: hit him, stun him, leave him in a shadow for dead, and then he would be there again to drive you mad.

Without another word she got up and went down the passage.

Rey was "drying out" in the chamber with the floor of broken bricks. She slid open the observation hatch. He was folded, naked, into a corner, with most of his weight against the wall. And asleep.

She unlocked the door. Sletin had followed only as far as the beginning of the passage.

Even in shoes it was hard to keep balance walking over the upturned bricks. She slipped once. Rey remained inert. There was very little light—outside the sun was fading and the high, narrow grille admitted a weak beam on one wall. Rey seemed, as her eyes adjusted, to be as white as lime. She stood over him.

His right arm burst out, as if on a steel spring, and held her at the calf, pulling her toward him. She lost balance and fell against the wall. Now his eyes were on her. Her trousers had ripped on a brick. She felt a trickle of blood on her ankle. Rey moved to a squatting position. She realized that he could not properly see her; his eyes had the glaze of the blind. His lunge had been lucky. She could smell him—him, his shit. There was shit all around.

"El Calentito," he hissed. *"El Calentito!"* The hand that had taken her leg kept groping out toward her.

She pulled herself up the wall, using her back on the stone to get balance. They were but inches apart. His hand nearly found her waist. Her feet were wedged firmly between bricks and her buttocks pressed into the wall—she could not be dislodged, and she felt the strength and the power rise in her.

His face came forward to hers. *"Calio,"* he whispered, and his breath hit her like a rancid wind.

He had delivered his head. Her arms came out and her hands locked into his neck. She felt the nails go into a vein. Blood splashed into her face. She had a surge of strength. Her fingers met at the nape of his neck and she felt something under a thumb—something that was hard, and cracked. Bile and blood sprayed her, but she kept her grip and was able to lift his head slightly and shake it. The bulged eyes were laughing like an insolent puppet's. She crashed the head back into the wall and kept crashing it until the sound of the impact softened.

Sletin stood framed in the door.

She saw him when she finally let go of Rey.

Sletin turned on the lamp. What he remembered afterward was not the gore nor even the orgasmic moistness in her eyes but the clear impress on Rey's neck of her fingers, singed into the flesh as distinctly as if by a branding iron.

■

"No, Nicolás. I want to walk. Just take my hand."

Álvaro stood by the car and watched: Mary and Cordón stepped from the road to the beach, going slowly down to the water. Under moonlight the sand glinted as though covered by frost. The water line was barely perceptible, just a change from crystal to a surface like folded silk. Kelp and salt in the dead air.

"Is that a castle?" she said.

"Yes. Peñíscola. Where we will stay, in the town."

They had driven across a narrow isthmus to the island, and she felt that the whole thing—castle, town, and beach—was ready to be detached to float out to sea.

"It's magical," she said, tightening her grip on his hand as they stopped at the edge of the water. "But you didn't choose it just for that, did you?"

"No." His grip responded to hers.

"Álvaro knew every inch of the road."

"Still the reporter."

"Of course."

He pushed a pebble into the water with his foot. "We brought people here from Barcelona. It's as safe as any place can be. We have friends here—people who like to help."

"Is that why you didn't go into Valencia?"

"I thought you were asleep."

She kicked off her sandals and pulled him into the water. "It's where I want to be—with you. But I don't want to be a burden or a danger to you. I'm really not ill. I'll soon get my strength. There is a story I have to finish."

"You are not a burden. We both need the time to think. Things have—there are things I must tell you."

"I know."

They stood silent, with the tepid water lapping their feet. There was no longer—Mary was sure of it—there was no longer anything withheld between them. Cordón had no barriers left. As he had come closer to her he had stepped away from something else—something umbilical.

"Nicolás." She closed her hand on his again. "I lost our child."

"Yes."

"I'm sorry."

He took her in his arms, face pressed into her hair. "There is no blame. Perhaps—perhaps it is for the best."

He was covering a disappointment, and that in itself confirmed the change in him.

And yet he was not at peace with peace. They had a small house to themselves, a two-story flat-roofed whitewashed house on the edge of the town. A reed-covered patio looked out over beach and sea. During the day a blue-white light invested the rooms, even with the reed blinds down. The whole character of the place discouraged darkness. There was no war. And that was what nagged at Cordón.

He made several trips north, always at night. The fourth time he did not return the following morning, as usual. She spent the day on the patio, making notes and trying not to show her anxiety. The old woman who looked after the house, Irina, came back from the market with a huge lobster. She demonstrated an obscene trick: by sticking a skewer in the lobster's spine she made it contract and jump off the table. Irina's toothless laugh, ringing in the rooms, was her way of taking Mary's mind off Cordón. That, she thought, was Spanish humor: callous, oriental, complicit, all in one gust.

She was picking at the lobster without appetite when Cordón and Álvaro came in. Álvaro was Irina's pet. She pulled him into the kitchen while Cordón went to Mary.

"I'm sorry," he said. "Something happened." He pulled a chair to her side. "Do you feel well enough to leave?"

"Look at me. I'm fine, you know that. What's happened?"

"I have to go to Aragón."

In the kitchen Álvaro was laughing as obscenely as Irina.

"Back to my own country."

"Back to the war?"

"Are you ready for that?"

"Nicolás." She took his head between her hands. "Your own country? That's the piece of you I've never seen. You certainly don't belong here."

He smiled with boyish relief and momentum. "This is for tourists. This is not real. I want you to see Aragón. I want you to see why it *is* a part of me."

"And the war?"

"We have to leave in the morning."

■

"You have a wife, a mistress, and quite a shocking reputation."

"The reputation I don't know."

"You're a Jew, aren't you?"

Koltzov's pebbled eyes had wandered to Serena's breasts but now came point-blank to her face.

"I'm sorry," she said. "Non sequitur. What I meant was—"

"What you meant was we have to be twice as good."

"Well . . ."

"Yes," he insisted.

"Is—is that true?"

"You. You are—*what*? Intelligent, certainly. Attractive, certainly. But where do you come from? You want to be something against your blood. A masquerade."

"Blood? Blood has no mind of its own."

"You think not?" He moved a restless hand to the table. It was the only stray part of him. "You think not?"

In that instant he seemed to her no longer familiar but balefully ancient. Yet the last thing he invited was pity. His danger was to be attractive for the wrong reasons. She poured herself more vodka, noticing that her hand was as cold as the bottle that he kept in ice. She drank in one swallow. What the hell. Why not?

This was Spain reduced to bone. A treeless place, virtually desert. Esparto grass patched a white-gray plateau like stubble on an old man's jaw. And a heavy, saturating heat mist.

"God—I don't think I've ever *been* so hot."

Mary's arm, hung out the car window, was coated in white gypsum dust. The Packard was the only moving thing. Everything was deadened, bloodless.

"They must be, they have to be mad," she said.

"No. No, not mad," said Cordón. "They have waited a long time. A long time. And chosen a good moment."

"*Jesus.* I can't believe it."

"The perfect time. The harvest gathered. All our best units at the front."

"Can you stop it?"

"If they succeed, our movement, our *idea*—all finished."

She remembered Álvaro's face when they had left him at Lérida. Veteran that he was now, Álvaro still hated to part from Cordón. That last look at Álvaro's eyes had told her more than had Cordón. The Packard rode high in the front and low in the back. There was a dismantled Maxim in the trunk.

An hour before dark the road descended steeply, the mist thinned and then broke, and they were in a watered plain, a *huerta,* with a river joining the road. Cordón stopped. There were ripe figs in a strip of trees dividing the river and the road. He picked some, and they sat in the car with the doors open to the river.

"Just when you think the heat will never end . . . " she said.

"Aragón has two faces."

"It's still your home, isn't it?"

"Everything I believe in is here."

"I—I don't have a single place, a home, that means anything."

"The people who first settled in America—they must have had that feeling. Otherwise they would not have survived."

"They were Puritans."

He looked at her sharply. "What happened to them?"

"America happened to them."

"Ah." He sucked at a fig held with fingers turned blue. "The people who want to destroy us, they say Aragón is a law unto itself. That is true. That way, we survive."

There was a concession of humor in his voice, but also an arrogance that was beyond argument, that selfsame arrogance that had been offensive to her when they first met, but which she had long accepted as ineluctable. Tricks of time in the mind: he was a whole life to her. And that trick you learned in war—to take what was there. She stretched out her legs and lay back on the seat. A sound could give the illusion of coolness: the sound of the river, clear water over white stone. She rubbed a bare foot in the grass. One line of a poem she kept to herself—"The light of understanding has made me most discreet," but she spoke the rest of the verse aloud:

"Smeared with sand and kisses
I took her away from the river.
The swords of the lilies battled with the air."

He nodded. "Lorca." Then wryly smiled. "From the Faithless Wife."

"I'll never be that." Her brief smile met his. "I could never get Lorca right in translation. So much of it is in the way it sounds. It's really music."

"Gypsy music. Yes. Poor Lorca. Murdered in the first days of the war. One thing the fascists cannot tolerate—a poet with the eyes of God. *That* is subversion."

She slid out of the car and went down to the river, slipping off her shirt and then her skirt.

■

The horseman's hair was thick and white and so was the mane of his stallion. They were both ebony and white, the horse's skin glistening after the gallop and the man's face grained dark in the morning sun. He held the reins loosely and came down the hill at the horse's own pace, stopping short of the road once he heard the car.

Mary first saw him like that: a sentinel figure nearly as still as stone, something risen from the rock.

Cordón slowed and stopped within a few feet of the horse. He got out without a word.

Before the two men spoke Mary had seen the likeness—in the bones.

The horseman's voice was melodic and baritone, pitched to rise at the end of each sentence.

"Always the companion of trouble," he said.

"Don Pepe." Cordón was formal. "I did not know you were here."

"The pleasure lies in living long enough to see it. That is the only pleasure."

"Is it safe for you?"

The horseman slackened slightly, thighs settling in the ornamental saddle, boots splayed out from the horse.

"Safe? Oh yes, I am made safe by the future."

"You know what's happening?"

"Oh yes. The Council of Aragón is dissolved by decree. Its offices are burning, burning. The produce of the collectives will be confiscated. Money, machines, transport, tools. The end of your dream, Nicolás. Who am I to thank for this deliverance?" His laugh rose to the hills. "I am to be given back my land by the Bolsheviks. Oh yes—I am safe." He looked from Cordón to the car. "You have left your manners in Barcelona."

□

It seemed for a second that Cordón might lose control, but he steadied himself and opened the car door for Mary.

"Miss Mary Byrnes."

The white head bowed.

"Mary. Don Pepe Cordón. My father."

It was like looking at Cordón thirty years hence—but without any intimacy.

"Mary is an American journalist."

"Miss Byrnes." He bowed again. "It shames me that you should see me like this. No better than a gypsy. A victim of dreams." He looked at Cordón. "No doubt my son will show you the family estate, the house. They use the house to store the seed grain—and for other things."

"Yes," said Cordón, "and we will keep it."

The chasm between the two men had worn out words. Don Pepe straightened himself as though braced by a corset, gently heeled the horse, and rode across the road and down into the valley.

"An anachronism," said Cordón.

Mary took his arm. "He loves you."

Cordón watched the figure disappear—for a moment just a totem borne on an invisible horse—and then shook his head.

"No. He cannot love. He cannot forgive."

■

The village sat with its back to the Pyrenees, at the edge of the *huerta.* A river, the Vero, came down from the mountains at that point. Looking south from the village, the plain opened up into a swathe of well-irrigated land producing almonds, olives, figs, and vines. Beyond the plain the heat mist already curtained the horizon where the plateau began. The village seemed held aloof from the plain, placed so that it could exist independently—and, as Cordón pointed out, it had an ideal defensive position that had saved it in the past.

The whole valley was in the hands of anarchist collectives. For its part, the village provided men and a center for storage, as well as an olive press and a winery. There was only one street, a bodega, a handful of houses—and the Cordón property. The family house, the *solar,* was, like the village, Moorish in style and surrounded by an extensive stone wall. The winery was an extension of the house.

When Cordón and Mary arrived, the car had to be left outside the gate. The drive to the house was blocked by mule carts and two trucks, unloading grain. As Cordón led Mary to the house, the men kept on working but welcomed him as "Captain."

"This was where you grew up?" she said.

"Until I went to Barcelona. To school."

"It must have been beautiful."

"At first, it seemed beautiful."

A man came out of the house—a well-braced middle-aged man with face shadowed by a wide-brimmed leather hat.

"Nicolás!"

"Miguel! Miguel, this is Mary, Mary Byrnes. Mary, this is Miguel Fonz, secretary of the collective."

Fonz bowed in the same manner as had Don Pepe.

"Nicolás—everything that we could move is in here. We are using the winery cellars for the grain. The house is full—except, of course, for the upper floor."

"We met Don Pepe."

Fonz took off his hat to wipe his brow—he was bald and had a skull with prominent veins.

"Yes," he said. "Don Pepe appeared five days ago. He just rode up to the house, walked around—he went upstairs—and then he rode off. Where he lives I do not know."

"He seems to know everything."

"Come—come inside."

They went through a bare-bricked hall to a kitchen at the back of the house. A wisp of a woman, unusual for her golden hair, was washing vegetables at a standpipe.

"Mercedes!" said Cordón.

The woman clasped him with wet hands slipping down his shirt.

"Nicolás—you come back!"

Cordón introduced Mary: Mercedes stood nodding at her, tongue-tied as through stricken shy. It was impossible to judge her age within twenty years. The sun seemed never to have touched her.

Fonz laughed. "Mercedes, she treats Nicolás like a son. Always."

Mary smiled at Mercedes. "I can see that Nicolás, he has come home."

"Yes," said Mercedes, finding a voice weakly. "Yes. He has come home." She surveyed him more critically. "And he must eat. You are tired, I can see." She permitted herself a tentative warmth in the eyes for Mary. "Your friend could also put on some weight."

Cordón held her hand. "Mercedes—look at you. Always feeding people, but a light wind would blow you away."

"It never has."

"No." Cordón became solemn. "No. She would never run away with me."

They all laughed, Fonz with a deep, thunderous roll, and Mercedes with a reedlike song.

Later, when Cordón and Fonz went outside, Mary remained in the kitchen, sitting at the table.

Still working, Mercedes looked at her with less reserve.

"You will marry Nicolás?"

Mary was unprepared for the sudden directness. She took a few seconds to meet the exacting eyes.

"War is not a time for marriage."

"He likes to seem all the libertarian. In some ways, he is conventional."

"Mercedes. Can I ask you—ask a personal question?"

The eyes neither dissented nor relented.

"Where is Nicolás's mother?"

Mercedes's mouth tightened. "Nicolás did not tell you? His mother? One day his mother went out of here on her horse; it was early, she often went riding very early—she went out that day, just like any other, out through the village, down to the river. She did not come back."

"What do you mean?"

"She did not come back."

"But—what—?"

□

"Nicolás was two years old. She did not come back. Nobody saw her, or the horse again."

Mary looked out the window. Cordón and Fonz were standing in the sun, Fonz sweeping his hat through the air to indicate dispositions of the men on the grounds, Cordón nodding. Everyone, including Fonz, moved around Cordón in a way that revealed custom. Anarchism had not eradicated every vestige of tradition. Cordón would not have welcomed this perception, but it was as clear to her as was Mercedes's love for him.

"What was she like, his mother?"

"Free. As Nicolás tries to be."

Cordón returned.

"Take Mary upstairs," said Mercedes.

"I was going to do that."

"It's all in order."

He led Mary to the wide stone stairs.

"She is amazing. You know how old she is?" said Mary.

"She—she must be . . ."

"She's sixty-two. *Sixty-two*"

"To me she seems never to change." He put his arm around her waist as they went up. "It pleases me that she likes you."

"Nobody gets by her."

"Gets by? What do you mean?"

"I'm sorry. I'm being American. I mean, she's very shrewd. And very, very caring." This she said with an eye on Cordón's response.

But he did not want to follow; he knew where it was leading, and deflected her attention to the house. There was a sudden and strange change in the coloring, from stone walls to wood paneling, low ceilings, and oriental carpets. It was gothic—except that where there might have been battlemented casements there were deep and airy windows.

"It's beautiful."

"A museum." He went to double doors. "Mercedes will not allow it to be changed." He opened the doors. They seemed then to walk into a cascade of light, sun filtered into great stripes, almost liquid, across a brilliant carpet. There was a smell of wood and of age. When her eyes adjusted to the light, she saw that it was a bedroom. An oak bed, large enough to sleep six, was covered in a tapestry, woven in a bluish-brown Moorish design.

"No one has slept here for twelve years."

He said it adamantly, as a man might announce the edict of a high church.

"Nicolás."

She walked a few paces from him, caught between bars of light but with her own color intensified, hair flicking with the purpose of her voice.

"Nicolás. Why did your father give up this house?"

She waited as he decided whether to reply. He was relating the question to something else—probably to his speculation about what had passed between her and Mercedes.

"My father," he said, the hesitation discarded in an impulse, "chose to go. When the village became a collective, all of the proprietors—the landowners, the farmers, the small and the large—they were all invited to join, but they had to accept the principles. The principles were equality in all things, the abolition of money, the use of barter. My father—Don Pepe Cordón—" He said it as though of a stranger. "Don Pepe laughed. He just laughed at me. *At me.* He said, 'I am not equal.' We have a phrase, *Agua robada.* It means, water diverted, stolen, from the communal stream. My father said, 'I am *agua robada.'* He laughed at the idea of banishing money. And removing the value of money, that was the real success. Removing the value of money had given back the value of people. Barter works. The dentist works for—" His risen enthusiasm was suddenly checked. "You understand me?"

"I was thinking of my own father. The banker."

"Well—my father, too. He is an anachronism."

"He chose to go?"

"He could not remain. I opened this house to the collective. The winery, our land, everything."

"But not this room."

"I told you—Mercedes . . ."

"Ah yes. Mercedes."

She went to him and put each hand lightly on his shoulders. "Mercedes knows you better than you know yourself."

□

Looking beyond his head, for the first time, she noticed in the way the light fell on the plaster behind and above the bed that there was a faint impregnation of what had once hung there: a crucifix.

■

At the end of the upper floor a narrow staircase led up to a tower. Cordón took Mary to the castellated gallery. It gave a view over the village and most of the plain. By now the heat limited the visibility: behind them the peaks of the Pyrenees were under a rolling line of storm clouds, purple-black and yet oddly yellow, too.

"The *carabineros* can come only one way—up the road from the valley. We have lookouts in the foothills beyond the village. They cannot approach without being seen, and they cannot overrun a position like this."

She saw that the Maxim was installed at the main gate of the estate, where it commanded the road from the village.

"It's all so crazy," she said, "that you should have to defend yourselves against people who are supposed to be on the same side. Crazy."

"Other collectives have driven them off. It's only a matter of time before we regain political control."

"Crazy. It could lose the war."

"In one sense, maybe. But if we lose the war we shall have won it. Really. We will be stronger at the end because the people have come alive, the will has come alive."

There was a silence between them, until she said, "You've never spoken of losing before. Never."

"There is a change."

"Nicolás." She held him. *"Nicolás."*

■

Fonz watched them. The tower was sharply cut against the turmoil of clouds. Mary's hair, too, was a turmoil, with a coloring like nothing Fonz had seen before. She was unexpected. Men had already asked him what she was doing there. Their suspicion, their prejudice was checked by their loyalty to Cordón, but it was almost as palpable as the sheath of storm clouds over the Pyrenees and rumbled, sotto voce, as the storm now did. Fonz went into the house, spitting once into the grain-dusted steps.

Mercedes sat at the kitchen table, sewing.

Fonz held his head under the standpipe. The water hit his skull hard and cold, giving it the look of one of the vegetable roots that Mercedes had washed earlier. She thought, watching him, that he resembled a thing torn from the earth, upended, his limbs the short, thick stalks, his bare feet the stubs of a pruned growth. A man grown so hard because the earth was so hard. She worked delicately over worn lace. Despite labor her hands were still those of a younger woman. She and Fonz had a clear view of their youth when they looked at each other. Her fineness and his power had concentrated with age and made them complementary, even interdependent in an edgy way. The Flower and the Weed they were called, in a tongue where the weed was strong—but only behind their backs.

"I was watching them," he said.

"So?"

Her reticence annoyed him. "She has him."

Mercedes drew a thread slowly through the lace and revealed nothing.

"He's like a *novio.*"

"He is in love."

He shook the last of the water from his head and glared at her.

"He is in love," she said again, laying down the work. "And she is trying very hard not to make him feel that being in love, being in love like that, is a weakness."

"She is a damn *Yanqui.*"

"Miguel." She squared up to him without rising. "Nicolás left here years ago. She did not take him. He lives in another world. She is a part of that world."

"He came back."

"Yes. Yes, he came back. I am pleased that he did. And to-night . . . " She looked up at the ceiling and then at Fonz. "You must realize that their lives may be very short."

□

■

"It will be dangerous," said Cordón. "I want you to realize that."

She stood by him at a window, watching the last of the carts bring in the grain.

"Nicolás, nothing that can happen here can be as bad as my dreams." She rubbed a hand along his forearm. "I feel as though everything has been a preparation for this, everything that has happened to us. That I have been brought here so that I should know something, that I should understand something. I felt it as we arrived. It's beginning to feel familiar in the way that something you have dreamed is familiar, later. Even—this seems so odd, but it's part of it—even the mountains. The mountains are the wall. I've been running, running. Running for a long while and now I can't run anymore. The wall is there—up there, I can't run through or over it. So I have to stop running."

Her hand rested on his wrist.

"Does that sound crazy?"

He shook his head. "When I saw my father on that horse, I knew I had seen that before, the white hair and the white mane."

"It's frightening."

"No." He held her at the waist and spoke firmly. "It should not be frightening. We are not a dream. We are real."

"I feel you, Nicolás. You are real. I feel you. I want you. *Now.*"

But the tangible and the intangible remained interwoven like the tapestry on the bed. A casual glance at the tapestry suddenly drew you into a section of the design, and your mind was entrapped, looping inward to another dimension. On the pale stone of the ceiling the light and the shadow seemed similarly to lock together, but in a fluid and elusive pattern that one moment suggested a landscape, a landscape that she felt she had previously inhabited, but the next moment became an ocean in passage between peace and turbulence. It lapped the walls with a rim of crimson. The bed was cold to the skin—the surprise of cold linen in a torpid room was another dislocation. The bed had long been withdrawn from life. They brought life to it with a sudden and rude energy; they violated it. Uncowed by the imposing piety of the chamber, they claimed back the bed for the cause of life. Mary's long, low cry was the final defiance of her spirit to the dead things around them, to the wall above with its faint stigma.

■

The *carabineros* came two days later. They were seen on the road several miles away from the village. Two trucks led three cars. Looking through his glasses, Cordón guessed that each truck carried at least a score of men. The trucks had wire grilles over their windshields and improvised armor plating over their hoods. Spare tires protected the sides. The *carabineros* were learning.

When they saw the barricade blocking the narrowest part of the valley leading into the village, the trucks stopped a quarter mile short. An officer got down and scanned the barricade through glasses—Cordón had the strange sensation of glasses on glasses. Two other officers appeared from the cars in the rear. The man with the glasses read the proclamation strung across the barricade: FEDERACIÓN ANARQUISTA IBÉRICA: COMMUNE OF OLVENA. NO SURRENDER.

The three men conferred and then the one with the glasses began walking, alone, toward the barricade.

"What's his game?" said Fonz.

"Talking," said Cordón.

"A trick."

"He's got balls."

"What do we do?"

"I will meet him."

From a room above the bodega Mary watched him go over the barricade and walk toward the officer. She had her camera focused on them.

The two stopped a few feet short of each other.

The officer was surprisingly young. Cordón had expected an old reactionary's face and instead found himself looking at a pale-skinned and clean-shaven martinet.

"I have a copy of the government decree empowering me to dissolve this collective by law and to hand back the land to the peasants."

Cordón smiled. "The peasants?" He waved back at the barricade. "You see the peasants."

"Your name?"

"It is the peasants who run the collective, and the peasants who own the land. The peasants await."

"Your name?"

"Cordón. Nicolás Cordón."

"Is this your village?"

"My village? It is the people's village."

"I know the name."

"You think perhaps of Antonio Cordón. The communist who runs the army. No connection."

"I think of Don Pepe Cordón."

For a moment he had surprised Cordón.

"That does have a connection," said the officer. "I see that."

"No more."

"This is not the place for a debate. Do you accept the decree?"

"How does it seem to you?"

"Then I am sorry." He turned his back on Cordón without any hint of emotion or fear and walked back to the trucks.

Before he reached them, men began to spill out, all with light automatic rifles, and from the rear truck other weapons were wheeled down a ramp—two field guns.

By the time Cordón returned to the barricade the *carabineros* had been deployed—some sent on each side up into the hills and the field guns lined up in the road. The trucks and cars turned and withdrew down the road toward the plain.

"They have learned a lot in a short time," said Fonz.

"Yes," said Cordón. "This captain is too bright-eyed. His pistol is German."

Mary came running from the bodega.

Cordón waved her back but she ignored him.

"Those guns," said Cordón, "they will make a mess."

"There are men in the hills," she said.

"They will be taken care of."

□

At that second firing broke out somewhere on the slopes above.

"We were ready for that," said Fonz.

"They will depend on the field guns," said Cordón. "Get everyone out of the village and into the *solar.*"

"What will you do?" said Mary.

The answer was a sudden detonation—distant, as though from a quarry. Then a plume of smoke, black with a surging flame beneath it, came up from behind a foothill by the road.

Fonz and the other men waved and cheered.

"One of the trucks," cried Fonz.

There was a second blast.

"And the other," said Cordón.

The officers and men at the field guns were in confusion, and some men ran back down the road, where the trucks had gone.

"What happened?" said Mary.

"Mines," said Cordón. "We let them come through and then mined the road. That way we get the field guns."

But the *carabineros* had already loaded the guns, and the first salvo came over with a high scream and fell in the back of the village, throwing up brick dust and fragments.

Only then did Mary realize her lack of fear. Each explosion was addictive. It was not a question of nerve: it was again like the first weeks in Madrid, the adrenaline closed down all caution. She had little sense of time passing. Before the guns fired a third salvo, there was more confusion among the *carabineros*. From one side of the hill behind them rifles opened up. Through her viewfinder Mary picked out the captain who had parleyed with Cordón. He alone was calm. He tried to get the field guns loaded again. Rifle shots from the hills were selective and accurate—one man at the breech rolled over. A shell fell from his hands and rolled with him. Mary held the captain in the center of her lens. All around him men were looking for cover, but he had his pistol out and was firing toward the hill. His men were wasting their own fire in panic. She saw that the guns were about to fire again, and their angle was lower. She lay across the sandbags of the barricade. The shells went overhead. One made a direct hit on the bodega—on the very room where she had been.

□

The other landed in the road. Part of the building wobbled; the wall fractured and then fell into the crater of the second shell. She swung back to the *carabineros.* A sheet of flame erupted among them. The men from the hill had worked down close enough to lob their crude firebombs. Her view was suddenly blocked. Cordón was leading an assault—men were pouring over the barricade, rifles in the air, and rushing the field guns. She moved to get a sighting. The captain stood by one of the guns leveling his pistol at Cordón, waiting for the range to close. She wanted to cry out but had no voice. She lowered the camera. There was another flare of flame and smoke. There were too many men for her to see Cordón. She went over the barricade and ran.

The smell she knew. Gasoline and burning flesh. And that curious madness of the senses mixing death and life. Sour smoke, flakes of ash, and the scent of wild thyme in the rocks. Death and life and the voices of both. Also a strange percussion—boots in stampede. The *carabineros* were running. From men in bare feet. A pair of bare feet lay upturned in the esparto with blood in the grass—some of the grass was just tipped with blood, as though lightly brushed. The captain of the *carabineros* had lost his hat and looked even younger without it. He sat, on his knees, resting one hand on his pistol on the road. He looked at Mary with slowly gathered interest. She noticed his thin and waxed mustache, waxed into a smile that the mouth could not follow. He blinked as if remembering something and tried to lift his hand from the pistol. The effort forced a frown. A jet of blood, very fine, shot from his left ear. His eyes were locked onto her but no longer blinked. A man behind put his foot on the captain's back and the captain fell forward into the road.

"The only man among them," said Cordón, at her side.

"He's so young."

She looked at the bodies, some still burning, and the discarded weapons. One of the village men had a newly acquired automatic rifle and held it to his chest. She took his picture.

Because she was there, because she was with Cordón, because Cordón's tactics had been so devastating, and because it was obvious that she had been in battle before, the men looked at her differently.

□

Not with warmth—but with a degree of acceptance, as they might admit a stranger on sufferance for the sake of having something new to talk about.

Fonz was mindless of a bleeding arm. His trousers hung adrift of his paunch. He walked around the two field guns in a joyous, half-dancing movement.

But Cordón looked elsewhere.

"Only eight shells," he said.

Fonz did not hear. He was a child with the most magnificent toys of his life.

■

That night Mercedes produced caldrons of stew. The whole village danced in the grounds of the house under the light of a half-moon. Silver faces and shrill voices. Mercedes wore black and danced with Fonz. Cordón was persuaded to play the guitar. He began with a nod to Mercedes.

"This is by Francisco Tárrega, the great Tárrega. It's called—" He plucked a chord. "—it's called the Minuetto Mercedes."

She blushed like a girl.

Mary sat with her.

"He always was a beautiful player," said Mercedes. "He has the hands."

It was hard to remember that only hours earlier many of these men had fought, and lost companions. Women and children had been injured in the shelling. But, as in the early days in Madrid, killing had closed the ranks and given them the manic spirit of survivors. Mary shivered; it was like a carnival of the dead.

Mercedes knew. She took Mary by a hand. "There is always pain, always sorrow," she said.

For a moment Mary wanted to leap forward in time, to be Mercedes's age—to get through what was to come and to find the serene resignation—it was not cynicism—that Mercedes wore as naturally as the black dress. Sometimes reality seemed easier to survive than the nightmares.

■

She turned over and reached out for Cordón. The bed held the adhesive mist of sex in the linen. He was gone. The sheet was still warm and damp. For a few seconds she lay still, keeping her hand where he had been, not sure whether she was awake or dreaming, not sure of the bed's substance. There was already a faint light. Then she heard steps and voices outside.

She slipped out of bed and looked down to the patio.

Cordón was there—walking slowly and talking to Álvaro.

When she came out to the patio they stood as she had often seen them: Álvaro deferring while Cordón stressed points with little thrusts of his head. It was Álvaro who saw her first.

"Álvaro."

"Mary."

"I did not want to wake you," said Cordón.

"You didn't."

"No."

"What is happening?"

"Could we have some coffee?"

"I'll make it."

When they came into the kitchen the two men were decided on something—Cordón, still bed-rumpled, had no bed memory, she knew.

"We have to leave," he said, "Álvaro and me. This morning. For Huesca."

"The front line," she said.

"Yes. The front line. Álvaro came from our people in Lérida. We have been too successful dealing with the *carabineros*. They are being withdrawn. The communists are sending in three divisions, under Lister. Three divisions. They call it maneuvers. Three divisions, and Lister's tanks. They mean to wipe us out."

"They're sending *tanks* against their *own* people?" she said, already as angry as incredulous.

He nodded. "But we are not their own people. They have Barcelona. Now they want Aragón."

"What will you do?"

"There are three anarchist divisions at the front. No mystery why they have been kept around Huesca. They do not know what is happening. I have to reach Mera."

"You mean—pull out the anarchists from the front line to stop Lister?"

"There is no other way."

She was furious in despair. "Franco needn't bother. He can just sit and wait for you to destroy each other. It's—it's *sheer fucking lunacy!"*

"I know that," said Cordón, as calm as she was inflamed. "Do you think I want it this way? Do you think I have any choice?"

She subsided a little, but was on the edge of tears.

"We have no choice," said Álvaro.

"I'll go with you," she said.

"No." Cordón's eyes and voice left no room for argument. "No. We cannot take you. We have to go through the reds who hold the rear. They have a line of reds behind the anarchists—to stop desertions, they say. We cannot take you."

Reluctantly she conceded, still openly upset.

"Fonz will take care of everything here."

She knew he meant that Fonz would take care of her.

"I'll be okay. I just want—" She pulled herself together. She had to order every limb, be strict in every movement, to carry it off. "Of course, I would be a danger to you. I see that. But I have to say—" She put down her coffee. "I *have* to say this. I can't see how you can any longer *believe* in this."

"It never was one war."

"It's a *hell* of a thing." She walked to the window to conceal her face. The wooded foothills gave no sign of habitation or of life. Not a bird stirred in the dawn. *"This* country. What is it about this *country?"*

"I will get the car," said Álvaro.

"No," she said, very insistently, and turned to them. "Not yet, Álvaro. Not yet. Listen to me. You are two of the finest people I've ever known. That's true. You're too damned fine for a country like this. I know I shouldn't be talking like this. I know that. But I love you both."

□

Cordón went to her and let her head fall into his shoulder.
"We will be back," he said.
"Be sure," said Álvaro, awkward with their intimacy.
"We say good-bye too often," she said.

■

Fonz stood with Mary as Cordón and Álvaro drove through the gates, into the village, and down into the plain. The Packard was swallowed in dust before it passed from view. Already she regretted her loss of control with them, what she had said. Cordón hadn't liked it, though he hadn't shown it. She had indulged herself, she felt—and implied that she was more outraged than he, which wasn't true. In the windless early heat Fonz's earthy smell reminded her of finding a familiar horse nuzzling up to her in a paddock.

"Everybody loves Nicolás," he said.

She nodded.

"Nicolás was right about his father." His eyes were narrowed in the shade of the wide leather hat. "Don Pepe was not loved. He took care of the village, in his way, but he was not loved. This place is like a small planet. We have all we need. We can exist on our own. We have had good years here. Nicolás was right."

"You think I will take him away." She surprised herself by saying it, saying it so adamantly. Still not in control.

He surrendered distance slowly. Finally he said, "Is that what you want to do?"

"I thought so." She felt able to be totally honest. "I thought so. Miguel, I know now. He will always come back."

"You are a good woman. He is lucky. Once—"

"Once?"

"Once he came here with another woman. Spanish, but not from Aragón. *La mujer celosa.*"

"The jealous woman?"

"Worse. She was bad. A blackness in her."

"And Nicolás—he was in love?"

"He was blind."

□

"I know that woman. She was in Madrid."

Fonz took off his hat and held it to his chest. "Mary. You are named for the Holy Mother. But you are not a believer?"

"I don't know anymore."

"You pray. I think you pray."

"Yes."

Bareheaded, he was avuncular without being remotely like a priest. "You are welcome here," he said.

■

Months of war traffic had smashed the metal roads. Winter mud had turned to baked ruts. The first town that Cordón and Álvaro had to get through was Barbastro, and there they found themselves blocked by a convoy of trucks. Álvaro recognized someone in the cab of a truck and went to talk to him.

He came back looking worried.

"They're going to Lérida for supplies," he said, but once in the car and leaning on the wheel to light a cigarette he added, "I knew him in Barcelona, an honest man. A socialist, but an honest man. He says all the anarchists at the front are being kept apart from the others. They've wiped out the POUM units. We would be lucky to get through."

"This car is too conspicuous," said Cordón.

Álvaro nodded.

To have an emotional attachment to a car was irrational; but it was more than that, a political attachment, too. The disintegrating Packard was their last tangible link with Durruti. Durruti, thought Cordón, was better spared this view of the war.

Álvaro reversed into a yard. "What now?"

"Out of the town."

Barbastro was in a valley and the river Vero came through it from the north. Cordón directed Álvaro to a dirt track that followed the river toward the mountains. In a few minutes they were well above the river, against a steep face.

"Here," said Cordón.

He took a pouch of papers and his canvas bag. Álvaro went to the trunk.

"What about this?" he said, lifting out his carbine.

"No. We cannot carry anything but our pistols."

They stood at the driver's side of the car, Álvaro lighting another cigarette and suddenly stepping back to take a kick at the running board.

"Damn! *Coño!*" he snarled. "We could never make a fucking car like this. Hispano-Suiza is for pimps."

It still smelled of leather, and the leather still had the stains. The Packard seemed in pathos to be animate and the most dutiful compatriot they had. Dutiful and dumb enough for sacrifice.

Cordón leaned inside and released the brake. He held the wheel as they both pushed. The car rolled across the track and over broken stones to the edge of the cliff, where it got stuck on a small caper bush. They gave a concerted push and, with a sudden surge, it was moving over the edge. The muffler scraped stone, the car slewed a little, and was gone.

It never reached the river. Shedding pieces of coachwork and glass, it fell to a ledge where it was caught by the trunk of a scrub oak. There it lay, belly up, and totally inaccessible. The rear axle was half torn from the chassis; otherwise it was surprisingly whole.

Cordón stared down. "A kind of memorial."

Álvaro stepped back and picked up his bag. It was hot and there was no cover. From nowhere, the mosquitoes had found them.

"Amen," he said.

■

Mary persuaded Mercedes and Fonz to sit together at the reed-covered end of the patio. They didn't touch. Mercedes looked directly into the camera, composed in a way that made her almost aristocratic. Her one vanity was to wear shoes—pointed, patent leather shoes that must have come from a city. Fonz remained bare-footed and was uneasy. His concession to formality was to button his shirt one place higher than usual, with the result that the shirt came close to choking him. She got him to put the hat on his lap. The picture was redolent of a time, but not this time. Mary, framing them, was conscious that they had both in some way eased out the present and were presenting to the lens—the act of posing had conjured it—the manner of two lovers at the time of engagement. The two wooden chairs were separated by the false propriety of the portrait.

"And again. That's *good.* Once more."

The final shot was the one—Fonz forgot his shirt.

Afterward, when Fonz had made a display of relief and gone back to work, Mary went into the kitchen with Mercedes.

The patent leather shoes clacked over the flagstones. The extra height they gave stressed Mercedes's calves, gave her a swing of the hip that was carnal in an unconscious, natural way.

"I like the shoes," said Mary.

"From Madrid."

"You have been to Madrid?"

For a moment Mercedes was injured by the implication of surprise, for another moment tempted to fantasize, but—finding her more usual self-assurance—she said, "No. No, I have never been to Madrid. Barcelona. But not Madrid." She pushed the shoes away from a foot, flexing her toes like a child released for unwanted constraint. "No. The shoes belonged to Nicolás's mother."

So was discarded a great deal more than the shoes and the thought of their owner. The romance of the portrait was kicked away too. Romance was a mood too fragile to have any staying power in the house, dismissed as the intruder it was.

■

Cordón and Álvaro had slept for two hours in the late afternoon under an olive tree in an orchard that had not been tended for some years. The trees were old, with little fruit. Half a mile below was a small river and beyond that the Huesca road. A convoy of trucks, stopped at a hamlet on the road, was still there when they awoke.

"Won't move up to the front until dark," said Álvaro.

"No. They must be worried about planes."

"Franco has been quiet. Nothing has moved here for weeks."

Cordón got up, realizing that the mosquitoes had feasted off him while he was alseep. "We should not go down there until dusk."

"They're socialists, all the truck drivers."

"There are always commissars. You know that."

Álvaro spat out a sour olive. "Red bastards."

The trucks began to move before dusk. They heard a man going along the line to rouse the drivers. He banged the cab doors with a rifle and shouted obscenities. Soon the air was sulfurous with the exhaust of ill-kept engines. The fumes drifted up to the olives, a peach-colored mist in the dying light. Several trucks balked and one was left behind, stalled.

Cordón and Álvaro made for this truck. Two men were bent under the hood.

"What's the problem?" said Álvaro.

"If I knew that I would not be in this shit hole." An irascible and unshaven face appeared.

"American truck." Álvaro nodded. "Ford."

"A pig."

"Always the same thing," said Álvaro ignoring the hostility and leaning under the hood.

"What do you know?" said the other man, the driver.

"I know these engines. Tough. Very basic. One weakness in the heat. Fuel pump."

"Where are you from?" said the driver, no less hostile.

"We are just like you, comrade—up the creek without a paddle. Our rear axle went in Barbastro. We were bringing beans."

Cordón had seen that the truck was taking ammunition to the front. There were Russian crates in the back.

"Beans!" The driver finally relented. "You should be able to fart your way to the front."

"I can fix this," said Álvaro. "Give me a wrench."

Within half an hour they were moving. Cordón and Álvaro sat on the crates.

As they pulled out of the hamlet, Cordón glimpsed a familiar face on a wall, under a lamp over the Civil Guard post: Dolores Ibarruri. La Pasionaria's injunction on the poster was, BEWARE THE ENEMY IN THE REAR! PURGE THE REAR! ORDER IN THE REAR!

■

Fonz had put the two captured field guns between the house and the village. With only eight shells they were a last resort. But Mary watched him fussing around them, and saw that their value was as much psychological as actual. She was standing there with him when they heard a plane.

It came out of the east with the sun behind it, at first just a flash of metal. It remained high, banking over the foothills of the Pyrenees before passing over the village.

"Fascists!" said Fonz.

"No. That's a Chato. Russian."

The plane was circling with its wings dipped.

Fonz lifted his hat for more shade to see it. "Russian?" he said. "Why?"

The plane turned away and disappeared into the sun, leaving its dislocating sound lingering in the valleys.

"Reconnaissance," said Mary. "Only the one plane."

Fonz followed her train of thought. She was the expert, but he had the instinct. "I will check the barricade," he said.

As a child she had imagined where the sun that she saw was to the people in the next state, and the one beyond it, as far as California. She looked at the Pyrenees, the usual storm already forming. She saw herself on the other side of the Pyrenees, watching the same cloud from the terrace of an auberge. France, so close. So far. France, where they could still take three hours over lunch without a thought for the other side of the mountain.

It was she who first distinguished the sound of tanks from the sound of the storm. It was felt through the feet. They were coming from the plain. Six abreast when they appeared around the curve in the road. That was different. Lister had been criticized at Brunete for not concentrating his tanks. Trying again, an experiment.

Two remained on the road, while the two on each flank deployed on the low slopes.

Mary knew what Cordón had told Fonz.

They stood at the barricade together, with all the men around them. The men sighted their rifles.

The two central tanks stopped and began ranging their guns.

Behind the first six tanks, four more appeared on the road.

"You can't stop them," she said. "Miguel. You *can't.*"

There were tears in his eyes. "Nicolás knew."

"He hoped he was wrong."

Fonz clambered to the top of the barricade and raised the white flag.

The lead tanks' guns had stopped moving. The other tanks continued to roll foward. A gun fired.

Mary had seen what was going to happen. She rolled her back against the sandbags and covered her head. There was an orange blast and a white blur in the air. Sand spilled over her. She passed out.

■

"Papers," said the commisar.

Cordón handed over a soiled envelope from his pouch.

Álvaro pulled out his cigarettes and offered one to the commissar.

The commissar shook his head and half-turned to bring the paper out of the shadow of the truck. He was middle-aged and myopic, with an incongruously white face although his hands were burned brown.

The truck driver and his mate were unloading the ammunition crates with other men.

The commissar handed back the papers.

"Over there. The green door."

Álvaro looked at Cordón. Cordón nodded, and they crossed the road without a word, watched by the commissar. Outside the green door was a *carabinero* guard, leaning on his rifle disinterestedly.

They went inside.

□

A handful of men were in there, two asleep on the floor and the rest on a bench. No one said anything.

Cordón had noted that beyond the green door was another, of plain wood, and that at that end of the building a telephone line was tacked into the wall and through a window which, in consequence, did not close properly. Before they went through the green door the telephone had been in use. He heard a Russian voice.

■

Mercedes had a concentrated fury. She stood in the middle of the kitchen, legs slightly apart and rocking as she spoke.

"You talk of peasants! What do you know of peasants! Your hands. Look at your hands!"

The young tank commander tried to conceal his hands. He was light-bearded and had a rim of grime over his brow stamped by his goggles, goggles now hanging at his neck. He looked plebian. There was no rank on his uniform. But what had given him away—as well as his hands—was his fine *madrileño* accent, as novel here as his tank.

"I will tell you something, old woman," he said. "About your leaders, the anarchists. I went to their headquarters when we arrested the Council of Aragón. It was like a brothel. Those men were living off the peasants. *We* are here to return the land to the peasants."

But she was more inflamed.

"Look around you. Do these people look at though they need liberating?"

"They were misled."

She let out a shriek that was half derision and half venom.

It was this that Mary first heard as she came around.

"I tell you," said Mercedes with a more measured and prevailing intensity, "these people who come forward now to welcome you would rush from their houses to embrace Franco. The same people."

The tank commander was tired. He saw Mary moving—she was lying on a bench with a folded coat under her head.

"This is the woman I came to question," he said.

□

As Mary looked at Mercedes she wondered who the angry woman was, where she was. All she recognized as familiar was her own smell, and she wondered why there was sand in her hair.

■

Cordón and Álvaro were the first to be led from the room with the green door. It was late afternoon and artillery fire had been audible for over an hour, coming from the direction of Huesca. They also heard tanks moving somewhere ahead.

An armed guard took their pistols and led them out with another guard behind them. They were marched past trucks that looked like the convoy that had left behind the stalled Ford—an assortment, some American, some Spanish, some Russian.

Then there was a stretch of clear ground, baked and matted stubble, and a cherry orchard. The cherries were already white.

Under a tree at the edge of the orchard was a small table, an antique with griffin feet and a polished walnut veneer. Seated behind it was a man whose most striking garb was his suspenders, brightly polished leather with brass buckles holding up baggy black corduroys over an impeccably crisp white shirt. On the table was a bowl, another antique of crystal glass, holding cherries in water. It was difficult to see any distinction of feature. In the shade the face was almost a blank. Barbered, shaved, and very young.

The guards led them to the table and then, with a nod from the man, fell back under the trees.

"Papers," he said—the same voice Cordón had heard on the phone, hardly a trace of Russian in the Spanish.

Cordón gave him the papers. He spread them out on the table, sucking a cherry at the same time, sucking it free of the stalk.

"Deserters," he said in the same neutral tone without looking up.

"How—how could we be deserters?" said Cordón. "We were coming here. Not going."

"Why?" He spat out the pit and selected another cherry from the bowl, looking up casually.

"We are on the staff of Cipriano Mera."

"Mera."

There was a prolonged pause during which two more cherries were sucked like lollipops, sucked without sound on a tongue that waited to find words.

"Where do you come from?"

"Barcelona. We—"

Suddenly the man was leaning over the table with widened Mongolian eyes, cutting off Cordón. "Your papers say Fourteen Division. The anarchist divisions on this front are Twenty-five, Twenty-six, and Twenty-eight. These are old papers. You are deserters. Like the rest of that scum."

He nodded toward the guards.

They were marched back to the room with the green door.

■

"She spoke perfect Spanish," said Mercedes. "As good as yours," she added with a snap. "It must be the shock."

"She can stay here for the night," said the tank commander. "When we pull out, she has to come with us."

They stood at the foot of the tapestry-covered bed. Mary had been put on the pillow with the tapestry lightly over her. She was deeply asleep.

The tank commander surveyed the room with the care of a connoisseur. "This was a beautiful house."

Not conceding to any of his gestures—giving no inch to him—Mercedes turned to go.

But he lingered. "According to my conscience this is obscene. According to my heart it is beautiful." He collected himself. "Beauty so easily corrupts."

She looked at the imprint of his grime, sand, and oil on the brilliant carpet. "A dog has more respect for it."

A few hours later Mary found Mercedes asleep in a chair by the bed. In sleep and in the dusting bleach of the night she looked like a finely crafted Madonna, something Liam's mother might have collected. Liam. In recalling Liam she found herself with other faces gathered at the bed. They assembled at random, with only solemnity in common. Tom, Abe Sachs, Tom Esposito, Ike Mandel, Pat Byrnes, Jack Casey; a bone rattled on her mother's wrist; the man called Matthew held the chow at his chest, and he alone was happy. Some of these faces gave way to others. Max Praeger appeared, Delphic with pipe. Another stirring. Here was Nicolás at last, clearer than the others, absolutely resolved in a light that outshone all the others.

■

Four trucks were lined up facing the cherry orchard. The table and chair were gone. The strength of the headlight beams fluctuated with the uneven running of the trucks' engines. From a distance the clustered cherries looked like fairy lights strung in the trees as the wavering yellow beams caught them. Exhaust smoke drifted low over dewed stubble. The racket of the trucks, occasionally gunned by drivers, swamped steps and voices.

The starting of the first truck had woken Álvaro. Cordón had not slept.

"What's happening, Captain?"

"Trucks."

Cordón was at the window. The other men remained in their torpor.

The first truck moved to the orchard as the others kicked into life.

Álvaro joined Cordón, still drowsy.

"Where is the cocksucker?" he said.

"He's there."

Brass buckles flashed in a beam.

It was some minutes before the green door opened. This time there were six *carabineros* to take them, and others by the trucks.

"Where are we going?" said one of the other men.

Nobody answered.

It was when they walked across the stubble that Cordón apprehended with the clarity of a diagram what had been arranged. The style was as familiar as a page in a textbook. By the time they had marched into the lights the others realized it, too. One of them tried to break and run, but was knocked back into line with the butt of a carbine.

The Russian stood to the left, arms folded. In the glare his face had more molding. Cordón thought, Lenin's cheekbones and Stalin's eyes.

"I can't even shit myself," said Álvaro.

"You are the best of men."

Álvaro touched Cordón's hand. "Captain. Captain—Durruti was right."

"Silence!" screamed a *carabinero,* unable to pin the source of the voices because of the noise of the trucks.

The Russian moved out of the light to somewhere in the trees. The smell of exhaust was almost choking. A single *carabinero* stood ahead of them. He directed the others to string out the men in a line facing the trucks.

Cordón, like the others, was virtually blinded by the headlights, but thought he saw a movement above the cab of a truck, where the canvas canopies began. When the guards withdrew they divided to each side of the line, but made no move with their carbines.

The Russian, still out of sight, raised his voice over the engines. It was not a voice suited to force; it was pitched high.

"The penalty for desertion is common to all armies. You know it."

And suddenly he was there, with a hand raised under the cherries.

"Cocksucker," screamed Álvaro.

The hand fell.

■

Mary screamed out, convulsing and kicking off the tapestry. Mercedes woke to see the red hair, before she saw anything else, drawn out and upward in Mary's hands; it was like she was trying to rip the hair from her head. She was on her knees on the bed with wide, staring eyes and trying to scream again, but nothing more than a sob came.

Mercedes got to the hands and forced them down, leaning over the bed and using all her strength, her face eye-to-eye with Mary's.

"Mary. *Mary.*"

At first the two grips competed.

The sob drained into a choke.

Mercedes released her grip and with her right hand slapped Mary sharply across the face.

"Mercedes."

"Mary."

"Mercedes."

"You know me now."

"It—" Mary's voice was little more than a whisper, each word coming slowly. "—It was terrible, Mercedes. A dream."

"You have been suffering from shock."

Mary put her hands out for Mercedes. "I saw—I saw—what happened?"

"A shell at the barricade. You were lucky. Covered by the sandbags."

"I don't remember."

"But you remember me."

"Yes. And Miguel."

"Miguel is dead."

"Oh God." She let Mercedes guide her back to the pillows.

"Mary. Before, you only spoke English. The commander was trying to ask you questions."

"Miguel raised the white flag. I remember. I remember the barricade. They fired after he raised the flag."

"The commander said it was an accident."

"The commander?"

"Please. You talk too much. Wait until the morning."

"The light. The light was so bright. Did you—" She faded again.

Mercedes adjusted the pillows around her.

In the morning the commander was more brusque and, Mercedes suspected, less confident of himself.

"She will have to come, however she is."

Mercedes was about to resist when Mary appeared in the doorway.

□

"It's all right, Mercedes. I am well." She looked at the commander. "Where are you taking me?"

"Lérida. From there you will be taken to Barcelona."

"On whose authority? Are you arresting me?"

He looked uneasy. "No. I am not arresting you. They know about you in Barcelona."

"What if I don't come?"

The brusqueness was reasserted. "You cannot stay here."

She looked at Mercedes. "You see how it is."

"Are you well enough?"

"I'm well enough to remember everything." She looked at the commander. "I do remember what you did."

"Good," said Mercedes.

They kissed before Mary went outside.

The tanks had gone. A few trucks were being loaded.

"What are you taking?" said Mary.

"Fertilizer. It is needed in other places."

The men loading the trucks were spiritless. They were not being coerced—curiously, none of the communist troops she saw had their guns on anyone. Some of them were sitting outside the bodega as Mary and the commander left in a truck. The bodega had already been patched up. Under the Moorish stonework that had been unmarked by the centuries she thought she saw a white-haired man in riding boots, standing in the shade with another man.

The only sign of conquest was a new pole at the edge of the village—flying the Republican flag.

"The wrong flag," said Mary.

The commander, at the wheel, was puzzled.

"It should be the hammer and sickle."

This failed to provoke him. "You should stay out of other people's wars," he said.

"Amen."

This time he was surprised, and very nearly hit the debris of the barricade as he drove around the shell crater.

■

□

"I have read the notebook," said Sletin, in lilting English.

"I am a journalist. An American national. Call Barea, Arturo Barea, in Madrid."

Mary had refused a seat and stood over Sletin's desk.

"Barea has gone. Indefinite leave." Sletin was still casual and leaned back in his creaking chair, pressing fingers together as in prayer. "You do know where you are?"

"I know what the SIM is. What it does."

He nodded slowly. The hands parted, and he looked again at her notebook, open on the desk. "Yes. You know a lot. And you put it all in here. So this is how lies are made." He flicked pages. "Even in notes your views are very clear."

"Listen. No one has any complaints about me. No one has ever—*ever* taken my notes."

He stopped at a page and pressed a finger to hold it down. "Here, for example. Your interest in this hospital."

"I was trying to trace American casualties."

"I can read," he said, in a changed tone, looking less amiable. "What you write here—'This place is all wrong. The guys never come out. Find more evidence.' What does this mean?"

"I think you know that."

"What I know is that we have reeducation camps for comrades who exhibit the wrong tendencies. We make no secret of it."

"Reeducation camps?" She stepped back from the desk. "My God, is that what you call them? You people have put a new twist in the language, that's for sure. Reeducation. You mean, nuthouses for nonbelievers. That's what they are."

He closed the notebook and put it to one side.

"What were you doing in Aragón?"

"Work it out."

"That might take me a little time." He stood up and went to open the door. Two women were there, one florid and buxom and the other, as though chosen to be the antithesis, tall and shapeless. Both wore blue smocks.

"Take her," said Sletin, and left.

"Please," said the tall woman. "Strip. Take off all clothes."

□

■

Ferrer heard the shouting before Sletin joined her, carrying the notebook.

"She is arrogant," he said.

"She is American."

"We are taking a risk."

"She is poison."

"We should have asked for authority."

"We do not need authority."

Sletin listened to the increasingly belligerent curses.

"I think she is trouble."

"I take the responsibility."

"I know." Sletin seemed no happier. "A little shit can make a big mess."

■

They had pushed Mary into a chamber before she realized what it was. She could see little. The upturned bricks scored her feet. She kept balance only by crouching. The crevices between the bricks, as she felt her way along them, were moist. The whole chamber was clammy and fetid. There was a smell of excrement.

"Bastards," she said in a whisper, and then *"Bastards!"* in a shout that bounced back from all the walls. A light came briefly on—too briefly for her to establish the dimensions of the chamber. The light was somewhere high on a wall. Eventually she found a way of wedging herself, fetuslike, in a corner. The discomfort of the bricks was greatly lessened by spreading her weight and leaning on the wall, although the wall was slick. She resolved to treat the walls as finite. By knowing a limit she kept a hold on space. That was important. That was how you handled a dream—fixing your space. This had once been a dream.

■

"She has scars," said Sletin.

"You want her?"

"I am not an animal."

"You want her."

"Not like that."

"You want her."

Sletin went back to reading the notebook.

■

She had, she realized, slept, and slept deeply. But for how long? To be wakened by a voice. Quite close but as though filtered through metal, in a dialect she knew, Andalusian. And singing.

> *"They said, when there came to Spain*
> *The unconquered King Amadeo,*
> *You are not able to govern the Spaniards.*
> *Nor is Lucifer either."*

"Ni tampoco el Hucife"—she picked up the line and repeated it, almost laughing as she sang.

The other voice stopped.

She began to laugh uncontrollably. Her voice echoed through the same intestinal connection.

Then there was a scream. The scream and the laugh met and overlapped in disembodied and desperate consummation, like an extruded note from a diabolic Mass.

The silence that followed was fully populated. A thousand voices had died in this darkness. There was no other sound. The wall seemed permeable to the touch. Her skin was rank, and though it met the wall there was no barrier, no limit. Stone and skin exchanged properties. Nothing was solid. Nothing held. Her head slumped. She lay on the brick with the indifference of a fakir on nails.

■

The light was on, the door opened. She stared toward it. The buxom woman's voice said, "Put this on."

Something fell at her feet.

She waited for the woman to come into focus.

"Please. Put it on."

It was a blue smock. She gripped it, and it was the first dry thing she had held for—how long? She rubbed it through her hands.

"You come."

Both women came over the bricks in their boots, and the buxom one pulled her up while the other picked up the smock and slipped it over her head. Held between them she went out to the corridor and down a passage. She shook herself free.

"I walk," she said.

"In here."

They opened a door.

It was the same room where Sletin had sat at the desk.

This time it was Aneta Ferrer.

"You!" said Mary.

Ferrer seemed very white. "Sit," she said.

"No. No thanks."

Mary wiped her palms on the cotton at her hips. Her head felt clearer than it had ever been: everything was black and white, including Ferrer; there was no color in the room and it was very, very clear. A shadowless light.

"This is obscene," she said.

"No," said Ferrer, in a slow, leaden tone. "No. When I first saw you, I tell you now, you were taking photographs at the Segovia Bridge. You remember that? *That* was obscene."

There was no response.

"I always remember. You were taking photographs of men dying. What did you feel, I asked myself then—what does she feel—why is she here? You must remember that."

Mary stood resistantly waiting.

"I always remember that. So now, what I do now, is take you to the edge, so that you can look over. You have been to the edge. Now perhaps you do feel something. Now you know."

"I know you're mad."

□

"Oh *no.*" Ferrer's voice came cracking coarsely out of its constraints. "No. That would be too easy. I am not mad. I *am* a woman. A woman. More woman that you can ever be. I *am* a woman." Her body, with no slackness in the black *mono,* seemed to brandish itself with each emphasis. "Women like me are the betters of men. We best men. We are strong when men are weak. Where men are strong we do not need strength. We have our blood. The blood that men cannot bleed."

"That superstition?"

"Superstition?"

Ferrer rose and pushed the desk away. "Women who can make men of men." She pushed her face forward. "Would a man say he could make a woman of a woman?" She laughed. *"Eh?"*

There were steps in the corridor. New voices.

The door opened without breaking the footsteps.

Ferrer glared.

"Miss Byrnes."

Before she turned, Mary knew the voice. To want to see Koltzov felt almost wanton.

"Miss Byrnes. There was a mistake." He took in her appearance. "A serious mistake."

Behind Koltzov stood Tom Esposito.

"Jesus," he said, "what the hell have they done to you?"

"I'm okay."

Koltzov intercepted Ferrer as she came around the desk. He gripped her by a wrist and his glasses slipped forward with the momentum. "You are beyond your authority. Well beyond your authority."

Esposito offered Mary an arm. She took it.

"How did you know?" she said.

Esposito nodded to Koltzov. "He knows everything."

"Tom. You smell good."

"Well—you don't. Matter of fact, this whole goddamn place smells like—"

"Shit," she said. "It smells like shit."

"That's it."

Koltzov said, "There will be a proper diplomatic apology. I will see to it."

□

"Can I have my clothes?"

"Of course."

"And my notebook, my cameras?"

"Everything. In due course."

Ferrer was about to speak but Koltzov pulled her away.

Sletin—white on white—stood uncertainly at the door.

"Comrade Koltzov," he said, "I will get them."

"A bath would be nice," said Mary, still holding Esposito.

"That can be arranged."

He led her down the passage. She noticed a look exchanged between Esposito and Koltzov, although Koltzov did not follow them. They came to the vestibule next to the cloisters. A portrait of La Pasionaria, hand-tinted with far too much flesh tone, was caught in a block of sunlight.

"Mary," said Esposito, "there is some bad news."

"I know."

"You know?"

"It's Nicolás, isn't it? He's dead. It's in your face, and it was in my bones. I knew before. How?" She tightened her hold on his suit. "How?"

"He died at the front. On the line at Huesca."

"That's what they told you?"

"Yes."

"It wasn't like that."

She broke from him and looked up at the picture, the revolution's icon.

"They talk about passion. *Passion.* That's *shit.* It's one great bloodbath. The passion isn't love—it's *hate.* I've never seen—" Her voice rose to the vaulted roof. "I've never seen a place with so many *hatreds.* That passionflower blooms only in blood. *Tell me!* How many graves is that passion going to fill, in this god-awful country?"

She stopped and said, more calmly, "Is Álvaro dead, too?"

"Álvaro Ortiz? Yes."

"I must see María."

Koltzov had appeared, drawn by the outburst.

Esposito took her arm again. "You are not lingering. I want you out of this place as soon as possible."

□

"I have to . . ."

"I want you out."

"Of Barcelona?"

"Of Spain. I'm taking you to the border."

"But—*Tom.*" She looked at Koltzov. "That's the price. You've fixed it. I see."

"I am sorry," said Koltzov.

"I won't be sorry. *Jesus. No.* Not *sorry."* She slumped into Esposito. *"Hold* me. For God's sakes."

■

Koltzov stood in the sun and waved as they left.

Ferrer stepped out, once the Cadillac had turned out of the gate. In the sun she was waxen.

"Cordón," said Koltzov, "Cordón had an accomplice."

"Álvaro Ortiz."

"The commissar of Huesca says he reported their arrest to this headquarters."

"To Sletin."

"They were supposed to be sent to Caspe, to Lister."

"There was a misunderstanding."

"What kind of misunderstanding?"

"The telephone is unreliable. You know that."

Koltzov stepped a pace away from her and fanned himself with his hat.

"Once," he said, "you know, I questioned whether you should go to Moscow for training. I stopped Yanin taking you."

"What?"

Birds left trees.

"I was wrong. You are Moscow material. Most surely."

■

Esposito had rooms at the Barcelona Ritz.

"It looks normal," he said, "but it isn't."

The red carpets were soft and spotless. The brass was polished, the tableware and settings impeccable. It had kept all the court rituals of a grand hotel, down to the shoe shine. But the food was cold and the lighting sparse.

The best she could do for a bath was four inches of tepid water, but it was like a purging.

Esposito underestimated their problems. Her exit visa took four days of wrangling between Barcelona and Madrid. Four days in which she slept most of the time.

She wrote a note to María, who was in Madrid, and another to Serena.

She never saw Koltzov again. Her notebook came back intact. Three rolls of film were missing, all of the combat at the village, but her equipment was unharmed.

"You know, Tom," she said, checking out the cameras, "for a man with your views you seemed to be very buddy-buddy with Koltzov."

"We understand each other."

She brooded on this, and him. "Yes. Yes—you would I guess." She focused the Leica on him as he stood at the window. "You're really enjoying this, aren't you, Tom? I look and I see the smugness of vindication on your face." She took a picture. "There. The face that says, I told you so."

"Well. I did. Didn't I?"

"It ain't that simple."

"I never said it was simple. But now you know what these people are really like. You better than anyone."

She took another picture. His puppy-fat chin was dusted with talcum. He smiled too brightly.

"The camera also lies," she said.

■

It took three hours to move the final half mile to the French border at Le Perthus, where the road funneled into a narrow pass in the low Pyrenees. More people, refugees, were being turned back than allowed through. The progress of the Cadillac was through dust, heat, and misery.

The gendarmes were arctic in their decisions.

But once the Cadillac and its flag were seen, they were waved through.

"The French never change," said Mary.

Esposito demurred. "They do a lousy job well. We're on good terms."

"I see that."

"You're not *really* different, are you?"

"Well . . . ' she said, drawn out as she tried to get a view of herself in the mirror, " . . . if you want the truth, I feel I'm being punished. The hell of it is, I don't know what for."

He directed the Marine driver to a kiosk clear of the column of traffic.

"One other thing," she said, not taking notice. "I do understand cant. *Real* cant, whether communist, Catholic—or diplomatic—has one thing in common."

"What might that be?"

"It comes from the bottom of the heart."

"Okay, stop here." He smiled cursorily. "You're working up a piece. Already."

She pulled at his tie. "You really are an interesting man. So single-minded. Quite dangerous."

"You're not *looking.*"

She finally took notice, as the Marine got out of the car. Why it should be she did not know, but French trees and French sun looked better, though the same. The Ricard sign on the kiosk was bright with lacquer. The steps had been swept. There were tables to one side with starched cloths.

And Liam came out with a glass in his hand—no, two.

□

31

MADRID, FEBRUARY 25, 1981

"God, these *people.*"

His complaint assumed that he could speak for her, too. She was clearly a part of the world that functioned properly and, like him, not born to take this shit. Right? But now, looking her over again, he was less certain. He slipped the Hartmann carryon from his shoulder and put it between his feet, trying not to let it touch the floor, pulling out cigarettes.

"Looks like it might take a while. Cigarette?"

"Thank you, no."

He knew she hadn't been up front in first class, but the voice was classy and for a woman of her age she was in good shape. What age? Great hair, red, and good legs. "Flying I can take," he said, lighting up, " . . . *airports* I hate. These people couldn't organize their way out of a paper bag."

The line from the immigration desks was about thirty people long and hadn't moved.

"What the hell do you suppose is the trouble?" he said.

"The TV crew."

"Yeah." He looked ahead and then back to her. "Yeah, that figures. Plane was held for them. No one ever held a plane for me, but then I'm not media. *Media.* Magic word. Except it doesn't seem to work here." Irritation inflated a vein in his neck.

□

"No." She offered some sympathy. "From the sound of it, none of them speaks Spanish."

"No. Do you? You speak the language?"

"Mmmm."

"You do? Not me. English is the language of business. Every place. Thank God."

"The *lingua franca.*"

"Pardon?"

"Universal tongue. Have you done business in Spain before?"

"No." He looked ahead again, at the unknown, without relish. "They say the place is opening up. But this latest trouble doesn't help. Makes people nervous."

"Yes, I guess it would." Her sympathy was evaporating. She looked at the immigration desks. "Something is happening."

The TV crew were taken off to another desk. The line moved again. Moving with it she began to look for details that might be reassuring. The uniforms were not—not to her, not even on the customs and immigration men, certainly not the Civil Guard. That was all it had taken, she remembered—put a man in a uniform and he became a stranger. Had they really changed? The Civil Guard looked paramilitary; the officials seemed edgy.

"Hey," he said, "I have a car meeting me. I would be happy to give you a ride into town."

"Thanks, but I'm being met, too."

"Right. Well—" He picked up the Hartmann ready to step over the line to the desk, passport in his hand. "Nice talking with you."

He was gone in a moment, and then they were looking at her passport, slowly turning the dog-eared pages, examining all the visas, one man glancing over the shoulder of another, then looking at her, and back at the overlapping stamps and the variety of ink colors. The man with the stamp found a vacant corner. He smiled as he handed back the passport. The other man had written something on her disembarkation card and was still watching her as she passed into the baggage hall.

Her bag was already on the carousel, and she was through customs in two minutes.

María was there. She looked cold even in the shearling-lined leather jacket and, as she went to María through the twin doors the wind hit her, too—enough to make her shiver, the same wind; it carried too much memory.

A limousine pulled from the curb and the Hartmann man gave her a wave.

She embraced María, kissed her. María pulled away to look at her. "Good. Good. It was right that you came. Let me take the bag. The car is just over here." María's nose and lips were raw. "Who was that man?" she said.

"Someone I spoke to in immigration. That's all."

"We get a lot of people like him these days."

María's voice, given provocation, was just like her own—and a multinational executive would be enough provocation. The María of the sixties was still there. They each had their decade, the time they would never shake from their reflexes. But their decades didn't touch. María was hardening in a way that wouldn't have happened if she had had children. The face between the shearling collar, bleached cheekbone, white on white, had a touch of the paranoid. Now she had a fresh conspiracy to sustain her and could hardly wait to share it as she strode through the traffic to the car. Too eager, too headlong, *too*—too what? Too anxious to prove her faith?

"It's really good that you came," she said, once she was settled behind the wheel, turning the key.

"I don't know."

"Of *course* it is."

She allowed a smile. "It's good to see you, María."

The little Seat smelled powerfully of Gitanes, but María was making a show of not smoking. She pulled away into the traffic with sudden aggression, asserting her claim to be taken as a native, driving to kill.

"No hassle with immigration?"

"No. No—but I think one of them knew who I was."

"I'll bet. You'll make them nervous. Of course, they pretend to be very relaxed, no censorship. Open door to anyone. But they still keep the lists. They know who *you* are, for sure. The *same* people are still *there. Jesus,* do you want any more proof of that than this—this incredible fucking plot? Could you *believe* it? Going into the

Cortes with machine guns, shooting out the television cameras? Did you *see* it?"

"It took me by surprise."

"It's not over yet. Not yet. I mean, it's very *scary*. Of course, there's one question nobody wants asked, never mind answered. Did the king—did Juan Carlos *know?*"

"You mean, was he waiting to see if it worked?"

"What do you think, Mother?"

"I think he's walking on eggs, and I think he's pretty good at it."

"Fucking buses!" María cursed volubly in Spanish.

"He's bigger than you are. Now that I'm here I really would like to make it to the hotel alive."

"You're sure you don't want to stay with me? Félix won't mind."

"While I'm working it's better in the hotel. Phones. Telex."

"You stayed there before, didn't you? The Gran Vía?"

"Yes. I did."

"Forty-four years ago."

"Forty-five. I arrived in thirty-six. October."

"How does it seem?"

She remembered a field. The airport had swallowed it, but the hills were there, and she could fix where the field must have been, the pits. Superficially the place was transformed. But not enough. Not in a way that allowed her to feel easy. The road was wider but it was the same road.

■

She watched María's Seat cut in front of a Mercedes and snake off into the evening traffic. She couldn't remember ever having a view of the Gran Vía like this. They had given her a suite on an upper floor with three windows over the Vía, and the Vía, like the suite, seemed purged of history. She had to wait for details to register. On a roof opposite the low light picked out several odd tiles scattered at random. That was always a clue, in other cities: London or Berlin, where blast and debris had punctured a roof. You could spot new buildings where the old ones had been blown away. Light scars overlooked in the resurrection of cities. Madrid looked good. The people seemed taller. Why look for traces? She wasn't here to do that.

She took a shower. That oddly revved-up feeling of jet lag; she was an expert on jet lag, taking salt tablets and grapefruit juice on the plane, never booze, she could slot into a new time zone without missing a beat. For the first time the hotel did seem familiar, something in the bathroom: it was the water, the smell of the water.

Stepping out of the shower, she caught a glimpse of her scar line in the mirror, peppered like the tiles. No different in coloring from the liver spots on her hands. Okay to have booze now, needed in fact. Jack Daniel's in her bag, send for ice and Vichy water. Not to look for traces, but knowing all the lies.

The waiter had cut his hair like J. R. Ewing, and his English had TV American in it. He asked if she wanted dinner in the suite. She asked him to get her a table for one in the restaurant—a quiet table. She asked in Spanish, and for some reason this dampened his style, made him more wary.

How to get hold of this story? She had to keep apart from the other reporters. But how to begin?

She was crossing the lobby to the restaurant—bearings vaguely familiar—when intercepted by a man.

"Mary Byrnes?"

There was familiarity and yet uncertainty in his voice.

"I'm sorry, but—" she said, looking at him.

"You don't recognize me?"

There were stirrings of ill-kept memories; the voice was the beginning of it, an English voice. And a feeling about the eyes, as though she had known the eyes in another face.

"I'm sorry." She shook her head.

"Of course. We never really knew each other too well, though you knew my sister rather better."

"Serena? You—you must be—my God, of course!"

"Giles. Formerly Pollard. The title fell upon me, as titles do. I am so very pleased to find you here, Miss Byrnes." He gripped her hand.

But it remained difficult to fit within this heavy and patrician figure the gaunt and recessive Giles Polland.

"Mary, please," she said, still holding his hand as though touching might fully restore memory. "Do I still call you Giles, or—?" she said, at last ready to make a joke.

"Of course." His smile momentarily caught more of the young man's bone around the chin. "Giles Selmont. I am, after all, a *Socialist* peer."

"It's extraordinary, to see you, here."

"Not really. Historical inevitability. I imagine we have both to pick up old trails."

"Why are you here?"

"Leading a parliamentary delegation. Came to give our support to the government. Fortunately, I think that may turn out to have been gratuitous."

"Yes. I hope so. But—but, there are echoes."

"Oh, indeed."

But this was bland. He seemed, in his English way, to have made a career of propriety. Then she remembered his old nervous habit of apology, now swallowed in this smoother and practiced charm.

"I wonder," he said, "would you dine with me? It would be nice to compare notes."

"Of course."

And so the conjunction of past and present was forced on her, before she was really prepared for it, in the person of Giles Pollard become Lord Selmont of Aston, forced on her but in no way that she could feel angry about, just uncomfortable. He ran the dinner conversation as he must have run many a parliamentary committee.

"So you've not been back, ever, until now?" he said.

"No."

"I see."

But did he?

"No," she said again, then tasted the glass of Rioja he had knowingly ordered before speaking again. "You see, what I could never understand—I don't understand it now—is why they had to wait for Franco to die. Waiting for an old man to die before they even dared to stand up. I haven't any understanding of that. No respect for it."

He was uneasy with this. Too much to the point for him, she thought—not within his etiquette. So, to make slight amends, she said, "I guess I'd better do more listening than talking."

□

"I can tell you what I know, if it will help."

Nonetheless, she realized, his intention was to instruct.

"Please," she said.

"There was a list of people to be executed. All the left-wingers in the Cortes, for starters. They took Felipe González right there, in the Cortes, took him at gunpoint to a small room and made him face the wall. As the Socialist leader, he was at the top of the list."

"But they didn't shoot him."

"No. I don't know why. Nor does González."

He had sunk and spread in the chair as a man preparing to enjoy food, arranging his belly for it, pulling glasses from his breast pocket to scan the menu—dividing his mind between selection, narration, and her reactions, and still leaving room for glances around the restaurant, a man who ran things and who picked up, as he did now, a question before it was formed. He put down the menu and said, "Don't be under any illusions. Juan Carlos wasn't with them. I've talked to him."

Too oracular, she thought.

He bore down immediately on this visible doubt. "The captain general in Valencia had his tanks out on the streets. The code word was *'sin novedad'*—"

"Everything ready," she said, "the same as nineteen thirty six. So what stopped them?"

His mouth seemed to stray toward the menu, but his eyes fixed on her. "Only three of the four army commanders can be considered loyal to the constitution. I don't know about the air force or the navy. But it was all settled in the night. Juan Carlos spent the whole night on the phone. Then it was finished." More reflectively he added, "Franco's ghost is still here. But it *is* only a ghost, you know."

"He died—Franco died—with the mummified arm of Saint Teresa of Ávila beside him."

He smiled. "Your kind of detail."

"Well—" She held up the glass of wine in friendship. "—I believe in details."

"I'm not sure about symbols."

"In *Spain?"*

"Ah," he said, with the pleasure of having provoked her into a

cadence that he recalled, with the same kind of pleasure he would have got tasting a port of the same vintage. "Well—look here, let's see how well they can live up to the menu, shall we?"

■

What most annoyed her later, thinking over the dinner, was his assumption that she would regard his former self as as much of a spent force as he obviously did, that it was something not worth talking about. He was glassy if she tried to press that. His implication was that she should see that he had learned how things were really done. And, of course, he had: Juan Carlos would talk to him. But not to her. Okay, she thought. I like it that way. I can sleep with that. But there were some things left to ask him that she was damned if she would let him slip away from. Like Serena. He had been platitudinous about her death—she had died in London in the blitz, "dancing at the Café de Paris"—and moved away from the subject swiftly. Really, he was a politician facing a natural adversary, good-natured about it but sure of it, too.

In the morning the story seemed already to be settling down to regular-sized headlines. What would be left for her? And then, suddenly it was there, in one picture. Dolores Ibarruri, La Pasionaria, 85 years old, at a window of the communist headquarters on Santisima Trinidad. Gray but vocal—the crowd called *Sí, sí, sí, Dolores está aquí*—Dolores is here. But it was a face behind the face that Mary knew better. Not gray, even now: the face of Aneta Ferrer. Not identified in the caption, hardly registered enough for that. But attendant.

It probably wouldn't be any good trying to talk to the party headquarters on the phone. She took a taxi. The driver knew the place and obviously had a problem with an association of her and it. He glanced at her in the mirror several times before he said, as they wove through traffic, "Communist party, yes?"

"The headquarters."

He gave up on the puzzle and began cursing other drivers.

The building was quiet; it had the appearance of a backwater.

The lobby was decorous; there was no strident posters and no icons. The receptionist, a crisp and bright young woman, repeated the names, "Comrade Ferrer—Miss Byrnes." And said, "You are not expected?"

"No."

The receptionist had to repeat the name Byrnes twice when she got through on an internal line and then, with a trace of embarrassment, had to look Mary over and describe her, and then become monosyllabic in response to questions, beginning to flush a little. Finally she put down the phone and said, "Follow me, please."

Mary was led into a nearby waiting room, aridly modern, with four leather chairs on each side of a low table. There was one picture hanging in the room, a large and good print of Picasso's *Guernica*.

"Please—take a seat," said the girl. "Comrade Ferrer will be with you shortly."

It was ten minutes. She wore a black suit—simple, unadorned black that managed to be ascetic and stylish at the same time. The face had aged without lines, except for knife-cut creases at the corners of the mouth.

The surprise was that she spoke English, but with a curiously Slavic heaviness.

"You were a long time coming back. Sit down, please."

She waited for Mary, then took a seat opposite, offered a cigarette, and when it was refused lit one for herself, taking her time. She had dried out tautly. The sensuality had gone: her body was now as withdrawn from life as a spinster's.

"What do you want?" she said.

"I would like to see Dolores."

"Dolores does not give interviews."

"But I've seen—"

"She does not give interviews. Dolores is eighty-five."

"I didn't know you were back, from Moscow."

"I came back in nineteen seventy-seven, with Dolores."

"Thirty—thirty-eight years in Moscow?"

Ferrer pulled on the cigarette and then siad, "It was a matter of waiting. History was—history *is*—with us. In the long view, history is with us. Perhaps that is something that you still do not understand.

□

But how could you? You are only a journalist. Here today, somewhere else tomorrow." The disdain seemed general, not particular. "I have followed your—your work. The war correspondent. Without a war you would have nothing to say. You have lived off war—France, Korea, Indochina, Algeria, Vietnam. Always there. I could always expect that." The cigarette was consumed again. "What would you want with Dolores? What can you understand of her?"

"Whether she really believes that the party has any future here."

"You are trying to settle a score."

"Oh, no. Oh, *no.* What would be the point?"

By then Mary had realized the echo in Ferrer's accent: it was like a ghost, of *Koltzov* talking through Ferrer.

Ferrer examined her and the question simultaneously, flicked ash to the table, became slightly less taut, and said, "You know, I do wonder why it took you so long to come back."

"You seem to have paid a lot of attention to my career. On my part, I've sometimes wondered what I would say if I ever saw you again."

"This is not what you expected it to be?"

"I remember the last time I saw you. I remember that."

Ferrer's eyes had yellowed at the rims and by leaning back she seemed to have lost focus, but her voice had no infirmity. "You make it sound important," she said.

"It would be important if there was any chance of you ever again having that kind of power. But look at you. And Dolores. Even in Moscow you must have seemed anachronisms. Stalinists. A Stalinist in Moscow is about as popular as a papist. And here—here the party doesn't even *talk* about Russia. Important? No, it's not important, anymore."

Ferrer nosed forward into focus again and snarled, "You were lucky to get out alive."

"Was I?"

"Have you—have you ever wondered, where are the anarchists now? *Eh?*"

Now Mary leaned forward. "Their mistake was seeing what you were. As Orwell said, the communists were not the extreme Left but the extreme Right."

"Orwell?" She rattled out a laugh. "I could never take seriously a man who had to change his name to conceal his class. How long was Orwell in Spain?"

"Long enough to understand." Mary gripped her bag. "Look—this was a mistake. I've had arguments like this before. They get nowhere. Nowhere. I don't want to do it anymore. This was a mistake."

Ferrer smiled and relaxed. "Now I know why it took you so long to come back."

"It was a mistake." Mary got up and went out without looking back, through the lobby and into the street, without looking back. It was not Ferrer whom she couldn't shake off, but Koltzov. It had been Koltzov who wrote the book, not she.

■

The Pyrenees were the only familiar line, sharp and white in a weak sun. Nothing else seemed to make any connections, nor to have any appeal. The road from Lérida was only lightly covered in wet snow streaked brown by trucks—mammoth tractor-trailers driven frighteningly fast. Rows of pylons carrying the power lines from the mountains straddled the plain and glinted with ice. Once out of the city María had become a defensive driver, not contesting the trucks; the slipstream and wash from a truck could slap the Seat out of its line. There was no heat in the car. They were both in shearling coats, but nothing seemed able to keep Mary's feet from freezing. They reached a crossroads and María pulled off. She switched the car off. Neither of them spoke. Wind came through the car's seams and outside, in the power lines, squealed at a constant pitch. A few feet from the car a small tin road sign, smeared with slush, pointed north to Vero.

Mary had a Michelin map on her lap but didn't refer to it.

The windshield began to mist. María wiped it clear with the back of her glove. "Well?" she said.

"No," said Mary. "Carry on to Huesca."

"You're sure?"

"Carry on."

María pulled out Gitanes. "I'm sorry, I have to. My God, my fingers are cold."

Mary took the lighter and lit the cigarette for her.

"I came here once before—" said María, "—in the summer. It was beautiful. Aragón. A place apart."

"You didn't tell me you had been here."

"No. They had just flooded the valley to make the irrigation lake. That was pre-Félix." She drew on the cigarette and laughed as she exhaled. "Félix wouldn't like Aragón. He's uncomfortable out of a city." She looked at Mary. "I should have told you, I suppose. But there was no one there who wanted to talk. Not about that time. So we went up into the mountains and got very drunk." She stubbed out the unfinished cigarette. "Okay. Huesca."

They waited for a truck to pass and then slid back to the main road, turning west. "Have you ever wondered, where are the anarchists now?" That voice warped to the same pitch as the wind in the wires. *No one there who wanted to talk.* The whole country wanted to forget, to eradicate. Probably right, *why not?* Over the Pyrenees the contrail of a jet slowly fluffed out and turned pale pink. Going north. María drove with only her left hand on the wheel; her right hand had regularly to clear breath from the windshield. Something in the utility of María's life, in her preference for cars, like this, the virtue of her simplicities—and something in the quality of her concentration—suggested the father.

She took María's right hand in her left and squeezed it. "I'm glad you came here, saw it in the summer. And you know you don't have to tell me anything, if you don't want to."

"Well, I *would* like to see more of you."

"Yes. I know."

"It's between Barbastro and Huesca, right?"

"Yes."

"This must be it; that's Huesca Cathedral on the horizon, just catching the sun, and this is the last village before Huesca."

Mary checked the map, and then folded it.

A street of medieval buildings had acquired a facade of illuminated plastic signs and a gas station. There was a truck park with a motel. Several of their rivals for the road were there.

□

"You stay with the car. I'll ask," said Mary.

María lit another Gitane and watched her walk down the street to the old *hostería* next to the gas station. They would take her for a tourist until she opened her mouth. In two days Mary's Spanish had passed from the gentle to the sharp, taking on old tones and shedding all traces of American, at ease in the vernacular. In Madrid this had seemed, to María, to be a little dated. But in Aragón it would be right. The impulse suddenly to come here had surprised María. What had happened in Madrid? Mary reappeared, walking more slowly, taking in the street. A famous mother most happy when shorn of her fame. And yet never happy at rest. The searching eyes with the gift for that finite piece of time in the lens, still as quick as . . . as before.

"You can leave the car here," she said, bending as María wound down her window. "It's just across from the motel, up there." She nodded to a place beyond the truck park.

When María was out of the car, Mary linked arms with her. "They knew the story," said Mary.

They had to step aside while a truck, spraying slush, came nonstop through the village. There was a rutted track leading up to a farm and, as they followed it clear of the truck park, it ran through trees—a cherry orchard.

"I think this is it," said María.

On the edge of the orchard was a cairn, about five feet high. On two sides the pyramid of stones was snow-coated, but on one of the clear faces there was a metal plaque, set into the stones. Eleven names were on the plaque, above the legend, "For Aragón, 1937." The plaque looked a lot newer than that; the names were carefully embossed and were bright in brass. "Nicolás Cordón" was two names from the top; "Álvaro Ortiz" two names below that.

María tightened her hold on her mother.

"It's okay," said Mary.

"It's well cared for."

"Yes. In the *hostería* they said it was—the cairn—it was unmarked for years. Three of these men were from the village." She began silently to cry.

"Oh, Mother."

□

"I'm sorry."

They stood for another minute with the wind at their backs.

"I knew Álvaro Ortiz," said Mary, clearing her voice. "He was a wonderful man. He always called Nicolás 'Captain'—it was from their time with Durruti. My *God* . . . Durruti." The memory, the man, was suddenly as sharp as the wind. "Come on. Let's take a walk."

They went above the orchard to a low ridge sheltered from the wind and walked south.

"Mother."

"Yes?"

"He died before he knew, about me—before you could marry."

"No." Mary shook her head. "I would not have married. It was never like that."

"Then why did you marry Liam? To give me a father?"

"Liam was a need. I could not have held together without Liam. Liam was a fine person. He *grew.*"

"I remember his laugh. And yours."

"Two graves. This. And Liam's, in Normandy. It's just beyond the cliff, at Omaha Beach. Two war graves, but different kinds of war. I don't know, they were so different, Nicolás and Liam, they liked each other, I think, and yet . . . I don't know. Are you happy?"

"In my way." María pulled close to her again. "I love you, Mother."

Mary raised her head so that María's could fall on her shoulder, and looked down over the village and beyond it to the plain. "I love you, *very* much. And I wish I could love this country. But I can't." She ended the apology and—María felt the change before she heard it—said, "In the end, love is a matter of trust."

■

ABOUT THE AUTHOR

Comrades is Clive Irving's third novel. Before taking up fiction, he had a career in journalism in both Great Britain and the United States. He was formerly the managing editor of The *Sunday Times* (London), head of Public Affairs Programming for London Weekend Television, an editorial consultant for *McCall's* magazine in New York and founding editor of *Newsday's Sunday Magazine.* He also writes for television. As a novelist he has taken some of the most momentous twentieth-century events—the appeasement of Adolf Hitler in the 1930s, the conflicts of Palestine—and portrayed them through the lives of fictional participants. Now in *Comrades* he finds a place, Spain, and a time, the civil war of the 1930s, that aroused deadly passions that have powerful echoes even today—a text and a theme, in fact, that are unforgettable in the human scale of the novel. Clive Irving lives in Sag Harbor, New York.

■